D1449201

By Steven South

Cover illustration and book design by Rebecca Weaver—

www.RebeccaWeaver.com

www.facebook.com/RebeccaWeaverArt

Map and logo by Naja Mesic— https://www.elance.com/s/majce/

 www.facebook.com/queenofsteelandfireseries

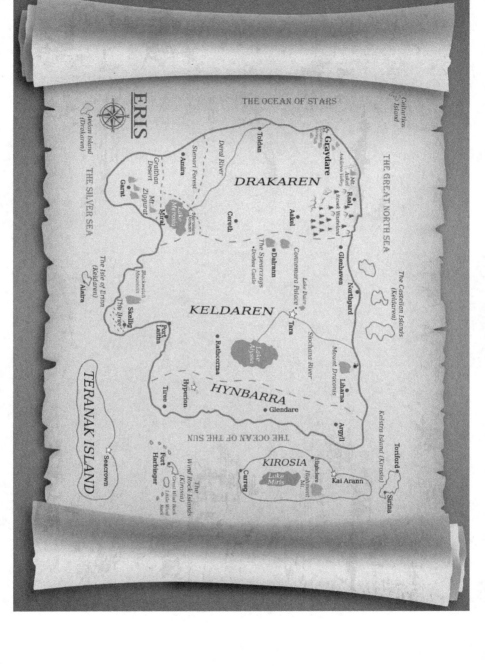

CHAPTER 1

Claire

Claire Erinn strode out of the palace, her guards hurrying to keep up. She held the surgeon by the elbow, pulling him along beside her.

"Please, Your Highness," the surgeon said. "There's no need for this. I've already examined the body."

"Then examine it again," Claire said. "Thoroughly. Before the gravesmen arrive."

On the far side of the courtyard, a line of oxcarts rumbled over the cobblestones. The drivers walked beside each team, heading toward the palace kitchens. One was a tall woman with long white hair, clad in a tattered black cloak. Dark, feathered wings arced high above her head. The other three were men, wearing peasant clothing.

Claire blinked. *Wings?* She looked again. The winged woman was gone. Only the three men walked beside the oxcarts. *I'm seeing things,* she thought, rubbing a hand over her eyes.

Kerry Bradaigh emerged from the barracks across the courtyard. The commander of Claire's Crown Guard detail wore silver armor over the royal blue of her uniform. The high collar hid most of Kerry's scar, but a thin, pale line was still visible on her cheek.

"Your Majesty," Kerry called out to her. "Where are you going?"

"Majesty? What happened to calling me Claire?"

"Things have changed."

There's an understatement, Claire thought. A twist of pain wrenched at her heart, and she fought it down, pushing it back deep inside herself. Back down to somewhere safe. *There'll be time for tears later,* she told herself. *Focus.*

"You're Queen now," Kerry continued, falling into step with her. Claire released the surgeon's arm, but gestured for him to follow.

"The coronation isn't until tomorrow. And too many things have changed, Kerry. I won't have you getting formal with me now. Call me Claire."

"All right. Where are you going, Claire?"

"Father's body was moved to the barracks infirmary, wasn't it?"

"Yes. The gravesmen will…do their work there."

"Then that's where the doctor and I are headed," Claire said. "I just heard the investigation was closed. I'm re-opening it."

"I spoke out against ending the investigation so soon," Kerry said. "But the Captain…" her voice trailed off.

"Father was too young and healthy for his heart to give out. No matter what the surgeons say. And he had enemies. The Captain of the Crown Guard shouldn't need me to point out how suspicious his death is," Claire said.

Kerry nodded. "I agree. I'll go with you."

The granite buildings of the Guard barracks ringed the outer square. Kerry led them to the wing on the far side of the plaza. They came to the infirmary, where two guards watched over the door. Kerry waved them aside, and opened the door herself.

The room had an arched ceiling, with tall windows that let light stream in. The sunlight glowed on the white cloth that covered the table in the center of the room. Beneath the cloth was the shape of a body. Claire's throat tightened. Her father's body.

"Get to it, Doctor. Make sure you didn't miss anything."

"Yes, Your Highness." The surgeon lifted the cloth. The minutes passed in agonizing slowness as he carefully checked over the body.

Finally, he turned to her. "I'm sorry, Your Highness. I can't find any sign of poison or injury. There's no indication of anything other than a natural death."

"Even I know some signs can only be seen from inside a body," Claire said, silently cursing the tremor she heard in her voice. "You're not finished yet, Doctor."

The surgeon's mouth dropped, and his eyes widened. "You want me to dissect the *king*?"

The thought of it sent a cold, sick feeling curling through Claire's stomach. She took a deep breath, steeling herself. "Would it show whether he was murdered?"

"Possibly, but…"

"Then do it."

The surgeon swallowed. "As you command." He went out into a small storage room, and opened one of the cabinets that lined its walls. Removing a roll of canvas, the surgeon brought it back into the main room. He unrolled it, revealing a line of pouches, each filled with gleaming steel instruments. Claire looked away, her stomach churning. "I'll be outside, Doctor," she announced.

Kerry followed her out. Claire paced the hallway as they waited, trying to push the image of her father's body out of her mind.

The surgeon finally opened the door, and beckoned them back in. Claire looked away from the shrouded body, and tried to swallow back the sick feeling in her throat. "I found something. I had to look it up in my texts to be sure of what I was seeing," the surgeon said. "But there were signs of verlinis in the body."

"I've never heard of that disease," Claire said.

"It's not a disease. It's a poison. A particularly subtle one. It closely mimics a natural death," the surgeon said. "I owe you an apology, Your Highness. It would seem the king was murdered."

Claire looked at Kerry. "You suspected it too, didn't you?"

"Yes," Kerry said. "A Crown Guard should always be suspicious. Especially when a king dies. I told the Captain as much. But he had already made up his mind to close the investigation."

Claire looked at the surgeon. "Thank you, Doctor. You may return to the palace."

He bowed, and left. When the door had closed behind him, Claire glanced back at the table. She shuddered, and took Kerry's elbow, pulling her along into the storage room. With her father's body out of sight, Claire took a deep breath, the sick feeling in her stomach easing. "You should have brought your suspicions to me."

An uneasy look passed over Kerry's face. "I wanted to. But it wasn't my place to contradict the Captain."

"Your place is leading my guard detail. That's the only place you need to worry about. Who did this, Kerry? Who killed him?"

"This sounds like a Drakari plot. Poison is one of Minerva's favorite weapons. Perhaps she's getting ready to start another war."

"Do you think Drakaren will invade?" Claire asked.

"I would, if I were Minerva," Kerry said. "A dead king…a young and untested queen…this would be the perfect opportunity to attack us."

"Send a warning to the Citadel. Tell the General to take whatever steps he feels necessary to secure the border." Claire hesitated, uncertainty gnawing at her. Her father's advice echoed in her head—*a ruler has to seem strong. Never let anyone see your doubts or weaknesses.* Claire sighed. *But this is Kerry,* she reminded herself.

Claire twirled a few wisps of hair that had come loose from her braid, twisting the auburn strands around her finger. "Is that right?" she asked quietly.

"It's what I would do," Kerry said. She reached out and squeezed Claire's arm. "You can do this, Claire."

"I don't feel like I can. I'm not ready. Father was supposed to have years to teach me how to rule."

"Others have taken the throne at sixteen. Some even younger."

"Those were kings. Not queens. But I suppose you're going to tell me that I'm just as good as them?" Claire asked.

"No. I know you, Claire. You're not as good as they were. You're better." Kerry smiled at her. "I think you've dealt with enough for today. Should I send Quaestor your regrets?"

"No. I have to go. He's Grandmaster of the Syncrestry. I can't refuse an invitation from him. If he were to disavow me before the coronation…" Claire shook her head. "I have enough enemies. I can't afford to make another. I'll meet with him to plan the funeral. I'll listen to his advice. And then I'll ignore it."

"I think he already is an enemy," Kerry said. "Some enemies might want to kill you, but others want to control you. Quaestor and the rest of the templers are spiders. And if you go to the temple, you'll be walking right into their web."

"Quaestor might be a spider. But I'm no fly. And any web of his will have a hard time holding me. But I have to meet with him. I can't risk offending the Grandmaster. No matter what I think of him and his gods," Claire said.

"It's your choice," Kerry said.

"We'll have to re-schedule my lesson," Claire said. "I won't have the time today. We'll spar tomorrow, though."

"That's fine. One day off shouldn't hurt your sword training," Kerry said. They walked back into the infirmary. Kerry glanced out the window. "The carriage is waiting, if you're ready to go."

Claire turned to look at the shrouded table. Tears suddenly blurred her eyes, and she wiped them away. "Yes. I'm ready."

They left the barracks, and crossed the outer courtyard again, heading back toward the palace. A wooden coach, resplendent in ivory paint and gilt trim, waited at the gate of the inner courtyard. Claire settled into the carriage. The driver cracked his whip, and the horses began pulling toward Tara. Kerry swung into the saddle of a waiting horse, and led an escort of guards after the coach.

In a short time, the city's walls loomed ahead of them. Passing through a gate, they made their way down the broad streets to the northern edge of Tara. A hill stood there, rising above the winding course of the Siochana River. Atop the hill was a massive sandstone rotunda, crowned by a bronze dome. The coach came to a stop, and a footman jumped down to open the door for Claire.

Kerry joined her at the base of the marble stairs. "It's been a long time since I last climbed the Holy Hill," Kerry said.

"I haven't been to the temple myself lately." Claire started up the steps. "I hope the gods pardon my lack of piety."

"The templers won't. Quaestor will certainly mention your temple attendance," Kerry said. "He spoke of mine when I was last here."

"What were you doing visiting the Grandmaster?"

"I came to consult the oracle spirits. I had just about given up on the gods, but I wanted to try turning to them one last time. So I paid the templers' price, and made an appointment to see Quaestor," Kerry said.

"Their price?"

"They don't charge the nobility or royalty. But for a commoner to consult the oracle spirits...that takes a great deal of coin," Kerry said.

"And what did you get for your coin?"

"It was quite a piece of stagecraft. Rivaling anything you'd see in a theater," Kerry told her.

"And that's what turned you away from the Syncrestry for good?"

"Yes. It felt more like duplicity than divinity," Kerry said.

They reached the top of the hill, where two bronze doors pierced the swirled sandstone of the temple walls. A woman and a boy waited there, both wearing the bronze-colored robes of templers. The boy's bare head was shaved, while the woman wore a headcloth made of coppery-brown fabric. A matching scarf was wound around her neck.

"Welcome, Your Highness," the woman said. "I'm Templer Garina, and this is my acolyte. The Grandmaster is expecting you within." She opened a door, and they followed her inside.

Their boots clicked on shining marble as they walked through the temple. A round skylight in the center of the dome let a shaft of sunlight stream down into the huge gathering hall. Garina led them down an aisle between rows of chairs.

A towering wooden pulpit stood at the end of the aisle. Behind it, a silver wall stretched to the top of the dome, dividing the hall into a crescent. Garina pulled aside a curtain of silver cloth, uncovering a door in the wall. She opened it, revealing a short hallway that ended at another door.

"No weapons are allowed in the sanctum," Garina said, her gaze dropping to the scabbard on Kerry's belt. Kerry scowled, clasping her sword hilt.

"Wait for me here, Kerry," Claire told her. "I won't be long."

Kerry nodded, still frowning. Claire stepped into the hallway, and Garina closed the door behind them. She opened the door to the sanctum. Inside, three curtains of heavy white cloth enclosed a square of marble floor. A golden wall stood at the far end of the room.

A raised platform was set in front of the wall, with a polished bronze firebowl standing atop it. Braziers were positioned at each corner of the platform, adding their light to the flickering glow of the firebowl. A gilt throne, padded with red velvet, stood on the platform, rising regally above a plain wooden chair sitting below the dais.

"If you would wait here, Your Highness, I'll summon the Grandmaster," Garina said, gesturing to the lower chair. She drew aside an opening in one of the curtains, and disappeared behind it.

A map of Eris hung above the platform, glistening as brightly as the golden wall it hung on. Claire went over to it. The map was made of gemstones, with the land surrounded by seas of sapphires.

On the western coast of the world, Drakaren was a sheet of onyx. A sweep of emerald representing Keldaren stretched across the center of the continent, and Hynbarra was a narrow strip of amber along the east coast. The Kirosian islands were spots of turquoise along the eastern edge of the map. Small amethysts were scattered across each country. *One for each temple,* Claire realized. A ruby marked the capital cities of Drakaren, Hynbarra, and Kirosia. *A ruby for each High Temple.* A single diamond marked Tara…*the Great Temple.*

She turned at the rustle of cloth behind her. Garina stood there, holding back a curtain. A man stepped out into the light of the braziers. "His Grace, Quaestor; Grandmaster of the Divine Syncrestry, and Lord Spiritual of Keldaren," Garina announced.

Quaestor's robe was made of golden cloth, with a matching headcloth held in place by a silver diadem. He wore two sashes crossed over his chest—the ruby-studded sash of a Lord Spiritual, and the diamond-encrusted sash of the Grandmaster. Quaestor raised a hand in blessing as he strode toward her, golden rings flashing on his fingers.

Two templers followed him, each carrying a short, golden scepter. One scepter was crowned with a large ruby, and the other was topped by a large diamond. "All blessings upon you, Your Highness," Quaestor said.

Claire bowed her head. "Your Grace."

Quaestor took the chair, the templers taking up positions beside him. Quaestor took the scepters from them, cradling the golden rods in his arms. Once he was suitably enthroned, he turned his attention to Claire.

"I can see why you display the map, Your Grace," Claire said. "What a beautiful reminder of your power."

Quaestor smiled. "You mean the *gods'* power, Your Highness. I'm simply their humble servant."

"Of course," Claire said.

Quaestor's smile faded, a serious look coming over his face. "You have my sympathies for your loss, Your Highness. King Colin was a great man. I assume you'll want the traditional funeral ritual?"

"No. I don't think I have strength enough to make it through the entire litany. I'd like the shorter service, Your Grace."

Quaestor nodded. "As you wish. But I'm surprised, Your Highness. Most of the faithful are comforted by the litany."

"I suppose I'm not like most of the faithful," Claire said.

"No, you're not. In fact, some templers wonder if you even *are* one of the faithful."

Careful, Claire told herself. "Faith moves like water. Sometimes faith is a quiet stream. Sometimes it is a mighty river. But faith always flows toward the ocean of truth," she said.

"Book two, chapter four. I'm impressed, Your Highness. I wasn't expecting you to quote from the Holy Texts." Quaestor smiled benevolently. "Perhaps if you attended temple services more often, your faith would be more of a river than a stream."

"But your faith is one of the reasons I invited you here today," he continued. "I want to share something with you, Your Highness. Something that will guide you as you take the crown. Something that will deepen your faith. I'll call on the oracle spirits, and ask them to give you their prophecy."

Claire returned his smile, mirroring its false warmth. "Very well."

Quaestor clapped his hands together.

Garina appeared from behind the curtains. "Your Grace?"

"Bring me the stone," Quaestor ordered.

Garina bowed, and left. She reappeared a moment later, carrying an ebony chest adorned with swirls of silver. She held the chest out to him.

Quaestor handed the scepters back to his attendants, dismissing them with a wave of his hand. They bowed, and left the sanctum. Quaestor reached into his robe, pulling out a small key that hung from a chain around his neck. He unlocked the chest and pulled a purple, melon-sized crystal out from it.

"The oracle stone," he said, nodding to Garina. She handed him a pair of bronze tongs, and extinguished the fire in each of the braziers. The dancing flames in the firebowl were now the only light in the room. Quaestor pulled a golden scarf up from around his neck, using it to cover his mouth and nose. Garina did the same with her scarf. "We cover our faces before we dare address the oracle spirits," Quaestor explained.

Garina drew a pinch of sparkling blue incense from a pouch in her robe, and threw it into the fire. Quaestor grasped the crystal with the tongs, and held it above the firebowl. The heavy scent of the incense oozed through the room, seeping into Claire's nostrils. "Wise oracles," Quaestor intoned, "use this sacred crystal as your mouthpiece, and give your servant Claire your prophecy..."

With each breath of incense-tinged air, a warm, blurry light glowed brighter in Claire's head. Her mind drifted, as if afloat on too much wine. She felt herself teetering on the edge of slipping into a trance. *It's the incense,* she realized. She pulled out a handkerchief, and covered her mouth and nose, blocking out the blue haze.

Clarity returned, and the glow in her head faded. Quaestor finished his prayer, and lowered the crystal into the fire. Garina bowed to the firebowl, and backed slowly out of the room, slipping between the curtains.

A violet light shone out from the flames, reflected by the polished sides of the firebowl. The flickering light danced against the white curtains surrounding the room, coloring them with flashes of purple. Quaestor folded his hands, and stared at the curtains, watching the lights intently.

"Your Grace..." Claire began.

He held up a hand, his rings glistening with purple reflections. "I must concentrate on reading the omens."

Claire fell silent, watching the lavender hues playing against the curtains. A whisper of bells floated into the room, and a voice began chanting. The chant was soft at first, but grew into a harsh, droning, deep-throated melody.

"It's the oracles," Quaestor said. "They're singing their prophecy." He listened for a few moments, and then turned to Claire. "I'll offer a sacrifice to thank them. Wait here while I bring it, Your Highness. I'll be just a few moments. Pray, and give thanks to the gods while you wait." Quaestor bowed to the firebowl, and left the sanctum.

The chanting continued. The voice was ethereal enough, *like you'd expect a spirit to sound,* Claire thought, but something about it seemed wrong. *It's too close,* she realized. She stood, and crept to the edge of the sanctum, slipping a knife out from her boot.

Claire thrust the knife into the curtain, cutting a few inches of cloth. Pulling the tear apart with her finger, she pushed the knife in deeper. She peered through the hole at the polished blade, using it like a mirror. The knife showed the reflection of a templer standing beside a shrouded lantern.

He was turning a crank on some sort of pump encased in a box. Bellows moved as the crank turned—bellows with long, slotted wooden pipes coming out of them. As the templer cranked the bellows, he pulled on levers and wires. Each time he pulled one, the sound of the chanting changed.

So this is the voice of the oracles! I should rip down the curtain and expose them as the frauds they are. Claire bit her lip. *But I can't confront Quaestor. Not yet. He's too powerful. And I have other enemies to deal with first.* She withdrew the knife, careful not to let it flash.

She folded the curtain over the tear, pulled a hairpin from her braid, and used it to pin the fold together. Claire went back to her seat. The chanting continued for another minute, and then the whispering bells sounded again as the voices faded away.

Quaestor returned, holding a pigeon. Murmuring a prayer, he drew a knife from his robe. He held the bird above the firebowl and slit its throat. He let the blood drain, and then dropped the body into the flames.

Quaestor re-lit the braziers, and slumped back into his armchair. "The oracles gave me a disturbing prophecy, Your Highness."

"Is that so?"

"They warned me of a grave danger facing you—and Keldaren," Quaestor said.

"And what might that be?" Claire asked.

"The oracles told me your father was taken from us too soon. They said you're unprepared for the throne, and that disaster will befall our people if you try to rule without help."

"And did the oracles propose a solution?" Claire asked.

"No. But I have one, Your Highness. I suggest you appoint a Viceroy to help you rule. Choose a wise, experienced leader to guide you in your royal duties."

"But the Chancellor already handles most of the daily affairs of government. How much more help would I need?" Claire asked.

"You need someone higher than the Chancellor. Someone who can help with the decisions that only the sovereign can make…matters of diplomacy and state. A Viceroy."

"I see. And I assume you have a candidate in mind?"

"Yes." Quaestor said. The warmth left his face, his expression turning serious. "I'll come right to the point. You should choose me."

Subtle, Claire thought, raising an eyebrow. "You're very direct, Your Grace. Some might think it improper for the Grandmaster to grasp at power like that."

"When the gods offer an opportunity, the wise man grasps it," Quaestor said. "The gods are offering both of us an opportunity here, Your Highness."

"Really?" Claire asked.

"Yes. You need my help. There are rumors you are an unbeliever. The people aren't sure of you yet. But the support of the Grandmaster would put an end to all that. And I can offer you something else as well. The support of the Guardian faction in the Senate," Quaestor said.

"How?"

Quaestor leaned forward. "The Guardians have made it clear they disapprove of a woman ruling Keldaren. They are traditionalists, after all, and we've never had a female sovereign before. But if you were to appoint me as Viceroy…who better to appeal to traditionalists than the Grandmaster? Not only would that quiet the criticism against you, it would strengthen your hand in the Senate."

Claire raised an eyebrow. "If I did appoint a Viceroy, surely one of the Senators would want the position."

"I'm sure they would. But not if I was a candidate. Most of the Senators are members of the Syncrestry. They would certainly step aside if they knew the Grandmaster was interested."

"Of course," Claire said. *Since you would disavow anyone who didn't,* she thought.

"Name me as Viceroy, and I can deliver the Guardian faction…and the support of the people."

"And what would I have to deliver?" Claire asked.

"Your public support for the Syncrestry...and for a few laws we would like to see passed."

"What laws?"

"A small increase in the government's payments to support our work. The appointment of a few High Templers to represent the Syncrestry in the Senate," Quaestor said.

"I see." Claire forced a smile onto her face. "Well, you've certainly given me a lot to think about, Your Grace," she said, standing.

He rose as well. "Let me know what you decide, Your Highness."

Claire nodded. "Thank you for seeing me today, Your Grace. This visit has been most enlightening."

"I hope it's also strengthened your faith."

"I've been troubled by doubts in the past, Your Grace. But after what I've seen today, I don't think those doubts will ever bother me again."

"I'm glad to hear that." Quaestor held his hand out, palm up. "Control over the senate. The support of the people. All right here in the palm of my hand."

Right where you'd like to have me, Claire thought.

"I'm holding my hand out to you," Quaestor said. "Take my hand, Your Highness, and it can all be yours."

"I can hardly make such a decision without giving it some thought, Your Grace."

"Of course. But when the gods offer an opportunity, they often don't offer it for long. I'll give you some time to think. But I can't keep my hand out forever," Quaestor said. "Walk with the gods, Your Highness."

Claire turned to find Garina standing by the door. She followed the templer back into the gathering hall, where Kerry and the acolyte waited.

"A worthwhile visit?" Kerry asked, falling into step with Claire.

"Definitely."

Garina let them out the front doors. She bowed, and withdrew into the temple.

"Back to the palace?" Kerry asked.

"Yes, but ride with me in the carriage. We have a great deal to talk about."

"What is it? What happened in there?"

"I saw the future."

"Quaestor showed you the future?"

"Yes. But not the one he wanted me to see. I saw a great deal more than His Grace meant to show me."

They climbed into the coach. As they rolled through the city gates, Claire looked out at the beggars huddled beside the road. One of her guards rode over to distribute the customary coins to them. There was the usual assortment of old men and cripples, along with a few orphans. And one old woman wearing a tattered black cloak. The woman sat bent over, the hump of her back rising behind her.

She raised her head. Her hair was as white as bleached bone, but her face looked young. Her skin was the color of frost. The woman's eyes met Claire's gaze. They were solid orbs of black...and as the eyes stared deep into hers, a shiver ran through Claire's stomach.

The woman's back *moved*. The hump unfolded, turning into two black-feathered wings stretching out above her.

Another shiver seized Claire. As the coach passed outside the city wall, Claire leaned over to look back at the woman. She was gone. Only the usual beggars sat under the arches of the gates.

"Are you all right?" Kerry asked.

"I think the lack of sleep is catching up to me. I'm starting to see things."

"See things?" Kerry asked, a concerned look on her face.

Claire shook her head. "Never mind. I'm sure it's nothing. I need to tell you what happened at the temple."

They had reached the palace courtyard by the time Claire finished telling the story. "I knew the gods were a lie!" Kerry shouted. "I knew it! You should publicly denounce Quaestor!"

"And then what? Most of the people belong to the Syncrestry. If I speak out against the Grandmaster, the streets would be swarming with protesters. I would just be giving the Guardians another weapon to use against me in the Senate."

"The people would turn against Quaestor once they knew the truth!"

"I have no proof. And who would the people believe? A newly-crowned sixteen year old? Or the Grandmaster of the Divine Syncrestry?"

"You have to do *something*," Kerry said.

"Quaestor will answer for this. But not yet. I'll deal with him when my position is more secure." The coach stopped outside the gate of the inner courtyard, where her cousin Elsie was waiting.

Claire stepped down, and Elsie gave her a hug. "Are they finished?" Claire asked.

"Yes. The gravesmen just left," Elsie said.

"I want to see him."

Elsie nodded. "I thought you might." They went into the palace, with Kerry and four guards following them. Claire stopped a servant in the hall. "Have a glass of wine brought to me," she told him.

They continued on, until they came to the door of one of the cellars, where two Crown Guards stood watch, their silver armor glistening over the royal blue of their uniforms. One opened the cellar door for them. Claire, Elsie, and Kerry went down the winding staircase, while the guards waited in the hallway.

The cellar was hewn from rough, white-washed rock. The room was empty, except for a granite table standing near a fireplace. The statue lay atop the table. Claire stared at it for a moment, and then she turned to the others. "I need some time alone with him," she said.

Kerry stiffened, her armor clinking. "I shouldn't leave you alone, Claire. Not with an assassin on the loose."

"What could happen in here? There's only one door, and there are six guards upstairs watching it. I need to say goodbye to my father, Kerry. And that's something I need to do alone."

Kerry sighed. "I'll wait outside."

Footsteps sounded on the stairs, and one of the kitchen stewards came down, bearing a tray with a pitcher and cups.

"Pour me a glass, and then leave the pitcher on the mantle," Claire told him.

"Wait," Kerry ordered. "Has a taster sampled that wine?"

"Of course, Legate," the steward said.

"You're sure?" Kerry asked.

He nodded. "Quite sure."

"Then pour yourself a drink," Kerry ordered.

"For myself?"

"Yes. If you're sure it's been tasted, then take a drink."

The servant looked at the wine, and then at Kerry. Then he nodded. "Of course." He poured a glass, and took a sip.

Kerry nodded, and gestured for him to proceed. The steward poured a cup for Claire, and handed it to her. He set the pitcher on the mantle, and left the cellar. Claire lifted the cup to her lips, the cool liquid sliding down her throat. She put the cup down as Elsie came over and hugged her.

"Stay strong, Claire," Elsie whispered. Elsie turned to the statue, put her hand over her heart, and bowed before she left.

"I'll walk you back to your rooms when you're done," Kerry told Claire, as she headed up the stairs.

Claire took another drink of wine, staring at the statue. She put the cup down again, and walked over to the table. The heavy granite seemed to exhale cold as she stood next to it. The statue lay on its back, its stone eyes glaring blankly at the ceiling. Claire gazed into them, with a half-hope the stone might melt, and there would be light and life in them again. She knew better. But for a second, it almost seemed possible.

She ran a hand over her father's face. The gravesmen had done excellent work pouring the stone-resin. His whole body was petrified now into a life-sized statue. His face, frozen under the thin layer of stone, looked almost the same as it had in life. *Perfectly preserved for the tombs,* she thought.

"That's all I have left of you now. A statue," Claire told the stone-clad body. *And a legacy. A kingdom to rule. A people to lead,* she reminded herself. "I'll do my best," she said, leaning down to kiss his cold, stone cheek. "For you. For our people."

Don't cry, Claire thought, feeling her throat tighten. She took another sip of wine. A sharp, queasy pain twisted inside her stomach.

The air rippled in front of her, coalescing into the form of a woman—a woman dressed in a tattered black cloak, with towering wings rising from her back. The wings shivered, ruffling the raven-black feathers.

What the nether? Fear clawed through Claire as she stared at the woman. Skin the color of frost stretched taut over the sharp bones of her thin face. A circle of gold, studded with black-diamond skulls, rested atop her head. Long, white hair framed the woman's ashen face. Eyes, black as pools of pitch, stared back at Claire. The same eyes that had met hers at the city gate.

The ebony orbs seemed to reach down deep into Claire. Their black gaze felt like they were pulling, *wrenching* at something inside her. The intruder reached out a hand, and clenched cold fingers around Claire's throat. The woman's icy grasp vised down, cutting off her cry for the guards. Claire flung the goblet at the specter's head. It passed right through, clattering to the floor.

"So you can see me?" The woman's voice was like wind over a frozen river. *"A little late for a warning."* But her lips hadn't moved. *"And you can hear me too,"* her voice echoed in Claire's thoughts.

A dizzying warmth spread from Claire's stomach, racing through her body. Her legs buckled, and she sank to her knees. The woman knelt, her dark wings encircling Claire.

"Don't be afraid. I'm giving you a gift," her voice whispered.

Pain ripped through Claire's stomach, like a knife twisting inside her. *What the nether is she?* Claire thought, fighting to hold back the panic thundering through her.

"I think you know," her voice said, inside Claire's mind. *"Yes, I can hear you. Just as you can hear me.* Should I speak aloud?" the woman asked, her lips moving, and the words reaching Claire's ears. "That makes it easier, sometimes. And I do try to make it easy for my prey."

She leaned forward, her white lips brushing Claire's ear. "This will be the hardest part. It's not a quick poison, I'm afraid. It will be a few moments before I can take you."

Poison? Claire glanced at the cup of wine.

The woman nodded. "Yes. Your father's was faster. But they chose a slower one for you."

Who? A fiery ripple of pain tore through Claire.

"It will be over soon," the woman said, almost gently. "I don't know who it was. I only hear a call when prey nears a trap. I rarely know who set the snare. But I will tell you what I can, Claire. That helps, sometimes. Especially during a long passing."

Claire clawed at the fingers clenching her throat, but her hands passed right through the woman's ice-pale skin. Pain burned out from her stomach, spreading in a warm wave of agony through her body. A fuzzy blackness crept up at the corners of her vision. *No,* Claire thought. *She can't be...*

"I am. I'm Death, Claire. I'm the end of the beginning. And the beginning of the infinite."

The blackness filling Claire's head grew, lapping over her in waves. She slumped over. Death gently lowered her to the floor. A fiery panic flared inside Claire, burning back the darkness. A light caught her eye, and she turned her head toward it.

The fire. Claire blinked. The fireplace came into focus. She reached out toward the light. Her hand closed around the end of a stick protruding from the flames. Claire jerked it free and slashed at Death's face.

She screamed, the shriek echoing through Claire's mind. The icy fingers released her. Claire's throat opened, her lungs heaving as she greedily gulped in air.

Claire turned her head, forcing herself to gag. She retched up the wine. The blackness lifted, her head clearing. Then Death's frozen hand clamped down around her neck again. Claire swung the burning stick back at Death, stabbing the fire into her. Her howl tore through Claire's thoughts. Death's body rippled as she dissolved into a cloud of mist. The mist shrank back from the flames, melting into the air.

"You've won this round. But you have no idea how many enemies you have. It's only a matter of time before you stumble into the next snare. You won't last a week," Death's voice whispered in her head.

CHAPTER 2

Claire

Claire stared at the spot where Death had disappeared. A frigid shiver shook her spine. *She's hunting me,* Claire thought. Sickness surged in her stomach again. But this time, it wasn't from the wine.

"Guards," Claire called, her voice croaking out from her throat. "GUARDS!" she shouted. There was a clamor on the stairs as the door burst open above, and the guards rushed down. Kerry was the first, her sword flashing in the lamplight.

"What is it?" Kerry shouted, her eyes darting around the cellar.

"The wine," Claire croaked, gesturing to the cup lying on the ground. "It was poisoned."

"Get a surgeon!" Kerry ordered the guards. "And go find that steward!" Two of the guards raced off. Kerry put Claire's arm around her neck. "Can you stand?"

"I think so."

"Help me get her upstairs," Kerry ordered one of the guards. He helped Claire to her feet. They both supported her as she walked shakily toward the stairs.

"It'll be all right, Claire," Kerry told her.

"No," Claire said, "I don't think it will."

The surgeons bowed, and left her apartments, leaving Claire in her bed, with Kerry sitting in a chair beside her.

"Did your men find the steward?" Claire asked.

"They found his body. It was smashed at the foot of the palace walls. And they found an open window on the top floor," Kerry said.

"Did he jump? Or was he pushed?"

"I think he jumped. He hesitated for a second when I told him to drink the wine. I think he knew exactly what was in it. And I think he didn't want to wait for the poison to do its work," Kerry said.

"He was willing to die in order to kill me. How can the Crown Guard protect me from enemies like that?" Claire asked.

"We will," Kerry said grimly. "Whatever it takes, we will."

"There are some things even you can't protect me from."

Kerry leaned forward in her chair. "Something more happened in the cellar. Something you haven't told me."

Claire nodded. "But I don't think you'll believe it."

"Try me."

Claire sighed, and absentmindedly twisted the bedcovers with her fingers as she told the story.

When she had finished, Kerry was silent for a moment. And then a moment more. "I understand why you were afraid I wouldn't believe you," she finally said.

"Because you don't?" Claire asked.

"I believe you think it happened."

"And just what's that supposed to mean?"

"Poison can make people hallucinate, Claire. I'm sure that's all this vision of yours was."

"No. It was real. I felt her hand on my throat. I looked into her eyes. Besides, Death appearing to me with a warning from the gods…that's something straight out of the holy texts, Kerry."

Kerry nodded. "That's the problem. You know what I think of the texts. I thought you felt the same way."

"I did. Until today."

"And now you believe in the gods," Kerry said, sounding mortified.

"No. Now I don't know what to believe. But I know this—there's something more out there, Kerry. Something more than just what we see. Whether it's the gods or something else, I don't know. But I know it's there."

Kerry shook her head. "I believe only what I see proof of. I learned that when I was a Constable. And I've never seen a god…or some black-robed demon claiming to be Death. I still say the poison was making you delirious."

"So, you won't believe me," Claire said.

"*Can't* believe, Claire. Not won't. You know how I am."

"I know. It's the worst part about being your friend." Claire rubbed a hand over her face. "Fine. You can't believe me. I suppose I can live with that. I suppose I have to." Claire threw the blankets off her, and got out of bed.

"Where are you going?" Kerry asked.

"I have to get ready. I have an appointment with Uncle Malcolm this afternoon."

"You're still going to meet with the Chancellor?"

"The surgeons said I'll be fine," Claire said. "And I want to speak with him before I'm crowned. I don't have time to waste lying in bed. The funeral is tonight, and the coronation is tomorrow."

"I have enemies on my borders. I have enemies in my Senate. And I have enemies in my own palace. I need Malcolm's advice, Kerry. Advice on how to survive the crown."

That afternoon, Claire watched the walls of Tara roll past her as the coach entered the city gates. She looked for Death among the beggars there, but the black-robed specter was nowhere to be seen.

The wheels clattered over the cobblestone streets. When they reached the park at the center of Tara, the coach rolled up a flagstone road to the Senate Hall. High glass windows lined the towering building. Flying buttresses, each crowned with a statue of a Keldari hero, supported its arched roof.

A tower of blue and white marble stood at the north end of the hall, and the coach came to a halt beside the tower. Claire stepped out, and climbed the steps to the Chancellor's office. Malcolm's own Crown Guards stood watch at the door, and Kerry joined them as Claire went inside.

Malcolm was sitting behind a desk piled high with papers. His skin wasn't the creamy complexion of most Keldari, but the pallid white of someone who rarely saw the sun. He was dressed in silk, the generous cut of his tunic not hiding a stomach going soft with age. The Chancellor's golden collar hung around his neck. A gold trinity knot—the blazon of the royal family—dangled from the links of the collar.

Malcolm looked up from his papers. A look flashed over his face at the sight of her. His eyes narrowed, and his lips curled back into a tight, hungry smile, his teeth glistening. A wolf's smile. It disappeared in a heartbeat, melting into Malcolm's usual warm grin. But a tiny shiver ran down Claire's back all the same. *You're imagining things,* she told herself.

"Claire. Are you all right?" Malcolm asked. "I heard what happened. I had thought you would cancel our meeting."

"I've been better, Uncle. The surgeons said I was lucky. Otherwise, you would be planning my funeral."

There was a strange look in Malcolm's eyes—a glimmer of something Claire couldn't quite put her finger on. *Concern? ...Disappointment?* she wondered, a shoot of misgiving sprouting inside her. She forced a smile onto her face. "I hope I'm not interrupting anything too important."

"Not at all. Writing speeches gets to be quite tedious," he said.

"I don't think I've ever seen you preparing this intently for a campaign."

Malcolm frowned. "I'm afraid this election will be quite a challenge. I don't understand what makes her so popular. It must be the novelty that's stirred so much interest."

She took a chair. "Perhaps it's more than just novelty."

"What else could it be? Isabelle Garenne isn't exactly the most prominent name in Keldaren," Malcolm said.

"She's served three terms in the Senate. She's hardly unknown."

"Her rants against the upper classes have certainly ensured that. But she's hardly a leading candidate. I think she's just trying to make even more of a name for herself by being the first woman to run for Chancellor," Malcolm said.

"Yet you still seem worried, Uncle."

"Not really. This election will just be closer than the last few. But enough about me. I asked you here to talk about your future."

"I'd welcome your advice," Claire said.

"Colin intended to teach you how to rule, to prepare you to be queen. But the gods obviously had other plans for him. You never had the chance to learn how to be sovereign. No one could expect you to be prepared to take the throne."

Claire shifted in her seat. Unease gnawed like a mouse at the back of her mind. "That's why I've come to you, Uncle. For help."

"I'm happy to help, Claire. I've been thinking about how to help you ever since Colin died. I recommend you appoint a regent to help you rule Keldaren—at least until you have enough experience to rule it alone. That's why I've drafted this law," Malcolm said, pointing to a paper on his desk. "If you sign it, the royal council can begin searching for the right man to assume the regency."

The twinge of unease became a nest of gnawing, gnashing suspicions. "I'd be interested in reading that."

"Of course," he said, handing her the paper.

A growing chill curled through Claire as she read. *I've walked into another web,* she thought. *With another spider waiting in it.* She looked up, forcing a taut smile onto her face. "I'll admit I have little experience with legislation, Uncle. But this law seems to give much of the sovereign's powers to the regent."

Malcolm's smile looked as stiff as hers. "I can see how you might read it that way, Claire. That's the advantage of having someone to help you understand the complexities of the law. Those provisions are merely legal technicalities. They're necessary to empower the regent to act in the name of the sovereign when necessary. The sovereign still has the final say."

"Unless the royal council agrees with the regent, and overrules the sovereign. A royal council the regent would appoint," Claire said.

He blinked, his smile slipping.

Yes, Uncle, I noticed that part. Even as well-buried as it was, she thought, meeting his gaze. She tried to put steel into her stare, but in her lap, hidden beneath the paper, her fingers fidgeted nervously with her bracelet.

Malcolm held her gaze for a few heartbeats. Then he looked away. "Well, perhaps that section needs to be re-written," he said, his smile tightening back into place.

"Perhaps it does. I'll consider your proposal. I'll consider it very carefully," Claire said.

"Please do." He leaned forward again. "There are enemies gathering, Claire. They see Keldaren as weak after the death of its king, with a young and untested new queen. The Guardian faction in the Senate will use this opportunity to try and unravel all the accomplishments of your father's reign."

"The Crusaders will try to stop them, but with their losses in the last election, they'll be too timid to be of much help to us. Appointing a regent will send a strong signal to both factions. It will put the Guardians on notice that we won't be intimidated, and it will put some steel into the spines of the Crusaders," Malcolm said.

"*We* won't be intimidated by the Guardians, Uncle? Aren't you a Guardian yourself?"

"Yes, but I know your sympathies lie with the Crusaders. And I am your Chancellor. I'll support whatever positions you set for the government," Malcolm said.

"How reassuring. But don't assume you know where my sympathies lie," Claire said.

"I'm sorry if I was presumptuous. I do know this, though. We face enemies from both within and without. The Drakari and the pirate clans will also see the king's death as an opportunity. Having an experienced regent ruling next to you would give our enemies pause in any plans they're making. And Keldaren has its share of enemies, Claire."

"I know exactly who Keldaren's enemies are," Claire said.

"I'm so glad." His smile widened. "I look forward to defeating them."

Claire matched his smile. "As do I."

Dral

Dral heard the office door close behind the girl. He turned a lever. The back of the bookcase swung out, and light flooded over him. He stepped out and swung the bookcase closed, hiding the passageway behind it again. Malcolm turned in his chair. The scent of defeat hung over him.

"Will she sign it?" Dral asked.

Malcolm smiled. "I think so. I just need more time to convince her."

"You're lying to me, Prince." Dral said it softly, with just the hint of a hiss. "I can smell the truth."

Malcolm glared at him. "Fine. No, I don't think she'll sign it. Tell your queen she'll have to deal with Claire."

"*You* were supposed to deal with her," Dral said.

"I answer to Minerva, not to you. Take care you don't forget your place," Malcolm said.

"I know my place, *Prince*," Dral hissed. He turned to the bookcase and opened it. Dral slipped into the passageway, closed the bookcase behind him, and climbed down a ladder to the tunnel.

He needs a lesson in humility. And the Queen will give him one.

CHAPTER 3

Minerva

Minerva sat in front of the fireplace, staring into the flames. There was a soft creak behind her. The sound of a turning hinge. She smiled. "Is this an assassination, Sis?"

"If it was, I would have made sure that hinge was oiled. How did you know it was me?" The voice echoed in the room.

"Only a Viper Knight could have slipped past my guards. And no Viper Knight other than you would have dared to come here." Minerva stood.

"And why is that? My knights have nothing to fear from your guards."

Minerva turned, scanning the room. "But they know their commander wouldn't approve of a knight practicing stealthcraft on the queen. A knight other than the commander herself, that is." Minerva stopped, facing one of the corners. "There you are."

"Wrong." There was a noise behind her, and a shadow seemed to part as a cloak opened. Black-gloved hands reached up and pulled down the hood, revealing a face framed by long locks of scarlet hair. "I'm here."

"How did you do that, Anastasia?"

Her sister turned the cloak, the light bending around it. "It's woven from shroudsilk. Ghost spiders on Aedan Island wrap themselves in it when they leave their burrows to hunt. It's like wearing a shadow."

"That must be very useful," Minerva said.

"It is."

"You should keep the hood up, to hide that head of yours. Your hair used to be like spun gold. If mother knew you'd dyed it that awful shade of crimson…" Minerva shook her head. "She'd turn in her grave."

"Some of us value faith more than beauty."

"You have your powers, Anastasia, and I have mine. Golden hair *is* power."

"One of *your* powers, sister. Mine are deeper," Anastasia said.

"Well, by the time this is done, we'll see about that, won't we?" Minerva asked.

"I have news on that front." Anastasia pulled a roll of paper from her robes. "A pigeon just arrived with a message from one of my knights. Malcolm failed. Claire won't sign the regency law."

Minerva took the paper. "I thought he might surprise me by succeeding."

"That was too much to hope for, apparently. He's been a useful source of information. But he lacks the subtlety for an assignment like this," Anastasia said.

"If he can't convince Claire to give up the throne, then we'll have to take it from her. Send a message to your men at Drohea. Tell them to set the plan in motion," Minerva ordered.

"And what of Malcolm?"

Minerva crumpled the message in her hand. "His usefulness has come to an end," she said, tossing the paper into the fire.

Anastasia smiled.

Claire

Claire and Elsie walked through the main hall of the palace, passing the portraits of Crown Princes lining the walls. Elsie paused at the last one. "I still can't get used to seeing your portrait there."

"I have trouble believing it myself, sometimes. But that's even harder to believe," Claire said, pointing to the black curtain painted over the face in the next frame.

"At least it's still there. The people burned enough of them over the past year," Elsie said.

"It's bad enough that people burn them, but for Father to allow Jared's portrait to be painted over, here in the palace…"

"He could hardly just leave it as if nothing happened," Elsie said.

"I know. It seems wrong, though, trying to erase all memory of him. He's still my brother, and I miss him. I used to wish Jared was still Crown Prince, so I wouldn't have to take the throne."

"Jared was always a bit too…unstable," Elsie said. "And he grew more troubled with each passing year." Elsie shook her head. "You were the best choice. Jared proved that."

"All Jared proved was that he wasn't the right choice. Now I have to prove that I am. I have to prove it to the people. And to myself." Claire turned, and went to a window next to the palace doors. Below, the inner courtyard was lit only by a few torches in the twilight. Guards stood at the corners of the small square, keeping watch over the coffin resting in its center.

The outer courtyard blazed with light. Rows of braziers stood amongst the aisles of chairs at the front of the yard, and many of the people standing in the commoner's section carried lanterns. Torches and lanterns also swarmed like fireflies over the hills surrounding the palace.

"It looks like all of Tara turned up for the funeral," Claire said.

"The people loved Uncle Colin a great deal."

"Some of them loved him. Your father was popular with *all* the people. But the crowd at his funeral wasn't this large."

"My father was only a prince. Yours was the king." Elsie looked at her. "Are you ready?"

"No," Claire said.

"We'll wait a little while longer, then."

Claire looked at her reflection in the window. A pale, stricken-looking face stared back at her. Even her freckles looked pallid. Unshed tears softened the bright green of her eyes. Claire set her jaw; willing the color back into her features. "We could wait a lifetime, and I still wouldn't be ready. We'll go now." She turned, and walked outside.

Crown Guards fell into step with her as she and Elsie descended the marble stairs. Claire looked around for Kerry, but she wasn't among the guards. They reached the inner courtyard, and Claire stopped for a moment at the bottom of the steps. She took a deep breath, and turned to face the casket.

Six guards stood watch over it. Claire walked to the casket, and bent down to kiss it. Grief surged inside her, and a crack opened in the mask she wore—a crack wide enough for tears to slip through. *Just get through the next hour,* she told herself. Claire straightened, wiping her eyes, and nodded to the Centurion standing nearby. He barked an order, and the guards stepped up to the coffin.

"Wait," Claire said. She gestured for one of the guards to step aside, and took his place next to the coffin. Bagpipers and drummers lined up in front of the casket, and struck up a funeral dirge. At the Centurion's order, Claire and the guards bent to lift and shoulder the casket.

The Centurion led the procession toward the iron gates of the inner courtyard, which swung open at their approach. They marched to a wooden platform at the head of the outer courtyard. Quaestor waited there, resplendent in his golden robe and headdress, flanked by a dozen templers. They climbed the steps to the platform, and gently laid the coffin down.

There was a chair set aside for her in the front row, and Kerry waited in the chair beside it. Claire and Elsie took their seats, along with the rest of the nobles and ministers. Quaestor walked over to the coffin.

"People of Keldaren!" Quaestor called out. "We are here tonight to mourn the loss of our great King Colin, and to beseech the gods to speed him on his way to the afterlife. May they welcome him with open arms!"

Turning to face the casket, Quaestor pulled a small knife from the folds of his robe. Putting the tip of the blade to his thumb, he pushed it into his flesh. When he pulled the knife away, blood glistened on his fingertip. Quaestor turned toward the casket, and traced prayers atop the coffin with his thumb.

When the Grandmaster had finished writing, he turned to face the crowd. "We gather together to celebrate the memory of King Colin…" he began.

Kerry leaned close to Claire. "I have something to tell you," she whispered, as Quaestor droned on. "Take out your handkerchief and pretend to cry. It'll look like I'm comforting you."

Claire pressed her handkerchief to her face. "What is it?" she whispered through the cloth.

"Lord Halen has arrested Senator Declan. He plans to charge him with conspiring to murder your father," Kerry said.

"Declan? But he and Father were both Crusaders. What would Declan gain by killing Father?"

"I know. It doesn't make sense," Kerry whispered.

"And why is the Captain of the Crown Guard personally arresting anyone, let alone a senator?"

"No one in the Guard knows much about it. Lord Halen is keeping the investigation sealed until he formally presents the charges," Kerry told her.

Claire looked at Quaestor, who was bringing his eulogy to a close. "He'll have to answer my questions. Whether the case is sealed or not," Claire whispered. "Go and tell Lord Halen I'm ordering him to explain what's going on with this investigation."

Kerry nodded. "I will. But I do have to prepare your coach and escorts for the coronation, and Lord Halen is overseeing the arrangements at the Royal Hill. I'll have to speak with him tomorrow."

Quaestor finished his speech. Everyone stood as he said his final invocation over the coffin. Claire joined the guards on the platform, and helped to carry the casket again. They processed back into the inner courtyard, where they lowered the coffin onto the stone slab.

Quaestor and his two attendants left, but the remaining templers followed the procession. They set up braziers around the coffin, bathing it in light. The templers sat in a circle around it, murmuring incantations as they settled in to sit vigil.

Claire walked to the staircase. There were statues carved into the hillside the palace stood on, and she stopped in front of them. Huge stone figures stood in a ring, their arms raised. A gigantic slab of stone, carved in the shape of Eris, rested on their upturned palms. There were five statues—one for each member of the high circle of the gods. The statues' gazes were fierce and confident. Their muscular arms easily bore the weight of the world.

Elsie came up next to her. "That's what I need to be," Claire told Elsie, nodding at the figures.

"A god?" Elsie asked.

"No, a statue."

"You want to become a statue?"

"I want to be like one. Look at them. They're carrying all of Eris. But they don't feel weak. They don't feel afraid. They just hold up the world, strong as stone," Claire said.

"That's because they are stone."

"Maybe to be a queen, you have to become stone," Claire said.

"Stone is strong," Elsie said. "But it's also brittle. A hammer could shatter one of those statues."

"It would take many blows to break them. And a very heavy hammer. I've already taken a few hammer blows lately, Els. And I have a feeling there are more ahead. Stone can withstand a hammer. That's what I need to become."

"Stone can't heal. It can only take the blows until it breaks," Elsie said.

"Stone can't run away. It can endure. And it can hold up the world. A queen can't run away. A queen has to endure. And a queen has to hold up the world," Claire said.

Elsie didn't reply. But there was worry in her eyes. *She doesn't understand,* Claire thought. She closed her eyes. She saw herself standing alone, naked in a sandstorm. The burning wind whipped sand against her, tearing the flesh from her body. *Stone can withstand the storm.* She saw herself turning to rock—turning into a statue.

The stone finished its crawl up her body, leaving a statue of herself standing strong on a pedestal—a fierce, confident gaze frozen on her face. *Let the winds blow. Let the sands fly. They can't hurt me now.*

Claire opened her eyes. She looked at the statues. *I'm as strong as they are,* she thought. *Strong as stone.* "Strong enough to hold up the world," she said aloud.

"What?" Elsie asked.

"Nothing," Claire said. "Let's go in."

At the top of the steps, Claire paused before going inside. She looked down at her father's casket, and the templers surrounding it. They sat in a ring around the coffin, swaying rhythmically as they intoned prayers. Claire remembered a Copperviper she had startled in the forest once. It had reared up on itself, rocking back and forth as it waited for a chance to strike. *It looked just like they do,* she thought, staring at the templers.

CHAPTER 4

Varin

Varin led the group across the wind-swept moors surrounding Drohea Castle. Clouds scudded across the sky above them, scattering the light of the low-hanging moon. He signaled a pause behind a hill. Varin lowered his hood, and the other knights did the same, revealing the steel serpent-faces of their helmets.

"Drohea was held by Drakaren for some time during the last border war," Varin said. "It served as General Magreve's headquarters. He had a tunnel built into it as an escape route. The Keldari never found it when they re-took the castle."

He reached up, feeling around the edge of a large rock set into the hill. A small piece of the rock sprang upward. He slid his hand into the open panel, grasping a lever inside. The entire rock slid soundlessly up on hinges.

Varin ran his hand over the crushed stone coating the metal form of the rock. Even up close, it was hard to tell it from the real rocks littering the hillside. He gestured for the other knights to follow, and stepped into the tunnel, feeling along the wall until he found the torch.

Varin struck a flint, setting the torch alight. He led the knights through the tunnel, passing under the wooden beams shoring up the packed earth. They followed the tunnel until it reached a small chamber. A ladder stood there, stretching up through a dark, narrow shaft.

"In the castle above," Varin whispered, "there's a spiral staircase, with a central stone column. The column looks solid, but it's actually hollow. This ladder goes up through the column into the rooms that were once General Magreve's quarters. That's where our target is. Stay absolutely silent. Any noise might be overheard by Keldari on the stairs."

The knights nodded. Varin started up the ladder, climbing with one hand and holding the torch with the other. They climbed for several stories, until Varin came to a stone ceiling. Varin blew out the torch, leaving them in total darkness. He felt the stones above him, and found the latch. He pulled it, and with a soft click, the trapdoor swung open.

Varin gestured to the other knights to wait, and climbed up into the closet above. He stepped to the side, closing the trapdoor after him. The stones fit perfectly back together, disappearing seamlessly into the floor.

Varin searched the room beyond, looking for heat. *He's alone.* Even now, it was unnerving to be able to see heat like a snake. *One of the many things to get used to as a Viper Knight. And one of the stranger effects of drinking the Venom,* he thought. Varin swung the door open. The room beyond was lit only by a few lamps and a flickering fire.

"So, Captain, is it time to go?"

Varin bowed. "It is, Your Highness. But please, don't call me by my old rank. I won't use a title granted by your fool of a father."

Jared leaned forward in his chair, his face emerging from the shadows. His eyes gleamed in the firelight. Varin stared at Jared for a moment. The prince's eyes always had an odd light in them—a look that seemed to dance precariously on the edge of madness. But it had grown worse since his imprisonment. And today, his gaze looked especially wild.

His voice, though, was calm, and controlled. "Of course. Forgive me, Sir Varin. I suppose I still think of you as the Captain Varin of my youth. The tutor who was more like a father than a teacher."

"I'm honored you think of me like that. Gods know you deserved a better father than the one you had," Varin said.

"Yes, I did. I should have rid myself of him when I had the chance," Jared said.

"It's better that you didn't, Your Highness. We can claim the Crusaders tricked your father into imprisoning you. But we could never restore your reputation if you had actually succeeded in killing him."

"You're right. I should have controlled myself better." Jared shook his head. "But you have no idea how angry I was, Varin. When he told me I wasn't good enough to be king…that I was too unstable, and that he sometimes thought I was out of my mind… I was so furious that I couldn't even see straight. But I didn't lose control until he told me Claire would be queen after him." Jared laughed. "What did he expect me to do when he gave *her* my birthright?"

"He probably didn't expect you to come after him with a dagger," Varin said.

"The guards didn't expect that either. But they were still too quick for me. And then my sister was free to steal my place as heir." Jared shook his head. "But the people call me a traitor."

"Many do call you a traitor, and worse, Your Highness. But there are those of us who know who the true traitors are. Your father has already paid the price for his treason."

"He really is dead, then?" Jared asked.

"Yes. His funeral is being held this evening," Varin said.

"Good. Let's be on our way, Varin. We have another funeral to plan."

"Is there anything you want to bring?" Varin asked.

"No, there's nothing I want from…" Jared stopped as Varin raised a hand.

Varin saw the approaching heat through the wall. "There's someone coming. Distract them," he whispered. Varin ran across the room, and ducked into an alcove behind a tapestry. He pulled a dagger out, and cut a small slit in the fabric, pressing his eye up against it.

The door swung open, and a Keldari Centurion stepped in, followed by a soldier. The soldier wore black armor over his crimson uniform, and a matching black helmet. The Centurion, though, wore no armor. *Not that any would fit him,* Varin thought. The Centurion was grossly fat, his uniform straining over his bulging flesh. *He's not even carrying a sword. The soldier dies quickly,* Varin decided. *That swine of a centurion won't be so lucky.*

Jared stood. "Ah, Centurion Elak. The brave commander of Drohea. To what do I owe the honor of your visit?" he asked, sneering.

"I bring bad news, Prince," Elak growled. "The King has died."

"I've already heard of my father's demise."

Confusion bloomed across Elak's fat face. "How could you know?" Elak turned to the soldier behind him. "Who's been talking to the prisoner?" he demanded.

Now, Varin decided. He whipped the tapestry aside and hurled the dagger. The blade buried itself in the soldier's throat, disappearing behind a burst of blood.

Elak stood frozen for a few heartbeats, staring as the soldier crumpled to the ground. Varin charged at Elak, knocking him to the floor. He squeezed his hand tightly around the fat throat, cutting off Elak's squeals of fear.

"Get the sword, Your Highness," Varin said, nodding toward the fallen soldier. Jared went over and pulled the sword from its sheath. "Open your mouth," Varin ordered the Centurion. The man's face went an even paler shade of white. "Put the blade in his mouth," Varin told Jared. "If he makes even the slightest noise, cut his tongue out."

"Gladly. I've waited a long time for this, Elak," Jared said, sliding the tip of the blade between Elak's jaws.

Varin went to the door, and drew his sword. He flattened himself against the wall and knocked. The guard outside unlocked the bolt. Varin kicked the door open, hitting the guard with it. A quick slash of the blade, and the guard's blood pooled at Varin's feet. Varin checked the hallway, and then came back into the room.

"You have a choice, Your Highness. We can escape quietly back through the tunnel. It will probably be an hour or so before anyone realizes you're gone. Or we can walk out the door, kill the garrison as they sleep, and send a message to the rest of the soldiers who are loyal to the traitor queen," Varin said.

"Let's send a message, Varin. And let's start with this filth," Jared said, kicking Elak.

"I have a better idea, Your Highness. Let's leave him right here. When a Keldari patrol comes to the castle and discovers what happened, he'll deliver our message to all of Keldaren."

"This castle is in the middle of nowhere. It might be weeks before a patrol passes by," Elak protested.

"Even if it takes that long, I doubt you'd starve," Varin said, glancing at Elak's stomach. "Stand against that pillar," he ordered, pointing to one of the wooden beams supporting the ceiling. Varin went into the closet, and brought the rest of the knights out. Taking a length of rope from one of them, Varin tied Elak's hands together behind the pillar.

Varin took a piece of paper from the desk, and wrote on it. He showed it to Elak. "Read it."

"Death to traitors," Elak read, his voice shaking.

"Will you deliver that message for us, Centurion?"

"Yes! I promise I will."

"Thank you," Varin said. He went to put the paper into Elak's hand. "Oh, forgive me. I tied your hands, didn't I? I'll just fasten it to your uniform."

Varin held the paper against the centurion's chest. He jerked a dagger out from his robes and stabbed it into the center of the paper, driving the blade deep into Elak's lung. Elak tried to scream, but all that came out was a strangled, wheezing gasp.

"You shouldn't have done that," Jared said.

"I'm sorry, Your Highness. I didn't think you would object to seeing him die slowly," Varin said.

"Oh, I don't." Jared tapped the reddening parchment. "But the blood is making the ink run. It's ruining the message you wrote."

"On the contrary, Prince. Blood *is* the ink. Shall we go down and write some more?"

Jared smiled. "By all means. I happen to have a pen at hand," he said, hefting his sword. Varin gestured to the door, and the other knights spread out, drawing swords from their black cloaks.

Two hours later, they stood in the Harva Woods, overlooking the moors surrounding Drohea Castle. Varin croaked a command toward the trees, and a croaking call answered. Enormous ravens emerged from the gloom, hopping toward them.

Varin held out his hand, and his roc bent down to him. He scratched its beak, rubbing it like a horse's muzzle.

Varin gestured toward the back of the double saddle fastened on the roc. "Minerva awaits you in Graydare."

"Then I shouldn't keep her waiting," Jared said, stepping up into the stirrup and onto the roc's back. Varin swung up into the saddle in front of him, and croaked down to the roc. There was a flurry of black wings as the huge bird hopped into the air, wheeling westward.

CHAPTER 5

Claire

Claire sat in front of a mirror, watching Elsie comb her hair. She had set aside the braided silver circlet she had worn as a princess. Claire stared into the mirror, examining the blue gown she wore. Elsie finished combing, and stepped back to admire her work.

"You look so beautiful, Claire. Why can't you wear things like this more often? You dress like a peasant milkmaid most of the time. Or like a soldier. You're going to be Queen. Why not dress the part?"

"If I'm going to be Queen, I should think I can wear whatever I want. And I don't like being dressed up like some doll," Claire said.

"Well, you can at least do something with your hair more often. Why not wear it down, instead of in a braid all the time?"

"Els, why do you care so much? I wear my hair the way I like to wear it."

"Because men prefer women who wear their hair down, who powder their faces, and dress like princesses. If you would just put some effort into it, you might catch someone's eye," Elsie said.

"I would think men would prefer a woman who's comfortable with herself. A woman who doesn't feel a need to hide behind powder or ball gowns. But whatever a man prefers, catching one's eye is the last thing I want," Claire said.

"And why is that?" Elsie asked.

"No man ever sees my hair, or my face, or my clothes when he looks at me. A man looks at me and sees a crown, a throne, and power. He sees those things and he wants them. He doesn't want me," Claire said.

"All men are attracted to a beautiful woman. No matter who she is," Elsie said.

"To a man, power is more attractive than any woman. And to a man, I'm nothing more than a stepping stone to royalty and power," Claire said.

"You're much more than that, Claire. You are beautiful. Even with the braid, and without the powder. And you have the sharpest wit I know. Men do value intelligence."

"To men, a sharp mind is like a sword. It's desirable only when they're the ones wielding it. Otherwise it's a threat. Especially if belongs to a woman."

"So, you plan on spurning all men?" Elsie asked.

"I'd rather have no man than a false one. But if I ever find one who seems worth the effort, I'll give him the chance to prove himself to me," Claire said.

"Not many men would wait around for that."

Claire shrugged. "That's their problem. Not mine. Besides, after tonight, I'll be a married woman."

"Married?"

"Tonight I'll take a vow to protect Keldaren, through peace and war, for as long as I live. Isn't that like a marriage?" Claire asked.

"I suppose it is. But are you marrying for love, or duty?"

"Both," Claire said.

The coach arrived at the Royal Hill just before midnight. A ring of guards held back the crowds. Cheers rang out as Claire stepped down from the coach. The guards cleared a path to the stone steps at the base of the hill. Claire and Elsie started up, the roar of the crowd filling the air around them.

Huge stone monoliths stood in a circle at the hilltop, with torches set into the ground beside each pillar. Claire reached the top of the steps, and turned, waving to the crowds below. They erupted in cheers, and she fought the urge to duck behind the huge stones. She forced herself to smile and wave. After a moment, she turned and slipped into the stones' shadows.

"You don't like this, do you?" Elsie asked from beside her.

"I hate being on display," Claire said.

"You're their Queen. The people want to see you. They were cheering you, Claire. Most rulers love to bask in adoration. Most rulers would have to be dragged away from a crowd cheering like that."

"I suppose I'm not like most rulers, then. I can lead the people well enough without being paraded around in front of them," Claire said.

"No. You can't. You were right before—this is like a marriage. You have to show Keldaren who you really are. If you keep yourself hidden, the people will never trust you. They'll never love you," Elsie said.

"And what if they don't love who I really am?" Claire asked.

"That's like a marriage, too. You have to be comfortable being yourself, and trust they'll see what makes you loveable," Elsie said.

"Assuming that I am."

"You are, Claire. Your father saw it. I see it. And in time, the people will see it too. Just be yourself, and they'll come to love you."

"I hope so. It's not as if they have much choice in this particular marriage," Claire said.

Elsie laughed. "And you're not exactly an eager bride!" She looked at the circle of people gathered at the center of the hilltop. "Are you ready?

"No."

"Good. No one ever is. Let's go," she said, pulling Claire's arm. Elsie led her over to the cluster of people. The High Arbiters, Quaestor, and Malcolm were all among the small crowd. Claire stepped into the center of the circle, and knelt down on a flat slab of granite set into the ground.

The Chief Arbiter walked toward her, followed by another Arbiter carrying a velvet cushion. A thin circle of spun gold glistened on the cushion. "Do you swear to preserve and protect

Keldaren, to stand between it and all dangers, through war and peace, for as long as you live?" the Chief Arbiter asked.

"I swear," Claire said. The next few moments were a blur, as he lifted the crown, and the golden circlet descended to rest atop her head. She put a gold ring bearing the royal blazon on her finger, and the circle of onlookers applauded. Claire stood, and Elsie gave her a fierce hug.

Claire took the crown off and turned it in her hands. Reflected moonlight raced like golden fire across its surface. She raised the crown up, and set it firmly into place atop her head again. Then she smiled at Elsie, and walked out beyond the pillars to the edge of the hill. The cheers roared out from below, crashing against her like a tidal wave. This time, though, she didn't shrink back. She let the cheering wash over her, and carry her away.

Dral

Dral sat behind the Chancellor's desk, his hands steepled together, watching the office door. The footsteps down the hall grew closer, and the door swung open.

Malcolm frowned as he shut the door behind him. "What are you doing here? Get out of my chair."

Dral didn't move. "Back from the coronation, Prince?"

"Yes. I told you to get out of my chair."

"And I told you that you were supposed to deal with Claire. Her coronation never should have happened without her signature on the regency law."

"I did my best. Now, get out of my chair and tell me what you're doing here."

"I have a message from the Queen." Dral gestured, and two black-robed Viper Knights stepped out from the shadowed corners of the room. They seized Malcolm's arms. One of them clamped a gloved hand over his mouth.

Dral stood. He drew a chain from his robes and wrapped it around Malcolm's neck. Malcolm struggled against the knights holding him, whimpers escaping from behind the hand covering his mouth. Dral looked into the prince's bulging eyes. "Your usefulness to the Queen is at an end, Malcolm. If you had been less arrogant, I would have done this in your sleep. Something for you to think about. While you still can."

Dral wrapped the chain around his hand and gave it a jerk. There was a soft snap, and Malcolm's body went limp. Unwrapping the chain, Dral slipped it back into his robes. "Bring the body down the tunnel," he ordered the knights. "We have to be clear of the city by dawn." *But we'll be back soon.* He looked out the window, gazing at the distant walls of the royal palace. *There's another neck here that needs snapping.*

CHAPTER 6

Claire

Claire was already awake and dressed when the sunlight first stretched through the palace windows. A knock came at the door. "Come in," she called.

Kerry walked in, closing the door behind her. "Did you sleep?"

"A few hours. I'll sleep better when Father's killer is caught."

"I just went to speak with Lord Halen. He wasn't in his rooms, though. He was called to the Chancery Tower," Kerry said.

"And what does Malcolm want with him? Will he try to turn Lord Halen against me now?" Claire asked.

"The Chancellor has disappeared."

"Disappeared? When?"

"No one knows. His guards last saw him go into his office after the coronation. The guards went in to check on him after a while, but they didn't find anyone inside. The guards swear he never left the room," Kerry said.

"Did they search the tower?"

"If I know Lord Halen, he'll tear the place apart for any trace of evidence," Kerry said.

"I should hope so. This doesn't look good for the Crown Guard, Kerry. First the king is murdered, and then the Chancellor vanishes."

"Lord Halen will bring this conspiracy to light. I'm sure of it."

"He'd better, and quickly. The royal family is running out of members," Claire said.

Jared

Graydare was aptly named. The buildings, the trees, and even the people plodding through the streets below all were the color of ash. It had looked so different last time. *Minerva and I could see all the way to the ocean from that watchtower. The entire city was glowing in the moonlight,* Jared remembered.

Daylight revealed a different city, however. *Faded paint and worn facades look better by night,* he thought, gazing at the buildings below.

"Your Highness? The Queen is waiting for you below," Varin said.

Jared turned away from the castle's parapets, and walked back to where Varin waited. Varin's roc was perched behind him on the edge of the tower, and Varin croaked a command to it. The huge raven squawked, then jumped off the tower, soaring away over the city.

"It will be good to see her again, Varin. Especially now that I don't have to worry about skulking back to prison afterward."

"Smuggling you in and out of Drohea was quite inconvenient. But you'll never have to worry about that again, Jared. Soon you'll rule Keldaren, and your enemies will be the ones in prison."

"The lucky ones will be in prison. The rest will be in the ground. Take me to Minerva," Jared said.

Varin opened a door, and led Jared down the stairs into the palace. They walked through hallways hung with the black and white colors of the Drakari royal family. Varin led him through the great hall, to a large door flanked by two palace guards. A crown was carved into the polished black wood of the door. The guards saluted, and one swung the door open. They climbed a short flight of stairs into the throne room.

The chamber was long, with a vaulted ceiling. Stone statues flanked the black carpet stretching from the stairs to the dais at the far end of the room. Above the dais hung a gray flag, emblazoned with the image of a raven clutching a black sword in its talons.

An ebony throne stood beneath the flag. The throne was carved in the shape of a raven, its wings flanking the chair's armrests. The raven's head, carved with cruel eyes and a gaping beak, loomed over the throne's occupant.

Her crown was the first thing that caught the eye. It was a bronze circlet, with four diamond-shaped spikes rising from it.

Each spike was capped with a ruby. Curly tresses hung like a cloud of spun gold around her head, and a slim white dress encased her lean body.

Her eyes met Jared's. It was if the sculptor of the throne had used Minerva as his model. Her eyes held the same cunning look as the raven's. Cunning, and fierceness. *Someone to be reckoned with,* he thought, not for the first time. *Someone for our enemies to fear.*

She stood, and held out her hands. Jared went to her, took her hands in his, and leaned in for a kiss. After a moment, she pulled away.

"I've missed you so much," he said, leaning toward her again.

She held her finger to his lips. "I've missed you as well. But I know you must be tired. And we have much to talk about before you can get some rest. There'll be time for more…pleasurable pursuits later."

He sighed. "Very well. When do we attack Keldaren? Give me command of the Drakari Army, Minerva, and I'll bring you victory."

"I'm sure you would, Jared. But this calls for something more subtle than a full-scale invasion. I want you to lead a contingent to take Connemara Palace. You'll kill Claire, and take her place on the throne."

"But Claire has supporters in the Senate also. They won't accept me as king if they know I've killed her."

"No one will ever know you did it. You'll kill everyone at the palace. The next day, you'll address the Senate, and tell them you've uncovered a plot to stage a coup. You'll tell them the plotters framed you, and tricked your father into imprisoning you," Minerva said.

"And I'll blame these conspirators for killing Claire," Jared said.

"Exactly. You'll say you learned about the conspiracy from loyal members of the government, and that you escaped from Drohea to try and warn Claire. But when you got to the palace, you found that you were already too late. Then you'll tell the Senate you're going to reveal the identities of the conspirators. You'll read out a list of names—names of those senators who are really Claire's strongest supporters. As you read off their names, Drakari soldiers in Crown Guard uniforms will arrest those senators for treason," Minerva said.

"An excellent plan. Very well, we'll do it your way," Jared said.

Her eyes seemed to flash. Her smile didn't so much as twitch, but he could have sworn that a dark look had sparked in her gaze for just a second. *You're imagining things,* he told himself.

"I'm so glad you agree." She sat down on the throne, pointing him to a chair across from her.

"That's something we'll have to change," he said.

"What?"

"I'll need a throne of my own. What happened to your former husband's throne?" Jared asked.

Minerva laughed—a dark, hollow laugh that sent frost down his spine. "This was King Valus' throne," she said, tapping the carved wing of the armrest. "Now it's mine."

"Ah, well…perhaps we can discuss my throne some other time," Jared said.

"Yes. Perhaps we can."

"When do I leave for Keldaren?" he asked.

"Tomorrow. After the Ravek arrive," Minerva said.

"Ravek? You're sending Berserkers?" Jared heard the quaver in his voice.

Minerva smiled. "I'm sorry, Jared. I didn't know you would be uncomfortable commanding Ravek. I can have Sir Varin take the command."

"No!" He swallowed hard at the knot in his throat. "I'll do it."

"It's all right, Jared. The Ravek make many brave men nervous. It's no wonder King Azeras conscripted them into the army after he conquered their homeland. That gray sandpaper skin of theirs… those fangs and claws…they have quite the chilling effect on enemies."

"You know what always bothers me the most about them, though? Those empty white eyes. It's like staring death in the face." Minerva smiled again. "I can understand why the thought of commanding a contingent of them unnerves you."

"It doesn't," he said, trying to put iron into his voice. *She's testing me.* "Lesser men may fear the Ravek, but I don't. I'll lead whatever troops you give me."

"Spoken with the courage of a king, Jared. Only Ravek Berserkers are swift and brutal enough to take Connemara before an alarm can be raised. They're going on this mission. No matter who commands it."

"It won't be a problem," he said.

"And what about killing Claire? Will that be a problem?"

Jared stiffened. "My mother died giving birth to her. That was the first thing she ever took from me. Then Father chose her as heir, and she stole my kingdom. It's time I start taking from her. First the throne. Then her life. I'll cut her throat myself."

Minerva smiled. "Good. Now, I'm sure you're tired from the long night. One of the guards will show you to your rooms."

"I'm tired of being apart from you," he said.

A warm smile spread across her face. "We'll have the rest of our lives together, Jared. But I need you rested and ready to leave tomorrow. And I have a great deal of preparations to make."

Jared sighed. "Very well." He rose, and walked up to the throne. He leaned forward, and kissed her. *The next time I see her, I'll be King. Then I'll finally be enough for her.* He smiled as he left the room. *Success and power are irresistible to her. And once Claire's gone, I'll have plenty of both.*

Minerva

The door closed behind Jared, and Minerva let the shudder she had been holding back ripple through her.

A laugh echoed through the room. "What a touching reunion. You must have missed him terribly."

"It's bad enough I have to put up with that fool. Must I endure your mocking also?" Minerva asked.

Anastasia stepped out from behind a statue. "I'm sorry. It was too hard to resist." She took a chair. "I had no idea what you've been putting yourself through these past few months."

Minerva's jaw clenched, her teeth grinding together. "I can barely stand to be in the same room with him. And to let him touch me…it's hard to keep myself from stabbing him."

Anastasia raised an eyebrow. "Just say the word, and I'll gut him like an eel. Or, I can arrange an accident if you prefer something more subtle."

"You have no idea how tempting that is. But I need him. His accident will have to wait," Minerva said.

"So it will be an accident, then? A pity. I'd like to disembowel the sniveling little worm."

"Either an accident, or in battle. The Keldari people would become too suspicious if he were to fall ill so soon after his father died. They might start questioning whether those deaths were natural or not. Especially in light of the rumors surrounding my late husband's death," Minerva said.

"Yes. Very ugly rumors about poison. Why don't you put a stop to people whispering such scandalous things about you?"

Minerva smiled. "Who do you think started those rumors? No one can ever prove I had anything to do with Valus dying. But knowing I'll kill those who stand in my way…well, that's something I want my enemies to know."

"You have the cunning of a raven, Sis."

"And the fangs of a cobra," Minerva said.

"Just how far are you going to let this go? Are you actually going to marry that cur?" Anastasia asked.

"I don't have a choice. Many Drakari kings have tried to conquer Keldaren before. They've only succeeded in decimating both our armies and the royal treasury. If he and I marry, and unite our kingdoms into an empire, then I'll conquer the Keldari without them even realizing it."

"But then Jared will be Emperor and rule alongside you. You'll only be able to control him for so long. He may be a fool, but he's a strong-willed fool," Anastasia said.

"I can manipulate him long enough to gain legitimacy in the eyes of the Keldari. When the time is right, I'll be a widow again," Minerva said.

"Widowhood agrees with you."

"Yes, it does. I wish it weren't about to be interrupted with another marriage. Especially one to Jared. I'll need you to restrain me from killing him before the time is right." She gave Anastasia a thin smile. "That might be a very difficult task."

Anastasia didn't smile back. Her face turned solemn. *So serious,* Minerva thought, torn between pride and bemusement. *My little sister. The cold-blooded commander of the Viper Order.*

"I'll do whatever you need me to," Anastasia said. "You've brought us this far. I'm with you, no matter where we're headed next."

"We're headed upward," Minerva said. "We've clawed our way from a gutter to a palace. No one will ever bring us low again. I swear that to you. An empire is our destiny."

"Even with commoner's blood in our veins?" Anastasia asked.

"Our blood is noble now. Not by birth. By power. By force of will. We've made ourselves royalty. Once we've done away with Claire and Jared, we'll destroy the other royal families. Then our line will be the last royal blood left in all of Eris. And we can complete our empire."

CHAPTER 7

Claire

Claire stood on the balcony in front of the palace, staring down at the courtyard below. Her father's casket rested on a wagon, surrounded by mounted guards. A huge column of guards on foot gathered in the outer courtyard.

"Do you want to go down?" Elsie asked.

"No. I said my goodbyes last night. I couldn't bear saying them again." Kerry came out of the palace. Her jaw was tight, and her eyes were restless.

"What is it?" Claire asked.

"I just spoke to Legate Brandon about the funeral procession. With everything that's happened, I want to forgo the tradition of having a large procession of Crown Guards escort the king's body to the tombs. But Brandon decided we must respect tradition. So Brandon will lead two hundred guards north to the Castellan Islands." Kerry grimaced. "It will be a *month* before they return."

"Did you speak to Lord Halen about that?" Claire asked.

"He's finally on his way back from the Chancery Tower. But I'm sure he'll agree with Brandon. Lord Halen is nothing if not a traditionalist."

"You're a Legate, Kerry. Can't you just order that more guards remain here?"

"I'm Second Legate. Brandon is First. Only Lord Halen can overrule his decision." Kerry sighed. "I'll try to convince him to do the right thing. But I suspect he'll be stubborn."

"Perhaps he needs reminding that his leadership has been lacking lately. Father is dead, and Malcolm is missing. And there's the small matter of the attempt to poison me."

"Until recently, Lord Halen's leadership has been flawless," Kerry said.

"I know. His record is the only thing keeping me from replacing him. If he doesn't get to the bottom of this soon, there'll be a change of leadership in the Guard," Claire said.

"Then I hope he understands the seriousness of the situation."

"Try to help him understand, Kerry. Before I have to make him understand."

"I'll do my best. I'll go see if he's returned." Kerry headed off toward the Guard barracks.

Legate Brandon strode out into the courtyard below, and swung up onto a waiting horse. He signaled to the wagon, and the driver snapped the reins. The mounted guards took up positions alongside the wagon, and as it rolled through the outer courtyard, the column of guards fell into place behind it. The North Road was lined with people waiting to catch a last glimpse of the king's casket.

"I should be going with him," Claire said.

"No, you shouldn't," Elsie said. "The kingdom needs you here."

"Why? Does the kingdom need me at the coronation ball? Does the kingdom need me to smile and wave and reassure people that everything will be all right?"

"Yes. That's exactly what we need. We've just lost our king. We need someone to make things seem normal again. We need someone to tell us it'll be all right," Elsie said.

Claire's eyes were hot and wet, and she wiped them. "And just how the nether am I supposed to tell people that? *I* don't think it'll be all right."

Elsie put her arm around her, squeezing her close. "It's up to you to make it all right."

The funeral procession reached a curve in the road, and Claire caught a final glimpse of the wagon before it disappeared. *He's really gone.* "It feels like I should pray, Elsie."

"Perhaps you should."

"Part of me wants to. Part of me wants to turn to the gods for comfort. Part of me wants to curse the gods. And part of me doesn't even believe in them," Claire said.

"Really?"

Claire sighed. "There's something false about them…something beyond the lies of the templers. There has to be something out there, some greater power. Death coming for me proves that. But as far as the Syncrestry goes…the templers never show us any proof, Elsie."

"Proof of the gods' existence is too much to ask," Elsie said.

"I want a sign, at least. Something tangible. A bridge between us and the gods. I don't think that's too much to ask. I think it's something we need. Otherwise we lose faith. Otherwise doubts take root."

"The Syncrestry is a sign. The templers are a bridge," Elsie said.

"The Syncrestry is a theater, and the templers are play-actors. If that's a bridge, then it's a bridge that leads *into* a chasm. Not across one," Claire said.

"Then someone should build a new bridge."

"But what mortal can build a bridge to the divine? Isn't that something only a god can do?" Claire asked.

"What god would do that, though? What god would stoop down to our level, and offer a hand to a mortal?"

"A queen who loves her people goes out and meets them. She doesn't expect peasants to come to her. A good queen doesn't sit in her palace and use her people like pieces on a game board. She goes out to meet her people where they are, and offers her hand to them," Claire said.

"Maybe being a god isn't the same as being a queen," Elsie said.

"Maybe not. But love is the same, isn't it? Wouldn't the gods reach out to their people if they loved them? Wouldn't good gods offer their hands to their people?"

"The holy texts don't describe the gods like that," Elsie said.

"No, they don't. And maybe that's what feels false about them."

Jared

"I'll never go back to sea after this," Jared said.

"I'm sorry it's not to your liking, Your Highness. The sea can unman even the bravest of us," the captain said.

Jared glared at him. "I can handle the sea. I just prefer to have solid ground beneath me."

"As you say, Your Highness. This ship, though…no one can build a ship like the Kirosians. A Kirosian ship is almost as solid underfoot as dry land."

"They may be good shipbuilders, but the Kirosians in this convoy were poor warriors," Jared said.

"One warship's contingent of Marines is no match for three ships full of Berserkers." The captain shook his head. "I don't like having those creatures aboard."

"Let me worry about the Berserkers. You worry about your crew. Are they ready?" Jared asked.

"They are. And so am I."

"After you, then," Jared said, gesturing to the cabin door. As the captain headed out onto the deck, Jared checked the fastenings of the Kirosian mail he wore. He picked up the helmet from the table. The world went dark for a second, and then reappeared, framed by the steel circles of the helmet's grille as he settled it into place. A Drakari soldier, also wearing a Kirosian uniform, followed him out onto the deck.

The ship approached the watchtower guarding the mouth of the Siochana River. Jared stood next to the captain, watching as the ship neared the dock next to the tower. A spyglass flashed from the top of the keep.

Jared looked back over his shoulder. The other two ships followed them in from the sea, sailing toward the inspection dock. Both of them flew the same flag as his ship did—a banner emblazoned with Kirosia's falcon and anchor blazon. All of the crews wore Kirosian clothing and armor. And all three ships carried the same cargo.

"Will it work?" Jared asked.

"Aye," the captain answered. "Look at this lot," he said, nodding toward the crimson and black-clad Keldari soldiers lined up at the dock. "If they were sharp, they wouldn't have their entire garrison out for the inspection, and they'd keep more than just one lookout in the tower. It'll work, all right. We'll be in Tara by nightfall."

"Good," Jared said. He nodded toward the Keldari. "Your audience awaits."

The captain made his way to starboard, where the crewmembers threw lines out to the Keldari soldiers ashore. The sailors dropped the gangplank, and a Keldari officer stepped aboard.

"I'm commander of this garrison. We'll need to inspect your cargo before you continue up the river to Tara."

"Of course," the captain replied. "Your men are welcome to come aboard."

The officer signaled, and ten soldiers came up the gangplank. The Keldari gathered around the hatch of the main hold. "Open it," the officer ordered, nudging the hatch with his boot. Two sailors slid the bolt aside and swung the hatch open.

An arrow shot up into the officer's face. A swarm of Berserkers boiled out after it, climbing up on nets from the hold. The Ravek warriors smashed through the Keldari, leaving broken bodies in their wake. They streamed ashore, their warhammers making short work of the remaining soldiers. The Keldari had left the tower door unlocked, and the Berserkers stormed inside.

One Berserker stood waiting on the shore, a longbow in his hand. There was a commotion atop the keep, and a pigeon burst into the air from behind the battlements. The Berserker drew the bow back, and sent an arrow flying. The arrow connected, and the pigeon gave a keening cry as it spiraled down to the ground. *No messages*, Jared thought with a smile. *No one will know what's happened here.* A moment later, a Berserker appeared atop the tower, and threw a crimson and black-clad body over the side.

Jared met the Berserker commander ashore. The Ravek warrior was over six feet tall, and wore black steel armor. Silver ridges on the armor outlined his bones, making him look like a silver skeleton. Pebbled gray skin showed underneath his armor. The Berserker's empty white eyes glared through the eye holes in his silver, skull-faced helmet. He held up his warhammer. There was a curved axe blade on one side of the weapon's head, and a heavy hammer on the other. Blood dripped from the hammer, steaming in the cool air. Jared clenched his hands together, trying to hide their trembling.

"That was the last one," the Berserker growled, his needle-point fangs flashing in his mouth. "The tower is ours."

"Burn the bodies," Jared ordered, in as commanding a tone as he could muster. "We have an appointment to keep at Connemara."

CHAPTER 8

Claire

Claire walked across the courtyard from the stables, a squad of guards escorting her back from her ride. The guard ahead of her stopped suddenly. "What's that?" He pointed with his spear to a dark shape in the sky, barely visible in the thin light of the autumn afternoon. "There's another one," he said, pointing.

"Whatever they are, they're getting closer," Claire said, straining to see. One of the guards gave a whistle, and signaled the nearest guard tower. A bell began ringing. Crown Guards rushed out, taking up defensive positions in the towers and along the courtyards.

Kerry came running out to the courtyard, her hand on her sword hilt. "What is it? Who sounded the alert?"

"Look," Claire said, pointing. "Are they rocs?"

Kerry squinted, staring into the sky. "No. Dragons."

A shiver of excitement ran up Claire's back. The dragons drew closer, their forest-green skin dark in the fading light. They passed over the palace, their bat-like wings beating powerfully. Claws curved like scythes from their feet. As they passed overhead, she saw the long saddles on the dragons' backs. A rider lay flat on each saddle, holding onto posts at the front, their feet secured in stirrups. *Dragon Knights.*

The dragons turned slowly, drifting almost lazily into the wind, and descended into the courtyard. They floated down, landing with a thud that shook the ground. A knight slid down from each dragon. Both knights wore black chestplates, greaves, and helmets. Their uniforms, colored the same forest-green as their dragons, showed beneath the armor.

The first knight walked toward Claire. A tall helmet covered the knight's head and face, except for a pair of sea-green eyes peering out through the eye slits. A sheathed sword was slung on the knight's back.

The knight dropped to one knee and lifted her helmet, revealing a long, brown ponytail. "Your Majesty, I am Dame Sloane of the Dragon Order. Our prefect, Sir Fulton, sent me to pledge the Order's allegiance to you. He also asked me to give you this." Sloane held out a package wrapped in cloth.

Claire took it, and unwrapped the cloth to reveal a sword. The hilt was the golden body of a dragon, its wings forming the hand guard. The dragon's mouth was open, the steel blade emerging from it. *Like a stream of silver fire*, she thought.

"This was your father's sword, when he served with us. He left it at Mount Draconis, with instructions to deliver it to his heir after his death."

"I never knew my father was a Dragon Knight."

Sloane rose. "He was a knight for five years. He left the Order when he married your mother."

"I'd like to hear more about his time as a knight."

Sloane nodded. "Of course, Your Majesty. But with your leave, we must attend to our dragons first."

"Certainly," Claire said. Kerry stepped behind Sloane, staring at Claire. Claire raised an eyebrow.

Kerry gave a quick shake of her head. *Alone*, she mouthed.

"The guards will show you to the lake," Claire said. "There's a grove there where the dragons should be comfortable. And I'll have the kitchens send out some meat. I'm sure they're hungry after the flight from Mount Draconis."

"Thank you, Your Majesty. I'll find you after the dragons are settled?" Sloane asked.

"Just have a guard bring you to me." Claire handed the sword back to her. "And bring this with you as well."

Sloane bowed, and she and the guards headed off. Kerry followed Claire into the palace.

"I spoke to Lord Halen," Kerry said, once they were alone.

"And it didn't go well," Claire guessed.

"Not at all. He told me he has evidence that Senator Declan plotted to have your father murdered. I asked him why a Crusader senator would want to kill a king who was a member of his own faction."

Kerry sighed. "Lord Halen said King Colin wasn't progressive enough for the Crusaders. He said he believes they killed the king to replace him with you, hoping to manipulate you into making even deeper changes than your father."

"Then why would someone try to poison me?" Claire asked.

"I asked him that. He told me the conspiracy must be deeper than he thought." Kerry hesitated. "He says he'll reveal the evidence tomorrow when he brings charges against Senator Declan."

"But you don't believe him?"

Kerry shook her head. "I've known him long enough to tell he was lying. There's something wrong with Lord Halen, Claire. Something very wrong."

"Yes, there is. And it's past time I put it right. Come with me," Claire said.

"Where?"

"To Lord Halen's chambers. You're about to become Captain of the Crown Guard," Claire said.

"Me?"

"I can't think of anyone better for the job."

"What about Legate Brandon?" Kerry asked.

"You mean the man who ignored your advice? The one who thought following tradition was more important than ensuring his queen's safety? He needs to leave the Guard, not lead it."

"But why me?"

"Because of your scar. Because of the blood you shed to protect my father. That was why he chose you as head of my guard detail. And that's why I'm choosing you now," Claire said.

"It's a great honor, Claire. But I don't deserve it."

"No one could deserve it more."

"But the Captain of the Crown Guard has always been a noble," Kerry protested.

"Then I'll have to make you a noble. You deserve that as well. You're like a sister to me. And the sister of a queen should be nobility. I think you'll make an excellent countess."

"I'm flattered, Claire. And grateful. But my family's blood has never been noble."

"Nobility comes from the heart, not the blood. And your heart is nobler than anyone else's I've ever known," Claire said.

Kerry looked at her, her eyes shimmering in the light from the lanterns. Claire stopped walking. "Are you crying?"

"No." Kerry's voice cracked. "But if you say anything more like that, I might. That's...that's the kindest thing anyone's ever said to me. Thank you." She smiled. "I think of you as a sister, too. Even though I'm almost old enough to be your mother."

Claire smiled back. "Hardly."

They kept walking, until they entered the corridor leading into the guard barracks. Shadows stretched around the corner from the next hallway. Kerry held up her hand, signaling Claire to stop. "Listen."

Voices were murmuring around the corner. "It's Lord Halen," Kerry whispered. They crept closer.

"The Queen's coach is leaving shortly. Get the men ready to ride out," Halen said.

"My Lord, what about the palace?" another voice asked. "If there's a threat, surely we shouldn't leave it undefended, even if the queen flees."

"Don't worry about the palace. There'll be a small force staying under the command of the Second Legate. She and the remaining guards will protect Connemara."

"I'll send a message to the Tara Legion," a third voice said. "They can be mustered and marched here within two hours."

"No," Halen said. "I have word there are spies in Tara. If they see the Legion gathering, they'll know they've been discovered, and they'll send word to their troops to attack immediately. We must get the queen to safety first. I'll have Legate Bradaigh send for help after we leave. The queen is waiting in her coach in the stables. Go and guard her. There may be spies in the palace as well. I'll join you as soon as I've found Legate Bradaigh."

The voices grew distant as the guards walked away. Kerry and Claire crept back down the hallway.

"What the nether is going on?" Claire whispered. "Has Halen gone mad? I should go demand some answers from him."

"No, you absolutely should not. Not until we know what's happening here." Kerry stopped, listening. "Someone's coming this way. Put your hood up. And stand over there, in the shadow. Stay quiet."

Claire raised the hood of her cloak, and slipped into the shadows between the lanterns on the walls. A Crown Guard centurion came around the corner. "Legate Bradaigh. You startled me. Who is that?" he asked, gesturing toward Claire's shadowed form.

"Never mind her," Kerry said. "What's going on?"

"Lord Halen is looking for you. He wanted to let you know not to send for help until we've left the palace."

"And just why are you leaving the palace? And why would I be sending for help?" Kerry asked.

"I don't understand. Lord Halen said you had already been informed of the conspiracy," the centurion said.

"I haven't been. Enlighten me."

"Lord Halen received word from an informant that there's a plot to attack the palace and kill the queen. There are enemy soldiers marching toward the palace. Lord Halen is going to lead a contingent of guards escorting the queen as she escapes. He said our best hope of getting the queen out alive is to bring her out in a plain coach with a heavy escort. I don't understand, Legate. Lord Halen said you had volunteered to stay behind and defend the palace."

"And just where does Lord Halen say the queen is now?" Kerry asked.

"She's waiting in a coach in the stables below," the centurion said.

"She's there right now?"

"Yes, Legate. Lord Halen ordered me to go and help guard her until he arrives. He went to look for you before we leave," he said.

Kerry gestured to Claire. "The queen is right here."

Claire stepped forward, pulling her hood down.

"Legate, what's going on here?" the centurion asked.

"I mean to find out," Kerry said. "Follow us to the stables."

Claire and the centurion followed Kerry to the main hall of the stables, where a large contingent of guards was gathered around a plain wooden coach. "Wait here with the queen," Kerry told the centurion.

Kerry stormed up to the line of guards surrounding the coach. "Step aside," she ordered.

"Legate...Lord Halen ordered us not to let anyone near the queen," a lieutenant said.

"I'm sure he did. Step aside, Lieutenant. That's not the queen."

"What? Legate, I have my orders..."

"Step aside!" Kerry roared.

The lieutenant went white, and stepped out of her way. Kerry wrenched the coach door open. "Get out," she ordered.

A thin girl, wearing a heavy white cloak and hood, stepped down from the coach. Kerry reached up and yanked her hood back. *A kitchen maid*, Claire thought, recognizing the girl.

"Does this look like the queen?" Kerry shouted. "A contingent of Crown Guards fooled by a scullery girl! Your lack of vigilance is appalling. It's a wonder the queen hasn't been killed already, being guarded by the lot of you!"

"Please, Legate," the servant girl said, cowering back from her. "Lord Halen swore me to secrecy, and told me to put this cloak on and sit in the coach. He said I must keep my hood up, and not say a word to anyone. He told me I'd be helping to protect the queen from a great danger."

"He lied. Centurion!"

The centurion came hurrying to Kerry. "Detain her until I return," she ordered, gesturing to the servant girl. "And when Lord Halen arrives, arrest him."

"Arrest him? On what charge?"

"Treason."

"You want me to arrest the Captain of the Crown Guard for treason?"

Kerry stabbed her finger out at the centurion. "I'm ordering you to arrest him. Follow my orders, or I'll arrest you. Understand?"

The centurion nodded. "Yes, Legate."

"Listen to me, all of you. The queen is right there," Kerry said, pointing to Claire, who stepped into the hall. "I don't know what Lord Halen is up to, but it's nothing good. When he comes down here, take him into custody. I'm going to take the queen to safety. I'll deal with Lord Halen afterwards."

Kerry took Claire by the arm, steering her out of the stables. "Shouldn't we take some of them with us?" Claire asked as they hurried up the stairs. "Especially if Lord Halen is loose in the palace?"

"Some of them might be in league with Halen. Until I know which of them I can trust, I won't trust any of them. I don't know what Halen's doing, but it's something big. He must have help. I wouldn't put it past him to have accomplices in the Crown Guard."

"Where are we going?" Claire asked.

"To find the Dragon Knights. I'll have them fly you to Tara. They can bring you back along with the Tara Legion. They'll help me protect you until I know who I can trust in the Crown Guard. Some dark plot is brewing here. This palace won't be safe until it's guarded by the entire Tara Legion," Kerry said.

They were walking quickly now, almost running through the deserted halls of the palace. "And where will you be while I go off with the dragon knights?" Claire asked.

"Chasing Halen down. He's too clever to just walk into the stables and be arrested. You won't be safe until he's in a cell."

Claire stopped. "No. I won't leave you to face him alone. Either you come with me, or I'm not leaving."

"He's too dangerous, Claire. I have to find him. And I won't have you here while I'm hunting him down. I have to keep you safe."

"I told you, I won't be leaving without you. So either you come with me, or I'm staying to help you," Claire said.

A quiet footfall came from the hallway behind them. Kerry spun, her sword flashing in the lamplight as she jerked it clear of her scabbard. Lord Halen walked around the corner.

Lamplight glistened on his shaved head. He wore his uniform and armor, and held his sword at the ready. "Don't worry, Your Majesty. Kerry won't be going anywhere."

CHAPTER 9

Claire

"I never understood why you wanted to close the investigation of the king's death so quickly," Kerry said.

"And do you now?" Halen asked.

"No need to investigate when you already knew what happened. Did you do it yourself, or have someone else kill him?"

"I poured the poison myself," Halen said.

"And how did you get it past the taster?" Kerry asked.

"I've taught you well enough, Kerry. Put the pieces together. The only way to protect someone is to be able to think like an assassin. Tell me, how would an assassin get poison past a taster?"

"You'd slip an antidote to the taster in something else. Something that wouldn't reach the king's table," Kerry said, realization dawning on her face.

"Tasting an entire meal can be thirsty work. What taster wouldn't appreciate a glass of water, especially one personally delivered by the Captain of the Crown Guard?" Halen asked.

Claire couldn't contain herself any longer. "You've served the kingdom for decades! How could you turn traitor?"

"Your puppy is whimpering, Kerry. Tell her to be quiet before I silence her," Halen said, pointing his blade at Claire.

"Answer her." Kerry said, raising her sword. "Why would you betray your country and your king? Why would you betray your oath to the Guard?"

"Did you ever wonder why it's called the Crown Guard? Why not call it the Royal Guard?" Halen asked.

"What?"

"Why the Crown Guard? Why name it that?"

"We protect the head that wears the crown. The sovereign *is* the crown," Kerry said.

"You're wrong, Kerry. We guard the crown itself. Not the head wearing it."

"A piece of metal. You're saying the Guard protects a piece of metal," Kerry said.

"No, of course not. The crown is more than a piece of metal. It's a symbol. An ideal. It's the honor of our country. King Colin sullied that honor when he made *her* his heir. He tarnished the crown. I had to protect it," Halen said.

"From what? From being worn by a woman?"

"From weakness. From our ideals being corrupted. No woman can rule Keldaren. No woman is strong enough to protect our country. Everything I've done is to protect Keldaren and the crown. I've done my duty. Which is more than I can say for you," Halen said.

Claire drew a knife from her boot. "She's about to do her duty, Halen. And I'll help her."

"Stay back, Claire," Kerry said. "I've trained you better than that. A dagger is no match for a sword."

"True. But if he starts getting the best of you, I'm going to stick him with this," Claire said.

"One of you at a time, or both together, it makes no difference," Halen said. "Prince Jared will be returning tonight. And I mean to give him both your heads."

He leapt at Kerry. She caught his sword on hers, but Halen kept coming at her, his attacks fast and furious. Claire edged closer as they traded blows. *Just give me an opening*, she thought.

Halen thrust his blade at Kerry's throat, but she deflected it with her own steel. His fist flashed out, punching her in the face. Kerry went crashing to the floor.

Claire charged at Halen, swinging her dagger. He spun, his blade nearly catching her, and she leapt back.

Kerry jumped to her feet and charged. Halen swung around. Their swords crossed with a shriek of steel, and Halen began forcing Kerry's blade downward.

Claire threw her dagger. It clanged harmlessly off of Halen's chestplate. But it was enough to draw his attention, and he turned toward Claire. Kerry slashed her blade into his thigh. Halen cried out as he crumbled to his knees, swinging wildly at her. Kerry sidestepped his blow, and stabbed him in the shoulder. Halen's sword clattered to the floor.

"Yield, Halen," Kerry said.

He bent over, wincing. "That's *Lord* Halen to you, peasant."

"Your title is forfeit, traitor," Claire said. "Surrender, before your life is, too."

Halen's other hand was a blur as grabbed his sword. He rose, throwing himself at Claire. Kerry's blade caught him in the side, just below his chestplate. He crumpled to his knees, coughing. Kerry kicked him onto his back, and held her sword to his throat. "It's over," Kerry said.

Blood bubbled from Halen's lips. He looked at Claire. "Your reign is over. Jared will be here soon."

"My brother is safely locked away in Drohea."

"No, he's not. He's coming for his crown. And your head. I wish I could have been the one to give it to him." Halen spat blood at Claire. He gave a wheezing gasp. His eyes fixed on her. Hatred smoldered in them for a few heartbeats. Then they clouded over.

Kerry pushed at the body with her boot. "He's gone."

"Do you think he was telling the truth about Jared?" Claire asked.

A dull, booming noise started outside. It grew louder, and faster. *The alarm*, Claire realized. The bells clanged frantically.

Kerry's mouth was set as tight as a knife edge. "Yes. I do."

CHAPTER 10

Claire

"We have to get you to the dragons," Kerry said, pulling Claire down the hallway. She stopped at a window overlooking the lake.

Dark shapes swarmed over the ground, charging toward the palace. Silver ridges on their black armor glistened in the moonlight, and warhammers swung in their hands. "Berserkers," Kerry said. "This is worse than I thought. Much worse."

"What now?" Claire asked. "They're between us and the dragons."

"The roof," Kerry said. "There are stairs to the watchtower down the next hall. Follow me."

"Wait!" Claire grabbed Kerry's arm. "Elsie."

"We have to get you to safety. I'll go back for her once you're on a dragon."

"No. We're going to get her now."

"Claire, please. Just let me get you out of here. I promise, I'll go back and get her."

"No, we're going now. Are you going to lead the way or should I?"

Kerry sighed. "I will." They raced through the halls until they came to Elsie's rooms.

"Elsie!" Claire shouted.

Elsie peered out from behind her door.

"Where's Damien?" Claire asked.

"In Tara, at the infirmary. He's the night surgeon this week. What's happening?"

"We're leaving," Kerry snapped. "Follow us."

They ran back upstairs. Claire and Elsie followed Kerry up the winding steps to the top of a watchtower. Chaos filled the courtyard below. The Berserkers had breached the outer courtyard and were attacking the inner gates. Crown Guards fought from the top of the inner walls, trying to hold back the surge of invaders.

The Ravek warriors muscled a ram into position at the gates. The guards shot arrows and threw spears, but their efforts barely made a dent in the waves of enemies.

"We have to help them," Claire said.

"No, we have to get you out of here," Kerry insisted.

"I can't just leave them! They'll all be killed."

"They're dying to protect you. If you go down there, you'll be killed. Then they'll have died for nothing. And so will you," Kerry said.

Claire bit her lip. "If I don't go down there and help, I'll be a coward."

"If you do go down there, you'll be dead. Not brave. Just dead."

A huge, dark shape flew overhead, blocking out the moon. Claire caught a glimpse of flashing, curved talons. A burst of wind followed the dragon, ruffling their clothes. The dragon shot down toward the outer courtyard. A geyser of flame erupted from its mouth.

The river of fire hit the cobblestones, exploding outward to rip through the Berserker ranks. Many of the Ravek warriors died immediately, but a few lived long enough for their screams to reach Claire's ears. As the dragon passed over the Berserkers, it reached down and skimmed the ground with its claws, tearing through those left untouched by the flames. There was another blast of air, and the second dragon shot overhead, screaming fire down onto the Berserkers. The first dragon turned, heading back toward the palace.

"Climb down," Kerry ordered. She helped Claire out onto the roof. After she had helped Elsie down, Kerry turned to the approaching dragon, holding her sword up. Kerry turned the blade back and forth, flashing reflected moonlight.

"What are you telling them?" Claire asked.

"I'm signaling them to come here."

The dragon turned, and spiraled down toward the palace roof. It floated in for a landing, shaking the roof as it touched down. The dragon's burning, golden eyes glanced over each of them, before moving to stare at the battle below. Its muscles tensed and quivered under its scales as it leaned forward, like a dog straining against its leash.

A knight slid down from the dragon. "Your Majesty," Sloane said, removing her helmet and bowing. "We were on our way to the palace when we ran into some Drakari scouts. We had to fight our way back to the dragons before we could get airborne and help the guards."

"Thank you for your help, Dame Sloane," Kerry said. "But what we need most is for you to get the queen to safety. Fly her and Princess Elsie to Tara, and bring the Tara Legion here. We'll hold them back until then."

"You're coming with us, Kerry," Claire said.

"I can't. There's not enough room."

"Each dragon can carry only two people in a saddle, Your Majesty. One knight and one passenger," Sloane said.

"You have to leave now, while you still can. The rest of the guards and I will hold them off until the Tara Legion arrives," Kerry said.

"If you aren't leaving, then neither am I," Claire said.

"Your Majesty," Sloane said, "if the dragons stay here, they and the Crown Guards can turn the Berserkers back."

"We can't risk keeping the queen here. We have to get her to safety," Kerry insisted.

"Then leave by horse, instead of by dragon," Sloane suggested.

"It would be safest to fly," Kerry said.

"Yes. But if the dragons stay here to fight, the palace can be saved. And so could the lives of many of your guards," Sloane said.

"All right," Kerry said. "I'll take them to Tara."

"If the Drakari attacked the palace, they might attack Tara as well. They've obviously come for the queen. They may have a contingency plan if they don't catch her here," Sloane pointed out.

"You think they have assassins waiting in Tara?" Kerry asked.

"They'll have spies, at the very least. Spies who might get word to the Viper Order of the queen's whereabouts. Unless there already are Viper Knights waiting in Tara for her," Sloane said.

"You may be right," Kerry said. "We could go to Liharna. There's a royal castle there."

"Why not go to Mount Draconis? It's only a two day ride from here. Closer than Liharna. You'd be most welcome there, Your Majesty," Sloane said. "Our prefect would like to meet you. And you'd be safe. I can't think of a safer place for you in all of Keldaren."

"Perhaps that would be best, Kerry," Claire said.

"A fortified mountain, guarded by dragons? That sounds ideal. We'll have to fight our way down to the stables though. And then fight our way out," Kerry said.

"Shanra will clear the way for us," Sloane said. At the sound of her name, the dragon turned away from the battle. Sloane drew a cloth-wrapped package out from behind the dragon's saddle.

"Us?" Kerry asked. "Does that mean you also?"

"I'll come with you. One more sword to help protect the queen. Two more, actually," Sloane said, handing the package to Claire. "You'll need this."

Claire pulled her father's sword out of the cloth wrapping. There was a belt and scabbard wrapped in the cloth as well, and she buckled them on. "Thank you, Sloane."

"We'll have to climb back into the tower to reach the stables," Kerry said.

"There's a faster way. Climb up behind me, Your Majesty," Sloane said, putting her foot into the stirrup on the dragon's saddle. "Kerry and Elsie, climb onto Shanra's feet and hang on to her legs."

"You expect us to just hang on?" Elsie asked, a tremor in her voice.

"It's just a quick hop down to the courtyard," Sloane said. "Faster than climbing back down through the palace."

"And what if I lose my grip on this quick hop?" Elsie asked.

"Els, you take the saddle," Claire said. "Kerry and I will hang on to the legs."

Once Sloane and Elsie were in the saddle, Shanra lifted herself up. The dragon's scaled belly was just inches above Claire's head. She locked her hands together around the nearest leg. It was like hugging a tree trunk with smooth, scaly bark. The smoky scent of the dragon filled her nostrils.

Shanra lurched beneath them and leapt into the air, her body shaking as her wings started to beat. They sailed down into the courtyard below. Claire's stomach sunk along with the dragon, and she clung tightly to the huge leg.

They landed with a shuddering thump in the inner courtyard. As they slid down from the dragon, Sloane leaned close to Shanra's head. "Go tell Sir Deran our plans. And then help him and Gorea clear the way to the stables." The dragon nodded, and leapt into the air, her wings beating furiously. She gave a roaring call to the other dragon, and they dove down at the Berserkers, burning through the survivors.

Sloane led them to the inner gates, where an officer was directing the defenders. "Lieutenant!" Kerry called. "Can you and your men hold the gates?"

"Most of the Berserkers are already dead. And the dragons seem to be doing a good job of mopping up the stragglers," he said. "We can hold them."

"Good. I need some of your men. We're taking the queen to safety."

The lieutenant signaled, and a squad of guards came running up.

"We're taking the queen out by horse. But there are still enemies between us and the stables. We'll be her shield." Kerry drew her sword. "For the crown! To the death!" she shouted.

The guards drew their swords. "For the crown! To the death!" they roared back.

Sloane pulled a slender metal tube from a sheath on her belt. She twisted the knurled metal, and thin blades slid out from each end of the tube. They expanded until the tube became a long, twin-edged lance. Sloane whirled the tube around. The blades of the twinlance spun through the air, whistling like wind over an empty grave.

Claire drew her own sword. *Father's sword,* she reminded herself. The hilt was cold in her hands. As cold as the fear curling through her. There was anger there as well, and its heat countered the cold. She stared out through the iron-barred gates at the invaders. *To the nether with all of you,* she thought, fanning the flames of her rage. *This is my home. You're not taking it. And you're not taking me.*

"Open the gates!" Kerry shouted. The guards unbolted them, and pushed one open enough just far enough for them to pass. Sloane led the charge, with Kerry following her. Claire and Elsie ran in the center of the cluster of guards.

They raced for the stables. A group of shadows moved near the stable wall, advancing toward them. Silver lines glittered on the dark shapes. *Berserkers.* The Berserkers charged, screaming a war cry. Sloane darted toward them, her twinlance spinning. She stabbed it through the eye slit of the first Ravek warriors' helmet. Slashing her blades around, Sloane caught another Berserker in the throat.

The guard in front of Claire crumpled. A Berserker wrenched his warhammer free of the fallen body, and turned his skull-faced helm toward her. He split the air with a roar, swinging the warhammer up. The axe blade flashed at her. She whipped her sword around and caught his blade on hers. Her arm felt like it would shatter with the force of the blow. Kerry's advice echoed in her head. *Fight smarter, not stronger.*

Claire let the impact carry her sword down. She angled her weapon as the interlocked blades descended. The arc of their steel passed her and she jerked her sword clear. She drove it down into the Berserker's foot. The Ravek roared and swung his weapon up for another blow.

Claire ripped her blade free. The Berserker's arm was raised, exposing a gap between his chestplate and the pit of his arm. She punched her blade into it. Claire twisted her sword inside him, as Kerry had taught her. Syrupy purple blood stained her blade. *Good gods*, she thought. *Purple blood.* The Ravek dropped his warhammer, and his arm went limp. He snarled at her, reaching out with his left hand. His claws flashed in the moonlight as he grabbed for her face.

A glittering steel point erupted from his throat, followed by a spray of blood. The point twisted, and the Ravek's body went limp. The blade withdrew as the Berserker fell. Kerry stood behind him, her blade glistening purple. "Fight smarter," Kerry said.

"Not stronger," Claire finished.

"Follow me," Kerry said. "We're almost there."

Ahead of them, Sloane spun a circle of steel around her, cutting down Berserkers. One Ravek remained between them and the stables. Kerry charged at him. They traded blows until Kerry slipped her sword under the Ravek's weapon. She jerked the blade against the Berserker's neck, just beneath his helmet. The sword tore through the gray flesh, slitting his throat.

Sloane finished off the Berserker she was fighting, and ran to join them at the stables. Claire looked around, counting the guards with them. *Five left.*

Kerry pounded on the heavy wooden doors of the stables. "Open for the queen!" There was no answer.

"We don't have time for this," Sloane said. She raised her head and roared like a dragon. The sound sent a shiver through Claire. Shanra turned away from burning Ravek, and came soaring back toward them. Sloane pointed to the stable door, and roared again.

"Get back," Sloane warned. Shanra angled toward the stables as she flew closer. She opened her mouth, and spat fire. The ball of fire crashed into the doors, erupting in an orange blaze. When the flames died down, only a charred frame remained. Sloane twisted her twinlance, and the blades collapsed down into themselves, folding back into the tube. She returned the weapon to its sheath, and entered the stables.

They followed her in, choosing horses from the stalls. They swiftly saddled and mounted the horses. Sloane and Kerry drew their swords and took the lead. They sped away from the palace, heading northeast.

CHAPTER 11

Claire

"We should avoid contact with people or villages along the way," Kerry said. "That way no one can tell the Drakari where you are."

"Is that really necessary? I doubt there are spies in every village in Keldaren," Claire said.

"The Drakari will hunt for you, Your Majesty," Sloane said, pulling her horse up alongside Claire's. "She's right. It's best we keep to ourselves, and only travel by night."

"So I have to skulk through my own kingdom like a fugitive? Hiding from my own people?"

"The Drakari will *hunt* you," Sloane said. "The Berserkers failed. Minerva will be sending something worse."

"Viper Knights?" Claire asked.

Sloane nodded. "If we stay away from the villages and only move at night, they might not find us. Let's keep what few advantages we have, Your Majesty."

"Very well," Claire sighed. They rode through the rest of the night, passing through quiet forests and dark moors. They found a few berry bushes and apple trees, and gathered as much food as they could. Just before sunrise, Sloane called the group to a halt near a stream. Everyone dismounted and led their horses to the water.

"We shouldn't ride much further. We can make camp over there," Sloane said, pointing to a wooded glen. "We'll continue after dark." They made their way into the trees. One guard took the first watch, while the rest of them bedded down on the dirt.

Exhaustion ground at Claire, and she quickly drifted off to sleep. When Sloane woke her for her watch, the long shadows of afternoon were stretching through the trees. When the sun had slid away, and night's cloak fell over the horizon, Claire roused the others. They ate from their meager provisions, and made their horses ready.

One of the guards loosened a bow and quiver of arrows from its strap on his saddle. He went over to Elsie, who was tightening the saddle on her horse. "Your Highness, I believe I've seen you shooting on the guards' archery range, haven't I?"

"I practice there from time to time," Elsie said.

"Then, please, take this," he said, handing her the bow and quiver. "I have my sword. You're the only one without a weapon."

"Thank you," Elsie said. "Hopefully I won't have occasion to use it."

"Best to be prepared," he said.

They all swung up onto their horses, and headed off again. Sloane led the way through the crisp autumn night. The moon and stars shone brilliantly, flooding the moor with an icy white light. Mist hung low to the ground, creeping across the grass like a stalking wildcat.

Claire rode up beside Sloane. "Can I ask you something?"

"Of course, Your Majesty."

"Do you belong to the Syncrestry?"

"No. I believe in the Fates," Sloane said.

"And why do you believe in them?" Claire asked.

"Look at life. One small happenstance can change everything. It all rests on chance. Why shouldn't spirits influence that chance? It makes as much sense as any other explanation for the twists of destiny that rule our lives. So I meditate on the Fates sometimes. When I want their help, I burn an incense stick and make an offering," Sloane said.

"And do they help you?"

Sloane shrugged. "I think so. I can't know for sure. But it's something to believe in, without all the rules and rituals of the Syncrestry. No offense, Your Majesty," she added.

"None taken. I have doubts in the Syncrestry myself," Claire said.

"Then what do you believe in, Your Majesty?"

"I'm not sure anymore. I suppose I'm waiting for a sign."

Sloane nodded. "Then I hope you get one."

Claire fell back, letting Sloane take the lead again. An unfamiliar voice rang out in her ears. "Above you."

"Who said that?" Claire asked, reining in her horse.

"Who said what, Your Majesty?" a guard asked.

The voice came again. "Above you."

Claire looked up, and saw nothing. "That. Didn't you hear?"

The guard shot a look at Kerry, and then back at her. "I heard nothing, Your Majesty."

Kerry pulled her horse up to Claire's. "I didn't hear anything either."

"Above and behind," the voice said.

Claire twisted in her saddle, looking back at the sky. Two shadows floated in front of the moon—shadows with wings and talons. A head with a hooked beak swiveled toward her.

"Rocs!" Claire shouted. They reined in their horses, following her gaze to the giant ravens above. The first roc tucked in its wings and dove down at them, a screech echoing from its beak. Elsie screamed and spurred her horse forward.

"Stop!" Sloane shouted. "Stay where you are!" She jumped off her horse, yanking her twinlance free. She twisted it and the blades snapped out of the tube. Sloane hefted the lance and hurled it. The twinlance caught the roc square in the mouth, cutting short its horrible screech. The huge raven shuddered and tumbled from the sky.

"Spread out!" Kerry ordered. Claire and the guards dismounted, drawing their blades. Sloane drew her sword as well.

Just before the raven's body slammed into the ground, a dark-robed figure leaped from a saddle on its back. He held a slim, straight sword. The figure hit the ground running. The wind blew back his hood, revealing a silver serpent-faced helmet. The Viper Knight closed in on Sloane, slashing at her. Sloane caught the sword with her own. They dueled back and forth, silent except for the screech of steel against steel.

"The other roc!" Kerry shouted.

Claire spun around. The second raven was landing nearby. The guards charged at it. A dark-robed Viper Knight slid from the saddle, a silver sword in his grip. He quickly cut his way through four of the guards. Now only one guard stood between him and Claire.

The knight's sword flashed through the throat of the last guard. He stepped over the guard's body, advancing toward her. There was a thundering of hooves behind Claire as Kerry rode at the knight. Kerry sliced her sword out, the blade biting into his hip.

As she passed, he slashed out, cutting the back of her leg. Kerry's cry echoed over the moor. The knight turned on Claire again and came limping at her. Claire moved her sword to block him. At the last second his steel twitched aside, swinging toward her chest.

Time seemed to slow as the sword arced closer. Claire darted back from it. She lost her balance and fell onto her back. The blade cut through the air above her.

The knight's boot smashed into her chest, pinning her down. Claire stared into the silver serpent-faced helmet above her. Behind the gaping mouth and its needle-point fangs, the knight's lips curled into a smile. His eyes blazed down at her. He hissed at her—a low, deep hiss that sounded straight from a cobra's throat.

An arrow suddenly embedded itself in his shoulder. He flinched, his boot coming off her chest. Claire rolled away from him, as Kerry charged on her horse. The knight spun to face her.

Kerry stabbed at his neck. The knight sidestepped the blade, and slashed through the horse's leg.

The scream was terrible, sending a sick chill through Claire's stomach. The horse collapsed on its crippled leg. Kerry went flying from her saddle and hit the ground. She tried to push herself up, but fell back into the dirt.

Claire leapt to her feet. He turned to face her, his sword swinging around. But she was already too close. Her blade bit into his wrist, nearly separating it from his arm. The slim sword flew from his hand.

For a heartbeat, he stared at the bloody ruin of his wrist. Then he charged at her. She slammed her blade between his ribs. He hissed again and struck her in the face with his good hand. Claire shoved the sword deeper into his chest. He reached out, clawing at her throat. She twisted the blade.

He crumpled to his knees, blood trickling from his mouth. His eyes still blazed at her. "Keldaren will burn," he gasped. Then he slumped backwards. Claire wrenched her sword free.

Sloane raced up, and stabbed her blade into the fallen knight's neck. "With a Viper Knight, you always have to make sure. The first one I killed managed to knife me in the back after I left him for dead. Quite a painful lesson."

"Where's the other one?"

"Dead, finally. These Viper Knights fight well. Not well enough, though."

"Where's Kerry?" Claire asked, looking around. Kerry's horse lay on its side in a pool of blood. A blue-clad body lay just

beyond it. Claire and Sloane ran over, and Claire knelt beside her.
Her fingers trembled as she pressed them to Kerry's neck. A warm
rush of relief flooded Claire when she felt a pulse.

They turned Kerry over. A large bruise marred her
forehead, and blood ran from the slash on her leg. Sloane drew a
knife, cutting the sleeve off of Kerry's uniform. Taking the strip of
cloth, she bound it tightly around her wound. "She has a pretty
large lump on her head. Doesn't feel like any broken bones,
though. Are you all right, Your Majesty?" Sloane asked.

"I'm fine, thanks to your aim with that arrow," Claire said.

"That wasn't me. I had my hands full with that other Viper
Knight."

Claire looked back in the direction the arrow had flown
from. Elsie sat on her horse a good distance away from them, her
face ashen. She gripped her bow tightly.

Kerry groaned, twisting on the ground. "Water," she
moaned.

Claire beckoned to Elsie, and she rode over. "Do you have
any water left?"

Elsie checked the water skin hanging from her saddle.
"No, it's empty."

Claire looked off at the forest over the next hill. She turned
back to Elsie. "Give me the water skin and your saddlebag. You
take care of Kerry. I'll go and try to find a stream, and maybe
some alvera in the forest." She squeezed her cousin's hand. "I'm
glad you kept up your archery practice, Els."

"So am I. It took you long enough to get out of the way and give me a clear shot."

"I was a little distracted. If I had known you were waiting to shoot, I'd have fallen down earlier," Claire said, smiling.

Sloane rose. "I'll go with you, Your Majesty."

"Stay here and help Kerry. And be on guard for any more trouble," Claire said.

Sloane bit her lip. "You shouldn't go alone."

"I'll be safe enough in the forest. Besides, you're the only one left to protect Elsie and Kerry," Claire said, gesturing to the fallen guards.

"And who's going to protect you, Your Majesty?"

Claire tapped the hilt of her sword. "I will."

Sloane smiled. "Spoken like a warrior. Keep a sharp eye out."

Claire walked to the forest. The air was cool and misty, with fog drifting low over the ground. There was a deer trail running through the trees, and Claire followed it until she came to a clearing. A tall rock stood there, like an island in the sea of mist.

"Claire," a voice called. It was the same voice Claire had heard before the rocs attacked. She looked around, seeing nothing but the trees circling the clearing. "Above you."

She looked up. A figure floated down toward her. It was a woman, clad in a long blue dress. Two sets of gossamer wings curled out from her back, fluttering as she descended. The woman settled on the rock, her wings folding behind her.

Her dress seemed woven from lapis lazuli—its fabric a deep midnight blue, flecked with specks of gold. She wore a chestplate that looked like solid pearl. The armor was a deep, pure white that flashed rainbows as it caught the moonlight. She wore a pearl helmet on her head. Two white wings rose from the helmet's temples, their points meeting above the helm. A sheathed sword hung from the woman's waist. A white, sparkling light gently shone from her.

Claire dropped to one knee. "You're a god."

"No, I'm not. Stand up, Claire. There is only one god, and I'm not him. I'm merely one of his servants," the woman said.

"What do you mean, only one god? There are many."

"No, there aren't. But there's no time to talk about that. I'm here to warn you again, Claire."

"Warn me? Of what?" Claire asked.

"That." The woman pointed skyward.

Claire looked up. A roc was circling above the clearing. The huge raven's eye glinted in the moonlight as it stared down at her. Then it dove. Claire drew her sword and stole a glance at the woman. She stood atop the stone, her hands folded together. *No help there*, Claire thought.

The roc cleared the treetops, its beak gaping wide. Claire leapt aside just before the claws caught her. She rolled away, the beak snapping above her head. Claire leapt to her feet. A huge black wing flapped in front of her. She brought her sword up and slashed it.

The roc's scream tore through the night. The bird flapped its wings, trying to fly, but the injured wing wouldn't hold its weight. It crashed to the ground. Claire dodged the raven's snapping beak, and slashed through its stomach. The raven screamed again, scrabbling away from her blade.

Claire charged. The roc reared back, opening its beak to strike. She punched the blade deep into its throat. The bird coughed, a wet, sucking noise coming from its throat. Blood welled up around the blade, and Claire jerked the sword free. The roc collapsed, gurgling as blood poured from its throat. The bird slashed at her with its claws. Claire stabbed her sword into the roc's neck. The raven gave a final, gargling cry as it died.

She turned to the woman. "You have a sword. You could have helped me."

"No, I couldn't. I could only warn you."

The air rippled next to Claire. *Not again*, she thought, a sick feeling curling in her stomach. The rippling dissolved into the black-cloaked figure of Death.

Death's eyes burned with black fire. "Again he warns her. Again he protects her. You violate The Law by preventing me from taking her."

"I merely warned her," said the blue-clad woman. "I didn't intervene. She changed her own fate, just as she did before. That is within The Law."

"He violates the spirit of The Law with these warnings. She would have been mine otherwise," Death said.

"He *is* the spirit of The Law. And if he chooses to warn her, he has his reasons for doing so. Do you think your judgment better than his?

Death lowered her black eyes. "No. But I don't understand. She's been marked. She should be mine."

"It's for us to follow his will, not to understand it. Remember your place."

"Remember your own place," Death snarled. "I'm a queen. You aren't."

"A queen, yes. But not of this world. There's no spirit for you to take here. Not today, at least. Return to your realm."

"And who are you to give me commands?" Death asked.

"One who serves your master," the woman said.

"We're both servants of The Emperor, valkyrie."

"But only one of us has any further business with Claire."

"For today." Death turned to Claire. "But one day soon, I mean to claim her." Death shivered, transforming into a mist that vanished with the wind.

Claire shuddered. *Evil witch*, she thought, sheathing her sword.

"She's not evil," the woman said.

She heard that? Claire thought.

"I did. She's not evil. Just bitter. And she's no witch. We serve the same master, and we each have our own roles to play. But she's not needed here today, thankfully."

"But who are you?" Claire demanded. "She called you valkyrie…is that your name?"

"My name is Astra. I *am* a valkyrie. One of many. Valkyries are warriors and messengers. Like the knights of this world. We serve The Emperor."

"Is that the name of this one god of yours?" Claire asked.

"No. It's one of his titles," Astra said.

"Then what's his name?"

"He needs no name. He's not one god amongst many. He's the only one," Astra said.

"I've never heard of this nameless god of yours."

"Your people knew him in the old world, before you came to Eris. But after people came to this world, they drifted away from him. They began to follow gods of their own creation," Astra said.

"Nothing in our histories says anything about that," Claire said.

"Your true history became inconvenient for those selling the lie of the new ways. So they turned the truth into a myth. And eventually even the myth was buried beneath the waves of centuries, and forgotten."

"You're saying the templers did all that?" Claire asked.

"The templers are just the latest in a long string of frauds who've claimed to speak for false gods," Astra said.

"Then why doesn't this god of yours do something? Why did he let the lies continue for all these centuries?"

"He is doing something about it. Even now he's moving in this world. He's started by warning you before Death could take you," Astra said.

"What do I have to do with any of this?"

"You have a role to play in his plans. A major role," Astra said.

"I'm supposed to believe I'm part of the plans of some god I've never heard of? A god I don't even believe in?" Claire asked.

"You certainly have reason to doubt, Claire. The gods of the Syncrestry are a lie, and those who claim to speak for them are frauds. But this god is no lie. He is the very source of truth."

"And I'm supposed to just take your word for this?"

"No. He'll give you reasons to believe," Astra said.

"How?" Claire asked.

"Go to the Isle of Erinn. A hermit named Sean lives there. He will be your guide."

"And what's so special about this hermit?" Claire asked.

"Nothing. And everything."

"I don't understand," Claire said.

"I know. But you will." Astra's wings spread out behind her, and she stepped off the rock, floating down. She landed in front of Claire, and drew her sword. The hilt was silver, but the blade was pure opal. Fiery greens and blues rippled across it in the moonlight.

Astra touched the tip of the sword to the rock. Water bubbled out of it, turning into a spring flowing from the rock's side. She waved a hand, and in a corner of the clearing, the mist blew away, revealing a cluster of bushes. "Alvera for Kerry," Astra said, pointing. "And food for your journey. I have to leave now. But I'll be watching over you, and your progress."

"Wait. I have questions."

"I know," Astra said, sheathing her sword. "But I can't give you the answers. Not now. Speak to Sean. He can answer many of your questions."

"But not all of them?" Claire asked.

"No. Not all," Astra said.

"Can he see the future?"

"No," Astra said.

"Can you?"

"I can see many possible futures."

"Please," Claire said, reaching out for her hand. "Tell me what you see."

Astra drew her hand back. "I can't."

"Please," Claire begged. The image of herself as a statue flashed through her mind again. She saw the statue crumble, the stone shattering and falling away. She sank to her knees. "Please," she said. "You have no idea how frightened I am."

Astra knelt in front of her, and took her hand. Faint, flashing tingles of warmth danced through Claire's hand where Astra touched her. "Oh, Claire," she said. "I know exactly how frightened you are."

She stared into the sky for a moment. Then she looked into Claire's eyes. "I see you victorious. I see you defeated in battle. I see you dying an old woman in your bed. I see Death taking you tomorrow. I see you living to see your first grandchild born."

"I see things worse than Death taking you. I see statues of you built all over Keldaren. I see you forgotten by your people after you die. I see an ocean of possibilities," Astra said.

Claire closed her eyes, a tear etching a hot path down her cheek. "And which one actually happens?"

"That's up to you. You write your own story, Claire. And the rest of your story isn't written yet." Astra reached up and wiped the tear away. The touch of her hand on Claire's face sent a warmth and peace through her like she hadn't known since she was a little girl.

Claire opened her eyes. Astra smiled. "Sometimes you can't be a statue."

Claire frowned. "Not when you have to hold up the entire world."

Astra helped her to her feet. Her wings unfolded behind her—gossamer shimmers in the moonlight. "You don't have to," Astra said. "He already does."

Her wings flared out, catching the air. She rose until she was just another tiny point of light in the sky. Claire stood, watching for a moment, until she lost Astra amidst the stars.

CHAPTER 12

Claire

Claire drank from the spring, then filled the water skin. She walked over to the bushes. Cream-colored ovals hung from the branches. Claire twisted one of them free, and pulled out her dagger, cutting into its skin. The outer rind of the fruit was hard, but the flesh inside was a spongy, milky white that looked almost like cake.

She took a bite. A rich sweetness filled her mouth. *Whatever it is, it's delicious,* she thought. Claire finished the fruit, and filled the saddle bag with more of them. Tube-like alvera sprouts grew beneath the bushes, and she snapped several off and put them in the saddle bag also.

Claire made her way back through the forest to the others. "She's awake," Elsie said, looking up from Kerry's side. Claire knelt next to her, and put the water skin to Kerry's lips.

Kerry drank, and then let her head fall back to the ground. "Sloane told me you went off alone." She sighed. Her words were frosted over with pain. "You shouldn't have done that."

"Let me guess," Claire said, breaking the alvera sprouts in two. Clear sap flowed out into the palm of her hand. "We should have left you here alone while we went to look for water."

"You should have left me and kept going to Mount Draconis." Kerry winced as Claire spread the sap onto her wounds.

"Well, it's a good thing we didn't. Otherwise I wouldn't have seen what I did," Claire said.

Kerry sighed again. "Let me guess. Another messenger from beyond this world?"

"Yes."

"Isn't it inconvenient that you're always alone when these messengers come calling?" Kerry asked.

Claire smiled. "The next time one appears, I'm going to grab them by their hair and drag them to you. But you probably wouldn't believe it even then."

A faint smile crossed Kerry's lips. "Any ghost you can drag by the hair wouldn't be much of a ghost, would it?"

Sloane was standing beside the horses, scanning the horizon. "Your Majesty, it'll be light soon. We should go deeper into the woods and make camp there for the day. We can continue on at nightfall," she said.

"Can Kerry continue on?" Claire asked.

"I'll be fine," Kerry said.

"I wasn't asking you," Claire said with a smile. "Will she be able to travel, Sloane?"

"I think so. You can ride with her and hold her in the saddle. We have surgeons at Mount Draconis. The alvera should help some until then. We should reach the mountain tomorrow morning if we don't meet any more surprises on the road."

They rigged a stretcher for Kerry from the saddle of a guard's horse. They carried her to the forest, where they made camp for the day. After seeing Kerry bedded down, Claire lay down herself.

She slept fitfully, and when night came, she was the first to wake. They readied their horses, lifting Kerry up onto Claire's mount. Claire sat behind her, holding her up in the saddle as they rode.

They traveled uninterrupted throughout the night. Finally, at dawn, they came over the crest of a hill. A field lay below, bathed in the drifting mist of morning. A black mountain jutted up out of the mist like a giant, jagged tooth. The sun rose behind the mountain, silhouetting the winged shape of a dragon circling the snow-capped summit.

Mount Draconis cast a long shadow over them as they rode toward it. Two walls, each dotted with towers, ringed the mountain. A third wall circled its base. "Wake up," Claire said, nudging Kerry in the saddle ahead of her. "You should see this."

"Impressive, isn't it, Your Majesty?" Sloane asked, riding up alongside her. "Even if one wall is breached, the level above can be held."

Kerry was awake now, staring at the mountain. "Good. You'll be safe enough here, Claire."

They rode up to the main gates. The thick, heavy portals were fashioned from ironwood and clad with steel plate. Two watchtowers flanked the gates—each manned by soldiers wearing crimson and black. One of them shouted a challenge to Sloane. She responded with a dragon roar.

The gates slowly swung open, revealing a line of soldiers. Sloane rode up to the officer at the head of the line.

He saluted. "Welcome back, Dame Sloane."

"Thank you, Lieutenant. I've brought the Queen with me, along with Princess Elsie and Countess Bradaigh."

The lieutenant bowed. "I'm honored, Your Majesty. Welcome to Mount Draconis." He waved a hand, and the line of soldiers parted.

Sloane led the way along the dirt road spiraling up the mountain. "Where are the dragon halls? And the knight's quarters?" Claire asked.

"Inside. The entire mountain is an ancient volcano. It's been dormant for hundreds of years. There are old lava caverns inside that serve as the dragon halls. We live in smaller caves near the summit. We have offices, mess halls, infirmaries, training chambers, and even a library. Back when the Dragon Order was founded, the original knights turned this mountain into a stronghold. They mined tunnels to connect rooms, enlarged caves, and raised the walls and gates. It took decades. But look at what they accomplished," Sloane said, waving a hand at the mountain.

They came to the next wall. Sloane shouted a password to the guards, and the gates opened. They continued on, until they reached the last wall, at the upper levels of the mountain.

Kerry had drifted off into a fitful sleep again, but the sound of Sloane yelling the final password woke her. The last gate swung open, and they followed the narrowing road into the entrance of a tunnel. Two soldiers stood watch there, beneath crystal globes hanging from the rock ceiling. The globes glowed with a soft yellow light.

"Bring a stretcher," Sloane ordered the soldiers. She and Claire helped Kerry down from the horse. As gentle as they were, Kerry still moaned with pain when they moved her. The soldiers returned, and they eased her onto the stretcher. Kerry reached up and grabbed Claire's arm. "Don't let them talk you into anything," she said.

"What?" Claire asked.

Kerry's hand loosened, and dropped from Claire's arm. "Don't let them..." she whispered, falling back into unconsciousness.

"Take her to the infirmary," Sloane ordered. "She'll be fine, Your Majesty. Our surgeons are quite experienced."

"I wonder what she meant," Claire said, as Kerry was carried off. "What am I not supposed to let you talk me into?"

"Joining us, I imagine. Our prefect intends to invite you to become a knight," Sloane said.

"Why would he do that?"

"He should be the one to explain. But I've seen you fight, Your Majesty. I'd be honored to have you join us."

"And why would Kerry object?" Claire asked.

"Training to be a knight is hard. Being one is even harder. A few of us die during training. More die in battle. Kerry is sworn to protect you. I'm sure the last thing she wants is to see you become a Dragon Knight."

"Some knights die in *training*?" Claire asked.

"Yes. At the end, mostly. The final test...well, there's no other word for it. It's brutal," Sloane said.

"And why would you want to see your queen exposed to such danger?"

"Combat is even more brutal. We train knights to survive that," Sloane said.

"But if I don't become a knight, I'll avoid combat," Claire said.

"All rulers must fight, Your Majesty. Whether with swords or with words, all rulers must fight. And most have to fight with both."

"I expected to spar more with words than blades. But so far, it's been more the other way around," Claire said.

"Be wary of both forms of fighting, Your Majesty. A tongue can be just as dangerous as a sword."

Claire sighed. "It seems there's nothing in a queen's life that isn't dangerous, Sloane. I'll speak with your prefect. Is there somewhere Elsie can go rest?"

"Of course. Show the princess to a guest room," Sloane ordered one of the soldiers.

"I'll see you later, Els," Claire said. "After we both get some sleep."

Elsie followed the soldier down one hallway, and Sloane led Claire down the other. At the end of the hallway stood a wooden door. A carving of a dragon was etched into it. The dragon's wings were outstretched, and it gripped a shield in its talons. The shield bore Keldaren's blazon of a harp and sword.

"The blazon of the Dragon Order," Sloane said, gesturing to the carving. She knocked, and a man opened the door.

He was older, but still looked lethal enough. A green Dragon Knight's uniform fit tightly on his tall, powerful frame. He wore no armor, but carried a sword and dagger on his belt.

"Prefect," Sloane said, saluting. "This is Queen Claire. Your Majesty, this is Sir Fulton, Prefect of the Dragon Order."

Fulton bowed. "Your Majesty. Please, come in. It's an honor to meet you." He gestured her to a chair. "Welcome to Mount Draconis. We heard of the attack on the palace. I'm relieved to see you're safe."

"Thank you." Claire sat down, looking around the small office. The same yellow globes that lit the tunnel hung here as well. "Sir Fulton, the captain of my guard warned me to not let you talk me into anything. I'll be blunt. Is there something you would ask of me?"

Fulton cocked his head. "Lord Halen said that?"

"Halen turned traitor, Prefect," Sloane told him. "He poisoned King Colin. Then he tried to kill the queen."

"A traitor. The Captain of the Crown Guard." Fulton shook his head. "There's only one way to repay such treachery, Your Majesty."

"He's already dead," Sloane said. "Her Majesty named Kerry Bradaigh to succeed him."

"Lady Kerry," Claire corrected Sloane. "I named her Countess as well."

"Pardon me, Your Majesty," Sloane said. "Lady Kerry killed Halen when he tried to murder the queen."

"You never answered my question, Sir Fulton," Claire said. "Were you planning on trying to talk me into anything?"

"Yes. I want you to consider becoming a Dragon Knight."

"Why?"

"Keldaren needs more than just a queen now, Your Majesty. We need a warrior," Fulton said.

"The attack on the palace can mean only one thing," Sloane told her. "Minerva means to start a war. And this won't be just another border skirmish. They tried to kill you. An opening gambit like that can only be followed by an invasion."

"But the attack failed. Doesn't that mean Drakaren won't invade?" Claire asked.

Sloane shook her head. "It means they *must* invade. The palace courtyard is littered with Berserker corpses. Minerva can't deny that Drakaren was behind this. She knows we'll retaliate. So she has to strike at us before we can attack them."

"It will be winter soon. They won't try to invade in winter," Claire objected.

"That's hard to say. Normally, no army would march in winter. Perhaps they planned to capture the palace, then Tara, and bring an army across the border to Dalrann. Then they'd control a corridor from the border into the heart of Keldaren. But now, they couldn't reach Tara before the snow flies. That doesn't mean they won't still try to take one of our cities before winter," Fulton said.

"Dalrann would be the obvious choice," Sloane said. "But Glenhaven is close to the border as well. Either would give the Drakari a secure place to winter in—and a foothold to launch a full-scale invasion come the spring."

"I should send troops to secure the border," Claire said.

"That would be wise, Your Majesty." Fulton leaned forward. "Kerry has taught you a good deal about swordsmanship. But there's still much for you to learn of warfare. We can teach you."

"Your father wanted the Dragon Order to give you his sword for a reason," Sloane said. "It was his wish that you join us."

"'Always at the front'. That's the motto of the Dragon Order, isn't it?" Claire asked.

Fulton nodded. "Yes."

"Kerry would say that no queen can fight in the front of every battle. She would say that a queen who always fought at the front would soon be dead," Claire said.

"Your Majesty," Sloane said, "she would be right. No ruler can fight at the front of every battle. Sometimes she must lead from behind. But consider this. If a queen watching from a hilltop gives orders to her soldiers, they'll march into battle. And they'll do their duty for her. But if a queen leads her soldiers herself, they'll *charge* into battle behind her. And they'll give their last drop of blood for her."

Claire bit her lip. "Kerry would say that I'd never be safe if I became a Dragon Knight."

"You're a queen. You will never be safe," Fulton said. "Never."

"I suppose that's true. But that's why I have guards. And why Kerry would keep me as far away from battle as she can."

"Dragon Knights believe the best security is skill and a sword," Sloane said. "You have the sword. We can teach you skill."

"If you can fight like one of us, then you'll be safer in the front lines of battle than you'd be in a fortress," Fulton told her. "Join us, and we'll make you the warrior Keldaren needs you to be."

"I've learned a lot from Kerry. But I have the feeling I can learn even more here. Very well. I accept," Claire said.

"Be sure you know what you're accepting, Your Majesty," Sloane said. "We can't make any special allowances for you. You must pass all of the trials. Especially the final one. It will be as difficult for you to become a Dragon Knight as for any other recruit."

"More difficult, even. Our training normally lasts at least two years. You'll have to complete it in a few months," Fulton said.

"This will be harder than anything you've ever done before, Your Majesty," Sloane warned.

"I've done hard things before, Sloane. But before I do this, I have to go back to Tara. The kingdom must be governed while I'm here training. If I'm here, then I'll have the ministers and the Senate come to me."

"We certainly have plenty of spare accommodations here. This is a wise move, Your Majesty. Even if Minerva's armies are unlikely to march in winter, her spies and assassins have no such constraints. You and the rest of the government will be well out of their reach here," Fulton said.

"My thoughts exactly. You said you heard from Tara after the attack?" Claire asked.

"Yes. Sloane's dragon returned, and told us what happened. The palace was saved. Most of the Berserkers were killed, and the rest fled. Sir Deran hunted down most of them. He found their ships moored a few leagues up the river from the palace," Fulton said.

"How did Drakari ships manage to get past the watchtower?" Claire asked.

"The ships were Kirosian."

"Kirosian? Are they involved in this plot too?"

"Sir Deran found blood on the decks. He believes the Drakari killed the crews and stole the ships," Fulton said.

"Still, the soldiers at the coast should have inspected the ships before they allowed them to sail down the Siochana," Claire said.

"Sir Deran flew to the watchtower at the mouth of the river. He found the entire garrison murdered," Fulton said.

"Where is he now? I have some questions for him," Claire said.

"After he checked the watchtower, he went back to continue searching for more Berserker survivors. He sent a full report back with Sloane's dragon. He'll return once he hunts down the last of the Ravek," Fulton said.

"Were there any human bodies among the attackers?" Claire asked.

"No, only Ravek. Why?" Fulton asked.

"Halen said that my brother was coming to the palace the night of the attack. Jared should be imprisoned in Drohea Castle, but it felt like Halen was telling the truth. About that, at least. Jared might be part of this conspiracy as well," Claire said.

"I'll have a knight fly out to Drohea at once. If Prince Jared was involved..." Fulton's voice trailed off.

"That would mean he's in league with Minerva," Claire said. "My brother has made some grave mistakes in the past. But to betray his country to the Drakari...I have a hard time believing that even Jared would go that far."

"We'll find out," Fulton promised. "Prince Malcolm is still missing, Your Majesty. It may be that he also has something to do with this."

"Perhaps he was one of Minerva's targets also," Claire suggested.

"That's possible. But if he was assassinated, where is his body? The constables and the Crown Guard have been searching everywhere for him. Even the charnel houses. No matter what's happened to him, though, the kingdom needs a chancellor," Fulton said.

"He's been missing long enough for me to appoint an acting chancellor. Something else to take care of when I get back to Tara." Claire stifled a yawn. "But I need some sleep first."

"Of course, Your Majesty," Fulton said. "Sloane, show the queen to her rooms."

"Yes, Prefect. I'll assign another knight to guard her before I rest," Sloane said.

"A guard? I thought you said I'm safe here, Sloane."

"You are. But I don't think *I* would be if Kerry found out I left you unguarded," Sloane said, smiling.

"I'll need dragons and an escort this afternoon for the trip to Tara. And send a message to the palace that I want to see Senator Garenne and General Aricet," Claire told Fulton.

He nodded. "I'll have a knight bring the message on his way to Drohea. And I'll arrange the escort. I'll speak with you later, Your Majesty."

Sloane led Claire out of the office, and down another hallway. They passed a servant in the corridors. "Fetch the queen a meal and bring it to her room," Sloane told him.

"Yes, Dame Sloane," the servant said, and hurried off.

Sloane opened a door. The room was large—especially for being carved out of a mountain. A rough-hewn wooden table and chair stood in the center of the room. A door to the washroom stood in one corner. In another corner, there was something that sent a swirl of pleasure and exhaustion through Claire—a bed.

Claire stifled another yawn. Above her hung the same globes that lit the rest of the fortress. "What are those?" she asked.

"I thought at first they were some sort of lantern, but there's no fire in them."

"They are lanterns, of a sort," Sloane said. "There's a glowing algae that washes ashore from the sea. The servants go collect it, and fill the globes with it. Much easier than lighting hundreds of lanterns every day."

"Ah." Claire turned her gaze away from the globes, and looked at Sloane. "What you were saying earlier about the training…you meant it, didn't you?"

"Yes. It will be the hardest thing you've ever done. But you can do it."

"I hope you're right," Claire said.

"I am. You'll see."

The servant returned, carrying a plate and cup. "Please, Your Majesty, eat and get some rest. You have another long journey ahead of you this afternoon," Sloane said.

"I'll see you later?"

Sloane nodded. "I'll go with you to Tara."

Claire followed the servant into the room, where he set the food and drink down.

"Enjoy the bed, Your Majesty," Sloane told Claire as she and the servant left.

The plate held a piece of fish covered in a rich sauce, along with slices of brown bread. She devoured the food, washing it down with the sweet wine in the cup. Her stomach was full for the first time since leaving the palace. With her hunger satisfied, she felt the exhaustion even more. Going to the washbasin, she rinsed away the dirt of the past few days.

There was a chest at the foot of the bed. Opening it, Claire found Dragon Knight uniforms inside. She changed into one, and then stretched out on the bed. It was like sinking into a warm sea, as the featherbed enveloped her in waves of softness. Claire let herself relax into the gentle darkness washing over her.

CHAPTER 13

Claire

A knock on the door woke her. "Enter," she called groggily. The door swung open, and a knight came in.

"Begging your pardon, Your Majesty. I'm Sir Brac. Dame Sloane assigned me to guard you. I was told to wake you at this hour."

"Very well." Claire yawned. "I want to go see Kerry."

"I'll bring you to her."

In the infirmary, she took a seat next to Kerry's bed. "How are you feeling?"

"Better," Kerry said. "They put some salve on my wounds, and gave me something to ease the pain."

"I'm glad." Claire raised an eyebrow. "How did you know they would ask me to become a knight?"

Kerry shrugged. "Why else would they give you the king's sword?"

"They told me that he wanted me to join the Dragon Order," Claire said.

"He may have. But when you were older. When your hold on the throne was more secure. When the kingdom wasn't on the verge of war."

"Sloane and the Prefect said I should become a knight because war is coming. Not in spite of it," Claire said.

"How can a queen oversee a war if she's busy fighting in it herself? And what if she dies in the fighting? What becomes of a kingdom at war when its ruler falls?" Kerry asked.

"I told them you would say that," Claire said.

"And what did they say?"

"That soldiers who fight for a queen who commands from the rear of a battle will do their duty for her, but soldiers that a queen leads into battle will spill their last drop of blood for her," Claire said.

Kerry was quiet for a moment. "That much is true. You already said yes, didn't you?"

"How did you know?"

"There's too much of your father in you for you to say no," Kerry said.

"And are you angry at me for saying yes?" Claire asked.

"Claire, you're the queen. It doesn't matter what I think."

"It matters to me. Are you angry?"

"No. I understand why you said yes. It will make my job harder…but my job isn't supposed to be easy." Kerry sighed. "And I think it's the right decision. I just worry about you, Claire."

Claire smiled, and reached over to squeeze her hand. "Worry like a sister, Kerry. Instead of like a mother."

Kerry smiled back. "I'll do my best."

"When are they going to let you out of here?" Claire asked.

"A few more days. The surgeon says I'll be well enough to travel in a week or so. If you're staying at Mount Draconis, I'll return to Tara. You'll be safe enough here, and I have a great deal of work to do rebuilding the Crown Guard."

Claire nodded. "I'm flying to Tara myself this afternoon." Concern flashed across Kerry's face. "Don't worry," Claire said. "I'll be taking along an escort of Dragon Knights. And I'll only be there long enough to make arrangements to move the government here."

Kerry took a folded piece of paper from a table beside her. "When you're in Tara, will you deliver this letter to Centurion Eloc? I'm promoting him to First Legate of the Crown Guard."

"I'll see that he gets it. Get some rest, Kerry."

Kerry nodded, and Claire left with Sir Brac. They met Sloane in a dining hall. "I've found a dragon to carry you," Sloane told her as they ate. "He'll be helping me train you. The journey to Tara will be a good opportunity to get used to each other. Would you like to meet him?"

Gods, no, Claire thought, suppressing the shiver seizing her. She forced a smile onto her face. "Of course."

Claire followed Sloane to the stable, where they mounted their horses and rode out. Midway down the mountain, they reached another tunnel, and left their horses in a stable before continuing down the passageway. They emerged into a giant cavern. Huge versions of the glowing globes hung from the walls, their light filling the vast space. Wooden walls divided the cavern into large compartments. Each compartment held a small mountain of dragon flesh, covered in dark emerald scales.

The dragons had long snouts, and their mouths were filled with rows of gleaming, saw-blade teeth. A ridged crest ran in a semi-circle above their eyes, ending in a short, curved horn on either side of the head. A long row of spikes ran along each dragon's spine, from the head down the length of the thick tail.

Sloane led her down the line of compartments. The dragons' breathing filled the hall—heavy, deep breathing that sounded like it was following Claire. More than once she shot a glance behind her, the back of her neck prickling. *Calm down,* she told herself. It had been one thing riding Sloane's dragon in the heat of battle. It was another thing entirely to walk through a cavern full of the huge monsters.

Sloane stopped in front of a sitting dragon. "Your Majesty, this is Breaus," she said. The dragon stood, his bulk rippling upwards in a smooth flow of scaled muscle. He towered over her, his neck curled back like a striking snake.

Claire stared at him. Breaus stared back, his nostrils flaring. His forked tongue snaked out amidst the rows of jagged, dagger-like teeth lining his jaws. The dragon lowered his head until it was level with hers. Golden flames burned in his large eyes.

"Are you afraid, girl?" His voice was thunder and stone.

"No." She took a deep breath. "No," she said again, stronger this time.

Twin puffs of fire burst from his nostrils. "You're lying. I can smell your fear. I can see your fear." The forked tongue flicked out again, just inches from her face. "I can taste your fear."

He turned his head to Sloane. "This is no Dragon Knight. This is a frightened little girl. This won't work."

"What do you mean?" Claire asked.

The burning eyes swung back to her. "Dragons are fire. Fire encased in scale and bone. To be a Dragon Knight, you must also be fire. You are ice, frozen by fear. You are no knight."

"I *am* a queen. You should give me more respect," Claire said.

"A queen you may be. But we dragons have our own clans, our own rulers, and our own laws. I may serve in the Order, but that doesn't make me your subject. And no dragon ever *gives* anyone respect. You must earn that. Fire respects only what it can't burn."

"Steel doesn't burn," Claire said.

"You are not steel," Breaus said.

"I can be."

"I wonder." He lifted his head and roared, rows of fangs glistening in his gaping maw.

Be steel, Claire told herself. She stood still, ignoring the urge to run that screamed through her. She forced herself to meet his gaze. The golden fire flared in his eyes. Then flames scorched out from his mouth.

Time seemed to slow to a crawl as the flames rolled out from between his jaws. Every fiber of her body howled at her to run from the inferno billowing at her. *I AM STEEL,* she roared in her mind. *STEEL DOESN'T YIELD.* She stood motionless, staring into the inferno burning its way toward her.

The heat blasted her face as the column of flame rolled closer. It was like falling into a sunset that lit every cloud in the sky ablaze. *One last, terrible sunset*, she thought, staring into the awful beauty of the inferno. The flames suddenly halted in their crawl toward her. The cloud of fire hung in the air, burning barely a foot from her nose. Then it stopped, the flames smoldering out, leaving only a wave of hot air to wash over her face.

Claire glared into the golden eyes above her. "Steel doesn't yield," she growled.

"There's fire in you after all," Breaus said. He smiled, his lips drawing back to show his fangs.

A test. It was all a test. "Did I pass?" she asked.

"This time," Sloane said.

"And I suppose I can expect more of these tests?"

"Many more."

Claire clenched her jaw. "We should be on our way. I have much to do in Tara."

Sloane waved to a servant. "Saddle the dragons," she called. "I'll go get the other knights of your escort, Your Majesty."

Servants brought out a long leather saddle. Breaus lay down while they fastened it to his back, just ahead of his wings. "I didn't care much for that little test of yours," Claire said.

"I didn't enjoy doing it," Breaus said. "But I would do it again. And worse, if necessary."

"Necessary for what?" Claire asked.

"To make sure you're ready."

"And what worse would you do?"

"I would watch you go into battle alone against monsters. I would watch you fight, and not help you, unless you fell," Breaus said.

"The final test?"

"The final test," Breaus said.

"And is all that really necessary?"

"Sloane tells me you've fought a Viper Knight. Were you ready for that?" Breaus asked.

"No," Claire admitted. "He nearly killed me."

"There's your answer, then. I once saw a knight I had trained die in front of me. He wasn't ready either."

"He didn't survive the final test?" Claire asked.

"He passed all the tests. He died in battle," Breaus said.

"Don't the tests make sure a knight is ready for a real battle?"

"They only measure skill. There's more to being a Dragon Knight than skill. Much more," Breaus said.

"And how was this knight lacking?" Claire asked.

"He was afraid. And he refused to admit it."

"So?" Claire asked, feeling her cheeks grow hot.

"People who say they're not afraid often feel the need to prove it. They take foolish risks. They get killed," Breaus said.

"And that's what happened to him?"

"Yes. You can lie to others about being afraid. There's no great danger in that. The real danger is in lying to yourself. That's the lie you were telling," Breaus said.

"You can see through me like that?" Claire asked.

"Fire reveals that which is hidden. A dragon's eyes see a great deal."

"And that's what you see in me. A liar," Claire said.

"No. I see someone who wants to be brave. But denying fear is not bravery. Fear is a mountain with no summit. Real bravery is to get up and climb the mountain. To keep climbing, every day. Not to deny how high the mountain is, or to wish it was lower. But to realize that the altitude is what makes the climb worthwhile. *That* is bravery," Breaus said.

"Then I'm not brave," Claire said.

"Admitting you're afraid is the first step up the mountain. Sloane and I can help you with the next step."

"Then I'll admit it. I'm afraid. I've been afraid every day since Father died," Claire said.

"Yet you carried on. You never gave up. You're braver than you give yourself credit for," Breaus said.

Sloane came back into the hall, along with four other knights. "Take this, Your Majesty," she said, handing her a helmet of black steel. "It will protect your face from the wind." Claire put the helmet on, and the world outside shrunk to the size of two eye slits.

Sloane helped her climb up onto Breaus. "Hold tight, Your Majesty," she said, showing her the posts at the front of the saddle. "And keep your feet in the stirrups." Sloane and the other knights mounted their own dragons.

Breaus stood, and followed Sloane's dragon to the far end of the cavern, where huge metal doors were set into the side of the mountain. Sloane gave a command, and servants started turning large wheels mounted on the walls. Each wheel set a chain in motion, and the doors slowly swung outward on their hinges. Cold air blew in, and sunlight pierced the depths of the cavern.

Sloane's dragon stepped outside, and Breaus followed out onto a ledge. The blue sky stretched out around them, and the wind howled, pulling and flapping at Claire's uniform. *It's like staring into an ocean*, she thought. *Just before you dive off a cliff.*

Claire shivered. Breaus swiveled his head back toward her. "Scared?"

"Yes," she said.

He nodded. "Keep climbing the mountain, Your Majesty."

"Breaus…call me Claire."

He smiled, his mouth gleaming with teeth. "Claire." Breaus' muscles moved under Claire's legs as he spread his wings. "Hold tight," he warned. Claire fought the urge to close her eyes.

Claire gripped the saddle posts tightly as she was jerked upwards. Breaus' muscles pulsed beneath her, his wings beating furiously. He turned to the left, banking around the mountain as they soared higher. The ground was dizzyingly far below, and Claire fought down the nausea surging through her stomach.

Claire looked away from the ground, focusing on Sloane's dragon in front of them. Breaus finished his turn and leveled off. The flight became smooth and peaceful, aside from the wind whipping against her. The churning in her stomach eased. She glanced down. *Incredible*, she thought. The emerald countryside was spread out in miniature below her. They flew over the moors and meadows of Keldaren, heading for Tara.

CHAPTER 14

Claire

After hours in the air, Tara finally came into view, the Siochana River twisting through the city like a sapphire snake. The dragons turned, heading for Connemara Palace. Breaus glided in for a landing in the palace's outer courtyard. Claire closed her eyes at the sight of the ground rushing up toward them, and squeezed the grips of the saddle. Breaus' wings snapped back, and their descent slowed. There was only a bump as Breaus' claws hit the cobblestones, and they came suddenly to a stop. Claire opened her eyes as Breaus folded his wings, and lowered his belly to the ground.

The other dragons landed around them in the courtyard. Claire loosened her feet from the stirrups and slid down from the saddle. Sloane and the other knights dismounted as well. A squad of Crown Guards came out into the courtyard, led by a centurion.

He saluted. "Your Majesty, welcome back."

"Thank you. I'm looking for a Centurion Eloc," she said.

"I'm Eloc, Your Majesty. I've taken command of the remaining guards at the palace. I'm afraid I'm the most senior officer left here."

"You're about to become even more senior," Claire said. She handed him the letter.

Eloc read it, his face growing pale. "Lady Bradaigh is putting a great deal of trust in me."

"Don't let her down," Claire said.

"I won't, Your Majesty. I received your message. Senator Garenne is waiting for you."

"And what of Aricet?"

Eloc frowned. "The general sent word that he would be here if he could."

"If he *could*? You made my orders clear to him?" Claire asked.

"I did, Your Majesty."

That pretentious churl. "General Aricet had best answer my summons by the time I leave Connemara tonight. Or else all he'll find himself commanding is a watchtower on the border." Claire shook her head. "I'll see the senator now."

"Escort the Queen to the throne room," Eloc ordered the other guards. "I'll fetch Senator Garenne, Your Majesty."

"I'll be back in an hour or so," Claire told Breaus. She followed the guards into the palace, accompanied by Sloane and the rest of the dragon knights. Two guards opened the throne room doors for her.

The room was circular, with walls of gilt-trimmed red marble, lined with tall windows. Frescoes depicting Keldaren's history decorated the domed ceiling. Sunlight streamed in through a circle of glass at the center of the dome, and glowed across the white marble floor. A dais of polished granite rose against the far wall of the room.

A marble canopy stood atop the dais, sheltering the throne beneath it. Carved from polished moonstone, the throne gleamed as white as winter. Where light reflected off it, though, shimmers of ocean-blue flashed deep within the stone. A royal trinity knot was etched in gold atop the throne's high back.

The knights waited outside while Sloane followed Claire into the throne room. The guards closed the doors behind them, leaving them alone in the marble rotunda. Claire climbed the granite steps to the dais and sat. The throne was like ice beneath her. The chill of the moonstone seeped through her clothes.

"You look uncomfortable, Your Majesty," Sloane said.

Claire grimaced. "It's cold. You'd think that over the years someone would have added cushions."

"I think it fitting they didn't."

"Why?" Claire asked.

"Ruling isn't supposed to be warm and comfortable. A cushioned sovereign would lose touch with that truth," Sloane said.

The doors opened. "Senator Isabelle Garenne," a servant announced. He led the senator to an armchair at the foot of the dais. Sloane went to stand at Claire's right side. *Where Kerry should be,* Claire thought, a flash of guilt pricking her. The servant bowed, then left the room, closing the doors behind him.

Claire watched as the senator took her seat. She was middle aged, yet still looked young enough. She wore her sandy-blond hair cut short, and was clad in a simple, but stylish, gray dress.

"Welcome, Senator Garenne. It's good to finally meet you."

"Please Your Majesty, call me Isabelle. It was an unexpected honor to receive your summons. What can I do for you?"

"Tell me why you wish to be Chancellor."

"Your uncle and I have very different ideas on how to govern the kingdom. I believe my ideas would serve the people better than his."

"My uncle warned me about you. He told me you were quite the raging populist."

"I imagine Prince Malcolm would call me that," Isabelle said.

"And just what are these better ideas of yours?"

"Our current laws favor the rich and the nobility. I would make things more balanced."

"How?" Claire asked.

"Taxes, for starters. Everyone in the kingdom pays taxes on their houses. That sounds fair enough, at first. Nobles and the wealthy have mansions and large estates, so they pay higher taxes than the poor. But wealthy merchants own ships, and docks, and warehouses. Nobles own farms and workshops, and country villas. None of these are taxed. Only homes are."

"What of it? The rich pay the taxes they owe," Claire said.

"Do they? Aren't docks and warehouses and farms all served by roads built by the kingdom? Aren't they all protected by constables? If any of them caught fire, wouldn't the Fire Watch turn out and fight the flames? And what pays for all of that?" Isabelle asked.

"Taxes," Claire said.

"Imagine I go into a shop and buy something. Then I take something else without paying for it. Would that make me a good customer, or a thief?"

"Some merchants give their best customers discounts, though. Especially when those customers spend a good deal of coin in their shops," Claire objected.

"Merchants make profits. That's why they can afford to give discounts. The profits from the large sales cover the loss of the discount. But a government doesn't make profits," Isabelle said. "Not any honest government. That's why we should charge everyone what they owe."

"Well," Claire said, "My uncle was right. You are a populist."

"I suppose I am, Your Majesty. Forgive me if I offended you."

"Not at all. I wanted to make sure we were in agreement before I appointed you Acting Chancellor," Claire said.

"I beg your pardon, Your Majesty? Did you say Acting Chancellor?"

"I did. I'll draft a royal warrant confirming the appointment. But as of now, you're the new Chancellor. Until the elections, at least," Claire said.

"I hardly know what to say, Your Majesty."

"Say you accept. Say you'll serve your country."

"Of course. But what if Prince Malcolm returns before the election?" Isabelle asked.

"He is the elected Chancellor. If he returns, you'll have to step down. But I have a bad feeling about my uncle's disappearance. I don't think we'll be seeing him again soon."

"And how will it look for me if he vanishes only a few months before an election, and I'm appointed to fill his office before the vote?" Isabelle asked.

"Only the most paranoid of Malcolm's supporters would say there was some conspiracy to replace him before the election, if that's what you mean. Besides, you're not the only candidate running against him. Alexander Odran is standing for election too," Claire said.

"There are some very paranoid people amongst Malcolm's supporters, Your Majesty. And I was the only Crusader candidate running against him. Odran and Malcolm are both members of the Guardian faction. Some will say I had some role in his disappearance."

Claire shrugged. "Let them think what they will. I chose you. If the people disagree, they can vote against you come election time. But for now, we have a great deal of work to do. I want you to summon my ministers and the Senate to Mount Draconis."

"The Dragon Order's stronghold? Why?"

"I'll be training there for the next few months, and I need the rest of the government with me to keep the kingdom running," Claire said.

"The senators won't like that, Your Majesty. But they will do their duty."

"Good. I'll expect to see all of you at Mount Draconis within the week," Claire said.

"We'll be there, Your Majesty." Isabelle stood, and bowed. "Thank you for your confidence in me."

"Thank me by proving I made the right choice."

"I will." Isabelle turned, and went to the door. She let herself out, and a guard stepped in.

"Your Majesty, General Aricet has arrived."

"Send him in."

Aricet strode into the room, his crimson cape billowing behind him. He was a slender man, with a thin, proud face and a beak-like nose. Rank tabs shaped like golden suns flashed on the collar of his uniform. He stopped before the dais and saluted.

"So good of you to decide to answer my summons, General," Claire said, shifting on the throne.

"My duties do keep me quite busy, Your Majesty. Thankfully, I was able to find some time to meet with you. I'm afraid I don't have long, though," he said.

"I'm sorry to inconvenience you so. Being Commandant of the army must be a heavy weight to bear."

"It is indeed," Aricet said.

Claire leaned forward. "Perhaps it's a burden you should be relieved of." She smiled. "Such stress can't be good for you."

He returned her smile. "That is most kind of you. But I'm happy to make the sacrifice to serve my country. And my army needs me."

"It's *my* army, General. Don't forget that."

"Of course, Your Majesty."

"And if I ever feel that the burden on your shoulders is too great, General, then I shall have to relieve you of it. Out of concern for your health."

"Your Majesty is good to be so concerned for me. May I ask why I'm here?"

"I assume you're aware of what transpired with Lord Halen? And the attack on the palace?" Claire asked.

"I am."

"I want you to send more troops to reinforce all of the watchtowers and keeps guarding the border with Drakaren. We must be prepared for an invasion," Claire said.

"Drakaren won't be invading any time soon, Your Majesty. It will be winter in a few months. They'd be unable to gain a foothold in Keldaren before the snow flies. It would be suicide for an invading army to fight in the dead of winter in enemy territory, without walls to shelter them or granaries to feed them. They won't attack until spring. I'll send more troops to the border then."

"The Drakari have already proven themselves unpredictable. You will send more troops now," Claire said.

"Your Majesty…that would be a serious disruption to our deployment schedule. An unnecessary disruption."

"General, where do your troops quarter for the winter?" Sloane asked.

"That's restricted military information," Aricet said.

"I'm part of the military, General," Sloane said.

Aricet smiled. "Not part of the army, though. I'm afraid I can't tell the Dragon Order all our secrets."

"Answer her question," Claire ordered.

Aricet's smile vanished. "We quarter them in castles and manor houses."

"I suppose the owners of those properties donate them, out of patriotism?" Sloane asked.

"We pay them rent, of course. A large amount of the army's coin goes toward paying our winter rents," Aricet said.

"That sounds quite lucrative for those owners," Sloane said. "And you personally make the choice as to where the troops spend the winter?"

"Yes. There's a great deal of competition amongst the nobles for our coin. That lets me choose only the best castles and manors for our soldiers."

"I'd imagine such high rents might lead to the nobles being tempted to offer...incentives to the person who chooses where the soldiers are quartered. It's a good thing you have the best interests of our soldiers at heart, General," Sloane said.

Aricet's face darkened, and he glared at Sloane. "Just what are you suggesting?"

"I'm suggesting, General, that we should be thankful you're too principled to be susceptible to bribery, or other such temptations." Sloane smiled. "Why, what did you think I was suggesting?"

"Nothing." Aricet glowered at her.

"The disruption to your schedule is regrettable, General, but necessary. You'll move troops to the border at once," Claire said.

"Your Majesty, I'm afraid I can't agree to your request. Moving the troops now is completely unnecessary."

"That wasn't a request. It was an order. And I don't need your agreement. Carry out my order, or I'll replace you with someone who will. Do we understand each other, General?"

Aricet's glare was as sharp as a sword. "Perfectly, Your Majesty." He turned toward the doors.

"You would leave without saluting your queen?" Sloane asked.

Aricet turned back. He came to attention and snapped a salute. Then he spun on his heel, and strode out of the room.

Claire sighed as the doors shut behind him. "That was unpleasant."

"I think we know why he was so reluctant to move the troops. If the soldiers are deployed to the border, they won't be quartered by the nobles. That would remove any reason the nobles would have to pay him bribes for choosing their lands," Sloane said.

"That could be. Or it may just be arrogance and stubbornness. I've never met someone so obstinate," Claire said.

"He's more than just obstinate, Your Majesty. That one will be trouble."

"I hope not. I have trouble enough already." Claire stood, and Sloane followed her into the King's office. *My office, now*, Claire reminded herself. She took paper and pen, and wrote out the royal warrant appointing Isabelle as Acting Chancellor.

"Time to be on our way," she told Sloane. They left the office, and the knights followed them through the corridors of the palace. It was dark outside now, and the lanterns were lit, their light reflecting off the polished granite floors. At the main doors, Claire gave the warrant to one of the servants. "Deliver this to the Royal Secretariat. And have a copy sent to the Senate as well," she ordered.

The air was chilly outside, proving fall's arrival. *And winter isn't far behind,* Claire thought. She and the knights swung back up into their saddles atop the dragons. The flight back to Mount Draconis wasn't nearly as jarring as the first flight, but there were still moments that made her stomach lurch.

It was late by the time they finally landed. The saddles were removed, and the dragons returned to their compartments for the night. Claire wearily made her way up the mountain to her room, and sank into her bed.

CHAPTER 15

Claire

The next morning, Claire met Sloane in a training chamber deep inside the mountain. "Are you ready for the first lesson?" Sloane asked.

"As ready as I can be."

"I'm going to throw something at you, and I want you to deflect it with your sword. Dragon Knights don't carry shields. We use our swords to redirect blows instead. This will train you to do that by instinct. Are you ready?"

"Yes," Claire said, drawing the training sword Sloane had given her.

Sloane hurled a green sphere at her face. Claire lashed out, but it sailed past her blade. The fruit smashed into pulp across her face, the pit dropping to the floor.

Claire wiped the mush from her cheeks, wincing when her hand touched the spot where the pit had hit her. "That hurt."

"An incentive to avoid getting hit," Sloane said. "And good practice for the next step in the exercise."

"What's the next step?"

"Rocks."

"You're going to hit me with rocks?" Claire asked.

"No. I'm going to throw rocks at you. You're going to deflect them. You'll only get hit if you miss," Sloane said.

"Then I suppose I'd better not miss."

"Once you can hit them all, we'll move on to the final step," Sloane said.

"And what might that be?" Claire asked.

"Arrows."

Jared

Proterian Palace loomed ahead of Jared as his horse galloped through the streets of Graydare. A single Drakari soldier was his only escort on the ride from the docks. *If I had taken Connemara, there would have been a victory parade to welcome me back.*

They rode up to the palace gates, where the guards let them in. A single Viper Knight waited by the stables. "Your Highness," Varin said, lowering his hood, "I heard things didn't go well."

"No. But it wasn't my fault, Varin! I didn't know dragons were there. Without them, we would have taken the palace," Jared said, dismounting.

"The queen is quite angry, Your Highness. Be on guard when you speak to her."

"Minerva loves me. I have nothing to fear from her," Jared said.

"She may love you, but her anger can be vicious. Be careful, Prince."

"Careful of what? Will she have me whipped? Will she throw me in prison? Will she scream at me?" Jared asked, smiling.

Varin's tone was dark. "Hope that she screams. If she's quiet, that means she's especially furious. And especially dangerous."

That gave him pause. The first twinge of doubt crept into his mind, along with a shiver he shook off. *She'll understand*, he told himself. *It's a minor setback. Nothing more.*

Varin led him into the palace. They passed through halls lined with dusty suits of armor, and chambers hung with faded tapestries. Finally, they came to the door of the queen's sitting room. Two palace guards stood watch outside.

"Remember what I said, Your Highness," Varin told him. One of the guards stepped inside. He emerged a moment later, and gestured for Jared to enter.

Minerva sat next to the fireplace, her face hidden in the shadows cast by the tall back of her chair. A second chair sat empty across from her. Jared sat down, crossing his leg over his knee.

"I didn't give you leave to sit," Minerva said softly.

Jared snapped to his feet. Fear twisted through him like a river of icy water. "I'm sorry," he stammered, "I assumed…"

"What do you have to say for yourself?" she asked, cutting him off. Her voice was still as soft and quiet as a forest stream.

"It wasn't my fault! There weren't supposed to be *dragons* there."

"You didn't send out scouts?" she asked.

"It took longer than I planned to march from the anchorage to the palace. There was no time to wait for scouts if we were to attack on schedule."

Minerva leaned forward into the light. Her eyes smoldered like the fires of the netherworld. "And what do you think now?" she asked quietly. "What was more important—keeping the schedule, or the surprise?"

"The surprise."

"Do you know what you've cost me? If you had taken Claire and the palace, Keldaren would have been ours. Now we'll have to fight a full-scale war in the spring," Minerva said.

"We'll win, though. Our army is much larger than Keldaren's."

"That's hardly the point. And victory certainly isn't guaranteed. They have dragons. We don't. Dragons change the equation, Jared. As you now know." Minerva sighed. "I'm sending you to the eastern army's winter quarters. You'll stay with them until spring."

He nodded. *I knew she'd give me a chance to redeem myself.* "I'll go take command of the army at once."

"You'll do no such thing. General Dalrush will still be in command. You'll perform whatever duties he sees fit to assign you. You'll follow his orders to the letter. And you'll ponder the price of failure. Understand?"

"I understand," Jared said. *Fool. She won't trust you again until you've earned it.* He stared at the floor. "I'm sorry for my failure. It won't happen again."

"Have you ever heard of General Magreve?" Minerva asked.

Jared looked up. "Of course. He was the Drakari commander during the last border war."

"I started that war to seize Dalrann Province from Keldaren. If Magreve had succeeded, we would have greatly enlarged our territory. But he failed. Your father defeated his army. And then, after Magreve and his soldiers retreated, the Keldari plundered the city of Cereth to teach us a lesson. Magreve failed me, Jared. He failed me miserably."

"I won't fail you again, Minerva."

"Did you ever hear what happened to the General?"

Jared shook his head.

"He came to the palace to explain himself to me. I removed him from command, of course. I had to, after such a failure. But I gave him a house to retire to, and a pension. I am a generous queen, after all."

"After he left the palace, though, he was set on by some criminals. He must not have been quick enough in surrendering his coin. They stabbed him. Several times, in fact. Such a vicious ending for such a petty robbery. He was already dead by the time a patrol of watchmen came across him," Minerva said.

The river of fear coiling through Jared now seemed to freeze solid. "You've always told me there's no crime in Graydare."

"That's what's so ironic—it's normally such a safe city. Magreve's murder was the only one in Graydare that year," Minerva said. "The watchmen never found his attackers."

"Then how do you know it was more than one criminal who attacked him?" He winced as soon as the words had slipped from his tongue. *Keep silent, fool,* he told himself.

"You're right, of course. How would I know how many there were? How very *perceptive* you are, Jared." Minerva's smile was as soft as her voice. Her eyes, though...her eyes burned like pools of molten iron.

CHAPTER 16

Claire

The cuts on her face still stung, but Claire fought the urge to rub them. That just made them hurt more. *Curse those rocks,* she thought. She shifted from one foot to the other, trying to take the weight off of her left hip. The wound there hurt worse than her face.

Sloane saw, of course. "At least the arrowhead was blunt."

"They won't be blunt in battle. Taking a real arrow there might have killed me," Claire said.

"Missing one arrow out of fifty isn't so bad, Your Majesty. And you didn't miss any the second time."

"One miss is all it takes. You told me that," Claire said.

"True. Draw your sword, Your Majesty. We'll start another exercise today."

She drew the wooden training sword, while Sloane uncoiled a long, braided bullwhip. Claire winced. "I suppose I have to block that, and if I miss, I get hit."

"Exactly."

"Isn't this the same as deflecting rocks?" Claire asked.

"This is a little different, Your Majesty." The door opened and another Dragon Knight came in. The knight uncoiled his own whip, and took a practice swing. Claire flinched as the crack echoed through the room. Sloane snapped her wrist, flipping her whip behind her. "This time there are two of us."

Jared

Jared rode along the trail, two Drakari soldiers following him. The castle stood atop a hill at the trail's end. The field below was covered with ramshackle wooden longhouses. *Those barracks will become iceboxes in winter,* he thought, shuddering. As they rode closer, though, he saw that the castle didn't look much better. The fortresses' walls were showing their age, dotted with gaps where stones had fallen.

Two soldiers stood guard at the main gate, wearing the gray tunics of the Drakari Army. Beneath the tunics, they wore leather armored with squares of steel. *This is the army that will win me my throne*, Jared thought, spurring his horse forward. The soldiers glared at him from under their wide-brimmed helmets.

"I'm Prince Jared. I'm sure you were told to expect me."

"No," one of them answered. "We weren't."

"Perhaps you didn't hear me." Jared leaned forward in the saddle. "I am *Prince* Jared. You'll address me as Your Highness."

"I heard you, Your Highness. And I've heard of you. Shame about the defeat at Connemara," the soldier said, smirking. "Oy!" he shouted up at the battlements above. "Open the gate for his high and mighty lordship, Prince Jared!"

Jared glared at him as the gate creaked open. "I'll have you whipped for your insolence."

"A thousand pardons if I've offended your magnificence," the soldier said, grinning as he leaned against his spear.

A flogging will teach you some respect, dog, Jared thought, jerking the reins. *It will teach them all to respect me.* He rode into the courtyard, and dismounted at the stables. "You!" he shouted at a stable boy. "Take me to General Dalrush."

The boy brought him to the general's office. Jared endured yet another smirk when he gave his name to the guard outside. *I'll have the entire garrison whipped if that's what it takes*, he thought, a white blur of fury filling his head. *They'll all bleed until they learn to respect me.*

Dalrush stood behind his desk, staring down at a map. He was of an average build, with thinning brown hair, and wore a gold-trimmed black cape over his army uniform. He looked up as the door shut. "Jared. Welcome to Grayspear Castle."

That's Prince Jared to you. Jared forced himself to bite back the words. "Thank you, General. Planning invasion routes?"

Dalrush looked at the map. "Yes. I'm devising strategies for the spring."

"Why wait until spring? I say we cross the border now. The Keldari won't be expecting an attack," Jared said.

"And with good reason. The snow will fly soon. If we attack now, we might be caught in Keldaren without adequate supplies or shelter. The Keldari wouldn't need an army. Winter itself would destroy us," Dalrush said.

"If we take Dalrann, we could hold the city over the winter. In spring it would become the tip of a spear pointed at Tara," Jared said.

"Assuming we could get across the border. The Keldari have doubtless stationed extra troops there since your attack on Connemara Palace," Dalrush said.

Your failed attack. Dalrush's eyes said the words, even if his mouth didn't.

"We would have the element of surprise," Jared said. "Unless they've stationed their entire army along the border, we'd still win."

"It's a bold idea, Jared. But not a practical one."

"So you're refusing to consider invading now?" Jared asked.

"Yes."

"We'll see what the queen says about that," Jared snarled.

"No, we won't. She already sent a message to let me know you were on your way. And her letter said she told you who was in charge here." Dalrush leaned toward him. "I'm in command, Jared. You'll be following my orders. See that you don't forget that."

Jared glared at him. There were a hundred things he wanted to say, most of them curses. But he wrestled down his anger, and held his tongue.

"I'll have someone take you to your rooms," Dalrush said. "But be back here in two hours. I have a meeting scheduled with the regimental commanders."

"I'll be happy to give my advice," Jared said, choosing his words carefully.

"I don't require your advice. I need someone to take notes," Dalrush said.

Another smirk, Jared thought, watching the hint of a smile curve across Dalrush's lips. *I'll see that smirk wiped off your face, General.* "I'll go to my rooms later," he said. "I have to see a sergeant first about a whipping."

"A whipping?"

Jared told him about the soldier at the gate.

"No sergeant in this army would give a whipping unless an officer orders one. You aren't an officer. And this is no whipping offense. These soldiers are veterans. You'll need to earn their respect, not demand it." Dalrush sighed. "You have to learn your place here, Jared."

No, Jared thought, *I have to teach you yours.*

Claire

The cloth was tight around Claire's eyes, enveloping her in darkness. She steadied her grip on the hilt of the sword, fighting back the urge to rip the blindfold from her face. A noise came from her left. Soft footsteps drew closer, and then retreated. There was a loud clang on her right.

Claire spun, slashing blindly. She sensed movement behind her and swung her sword around. There was a blow on the back of her armor, and the clang of a wooden sword against steel rang through the room. Claire yanked the blindfold off. "How did you get behind me? I heard you on my side."

"Did you?" Sloane pointed to an armored gauntlet lying on the floor. "You heard me throwing that. What you didn't hear was me stealing up behind you. Don't focus on just one sound. You have to be aware of everything. Not just the obvious."

Claire threw her sword to the ground. "This is pointless! When will I ever have to fight blindfolded?"

Sloane's gaze was cold. "I seem to remember fighting beside you once at night."

"That's different."

"How?" Sloane demanded.

"There was moonlight."

"Luckily for us. But the moon could just as easily have been hidden by clouds. Besides, the blindfold isn't just to teach you to fight in the dark. It's to heighten your other senses, to teach you to see without your eyes. If you find that pointless, then just say the word, and we can end your training," Sloane said.

Claire sighed. "No. I want to keep going."

"Then pick up your sword."

Claire reached down and picked it up. She winced as she bent over. She straightened, and reached under her armor to touch the spot where Sloane had hit her.

"Do you need a break, Your Majesty?"

"No. It hurts less than the whips, at least. Continue."
Claire fitted the blindfold back over her eyes. Sloane's footsteps
moved quietly off, and the hunt began again.

Jared

It's about time Dalrush sent me on a real mission, Jared
thought as he walked out to the courtyard. *I've wasted a whole
month playing his glorified steward.* A roc stood in the courtyard,
flapping its wings impatiently. A Viper Knight waited beside it.

The knight inclined his head. "Your Highness, I'm Sir
Dral. I was one of the knights at Drohea Castle."

"Of course. It's good to see you again, Sir Dral. I'm sorry
this is just a scouting flight, and not a raid. Still, it's good to be
commanding a mission again."

A ghost of a smile flashed across Dral's face.

Jared glared at him. "Did I say something humorous?"

"Not at all, Your Highness. After you," Dral said,
gesturing to the roc. Jared climbed up onto the back saddle, and
Dral settled into the saddle in front of him. Dral leaned forward,
and croaked out a command. The roc took a few running steps and
snapped its wings down, soaring into the air. Once they were aloft,
the bird turned and headed east.

An hour passed before a gray tower appeared ahead of
them. They flew past the Keldari watchtower, and continued along
the border, passing over Keldari keeps and towers. After they had

passed a score of fortifications, Jared leaned toward Dral. "There are no extra troops here, are there?"

Dral shook his head. "No, this is just the normal complement. A squad or two at each tower. No more."

"Then my sister is even more a fool than I thought."

"It would appear so," Dral said.

"Head back, Sir Dral. The General and I have much to discuss."

An hour later, the roc skimmed low through the air, and landed in the courtyard of the castle. Jared leapt down from the saddle and hurried inside. He found Dalrush in his office. *Where he always is. Sitting behind his desk, staring at maps.* "They haven't sent more troops to the border!" Jared exclaimed.

"What?"

"We flew over the Keldari defenses between us and Dalrann. There's only the normal number of soldiers there. Now's our chance, General! If we move quickly, we can take Dalrann."

"Slow down, Jared. Think this through. Why wouldn't the Keldari send reinforcements to the border?"

"Because they're fools. And we should take advantage of their foolishness."

"Only the worst of fools would make a mistake like this. Perhaps it's not a mistake at all. Perhaps they aren't as foolish as you think," Dalrush said.

"You think it's a trap?"

"I think that likely. But even if it weren't, and we were to take Dalrann, the Keldari would only have to lay siege to the city. They could cut off our supply convoys, and starve us out," Dalrush said.

"There's plenty of food in the city's granaries, General. More than enough to feed an army for the winter."

"And then what would the people of Dalrann eat?"

Jared shrugged. "Let them leave the city after we take it. Or let them stay and starve."

Dalrush pointed a finger at him. "This is the problem with all your plans, Jared. You lack experience. A good commander knows the people of a captured city can be very useful in a siege. Having thousands of their own citizens as hostages can dissuade an army from using catapults against a city, or poisoning its water supply."

Jared slammed his hands down on Dalrush's desk. "A good commander has courage, General. I bring you an opportunity, and all you give me are excuses. Perhaps you lack the nerve to command this army. Perhaps you should be replaced."

Dalrush stood. He leaned forward on the desk, until he was nose to nose with Jared. "*I* command this army. If you question my leadership again, I'll throw you in chains. And if you question my courage, then meet me in the courtyard with your sword."

His glare was razor-sharp as he stared at Jared. Jared stared right back. Dalrush was no muscle-bound brawler, like some of the Drakari soldiers. And he was no Viper Knight. But there was a menace in Dalrush's eyes that gave Jared pause. Fear overcame the fury boiling through Jared. *Too dangerous*, Jared thought, tasting the sour tang of fear in his mouth. *If we dueled, I'd lose.* He looked down.

Dalrush smiled. "Close the door on your way out. I have a great deal of work to do."

Jared hung his head. "Yes, General." As he closed the door, he heard Dalrush's scornful chuckle. *Good. Let him think me defeated and meek.* Jared smiled as he walked away. *Let him mock me, and think me a toothless tiger. And let him forget that a tiger has claws.*

CHAPTER 17

Claire

Claire walked into the training room, where Sloane was waiting. The rock-hewn chamber was filled with columns of different heights. A glass globe filled with oil stood atop each column. Wicks of braided rope burned on the lamps.

Sloane tossed a twinlance to Claire. "Let's see what you remember of lance handling. Put out one of the flames. Without hitting the glass."

Claire spun the twinlance as Sloane had taught her. The blades wailed mournfully as they whipped through the air. She sliced one of the blades over a lamp. The flame flickered, but didn't burn out. Claire tried again and again, but the flame refused to die.

"The blades are too thin for that. They won't move enough air to blow them out," Sloane said.

"Then how the nether am I supposed to put them out?"

"Cut the wick," Sloane said.

"You want me to cut a burning wick. Without hitting the lamp."

"Yes."

Claire spun the lance around again, slicing out at the nearest lamp. Her blade hit the globe, shattering it. Claire grimaced. "I suppose I have to put out every lamp before we can move on?"

"Of course," Sloane said, pulling another globe from a cabinet and lighting it. "And you have to extinguish them all within one minute." She set the lamp on the empty column, and pulled a tiny hourglass out from the cabinet.

Claire's knuckles whitened on the grip of the lance. She had a sudden urge to smash every lamp in the room. And Sloane. Claire glared at Sloane. She definitely wanted to hit her.

Sloane looked at her, and seemed to sense what she was thinking. "Every Dragon Knight has to pass this test," she said. "You have three choices, Your Majesty. You can walk away from training and be done. You can stand there wasting time seething. Or you can get to work mastering this. The choice is yours."

Claire glowered at her. *She's right. Get on with it.*

"Besides, we'll be working on hand to hand combat next. You'll get your chance to hit me then," Sloane said, smiling.

Claire gave her a tight smile in return, and swung the lance up into a ready position. She stared at the nearest lamp, and the bare inch of wick between the flame and the glass. Then she started the blades whistling through the air.

Jared

The room was freezing, despite the fire blazing on the hearth. The icy winds of the storm howled in through the chinks in the dilapidated walls of the castle. A knock came on the door. Jared opened it to find a soldier waiting.

"General says for you to meet him in the west tower. He's got a mission for you," the man growled.

"In this blizzard?"

The soldier grinned, showing the gaps in his teeth. "General says to make it quick." He walked away, chuckling.

Jared cursed, and went to get his cloak. He found Dalrush standing in the guard tower, staring out at the storm.

"I have an important assignment for you today, Jared. We must make this castle ready for battle before we attack in the spring. As you can see, there's a great deal of work to be done before this place is useful as a fortress." Dalrush pointed to a gap in the battlements a short way down the ramparts. Several large stones had fallen from the wall, leaving an opening that the wind howled through.

The sentry on duty came through on his rounds, passing through the tower before continuing down the ramparts. Dalrush paused to return the soldier's salute. "I want you to walk the perimeter of the castle, and make a list of the repairs needed," he continued. "I'll expect your report by tomorrow morning."

"You want me to do it now, in this weather?" Jared objected. "Surely it can wait."

"No. It can't. I suggest you walk quickly, Jared. It will help keep you warm."

Jared seethed, wanting to rip the General's throat out. He wrestled his anger under control, taking a deep breath. *What would Varin do?* he asked himself. As Dalrush turned to leave, the answer came to him. Jared quickly glanced around. The sentry was heading in the opposite direction, and had almost disappeared into the swirling whiteness of the storm. No one else was in sight.

Good. No witnesses. Dalrush walked away. Just as he was about to pass the hole in the wall, Jared charged at him, shoving the General toward the gap.

Dalrush pitched forward, his fingers scrabbling at the stone. For a second, they held, but then slipped loose. Dalrush fell as silently as the snow.

"Guard!" Jared shouted to the sentry. By the time he and the soldier reached the body, a red pool had spread across the white snow.

The sentry touched Dalrush's neck, feeling for a pulse. "He's dead."

A colonel emerged from the castle. "What's all this?"

"We were walking along the top of the wall, and the General tripped," Jared said. "I tried to catch him, but he fell."

"And he just happened to be by that gap in the wall when he tripped?" the colonel asked. His eyes were as gray and cold as flint as he stared at Jared. A white beard framed his tight-set mouth.

Jared stared back, trying to make his own gaze like stone. "Yes."

"I suppose you'll want to take command now?" the colonel asked.

"The queen sent me here to assist General Dalrush. It's only fitting that I replace him as commander. What's your name, Colonel?"

"Roche."

"How is it that I've never seen you at the commanders' meetings, Colonel Roche?"

"I don't command a regiment," Roche said. "I'm the stable master."

"That's an…unusual position for a colonel, isn't it?" Jared asked.

"Too lowly a position, you mean?"

"That was my meaning. I was trying to be more subtle in saying it," Jared said.

"There's no subtle way to say it. A colonel with twenty years in the army is responsible for overseeing the sweeping of horse scite. This one," Roche said, pointing to Dalrush's body, "said I was becoming too ambitious. He took my regiment away, and gave me a position that should go to a sergeant. All to humiliate me after I once dared to question his orders."

"I've questioned General Dalrush myself," Jared said. "He was a man in need of questioning, I think. A man too blind to see beyond his own arrogance. As the new commander of the eastern army, I'll need a second in command. Someone I would raise to the rank of General. Perhaps someone whose talents had been overlooked by the previous commander. Do you know of any officers like that, Colonel?"

Roche's eyes widened, then narrowed again. He nodded. "I'll advise the other officers that you're in command now, Your Highness."

"Thank you...General."

The next day, Dalrush's body rested in a simple wooden casket atop a stack of logs outside the castle walls. The entire eastern army was assembled beneath the hill. Jared stood at the head of the casket. Roche stood at his side, watching the soldiers. *He's done an excellent job of winning over the officers,* Jared thought. *Winning the men, though...that's up to me.*

Jared stepped forward. "Warriors of Drakaren! It's a bitter irony that a warrior like General Dalrush should be killed in an accident, instead of in battle. But we will carry on his legacy, and his plans for victory over Keldaren. As many of you know, I recently went on a scouting mission. I discovered that Keldaren hasn't reinforced its border defenses. The General and I made plans to capture the city of Dalrann, to hold it through the winter, and use it to launch an attack against Tara come spring. We won't let the General's death stop his plans. We'll invade Keldaren and take Dalrann!"

Jared paused for a moment, staring at the sea of faces below him. Some of the men looked excited, but more were grumbling. "I see that some of you are eager to fight, and some hesitate. Consider this—if the army stays here, you'll spend the winter huddled in these miserable iceboxes," Jared said, gesturing to the longhouses filling the valley. "Some of you will freeze to death. Some will lose fingers and feet to frostbite. You'll live on sparse rations in drafty quarters, hoping to survive the snows."

He paused again. "Or you can follow me to Dalrann. Once we've taken the city, we'll evict the people. You can quarter in warm houses, and eat from the city's granaries. Think how well an army can eat on the food stores for an entire city. That's your choice, men. You can starve in the snow here, or you can feast in warmth in Dalrann."

They were still silent. *I don't have them yet.* "In Keldaren, if a city was sacked, the spoils went to the Crown," Jared shouted. "Is it the same in the Drakari army?"

"It is!" one of the officers shouted back.

"Then we'll change that. Follow me to Dalrann and you'll be rich as well.

You'll keep all of the spoils you win when we take the city!"

One sword went up amidst the sea of gray uniforms. Then another. An entire forest of blades seemed to sprout before him. Cheers roared out as the men thrust their swords into the air. Even the officers joined in. Jared smiled. *I should have started with that.*

He signaled to Roche. "Light the pyre. Then have the men break camp and get ready to march. I want to reach Keldaren by tomorrow night."

A burning torch stood in the ground nearby. Roche carried it to the funeral pyre. He lit the logs, and the army fell silent, watching as the flames consumed Dalrush's body. *Soon all of*

Keldaren will burn as well, Jared thought. *And my kingdom will rise from the ashes.*

CHAPTER 18

Claire

Sloane was waiting for her in the training chamber again. *No weapons*, Claire saw. *More hand to hand combat. But no padded leathers or helmets.* She stifled a groan. She still sported a black eye from their last bout without padding.

"No training today," Sloane said, her face grim.

"No?"

Sloane shook her head. "Only a test."

"A test of what?" Claire asked.

"Everything."

Claire's heart seemed to shudder in her chest. "You mean the final test?"

Sloane nodded.

"You didn't tell me it would be today. I'm not ready!"

"We never tell a recruit when the final test is. All warriors must deal with the unexpected, Your Majesty. You're ready. Today will prove that to you."

Claire took a deep breath, but it felt like no air filled her lungs. "What do I have to do?" she whispered.

"There's a colony of wolfworms on the seashore, north of Liharna. We keep their numbers down so they don't threaten the city. Normally, dragons burn their nests from the air. For the final test, though, we send a recruit out to destroy them. On foot," Sloane said.

"And how many are in a nest?"

"Males keep a harem of two or three females. So, three or four adults. And then there's the young. Their tunnels are always crawling with nestlings."

"And I'll be alone?" Claire asked.

"Breaus, Shanra, and I will go with you. But we'll only help if you fall. If you do go down, try to hold them back until we can get to you. We'll come as fast as we can. But the wolfworms are vicious. And quick. Most who fall fighting them never get up again," Sloane said.

Claire's stomach churned. She coughed, and swallowed hard.

"You don't have to do this, Your Majesty. Say the word, and we'll end your training."

Claire shook her head. "I won't quit."

"Good. Get your weapons and armor. I'll meet you in the dragon hall." Sloane reached out, and squeezed her shoulder. "You can do this. You will do it."

Claire nodded. Her stomach roiled, threatening to expel her breakfast. She made her way to the armory, where a squire helped Claire don her armor. She sheathed her sword on her back, a dagger on her right hip, and her twinlance on her left hip.

The squire handed her a helmet. Claire tucked it under her arm and went to the stables. As she rode down to the dragon halls, she glanced at the helmet. *At least I have something to throw up in.* She felt a grim smile curl across her face. When she reached the dragon hall, Breaus, Sloane, and Shanra were already waiting.

"I'll find a nest from the air, and Breaus will set you down near it," Sloane said. "The adults will emerge when you get close to the nest. They tend to attack together. The twinlance is the best weapon for them. Once you've killed the adults, you'll have to go down into the tunnels to kill the nestlings. It'll be too tight inside the nest for the lance."

"Is it really necessary to kill the young?"

"If we don't keep their numbers down, the wolfworms will expand their territory. And if they expand much further, they'll be within hunting distance of Liharna. They'll feed on people just as readily as they do on deer and wild boar. Don't worry about the nestlings, Your Majesty. Worry about yourself. You won't be executing them…you'll be fighting them to the death. Wolfworm young are just as dangerous as a full-grown lion."

Claire swallowed. "And what about the adults?"

"I'd rather face ten lions than one adult wolfworm," Sloane said. She stepped up to Shanra, and climbed into the saddle.

Claire put her helmet on and went over to Breaus. He lowered his belly to the ground, and she climbed up. "Don't ask," she said. "The answer is yes. I'm terrified."

His head swiveled around, and his gold-fire gaze met hers. "You can do this, Claire. I've seen you fight. You can kill them."

"You'll help me, if I fall?" she asked.

"Yes. But don't fall."

Claire nodded, and fell silent as Breaus walked out the doors and into the sunlight. She stayed quiet, lost in thought, as they took off.

I haven't paid much thought to what Astra told me. Probably because I've been too busy getting bruised and battered in training every day, she thought. *Is this Emperor of hers really even a god? Should I pray to him?* Questions whirled through her mind as they flew on. When the coast came into view, she made the decision. "Let me survive this, and I'll seek out this hermit of yours," she whispered to the valkyrie's god.

They flew in circles over the shoreline, where holes scarred the ground below. *Nests,* Claire realized. Sloane gestured to Breaus from her dragon, pointing to a nest. He spiraled downwards, and landed on a hill. Claire climbed down from the saddle. She stood in front of Breaus and stared down into the gully where the nest waited.

"You have fire in you, Claire. Use it," Breaus said.

She turned to him. "I will. Thank you, Breaus. For everything."

"I haven't done much," he said.

"You've taught me a great deal on our flights together," Claire said. "And I appreciate it. No matter what happens."

"You'll win. That's what will happen," Breaus thundered. He touched his broad muzzle to the face of her helmet. Even through the steel, she felt the heat radiating from him. Claire smiled at him, then turned and walked down the hill.

As she entered the ravine, her fear began evaporating, like mist burned off by the sun. A hard, focused sensation took hold of her. Claire drew her twinlance and twisted it, feeling the blades click into place.

She came to a stop a short distance from the hole, and stood with her lance at the ready. Claire closed her eyes, focusing her senses. She felt movement in the ground, and heard a scrabbling noise. She opened her eyes.

A long, chisel-shaped head, the blackish-brown color of rotting leaves, emerged from the hole. Beady black eyes bulged from the sides of the head, and below them were two sets of sickle-shaped mandibles, clasped over a beak-like mouth.

The rest of the long body followed. Four sets of segmented legs emerged, and their heavy claws carried the wolfworm toward her. Its body swayed as it moved, its skin glistening like an insect's shell. A rattling noise came from its mouth. The wolfworm whipped the end of its tapered tail from side to side as it stared at her.

There was movement in the ground behind her, and she spun to see another chiseled head erupting through the dirt. The second wolfworm's mandibles snapped as it hauled itself out of the earth, leaving behind a freshly-formed tunnel. The same rattling sound came from its throat. Then the ground shuddered, caving in as a third wolfworm emerged on the other side of her.

The two creatures that had burrowed up were smaller than the first, but each was still twice the size of a horse. The bigger wolfworm stopped rattling, and hissed to the other two. *That must be the male,* Claire thought. The females hissed back to him. He charged at Claire.

Claire slashed with her lance. He reared his body back on itself like a snake, and her blade cut only air. She sensed the females charging behind her, and spun. Claire ran toward them, her lance spinning.

One skittered to the side, dodging her blades. But her steel connected with the side of the other female's head. The blade ripped through the shell-skin and emerged in a spray of white, soupy blood. The wolfworm screamed and snapped at her. Claire spun away and angled her other blade into the beast's side, the lance carving a channel through it. The female dropped, still screaming. Her side flooded milky-white with blood.

Mandibles closed around Claire from behind. They snapped down around her chestplate, screeching against the steel. The beak snapped out at her, tearing into her skin. Claire struck backwards with her armored elbow, slamming it into the bulging orb of the beast's eye. Now it was the male's turn to scream.

The mandibles released her, and Claire spun to face the male. He was far too close for her blades. She brought the grip of the lance smashing up, tearing through the mandibles. Hot blood pulsed from the fresh holes in his jaws. The male screamed again and reared back on his legs. But that exposed his belly, and Claire slashed through it. The wolfworm scrabbled away, blood streaming from the raw wounds.

Her own wound sent pain stabbing through her as Claire turned to face the second female. She circled Claire warily, then charged. Claire sidestepped and sliced her blade through one of the beast's back legs. The wolfworm screamed, scuttling aside.

The male charged again, and Claire took a leg from him also. Both wolfworms circled her, still moving well enough for their lost limbs. *They have seven more left, after all*, she thought. The female charged. Claire slashed out, her blade tearing a hole in the monster's face. She screamed and spit blood at Claire.

Her mate lunged forward. Claire dodged his snapping beak and rolled aside, cutting through another leg as he passed her. The wolfworm stumbled to his belly.

The female rushed at her. Claire hurled the lance into her face. The wolfworm hissed and shook her head, as if trying to shake the blade loose. She fell writhing to the ground. Claire drew her sword, stepping carefully around the female's flailing limbs, and slit the beast's throat.

A tail slammed into Claire, knocking her down. A claw stomped onto her chest, pinning her to the ground. The male reared up above Claire. His mandibles were gone, but his beak still snapped. He pulled his head back to strike.

With a flash of steel, Claire thrust her blade deep into his jaw. He screamed and scrabbled away, her sword still buried in him. He tossed his head from side to side, trying to shake the sword loose. The wolfworm turned, lashing out again with his tail. Claire dropped, rolling under it.

She leapt up onto the wolfworm's back. The shell-skin was smooth and slippery beneath her feet as she ran toward his head, drawing her dagger. The monster reared, and Claire stumbled.

She landed flat on the wolfworm's back, clinging to his body with her legs, until her hand reached the ridge in the shell at the back of his neck. Pulling herself forward, she plunged the dagger into his eye.

The wolfworm howled, shaking and shuddering. Claire stabbed into the center of his head. She held on until the death throes subsided. Then she withdrew the dagger, and freed her sword from his jaw.

Claire turned to the remaining female. The wolfworm lay in the dirt, blood still oozing from the ruin of her side. The creature tried to scrabble away, but her wound kept her from going far. She reared up, her beak and mandibles snapping.

As the wolfworm struck at her, Claire slammed her sword into its beak. A mandible caught Claire's shoulder, and she felt the warm flow of blood down her arm. Ignoring the pain, Claire thrust her sword into the beast's throat, burying it to the hilt. The female reared back, the sword protruding from her gaping beak.

The wolfworm coughed, as if trying to vomit the sword out of her mouth. She fell to the ground, still jerking. Claire drew her dagger, and plunged it between the creature's eyes. The body shuddered, and then fell still.

Claire freed both of her blades, and held her sword up to the sky. Breaus and Shanra flew low, and Breaus blew a triumphant ball of fire into the air. Sloane leaned down and pointed to the entrance of the tunnel. *The nestlings,* Claire remembered.

The tunnel was even wider than the holes that the wolfworms had burrowed out. Claire walked gingerly down into it, her sword ready. The earth seemed to swallow her as she made her way down.

She never saw the first nestling. It dropped onto her from a hole in the ceiling, knocking her to the ground. Its mandibles scraped along the sides of her helmet as it tried to bite her head off. Its claws slashed at her, some screeching across steel, while others struck where she was unarmored. The hardened leather under her uniform offered little resistance to the claws slicing into her skin.

Claire thrust her sword up into the nestling's face. She threw it off her and spun around. She slashed down, separating its head from its body. The nestling spasmed, then fell still.

The young wolfworm looked like its parents, but was only the size of a large dog. Claire turned back to continue further in. A rattling noise started, rising up from the depths of the tunnel. At first it was only one rattle, and then a second. A third joined in, and then a dozen rattles and hisses filled the tunnel. Claire swallowed hard, and held her sword ready as she started down.

Twilight had fallen by the time she limped back up to the surface, her uniform slashed and stained with blood. Breaus and Shanra circled overhead, and when she emerged, Breaus swooped down and landed. "I knew you could do it," he rumbled, flashing his teeth in a smile.

"I wasn't so sure. But I'm glad I was wrong. Take me back, Breaus. I never want to see another wolfworm again."

"I promise, no more wolfworms. You've earned your knighthood," he said.

"So no more tests?" Claire asked warily as she hauled herself into the saddle.

"The Order has no more tests for you. The world, though...that will be your next test." Breaus took off, and they flew back to Mount Draconis, with Shanra and Sloane following.

After the dragons landed, Sloane came up to her. "You did well, Your Majesty. Very well indeed. I imagine you'll want to get cleaned up, and I'll send a surgeon to tend your wounds. Get some rest. I'll be waking you early. You're to be knighted at dawn."

CHAPTER 19

Claire

It seemed she had been asleep only a moment when there was a pounding at her door. "Enter," she groaned. Sloane stepped in, carrying a uniform. It was black, instead of the usual green. Sloane laid it on the bed. Sloane also wore a black uniform.

"What's that?" Claire asked.

"A dress uniform, for the knighting."

"Why does this have to be at dawn? I could use some sleep," Claire said.

"You'll see why, Your Majesty. Get ready, and then we'll go to the armory."

Sloane stepped out while Claire washed and put on the uniform. When she emerged from her room, Sloane and a Crown Guard were waiting. They went to the armory, where a set of armor hung on a stand in the center of the room.

This wasn't the normal black steel of Dragon Knight armor—the greaves, gauntlets, chestplate, and helmet were all covered with gold leaf. The armor sparkled in the light of the lamps as Sloane helped her buckle it on. Claire slipped her sword into its scabbard, and fastened on her dagger as well.

"Today you'll choose a dragon," Sloane said. "Breaus has asked for you, and that's quite an honor. He's one of the most acclaimed dragons in the history of the Order."

"I'd be honored to choose Breaus."

Sloane put on her own set of golden armor, picked up a canvas bag, and led them to a winding stone staircase.

"Where are we going?" Claire asked.

"To the peak." They began climbing, spiraling higher and higher up the stairs. Finally, they emerged into a huge chamber. The walls were hewn from the stone of the mountain, but the floor was polished white marble. The room was a stone half-circle on one side, with a soaring wall of glass forming the other end of the chamber. In the center of the glass wall was the blazon of the Dragon Order—formed in crystal and bordered with lead. Suspended in the window, the crystal dragon looked almost as if it were flying through the sky, carrying a crystal shield emblazoned with a sword and harp.

The high stone walls at the back of the chamber were filled with hundreds of carved alcoves. Skeletons wearing golden armor filled most of the lower niches.

Fulton's voice came from behind her. "They're knights who died in battle." Claire turned to see the Prefect standing in the center of the room, resplendent in his gold armor and black uniform. "This is the Glass Hall, where we bring the bones of our fallen. And where we bring new knights to swear their oath. To remind them of the sacrifice they may have to make. And to promise them a place here should they fall in battle."

The first golden rays of sunlight crept up through the bottom of the glass wall, making the marble floor glow a radiant white. Fulton drew his sword. "It's time for your knighting."

Claire walked to him. The Prefect stood within a thin circle of silver embedded into the floor. Within the circle was the Dragon Order's blazon, also inscribed in silver. "Kneel, Your Majesty," Fulton said.

Claire knelt on the silver dragon. Behind Fulton, the sunlight struck the crystal set into the glass wall. Brilliant colors exploded from it, casting the rainbow shadow of the blazon over Claire. The silver she knelt on reflected the beams of color, setting the white marble of the floor aglow with rainbow light.

"Claire Erinn," Fulton said, "you have been trained and tried, and found worthy of the Dragon Order. Would you swear our oath?"

"I would. I swear my blood and my life to defend the kingdom, to protect the innocent, and to serve justice," Claire said.

Fulton's sword gently touched one of her shoulders, then the other. Claire gritted her teeth when the sword grazed the wolfworm's bite marks.

"I dub you Dame Claire Erinn, knight of the Dragon Order," Fulton said. He sheathed his sword, and held out his hand. "Rise, Dame Claire."

Claire took his hand, and stood. "Breaus is waiting outside," Sloane said. She led Claire to a door set into the corner of the glass wall. They walked out into a snow-covered meadow dotted with red bushes.

Claire turned, and saw that half the mountaintop was missing. The remaining half of the mountain's cone formed the Glass Hall. A stony peak rose above the wall of glass, and the dark shape of a dragon sat atop it. The other half of the mountaintop seemed to have fallen away, leaving the meadow she stood in.

Far below them, morning mist steamed off the moors surrounding the mountain, and the rising sun glittered over streams and lakes as it spread its rays across the country. Sloane drew her sword, and flashed it up toward the peak. The dragon stretched its wings out, leapt into the air, and floated down, landing in front of them.

It was Breaus. "I was told you would have me for a rider," Claire said.

Breaus nodded. "It would be an honor, Claire."

"The honor is mine," she said.

Sloane opened the bag she held, and drew out a bottle of red glass, along with a large steel goblet. "These are bloodberries," Sloane said, gesturing to the nearest bush.

The bush was covered with hundreds of small red berries. Claire looked closer. The berries themselves weren't red, but glowed with red light. *Not glowing*, she thought, *burning*. An intense red blazed deep within each berry. "How are they doing that?"

"There's a legend that two giant dragons once fought each other above this mountain," Sloane said. "One was killed, and fell from the sky. His body knocked half the mountaintop away when it fell, and formed this meadow. His blood soaked into the dirt, and later, these bushes grew. This is the only place in all of Eris that they're found. And the glowing...that makes the legend seem to have some truth to it. You've never seen a dragon bleed, have you?"

Claire shook her head.

Sloane took the bottle, uncorked it, and upturned it over the goblet. The crimson liquid that poured out glimmered, as if burning sparks were suspended in it. "Dragon blood glows like this. This is bloodberry wine. It's for the final ceremony to make you a true Dragon Knight. And to seal you to your dragon." She set the empty bottle down. "Breaus will give some of his blood, and you'll give some of yours. Human and dragon blood mixed together will light the fire."

"Light the fire?" Claire asked.

"The final step in becoming a knight. After we combine the blood, you'll both drink the wine. It will make you stronger and swifter. It will give you dragon's blood," Sloane said.

Claire drew back. "This is sorcery."

"No, it's alchemy. Every Dragon Knight has done this. There's power in a dragon's blood, Your Majesty. And mixing it with human blood and the wine enhances that power. There's no witchcraft in this. People drink wine to fortify themselves. This is like that. Only more powerful," Sloane said.

Claire took a deep breath. "What do I have to do?"

Breaus raised his arm over the goblet, and drew a claw across his flesh. A thin red line appeared against his emerald scales. He turned his arm, and scarlet blood ran out. Golden specks burned within the crimson liquid. He let the glistening blood run into the goblet. "That," he said.

Claire rolled up one of her sleeves, drew her dagger, and held her arm over the goblet. She put the cold steel to her skin, and cut. A dull redness trickled down her arm. As the first drop of her blood splashed into the goblet, red flames erupted across the surface of the wine. Claire snatched her arm back as the flames leapt higher. The fire burned out, but the elixir in the goblet still shone with the fire's scarlet light.

Breaus picked the goblet up, his talons delicately closing around the stem. His huge claws dwarfed even the large cup. He lifted it to his mouth and took a sip. Then he handed it to Claire.

She took the goblet. The wine steamed, hot against her lips. She gulped down a mouthful of spicy sweetness.

When the wine hit her stomach, it felt like a ball of fire exploding within her. Heat scorched through her, and her entire body felt as if it were melting. Claire cried out in pain and doubled over.

Sloane caught her, and lowered her gently to the ground. "Breathe, Your Majesty. It will be over in a second or two."

Claire took a deep breath, and the pain was gone. She opened her eyes. Everything looked clearer and sharper than it had before. She took another breath. Even the air seemed richer, and thicker.

"Better?" Sloane asked with a smile, helping her sit up.

"Much," Claire said. "Better than I ever felt before. What did that do to me?"

"It gave you dragon blood. Look," Sloane said, reaching out and squeezing the skin around the cut on Claire's arm. Blood oozed out. This time, though, the blood was as vividly crimson as Breaus'. Claire's breath caught in her throat. Glowing specks were suspended amidst the scarlet.

"And that's not all it gave you." Sloane helped Claire up, and handed her the empty goblet. "I want you to squeeze this as hard as you can. Hard enough to dent it."

"This is steel," Claire objected. "I can't do that."

"Try."

Claire took the goblet and squeezed. The steel felt as though it was giving way beneath her fingers. She gasped and dropped the cup. There were dents where her fingers had been. *That's impossible*, she thought.

Sloane laughed. "You look like you don't believe it."

"I don't."

"Then maybe you'll believe this," Sloane said. She walked a few paces, and turned to face Claire. Sloane drew her dagger from its sheath, and aimed it at her. "Catch," she said.

"Sloane, what do you think…" before Claire could finish, Sloane hurled the dagger. Time seemed to slow as the blade spun lazily toward her. Before she could even think, she reached out and plucked it from the air by its hilt.

Claire stared wide-eyed at the dagger in her grasp. Sloane laughed again. "It takes some time to get used to doing the impossible," she said.

"This will take a long time to get used to," Claire said. She cocked the dagger, and threw it back toward Sloane.

Sloane caught it, smiling. "You're a true knight now. I'm proud of you, Your Majesty. I knew you had it in you."

Claire smiled back. "Thank you, Sloane. Now that I'm a knight, I think I have to go be a queen again. At least for a while. I haven't been to a session of the Senate in days." Claire went to Breaus, and touched his muzzle. "Thank you for choosing me," she said. "I'll see you later."

Sloane walked back to the Glass Hall with her, the guard trailing behind. "Time to reacquaint myself with sparring with tongues, rather than swords," Claire said.

"Yes. But keep your blade sharp, Your Majesty. Come spring, it won't be words we'll be fighting with," Sloane said.

CHAPTER 20

Jared

Moonlight lit the way as Jared and the officers rode at the head of the army. A contingent of Stenari archers marched after the horses, with long columns of foot soldiers behind them. Jared signaled a halt when they reached a valley. Roche came up alongside him while they waited for a scout to ride ahead.

The wind changed direction, and blew the scent of the Stenari toward them. Jared wrinkled his nose. "If the wind doesn't shift, we won't have to worry about the Keldari seeing us," he told Roche. "They'll smell us coming. These primitives make useful conscripts, but I'd replace them with men in a heartbeat."

"Men can't shoot like the Stenari can, Your Highness."

"If their shooting is as lethal as their stench, they could destroy the Keldari army all by themselves," Jared spat.

The scout came riding back. "The border is just beyond the hill. There's a Keldari watchtower down there," he reported.

"Good," Jared said. "We'll crest the hill and sneak down on them. Have one of the Stenari come with us, General. No doubt the tower will try to send a pigeon as soon as they spot us. We'll see just how good these primitives are."

The scout went off to bring an archer. Roche gave the officers their orders, and they marched the soldiers into position. Jared dismounted, and he and Roche walked to the top of the hill.

The watchtower stood below them. A green flag, emblazoned with Keldaren's golden harp and silver sword, fluttered from its parapets.

"General, the archer you wanted," the scout announced.

Jared turned. The rat stood about four feet tall on its hind legs, average height for a Stenari. Its brown fur was matted and mangy, and its thick tail hung limply like a huge, dead worm. Its eyes bulged like black marbles from its dirty face. A quiver of arrows was slung across its back, and it held an ironwood bow in its pale paws.

"Can it understand me?" Jared asked Roche.

The Stenari chittered at him, working its large teeth in its mouth.

"They can't speak Erisian, but they understand it well enough," Roche said.

"The Keldari down there will be sending out a pigeon when they realize we're attacking," Jared told the archer. "Make sure that pigeon falls. Understand?"

The Stenari hissed, twitching its whiskers.

"Don't fail me," Jared warned. He stepped back from the rat. A single Stenari didn't reek nearly as much as a whole column of them, but this one still smelled badly enough. Jared looked back at the watchtower. "Order the advance."

Roche gave a signal, and the soldiers began moving around them, creeping over the crest of the hill. They kept silent as they skulked toward the tower. They were more than halfway there when a horn sounded.

The Stenari slid an arrow onto its bow. The alarm horn kept sounding, its shrill notes echoing through the night. Light bloomed in the arrow-slit windows of the watchtower. A figure in crimson and black appeared on the tower roof, ducking behind the battlements. A moment later, a pigeon fluttered up and wheeled eastward.

The Stenari's bow twanged, and an arrow streaked out, downing the pigeon. The soldier moved on the roof of the tower, and the bow spoke again, sending an arrow flying into him. The soldier fell, and the Stenari turned to Jared, snarling triumphantly.

But there was still movement atop the tower. "He's getting up!" Jared shouted.

The Keldari soldier stood again, cradling a pigeon in his hands. He tossed it off the far side of the tower. The Stenari turned, stringing another arrow. He shot at the pigeon, but the tower stood between them and the bird. The Stenari shot a second time, and missed again. Snarling, the archer sent another arrow flying into the Keldari. The soldier fell once more, and this time, he stayed down.

The pigeon climbed high enough to clear the tower. The Stenari shot again, but the bird was beyond his range. Jared watched the pigeon fly eastward, toward Tara. "Give me your bow," he ordered. The rat handed it over, chittering and squeaking.

Jared felt the heft of the ironwood. He bent the bow, testing its strength. Then he smashed it into the Stenari's face. He kicked the rat in its stomach, cutting short its squeals. The Stenari doubled over. Jared beat it with the bow until it dropped to the ground. Then he gave it one last kick. "I'll be generous with you, Stenari, and let you live. You'll serve as an example of the price of failure," Jared snarled.

The soldiers below moved the battering ram into place, and its booms against the tower door rang out through the night. "The pigeon will warn them that we're coming," Roche said.

"It doesn't matter," Jared replied. "Even if they started marching now, troops from Tara would never reach Dalrann in time. By the time they arrive, the city will already be ours."

Below them, the door gave way, and soldiers stormed into the tower. They emerged on the roof a few moments later, waving bloodied swords. Their triumphant shouts filled the air. "Remember that sound, General," Jared said. "You'll be hearing it again at Dalrann."

Claire

Claire was eating breakfast with Isabelle when the servant found her. "Your Majesty. Chancellor," he said, bowing. "Forgive me for interrupting you, but the prefect said she needed to see you urgently."

"Both of us?" Claire asked.

"Yes, Your Majesty."

He led them to the prefect's office. Fulton and Sloane were there, looking at a map spread across the desk.

Fulton stood as they entered. "Forgive me for the abrupt summons. We've received a pigeon from Tara. A Drakari army has crossed the border near Dalrann."

A sick feeling shot through Claire's stomach. "How did they get past the extra troops at the border?"

"The pigeon carried a letter from a captain at the Citadel in Tara. He told us they received a message from the border warning of an invasion, and that General Aricet immediately rode west with three centuries of cavalry troopers. But he also told us why the General left in such a hurry. Aricet ignored your order, Your Majesty. He never sent reinforcements to the border," Fulton said.

That arrogant fool. "He's gone too far this time. I'll have his command for this," Claire said.

"If he was Minerva's general, she would have his head for this," Sloane said.

"Don't tempt me, Sloane. I'm not Minerva."

"Aricet should count himself blessed that you aren't," Sloane said.

"Aricet should count himself a total lackwit if he believes that three hundred cavalry troopers can hold Dalrann against a Drakari army. I assume he sent legions from Tara also, for all the good that will do," Claire said.

Fulton nodded. "But it will take days for them to arrive. Even Aricet and his cavalry likely won't reach Dalrann before the Drakari."

"Then Dalrann is lost," Claire said.

"Perhaps not. I told you that the knight I sent to Drohea Castle found your brother gone, and the garrison dead. But I didn't tell you that Sir Deran wasn't the first to arrive at the castle."

"Who was?" Claire asked.

"He found the Sixth Legion quartered there. They had been on a patrol in the area, readying to return to Tara for the winter, when they came past the castle and found the garrison dead. Their commander wanted to stay at Drohea as long as he could, to keep more troops near the border. The Sixth Legion may still be there, Your Majesty. And Dalrann is only a day's march from Drohea."

"But Dalrann is less than a day's march from the border. The Drakari will be there before the Sixth Legion can arrive," Claire said.

"Unless we slow them down. Take all of the knights and dragons from Mt. Draconis, Your Majesty. Fly out to meet the Drakari and stop them," Fulton said.

"Even the entire Dragon Order couldn't destroy a whole army," Claire protested.

Sloane leaned forward. "The Spearcrags," she said, tapping the two peaks on the map. "The pass between them is narrow. As few as twenty dragons could hold it. You'll have fifty. Hold them there until the Sixth Legion arrives. Then destroy them."

"Will a single legion be enough to defeat their army?"

"Along with fifty dragons? Absolutely. Especially after you've ground down their numbers before the legion arrives," Fulton said.

"If it takes a day for the legion to get there, we won't have fifty dragons left by the time they arrive," Claire said.

Sloane nodded gravely. "Some will fall, to be sure. But more than enough will be left to destroy the Drakari."

"And if the Drakari choose not to go through the Spearcrags?"

"If they try to go around the mountains, that would add another day to their march," Fulton said. "The road runs right through the pass. They'll come that way."

"You'll be leading us, then, Fulton?" Claire asked.

"No. I believe you should take the command, Your Majesty. I'll go to Drohea and summon the Sixth Legion."

"Very well. Have the knights assemble in the dragon hall," Claire ordered. "I'll meet them there."

"Yes, Your Majesty," Fulton said.

Wait…what did I just say? Claire thought.

"Not what the old Claire would have said, is it?" Sloane asked, smiling.

"No. I would have said that I wasn't ready yet to command such a mission."

"And how do you feel, Your Majesty?" Fulton asked.

"I feel ready. I feel…eager," Claire said.

"It's the dragon's blood," Sloane said. "You have fire in your veins now. It will burn away the doubts. And burn away your enemies."

CHAPTER 21

Claire

Claire stood armored and armed in the dragon hall, with Sloane and Fulton beside her. Breaus waited at the head of fifty dragons, their knights standing beside them. Claire gestured to Breaus, and he lay down on his belly. She climbed onto the saddle, and stood up in it.

Breaus rose to his feet, lifting her up so everyone could see her. "A Drakari Army marches on Dalrann," she shouted, her voice echoing through the hall. "There's a hungry wolf on our doorstep. I say we feed it." Claire drew her sword. "With fire and steel."

The knights shouted in approval, raising their swords. The dragons roared, sending puffs of flame into the air. Claire gazed down at them, watching the fire reflecting off the bare blades.

The Spearcrags' shadows stretched long and dark in the late afternoon sun by the time they first glimpsed the Drakari. From the mountain ledge, Claire caught sight of a distant gray river winding its way across the snow-covered plains. She put a spyglass to her eye. The river was formed of columns of Drakari soldiers. Steel plate flashed as they marched.

As the Drakari drew close to the pass, a wave seemed to ripple through their ranks. Shouts rose up, and spear tips moved to point at the mountains. Sloane stood next to Claire, their dragons sitting on a ledge nearby. "They've seen us," Claire said, as the Drakari ranks moved into defensive formations.

"Let's light the way for them," Sloane said. She walked to her dragon, and signaled to the other dragons and knights spread out across the mountains.

Claire swung up into her saddle. "Time to feed the wolf," she told Breaus.

He leapt into the air, circling while four other dragons joined him. They flew toward the Drakari. When they passed over the gray-clad columns, the dragons tucked in their wings and dove. The Drakari archers raised their bows, and a black fog of arrows boiled up at them.

Breaus loosed a river of fire. It scorched through most of the arrows, burning them to cinders. But a few made it past the flames, and clanged like hail off Claire's armor. The arrows pelted Breaus also. He roared in fury as an arrowhead lodged itself in a chink between his scales.

Breaus fired an inferno down into the archers below. The other dragons joined him, pouring down fire. The streams joined together into a flood of flames engulfing the Drakari. Shrill screams rose from the burning soldiers.

Spears arced up from the Drakari ranks. One lance caught a dragon in the throat. He fell, trailing fire from his wound. The dragon crashed into the ground, crushing a dozen Drakari beneath

him. Their companions attacked him with spear and sword. The
dragon's rider leapt into the fight. But the knight couldn't hold
back all the Drakari. Gray-clad soldiers swarmed the dying
dragon. He tore through many of them, but the Drakari kept
coming, hacking at him with their blades. With a terrible howl, the
dragon collapsed beneath them.

Breaus and Shanra turned back, weaving a web of fire
around the knight and the fallen dragon. Their flames burned back
the Drakari, and cleared a space for Shanra to land and pick up the
downed knight. As Breaus flew around for another pass, the next
wave of dragons began their dive. Again and again the dragons
attacked, grinding down the Drakari columns. *We'll mill them like
corn,* Claire thought, *and grind them into dust.*

It was a long milling. The dragons attacked in waves, their
flames and claws killing hundreds. But as they decimated the
Drakari ranks, more dragons also fell. It was after nightfall by the
time Fulton finally joined them. The battlefield was lit by fire and
moonlight as the dragons fought, and burned, and fell throughout
the night.

At dawn, the first rays of sunlight flooded across the field.
But the ground itself was still black with scorched corpses.
Thousands of Drakari had fallen. But thousands more still stood
their ground.

The dragons came around for another pass. There was a
distant flash to the south, and then another. Claire nudged Breaus,

and pointed. He nodded, changing course. The distant flashes became a line of Keldari soldiers, their spears glinting in the sunlight as they marched closer. *The Sixth Legion.* As they swooped low over the soldiers, Claire drew her sword, and roared triumphantly. Breaus echoed her roar, and flew back to the battle.

They continued thinning the Drakari ranks with flame and claw. About thirty dragons still flew. Some lay dead on the fields below, and some injured dragons had been forced to quit the battle. *We've fed them fire*, she thought, as the Sixth Legion reached the mountain pass. *Time to serve the steel.*

She nudged Breaus and gestured to the pass, where the legion was moving into a spearhead formation. Breaus landed between the mountains. Claire leapt down, drawing her twinlance. She felt the familiar *thunk* of the blades expanding and clicking into place. She waved her lance, signaling the other dragons. Breaus took off and flew ahead, spewing a waterfall of flames down on the Drakari.

The other dragons answered her signal, landing to let their knights leap down to join her. Claire gave a roar, and charged the Drakari lines. The knights stampeded after her.

She charged toward a gray wall of shields, ignoring the spear tips bristling from it. Claire angled her lance, stabbing it into the chest of the closest soldier. She used the lance like a vaulting pole, letting her momentum carry her up and over the spears. Claire landed in the midst of the Drakari ranks. She jerked her lance free, and spun a circle of steel and blood around her. The enemy lines roiled as soldiers shrank from the swirling blades.

The other knights smashed into the Drakari lines behind her. Claire slashed through enemy after enemy, the dragon's blood singing hot in her veins. She let the fire roar through her body and blaze out through her limbs, moving her in a deadly, blurring dance.

She sensed the charge before she heard it. Rushing feet thundered like a raging river behind them, and a tide of soldiers crashed into the Drakari ranks. There was a flash of crimson and black next to her, and Claire found herself fighting alongside a Keldari soldier. The Drakari held for a moment. Then they broke, their lines crumbling as the soldiers fled.

The dragons gave chase, raining down rivers of fire. Claire left the rest of the fighting to them, and joined the other knights in tending to the wounded.

Fulton found her kneeling by the side of the Sixth Legion's surgeon, leaning over a knight. Claire held the knight's head in her lap as the surgeon sewed up his wound, trying to staunch the bleeding. The knight gave a soft gasp, and the rise and fall of his chest stopped. The surgeon felt the vein at the knight's neck. Then he threw his needle down with a curse, and moved on to the next patient.

"Your Majesty," Fulton said quietly, "General Aricet has arrived with the cavalry."

Claire stood. She started toward a waterskin, to wash the blood from her hands, but stopped. "No," she said. "Aricet must see this. This blood is on *his* head." Claire stormed off, the fire within her burning as hot and red as the blood dripping from her hands.

Aricet stood at the rear of the Keldari lines, amidst a cluster of officers, leaning over a camp table and a map. The officers parted at the sight of her.

"Your Majesty," Aricet said. "What are you doing here?"

"I'm doing your job," she snapped. "Stopping an invasion. Where are the legions I ordered sent to the border?"

"In Tara. I decided that the safety of the capital was the priority."

"That decision defied my orders," Claire said through gritted teeth.

Aricet sighed. "It wasn't your place to interfere in military affairs."

"Not my place? The sovereign is the supreme commander of the military!"

"The sovereign is a sixteen year old girl. Leave the military matters to me, Claire."

Claire lifted her hands, showing the dried blood staining them. "A sea of Keldari blood was spilled here today. All because you disobeyed my orders."

"Take my advice, and stay out of military affairs. Or there will be a great deal more blood on your hands." Aricet smirked, and looked back down at his map.

Claire kicked the table aside and drew her sword. "You're relieved of command, General. And you're under arrest for insubordination. Walk to the dragons. I'm taking you back to Tara for a court-martial."

Aricet laughed. "Put that away, Claire, before you hurt yourself. I have no time for games."

Claire moved the tip of the blade to his neck. "Walk to the dragons, or be carried on a stretcher. The choice is yours."

Aricet's eyes narrowed. "I'll teach you some respect, you arrogant little scitan. We'll see if you know how to use your steel. Boy! Bring me my shield," he called to his page.

'Traitor!" someone shouted. "Not only do you defy the queen, but you'd actually fight her? This is treason!"

An officer stepped forward. Sandy-brown hair topped his tall frame. He had a handsome face, with a small scar on his chin. There was a gleam of anger in his ocean-blue eyes.

"Major Dalraiden," Aricet said. "I wouldn't have expected you to be a lapdog for our little queen."

"The only dog here is you. A treasonous dog who would turn his back on his oath. If you want to fight someone, fight me," the major said, drawing his sword.

"Thank you for your loyalty, Major," Claire said. "But this is my fight."

"As Your Majesty commands." The major sheathed his blade, glaring at Aricet.

The officers and soldiers cleared a space for them while the page handed Aricet his shield. He drew his sword. "Did the Dragon Order give you a uniform, Claire? You're no knight. You're just a little girl playing at being queen," Aricet said.

Claire raised her sword. "This is your last chance, General. Put down your blade and walk to the dragons. Don't make me hurt you."

Aricet snorted. "I'd like to see you try." He charged, slashing at her. Claire ducked under the blade, deftly slicing her sword into the back of his knee. Aricet fell with a cry of pain.

He rose from the dirt, his face a burning red. "I'll kill you, you little wench," he gasped. He came at her more warily this time, limping on his injured knee. His sword flashed up. Claire met it with her own steel, knocking his blade away. Aricet swung his shield at her face.

Claire jerked her head aside. As his arm passed by, she reached out and grabbed it, twisting hard. Aricet winced and dropped his shield.

Claire kicked at his injured leg. Aricet screamed and dropped to his good knee.

"Surrender, General. Don't force me to kill you."

"How?" Aricet gasped. "How are you beating me like this?"

"I'm a Dragon Knight," Claire said.

Aricet was still for a heartbeat. Then his fist shot out in a blur, thrusting his sword at her.

Claire's blade flashed. Aricet's sword fell to the ground, followed by his thumb. He screamed, clasping his right hand to his chest.

Claire kicked his sword away. "You're finished, General. Now, walk to the dragons, or I'll take your other thumb."

"Kill the traitor!" a captain shouted.

"Enough Keldari have already died today," Claire said. "He'll be court-martialed. And then exiled."

Anger flashed on Aricet's face. "You'd banish me like a dog?"

"The penalty for treason is death, General. Exile is a mercy. A mercy you don't deserve," Claire said.

Aricet bit his lip. "Thank you for your *mercy*," he growled.

Claire pointed with her blade. "The dragons are that way. Move."

Aricet began limping off. Claire glanced over the troops, her gaze falling on Major Dalraiden. He smiled at her, his eyes gleaming more gently now. Claire turned to follow Aricet, but found herself looking back at those blue eyes.

Suddenly, Dalraiden's eyes shifted from hers, his smile vanishing. "Look out!"

Claire's eyes darted to Aricet. He shook his left arm, and a stiletto dropped from his sleeve into his hand. He spun, the blade glittering in his fist. Claire slammed her sword up into his throat.

Aricet coughed and choked, blood gurgling from his mouth. He dropped the knife and sank to his knees. Claire pulled her blade free, and Aricet slumped over. His coughing turned to a strangled wheezing, and then he fell silent. *One more death on this bloody day*, Claire thought.

CHAPTER 22

Claire

Claire sensed someone approaching from behind her. She spun, her sword at the ready. Major Dalraiden raised his hands. "Are you all right, Your Majesty?"

Claire lowered her sword. "Yes. Thank you."

He bowed. "I'm Adrian Dalraiden."

"I've heard of you, Major. You were quite the hero in the last war."

"I was no hero, Your Majesty."

"That's not what I've heard."

"I did my duty, as any soldier would. Nothing more."

"I was told that your men were wavering after your captain fell. If you hadn't picked up the standard and led the charge, the Keldari lines would have broken. Drakaren might have conquered all of Dalrann province if it weren't for you."

"As I said, Your Majesty, I was simply doing my duty."

"That was far beyond a sergeant's duty. I'm not surprised Father promoted you," Claire said.

"I was. To go from sergeant to captain is unheard of."

"You've been promoted since then. That shows the first promotion was deserved."

"I hope it was," Adrian said.

"I certainly think so. Keeping the Sixth Legion at Drohea shows that you have more sense than Aricet did. We couldn't hold the Drakari here forever. If it weren't for you and your men, they might have broken out and taken Dalrann," Claire said.

Adrian shifted his feet, his expression uneasy. "I questioned General Aricet about his orders for us to winter in the capital. But he insisted we report back on schedule. I had been planning to march the legion to Tara next week."

"Then it was our good fortune that they attacked when they did. You've saved Dalrann, Major. Again. Tell me, why did you question Aricet's orders?"

"After the attack on the palace, it was obvious the Drakari might try to invade. I wrote to the general several times, urging him to send more legions to reinforce the border. He refused. I asked him to at least let my legion stay near the border. But he refused that as well," Adrian said.

"And you respected his orders."

Adrian shrugged. "What else could I do? A good officer questions his commander when he disagrees, but he still obeys orders."

"Tell me, Major, was there anything else you disagreed with Aricet about?"

"Yes. Many things."

"Let's take a walk. I'd be interested in hearing your ideas," Claire said.

"Of course, Your Majesty. But first, might I ask you a favor?"

"And what would that be?"

"I hope it isn't too presumptuous, but please, call me Adrian. When someone calls me Major, I still look around for the officer I forgot to salute."

Claire laughed. "Only if you call me Claire."

His blue eyes widened. "I couldn't do that, Your Majesty."

She smiled. "You can address me as 'Your Majesty' in front of other people. But call me Claire when we're alone. That's an order. You told me a good officer obeys orders."

He smiled back, almost shyly. "You have me there, Your..." he shook his head. "Claire."

"Adrian it is, then," she said.

An hour later, they walked back to where the legion was setting up camp. The soldiers had pitched the headquarters tent, and the officers were gathered under the canopy. Claire sat in the commander's chair, while Adrian joined the other officers.

"The army has need of a new Commandant," Claire announced. "And I've chosen a new General. I've chosen someone with courage and initiative. I've chosen Major Adrian Dalraiden."

Murmurs spread through the officers. Adrian cleared his throat. "I'm honored, Your Majesty. But I'm too young for this position."

"I certainly can't hold your youth against you, Major," Claire said, smiling. "You're older than your queen, after all."

Adrian frowned. "Be that as it may, Your Majesty, I lack the experience a general needs."

A captain stepped forward. "Your Majesty, Major Dalraiden should be commended for his honesty. There are men in the army who have been officers longer than he's even been alive. I urge you, choose someone with greater experience."

"Experience, Captain, is no guarantee of a good commander. General Aricet spent decades as an officer," Claire said.

"Aricet lacked honor, Your Majesty. Choose someone more loyal than he was. But choose someone with more experience than Dalraiden."

"Aricet was also a fool, Captain. His experience didn't change that. I have chosen a loyal officer. The only officer who had the courage to stand up to Aricet when he turned against me. The only officer who had sense enough to keep his troops near the border to guard against the Drakari. Major Dalraiden."

"Your Majesty," Adrian said, "thank you for the compliment. But please, choose someone else."

"Are you refusing the promotion?" Claire asked.

"I wouldn't refuse my queen. I'm simply saying that I don't want it. I'm not ready," he said.

"I understand. I didn't feel ready for this," she said, reaching up to touch her crown. "And I certainly didn't want it. But it was thrust upon me. Thank you for your counsel. The promotion is yours, though, whether you want it or not. That is the will of your queen."

Adrian bowed. "Then what can I do but obey?"

Claire smiled. "Your first task, General Dalraiden, will be to re-deploy the army to the Drakari border, and to prepare for the invasion."

"Invasion? Do you think they'll invade again, after their defeat today?"

"No, I don't. But we'll be invading Drakaren come the spring," Claire said.

"We will?" Adrian asked.

"This isn't the first time Minerva's attacked us. The most we've ever done in return is to pillage a few Drakari cities. This time, we're going to Graydare to remove Minerva from her throne. That will send a message about the cost of attacking Keldaren," Claire said.

"Your Majesty, there's a good reason we've never taken their capital. We defeated Drakaren's eastern army today, but they still have two more. Their southern army is small, to be sure. But their western army alone is larger than ours. We don't have nearly enough troops to defeat them," Adrian said.

"Minerva is a dagger at our throat. As long as she sits on the raven throne, Keldaren will never be safe. No country in all of Eris will be safe until she's removed. I'll go to Hynbarra and Kirosia, and win their support for this war. If they join us, we'll have more than enough soldiers to defeat Drakaren. Make the preparations, General. I'll bring back the troops you need." Claire stood.

Adrian nodded. "I'll escort you to your dragon." They walked back together to where Breaus waited. "This has been a most eventful day," Adrian said, as Claire retrieved her helmet from Breaus' saddle.

"It's not every day you become a general," she replied.

"It's not every day you meet a queen, either. Especially not one so beautiful…" he stopped, his cheeks turning crimson, and he looked away.

He's actually blushing, she thought. *Like a little boy caught with his hand in the cake.*

"Forgive me, Your Majesty…I didn't mean to say that. It just slipped out."

"We're alone, Adrian. You promised you would call me Claire." He looked back at her, and he blushed even more, making her heart ache with the sweetness of it. "Whether you meant to say it or not, I hope you *meant* it," she said.

"I did." His smile turned the cold autumn air as warm as summer.

Several days later, Claire walked with Kerry through Connemara Palace. "They're all here?"

Kerry nodded. "The last coach arrived a few minutes ago."

They went into the throne room, where chairs were set up below the dais. The room was crowded with senators. As Claire entered, the buzz of their conversations died away, and the senators all rose. Elsie sprang up from her chair next to the dais, and ran to hug Claire.

"I'm glad to see you still in one piece," Elsie said. She drew back, looking at Claire. "What is it?"

"What?"

"There's something different about you," Elsie said.

"I'm a Dragon Knight now. That tends to change a person."

"No, it's something else. It seems like you're preoccupied with something…or maybe someone?" Elsie asked.

How did she see that? Claire's cheeks burned. "I have no idea what you mean."

Elsie smirked. "Of course you don't."

"Seriously, Els. The only thing preoccupying me is war."

"Strange," Elsie said, "I've never seen anyone smile like that when they're thinking of war."

"Was I smiling?" Claire asked. She had been thinking about Adrian again. *I have to forget about him*, she told herself. *At least for now. I have allies to win, and a war to plan.* But forgetting him was like trying to forget summer in the winter. Even though it was gone, there was still a haunting memory of its warmth.

Elsie's grin grew wider. "You were."

Claire smiled back. "I was thinking about the surprise I have for you."

"What surprise?" Elsie asked.

"You'll find out." Claire took her seat, fidgeting on the throne. The silk of her jade-colored court dress felt foreign against her skin after months in a uniform. "Senators and Chancellor Garenne, thank you for your service these recent months. Keldaren was attacked, and you endured hardship to serve your country in her time of need. Now we've been attacked again."

"We defeated one of Drakaren's armies. But two more remain. Minerva will never stop attacking us. So we have to stop her. I will go to Kirosia and Hynbarra to ask for troops to help us. And then we'll go to war."

Claire raised her voice to make herself heard over the growing murmurs filling the room. "We'll remove Minerva from power, and eliminate these constant threats."

Isabelle stood. "The Queen is right to take action against Minerva. She's brought war to Keldaren too many times. We'll never have peace until we're rid of her."

"It will be a costly war," Claire said. "But doing nothing will cost us much more. We came near to losing Dalrann a few days ago. When I became queen, I swore an oath to defend Keldaren. When the war starts, I'll go to the front, and lead the army myself."

Even more murmuring erupted amongst the senators. Claire waited for it to die down before she spoke again. "I'll be away from Tara a great deal over the coming months, but the throne will not sit empty for that long. Elsie," Claire said, beckoning to her.

Elsie rose, and walked up to stand before the throne. Her eyes were wide, and she bit her lip. Claire removed the signet ring from her hand, running her finger over the crown and trinity knot embossed into the gold.

Elsie's eyes grew even wider, and her face paled. *No*, she mouthed to Claire.

Yes, Claire mouthed back.

"I'm appointing Princess Elsie as my regent. She will sit the throne in my stead until I return." Claire held up the ring. "I'm giving her my ring, and I give her authority to sign laws and issue royal warrants in my name." She handed the ring to Elsie.

"Claire, I'm not ready for this," Elsie whispered to her.

"No one ever is ready, Els. I seem to remember you saying that before they crowned me," she said quietly.

Elsie stared at her for a moment. Then she slipped the ring on.

CHAPTER 23

Claire

Claire smiled at Elsie. "Thank you again, Chancellor, and Senators. I'll leave the running of the kingdom to you and Princess Elsie until I've returned from Graydare."

The senators stood, bowed to Claire, and started filing out of the throne room. "Chancellor Garenne," Claire called out, "one moment." She met Isabelle at the foot of the dais. Elsie still sat in her chair, twisting the ring on her finger, and biting her lip.

"Help Elsie while I'm away," Claire whispered. "I know she can handle this, but she seems rather less confident. I'm sure she would appreciate any advice you could give her."

"Of course, Your Majesty," Isabelle said.

Claire walked over to Elsie, who sat staring at the ring, a stricken look on her face. "You'll do fine," Claire said. "You're better prepared for this than I was."

"How could I possibly be more prepared than you?" Elsie asked.

"You're already married," Claire said. "I wasn't."

Elsie laughed. "I don't think marriage is really that much like ruling a country."

"From what you've told me, it is. You try to guide your people in the right direction, protect them from danger, and talk some common sense into them when you need to," Claire said.

"That does sound like having a husband." Elsie grinned. "I wonder what Damien will think of this second marriage of mine?"

"Tell him it's only a temporary one. That should ease his jealousy." Claire smiled. "All jesting aside, Els, you'll do fine. And I'll be back as soon as I can." Claire gave Elsie's shoulder a squeeze. "The throne is yours."

Kerry followed Claire out of the throne room. "Your First Legate has things well in hand?" Claire asked.

"Well enough. The Crown Guard will be fine under his command until we get back."

"You're not going to like where we're going," Claire warned.

"Kirosia and Hynbarra?" Kerry asked.

"We're going to the Isle of Erinn first," Claire said.

"Why would we go there?"

"I promised I would visit a hermit who lives there," Claire said.

"And just who did you make that promise to?" Kerry asked, suspicion tingeing her voice.

"A god. The one whose messenger I met in the woods."

"Our time would be better spent seeking troops from our allies," Kerry said. "But where you go, I'll go."

Claire stopped at her apartments. She emerged a few moments later, wearing her Dragon Knight uniform and armor. "It still seems strange to see you in that uniform," Kerry said, as they continued down the halls.

"It felt strange at first. But I've spent enough time now in uniform that it was odd to wear a dress again," Claire said.

"Some battles are meant to be waged in armor," Kerry said. "But some can only be fought on a different field, in a different sort of uniform."

"I'd prefer a sword on a battlefield to debate in a throne room," Claire said.

"A good ruler must be able to fight with both."

"I know. I suppose there'll be some verbal sparring ahead for me in Kirosia and Hynbarra," Claire said.

"Not in Kirosia. If you want help from Queen Alexis, all you'll have to do is ask. Prince Hesperian, though…he'll only give you troops if he sees some gain in it for him," Kerry said.

They walked to the courtyard, where Sloane was waiting with Breaus and several other knights and dragons. "Kerry will ride with me," Claire told Sloane. "We're going to Alaira before we visit Kirosia."

"Are you going to inspect the Fleet, Your Majesty?" Sloane asked.

"No." Claire waited. She saw the question on Sloane's face.

Kerry saw it too. "Believe me, you don't want to know," she told Sloane.

Sloane nodded. "Then I won't ask." She gestured to the dragons. "We're ready whenever you are, Your Majesty." They climbed aboard, and the dragons soared off into the sky.

Many hours later, silver flashes appeared on the horizon. As they flew closer, the flashes grew into a vast stretch of water, gleaming in the sunlight. Claire peered down as they flew over the Silver Sea. It was so clear and shallow that the reefs were visible below the waves—along with the sharks patrolling them. After another hour, an island appeared.

They flew to the eastern shore, where a cove was filled with anchored galleons. A huge fortress sprawled across a hill near the cove. A small city and harbor stood at the foot of the hill. Claire gestured to Breaus, pointing to the fort.

Breaus angled toward it, and landed in its courtyard, while the other dragons came in for a landing around them. A Sea Knight emerged from the fortress, wearing a dark blue surcoat over silver mail. The surcoat was embroidered with the blazon of his order—a golden sword rising from a silver wave.

Claire removed her helm and climbed down from Breaus. The knight looked at Claire's crown, and saluted. "Your Majesty, welcome to Fort Connalt. We weren't expecting a visit from you," he said.

"There was no time to tell you I was coming. I need to see the Prefect," Claire said.

"Of course, Your Majesty." The knight led her, Sloane, and Kerry into the fortress. He brought them to a door, and knocked. A muffled voice answered. They followed the knight inside, where a thick-chested man in a knight's uniform sat in an armchair, sharpening a sword.

"Her Majesty, the Queen," the knight announced. "Your Majesty, this is Sir Rion, Prefect of the Order of the Sea."

"Your Majesty," Rion said, rising and putting the sword aside. "I wasn't aware you were coming. Otherwise we would have had a more suitable welcome for you."

"This isn't an official visit, Sir Rion. I came here looking for someone," Claire said.

Rion dismissed the other knight. "Please, Your Majesty, have a seat. Who are you looking for?"

"I don't know his name. But I know he lives alone here on the Isle of Erinn. I thought that if anyone would know of a hermit on this island, it would be you," Claire said.

Rion nodded. "That would be Sir Sean."

"Sir? He's a knight?" Claire asked.

"He was one of our greatest knights. Until he caught the sweating sickness. He survived, but it left him blind. Ever since then, he's lived as a hermit." Rion shook his head. "He used to be a lion in battle. He was always the first over the railing onto an enemy ship, and always the knight with the most kills. He would have made Prefect one day. Until he fell ill, that is."

"And where is he now?" Claire asked.

"He lives in a small house on the western shore of the island," Rion said.

Claire frowned. "A blind man is living alone off in the wilderness? Is this how you treat one of your greatest knights?"

Rion shifted uneasily in his chair. "I tried to talk him into going to the veteran's infirmary in Tara, Your Majesty. He certainly would have been eligible for a place there. But he refused to go. Blindness changed him. He became very bitter. And angry. He wanted to stay here on the island, and to live alone. So we built a house for him, and let him be."

"How do you know if he's even still alive?"

"We do send him provisions from time to time, along with firewood. Other than that, we leave him in peace," Rion said.

"Is he sane, though?" Kerry asked. "A bitter and angry man who chooses to live as a recluse in the wilderness…that sounds a bit unbalanced."

"I haven't spoken to him since he left the Order," Rion said. "But the knights who bring him provisions saw a great change in him several years ago."

"What kind of a change?" Claire asked.

"They say he's lost his bitterness. And that he seems to have found some peace. Why, if I may ask, Your Majesty, are you so interested in Sir Sean?"

"I have to speak with him," Claire said.

"I see. I'm sure you have your reasons," Rion said.

"I do."

Rion nodded. "You can find his house on the western edge of the island. A creek flows down from a high hill and empties into the sea nearby. I would imagine he doesn't venture too far from the house."

Claire stood. "Thank you, Sir Rion."

"Of course, Your Majesty. After you speak with Sean, you'd be most welcome to stay the night here at the fort, if you'd like. It's been many years since we had the privilege of a sovereign visiting the homeport of the Fleet."

"Thank you for the invitation. But we will be at war with Drakaren soon. I have alliances to forge, and a war to plan. I promise I'll visit again when I can. Give my regards to Admiral Sheridan. I assume he's at sea?" Claire asked.

Rion nodded. "He left with the Fourth Squadron several days ago. We had reports of black sails off the coast of Skellig. The Admiral went to hunt them down."

"Then I hope he succeeds. One day we must remove the pirates permanently from Eris, instead of just chasing them from Keldari waters," Claire said.

"Both the Sea Knights and the Fleet would welcome the chance to do that, Your Majesty," Rion said, a surprised look on his face. "But we've never been given the troops we would need."

"We can't spare the soldiers now, but after the war is over, I'll send you more troops. And then you can end the threat of the pirates once and for all," Claire promised.

Rion smiled. "I'll look forward to that, Your Majesty." He bowed as they left.

Back in the courtyard, they climbed up onto the dragons. "Head west," Claire told Breaus.

CHAPTER 24

Claire

When they reached the western shore, Claire nudged Breaus toward the distant glint of a stream. The stream fell in a gentle waterfall from a hill. Atop the hill was a small lake, surrounded by trees. A small, simple house stood near the hill.

Claire signaled Breaus to land. She and Kerry slipped down from the saddle onto the warm sand beside the water. The other dragons touched down around them.

Sloane came up to them. "Where is this Sir Sean?"

"There," Kerry said. A man was walking up from the house, with a small brown dog trotting just ahead of him. He followed the dog, feeling his way across the ground with a wooden walking staff. He wore a simple blue robe of rough fabric, bound at his waist with a cloth belt. The man was tall, but of slighter build than Claire had expected. Streaks of gray ran through his brown hair. *He looks more like some scholar than a former knight.*

When the man came closer, his dog gave a single bark, and sat down. He brushed against the dog and stopped. "Welcome to the Isle of Erinn, Your Majesty. I assume you're Queen Claire?" His voice was as warm and gentle as the waves lapping against the beach. His hazel eyes were fixed straight ahead in an empty stare.

"Yes. But how did you know who I am?"

"I heard the dragon wings. I've seen you in my dreams, Your Majesty. And in my dreams, you rode a dragon," he said.

"I take it you're Sir Sean?" Claire asked.

"Simply Sean, Your Majesty. I gave up the title when I left the order."

"A knight is a knight for life, Sir Sean," Claire said.

"I chose to put aside the Sir. When I went blind, I was no longer any kind of knight. I felt I was unworthy of the title," he said.

"You said you've seen me in your dreams?" Claire asked.

"The Ancient has given me many a dream of you lately, Your Majesty."

"The ancient? The ancient what?" she asked.

"Not what—who. He is the god," Sean told her.

"A valkyrie spoke to me of a god. But she called him the Emperor," Claire said.

"He has many titles. That's the one Astra and the other Valkyries use."

"But what's his name?" Claire asked.

"He has no need of one," Sean said. "If you were the only person in Eris, you would have no need of a name. The only god doesn't need a name either."

"The templers say there are many gods."

"You've seen what the templers are," Sean said.

"And how did you know that?"

"He's shown me a great deal about you," Sean said.

"In your dreams?"

"Yes. Astra has told me much about you as well."

"You have me at a disadvantage, then. I know almost nothing about you," Claire said.

"Then I should tell you about myself. Would you care to walk up the hill with me?" Sean asked.

"The hill? Why?"

"It's part of my story."

"Can you climb a hill?" Claire asked.

Sean smiled. "I know the paths here very well. And I have Star also." The dog's ears pricked up, and it stood, wagging its tail.

Claire smiled down at the dog. "Star?"

"He helps me get around the island. He'll stop me before I walk off a ledge, or warn me about a snake in the path. When I sailed with the Fleet, the ship set its course by the stars. I thought it was an apt name for him."

"Very," Claire said. "Let's take that walk, Sean."

"I'll go with you," Kerry quickly said.

"Sean, this is Countess Kerry Bradaigh. She's Captain of my Crown Guard," Claire said.

"And she mistrusts an eccentric former Sea Knight," Sean said, still smiling.

"Sir Rion told us you were bitter and angry when you came here," Kerry said, falling into step with them. "That concerned me."

"Understandably so," Sean said. "But it's been over ten years since then. Things have changed a great deal."

"You certainly don't seem bitter now," Claire observed.

"When I went blind, I was no longer of any use as a knight. I was adrift, purposeless. I was more than bitter, Your Majesty. I was frightened. And furious. I'm afraid I didn't handle it well."

"What changed?" Claire asked.

"I found a purpose."

"And what was that?"

"The Ancient started speaking to me in my dreams, and showed me my role in his plans. And my role is to show him to you," Sean said.

"So you're supposed to convert me to your god?" Claire asked.

"No person can ever really convert someone else to anything. I'm supposed to show him to you. Whatever happens after that is up to you," Sean said.

"Then by all means, show him to me," Claire said.

"It's not quite that simple," Sean said.

"Of course not," Kerry said. "It's never that simple, is it? It's always mysteries, and rituals, and half-revelations. Why is that, Sean? Why can't you just show this god of yours to us and be done with it?"

"That's a good question," Claire said.

"It is," Sean said. "But a god at my beck and call wouldn't be much of a god, would he? And there's a reason he shrouds himself in mystery, and doesn't just go about openly in the world. The Ancient isn't a tyrant. He invites people to believe in him. He doesn't force them. Not showing himself gives us freedom to choose whether to believe in him or not."

"Revealing himself would hardly force people to believe," Kerry said.

"Wouldn't it? Without the possibility of a reasonable doubt, you'd have no choice *but* to believe," Sean said.

"Seeing isn't always believing," Kerry said.

"Did you believe the show Quaestor put on when he supposedly summoned the oracles?" Sean asked.

"I didn't tell you about that," Claire said.

"I know. I saw it in another dream. Did you believe it?"

"At first. But something seemed wrong about it. And then I looked behind the curtain and saw the truth," Claire said.

"Exactly. We believe what we see if it doesn't feel false. And if there's no curtain masking the illusion. You saw both Death and a valkyrie. How did that feel?" Sean asked.

"More real than anything else I've ever seen," Claire said.

"And now could you ever come to believe that you never saw Death or Astra?"

"No. It was too real, too vivid," Claire said.

Sean nodded. "It would be the same with seeing the Ancient. But even more so. He gives us signs to help us develop faith, but he won't show himself directly."

"How can you have faith in something you've never seen?" Kerry asked.

"Faith is trust. If I tell you that I'll do something, you have no proof I will. But if you trust me, you'll believe that I'll do it. That's faith. Belief without proof," Sean said.

"But trust is something earned," Claire objected.

"Not necessarily. You can give trust," Sean said.

"Not without a reason to."

"Like a sign? You've had Death and Astra as signs. Even I'm a sign," Sean said.

"You?"

"Yes. I know more about you than I could without it being revealed to me somehow, don't I?" Sean asked.

They reached the top of the hill, where a grove of trees stood before them. Kerry held the branches back for Sean.

Claire followed Sean through the trees, and found herself standing next to a small lake. A stream ran from it, burbling out to flow over the side of the hill. A fallen tree lay along the shore.

Sean found the tree with his staff, and sat down on it. He gestured for them to sit as well. Star curled up at his feet. "This is where Astra first appeared to me and told me about the Ancient," Sean said.

"Did you believe in the Syncrestry when you came here?" Claire asked.

"I did. I wasn't very devout, but I attended the temples, and I believed that the gods ruled my life."

"Why?" Kerry asked. "Why believe in something you've never even questioned?"

"That's not something you would do, is it?" Sean asked her.

"I would never blindly follow anything," Kerry said. "Not any god, or faith, or person."

Sean smiled. "Blindly. That's a good word for it. There was so much I couldn't understand until I lost my vision. When I had my sight, I saw only what others were doing, and I couldn't see the questions I should be asking. So I simply followed blindly."

"But that's exactly what you want Claire to do!" Kerry said. "You want her to blindly follow this new god of yours."

"Not at all. I want her to ask the questions I didn't. The questions she started asking the day she looked behind the curtain in the temple," Sean said.

"But you want her to believe in your god," Kerry said.

"No, I think the answers she finds will lead her to believe," Sean said.

"What made you believe?" Claire asked him.

"It was the sort of god that Astra told me of. A god that doesn't use you as a piece on a game board, like the templers say the gods of the Syncrestry do. A god who shows you a path, but who lets you choose your own way in the world, instead of ruling over you like a tyrant."

"So you found an appealing god, and that made you believe," Kerry said.

"That intrigued me. But there were other things that convinced me. Signs Astra gave me. Things she showed me," Sean said.

"More riddles and mysteries," Kerry scoffed. "I'd find a cruel god more convincing than a kind one."

"Why?"

"The world is cruel. How could a kind god allow it to be like that?" Kerry asked.

"Would you believe that I've seen this grove and this lake before? Astra showed it to me. She gave me back my sight once...for a few moments, anyways. I imagine on a day like today, you can see the sun shining through the leaves," Sean said.

"Yes, you can. What of it?" Kerry asked.

"There are both shadows and sunlight...they exist side by side. In fact, there can only be shadows when there is light. Otherwise everything would be dark," Sean said.

"You mean that both kindness and cruelty can exist at the same time," Claire said.

"Yes."

"But a kind god wouldn't allow misery to exist. He would make the world a paradise, not one as full of suffering as this," Claire said.

"If he decided to control people, he could stop them from choosing cruelty and evil," Sean said. "But then he would be no better than the false gods of the Syncrestry supposedly are. He would be a puppeteer pulling strings. So he allows us to take our own path, even if it takes us away from him. And even if that path causes misery."

"So he lets people who choose the wrong path suffer. But what about the child who goes hungry because her father spends all his coin on drink? What about the cripple who has to beg for food because he can't work? If this Ancient is truly a kind god, then why doesn't he protect the innocent from suffering?" Claire demanded.

"Did your father love you?" Sean asked.

"What?"

"Do you think your father loved you?"

"Of course he did," Claire said.

"Yet he chose you as heir to the throne, and wanted you to join the Dragon Order. Has any of that been easy?" Sean asked.

"No. It hasn't."

"My dreams have shown me how hard it's been for you. I've seen the pain and the fear its caused you. You've shed blood and tears walking down this path. How could your father love you and not protect you from all those hardships?"

"I see where you're steering me, Sean. But this is different. He had to make me his heir. Otherwise Jared would have become king."

"You have cousins," Sean pointed out. "King Colin could have named one of them."

"Why should one of them have to go through this instead of me?" Claire asked.

"Exactly," Sean said.

"That's different. I can understand why I had to become queen. Can the beggar understand why he's crippled? Can the child understand why she's hungry? And there's a reason I had to accept the crown. What reason is there for innocents to suffer?"

"It took years after I lost my sight before I could understand the purpose behind it," Sean said. "We often can't see the reason for things until long after they've happened."

"If this god of yours did allow people to suffer for some greater purpose, if he was truly a kind god, he would tell them the reason for it," Kerry said.

"What if we couldn't understand the reason?" Sean asked.

"What kind of god couldn't explain it?" Kerry demanded.

"Do you know the history of Keldaren?" Sean asked. "The story of how we came by ship from Edera, and how King Connalt Erinn first led our people to this very island?"

"Of course," Kerry said.

"Then explain it to Star," Sean said, reaching down to scratch the dog's ears.

Kerry glared at Sean. "I don't think he'd understand."

"And does that say something about your limitations, or his?" Sean asked.

"His, I suppose. So I shouldn't bother to ask any questions about your god, because I'm too limited to understand the answers?" Kerry asked, her voice heavy with sarcasm.

"Not at all," Sean said. "Honest seekers who question truth are much closer to it than those who just follow something blindly. Just accept that you can't understand *all* of the answers. That's why there are mysteries. And why you need to have faith to believe. Faith isn't acceptance that there are no answers—just that there are some answers you can't understand."

"I suppose I'll never have faith, then," Kerry said.

"Do you believe Claire will be a good queen?" Sean asked.

"Absolutely."

"Why? You can't know that she will be. You can't see into the future," he said.

"She has wisdom and courage. She puts the kingdom before herself. Look at everything she's done, and all that she's sacrificed for the good of Keldaren," Kerry said.

"So you know she has those qualities, and you reason that those will make her a good queen?" Sean asked.

"Yes."

"And you trust that she'll be a good queen?"

"I see where you're heading with this, Sean. It's different. I know Claire."

"That's exactly what you need in order to believe in someone, Kerry. Reasoning, trust, and knowing them. You don't know the Ancient. That's one of the reasons you can't believe," Sean said.

"How are we supposed to know him when he won't reveal himself?" Claire asked.

"He does reveal himself. Just not directly. He reveals himself most fully in the Gift," Sean said.

"What's that?"

"Another mystery, I'm afraid. But one he shows to those who believe in him."

"And what of those who can't believe?" Claire asked.

"Speak to him. Ask him to show you who he is. Perhaps he'll give you a sign that will let you trust him enough to believe."

"Pray, you mean? I wouldn't know his prayers," Claire said.

"Just speak whatever's in your heart. Come back tonight, and ask him for a sign."

"Why tonight?"

"The stars will be out then," Sean said.

"And that's important?"

"Very."

Kerry leaned close to her. "We have to reach Kirosia and Hynbarra. They have real soldiers to help in the fight against Minerva. We don't have time to waste looking for imaginary help here," she whispered.

She's right, Claire thought. *There's no time for this now.* "We should be on our way, Sean. We have allies to make, and a war to win. I'll return when the war is over, and seek your god then."

"As you wish, Your Majesty. But it seems to me that he's seeking you now. Are you sure you aren't leaving because you're afraid he'll find you?"

"Of course not." *But maybe I am,* she realized. "I just don't have the time now. Later. When the war is won."

"You're welcome here any time," Sean said.

Claire stood, and held out a hand to help Sean up. The wind blew, rustling the leaves of the trees ringing the lake. "Stay," a voice whispered amidst the blowing leaves. "Stay and see."

CHAPTER 25

Claire

The voice wasn't Astra's. This was a man's voice, as soft as the wind, but as deep as an ocean. The words echoed in her mind, tugging gently at something deep inside her. A decision snapped into place in Claire's mind. "We're staying the night," she told Kerry.

"What? Why?" Kerry asked, exasperation creeping into her voice.

"I want to see what happens tonight."

"And when nothing does happen, will you finally stop chasing ghosts and gods all over Eris?" Kerry asked.

"There are worse things to chase than hope and meaning," Claire said.

"You can find those without resorting to this folly," Kerry said.

"Perhaps. But I haven't found them yet. So I'll indulge this folly. I value your counsel, Kerry. But I've made up my mind. Tell the others to make camp. Hynbarra and Kirosia will keep until tomorrow."

The sun was setting as Claire made her way back up the hill with Sean and Kerry. At the top of the hill, Claire held the branches back for Sean, and then followed him into the grove. The water glistened silver in the moonlight, and there was a cool, tingling charge to the night air.

Sean made his way to the fallen tree and sat down. Claire took a seat next to him. "I should ask for a sign?"

"Ask him for what you need to help you believe," Sean said.

Claire closed her eyes and whispered a prayer. She waited for a few moments, then opened her eyes. "And where might this sign be?"

"Have patience, Your Majesty. As I said before, a god is not there to be at one's beck and call," Sean said.

"Perhaps because he's not there at all," Kerry muttered.

The hours passed, and still nothing happened. *Show me a sign,* Claire whispered over and over in her mind. *Help me to believe.* There was no answer. Wind blew in the trees, but there were no voices in the rustling of the leaves. The creek babbled, and water lapped on the shore of the lake. Other than that, all was still. The entire world seemed asleep. Claire's heart felt as dark and bleak as the empty night. *Why lead me here and then show me nothing? If he's real, why doesn't he answer me?*

Kerry stood. "It's late, Claire. And we have a good distance to travel tomorrow. Perhaps it's time to catch a few hours' sleep."

If Sean's god does exist, it seems he's turned a deaf ear to me, Claire thought. She stood as well. "Are you coming down, Sean?"

"No," he said. "I'll wait a while longer, I think. I have a feeling something will happen tonight."

"We'll lose sleep. That's all that's going to happen," Kerry snapped.

"I think I'll wait a while longer also," Claire said, frowning at Kerry. She took her seat again. Kerry sighed and sat back down.

The minutes dragged on. Claire's head nodded. A tendril of mist crept across the ground toward her, curling around her feet. She snapped her head up.

Kerry turned to look at her. Then she jumped to her feet, yanking her sword from its scabbard. "Who are you?" Kerry shouted. "How did you get up here?"

Claire looked behind her. Astra stood there, mist swirling around her. The mist glittered white as it caught the light glowing out from her. Her wings, transparent and glistening in the moonlight, fluttered delicately in a gentle breeze.

"Astra," Claire said. "Are you the sign I asked for?"

"No. I'm here for Kerry," Astra said.

"Do you know this…whatever she is?" Kerry asked Claire, her sword at the ready.

"Yes. This is Astra. She's the messenger that appeared to me on the way to Mount Draconis."

Astra took a step toward Kerry. "Stay back." Kerry gestured with her sword. "Costumes and trickery don't fool me. You're no ghost or god. I don't know what your scheme is, but I see you for the fraud you are."

"I am none of those things," Astra said, taking another step toward her.

"I told you to stay back. Come any closer, and I'll cut you."

"Kerry, stop…" Claire began. Astra raised a hand to quiet her.

"Let her do what she feels she must," Astra said. She stepped closer to Kerry.

Kerry's sword flashed up, arcing into the midnight-blue sleeve of Astra's dress. It was a glancing blow, one that should have merely grazed her. But the tip of the sword passed through her arm as if it weren't there. Kerry stared, her mouth open in disbelief. Then she slashed out again. Her blade sliced straight through Astra's pearl chest plate, as if the blade was cutting mist.

Kerry gasped, lowering her sword. Astra put her hand on Kerry's shoulder. "Don't be afraid," Astra said. "I was sent here to talk to you. Nothing more."

A deep, silvery light flooded the glen. Claire looked up at a ball of silver fire descending toward them. As it grew closer, the ball took on the shape of a woman. Her body appeared to be ablaze with silver flames. Huge wings stretched out of her back, and flared to catch the air as she landed in front of them.

The woman was a giant, at least three times Claire's size. Her body wasn't on fire—it *was* silver flame, burning and rippling in the shape of a head, torso, arms, and legs. Orbs of golden light formed her eyes.

Kerry fell to her knees, crying out in terror. She dropped her sword and covered her face.

The giantess looked down at Claire. "ACERA DES ICANA," she boomed, her voice thundering like a tidal wave against the shore. Claire's knees trembled, and she fought to stay standing. The silver woman was both beautiful and terrifying.

"ICINEA SES ERENESA," Astra rumbled.

The giantess looked at her. "ESERA." She turned her gaze back to Claire. "Can you understand me?" Her voice was now as soft and quiet as a gentle rainfall.

"Y…yes," Claire stammered, shivering.

"It has been some time since I was last in this world. I had forgotten not to use the Startongue."

"You're a star. And the sign," Claire realized.

"Yes. My name is Caeli. I will show you what you seek."

"Him? You'll show me him?" Claire asked.

Caeli shook her head. "I cannot show you him directly. Not while you are still part of this world. But I will show you what I can. It will be enough, I think."

Caeli knelt. "Come," she said, spreading her silver-fire arms.

She'll burn me, Claire thought.

"It's not that kind of fire," Caeli said.

Claire looked at Kerry, who was still covering her eyes.

"Astra will care for her."

Claire stepped toward Caeli. Feathers of silver fire burned across the surface of the wings as they encircled her. Caeli reached out her hands; Claire hesitated, and then took them. The silver blaze forming her fingers was cool to the touch.

Caeli pulled Claire to her and picked her up, cradling her against her chest like a child. The silver flames licked at Claire, cool and soothing against her skin. Caeli snapped her wings down, and they soared up into the sky. They flew faster than Breaus had ever carried her, but there was no wind against her face. Even as they shot upwards, the air was absolutely still around them.

"Look down," Caeli told her. Claire peered hesitantly over the burning arms. The Isle of Erinn was a tiny green dot in the Silver Sea below. The entire continent of Eris was spread out beneath her feet. A trail of silver fire burned behind them as they streaked upward.

The Walls of Eris came into view. The solid bulwarks of impenetrable mist circled the seas and oceans, forming the ends of the world. Beyond the walls, league after league of waves rippled across the midnight-blue water of an endless ocean. Now all of Eris looked like a distant island floating on the ocean below.

There were other islands afloat on the dark blue sea, surrounded by their own walls of mist. Some were green and lush like Eris, while others looked brown and barren. Some were a bleak, bone-white, and others were an angry mix of red and black.

"Other worlds," Caeli said. "And the light that shines on them all." She pointed. A mountain rose from the center of the endless sea. Mountain was the only word for it—but mountain didn't nearly do it justice. This peak soared to impossible heights, and made the mountain ranges of Eris look like anthills. The mountain was sheathed in an outer layer of clear crystal, with a heart of glistening, golden-orange stone. A waterfall tumbled from the peak, thundering into the dark-blue sea below.

The summit was hidden by a blinding corona of golden light. The entire peak glowed with its reflection, radiating out through the black void surrounding it. Caeli lifted her head to the summit and started singing.

It was a song unlike any Claire had ever heard. Caeli sang music, not words. A shimmering, dancing song of harps floated from her mouth. The music resounded so vividly that Claire could almost see the notes swirling their way across the sky.

Silver lights descended toward them, growing brighter as they emerged from the golden aurora at the summit. The lights were silver fire, shining against the blackness. *Stars*, Claire realized. Caeli sang louder, her harpsong ringing out across the divide. The stars sang back to her as they drew nearer.

A constellation of stars shone around them. They sang gently in the Startongue, in a chorus of almost unbearable beauty. The notes of their song swelled, then receded, then surged again, pulling at Claire's heart. The song carried her on a rushing tide of transcendence. She felt every pulse of her heart being tugged up toward the golden light.

Claire began to cry, the music flooding through her. Caeli spread her arms as the song itself took hold of Claire, lifting her up through the sky. She passed star after star, their chorus propelling her up toward the summit of the mountain. There was a power in the song—a power like she had never felt before.

Then the song slowed, growing quieter. She felt herself floating gently down again, until she settled softly back into Caeli's arms. They slowly descended, the circle of stars above receding. Caeli nestled Claire close to her, wiping the tears from her cheeks. "Why are you crying?"

"I felt like a little girl again, running to her father. Tell them to sing again, Caeli. Send me back, please," Claire begged.

"I can't, Claire. We sent you as high as you could go. Why do you want to go back?"

"I felt him, Caeli. The higher I went, the stronger I felt his presence. I want to feel that again."

"Does that mean you believe, then?"

"After that, how could I not believe?"

The golden fire of Caeli's eyes flared. "Then I can show you. Close your eyes." Caeli touched Claire's forehead, and gently traced her fingertips down over her eyelids. "Now, open them."

Claire opened her eyes. The waterfall poured down the side of the mountain as it had before. Now, though, the water was alive with golden sparks. They rushed glistening down to the end of the waterfall, where it crashed into the dark sea. Golden sparks floated up with the mist, and flew like fireflies out across the ocean, swarming over the worlds below.

A single golden spark drifted up, and hovered near Claire. When she took a breath, it drew the spark into her. She gasped as the light entered her. A moment later, another golden spark drifted up, and was drawn in with her next breath.

"What is that?" Claire asked.

"The Emperor. It's how he sustains the worlds. He constantly breathes himself out into every living thing. Including you."

"Why couldn't I see it before?"

"You live behind a veil there," Caeli said, gesturing to the ocean below them. "The veil is a part of the worlds, and a part of those who live in them. You have to be lifted up before you can see beyond the veil."

Another spark floated up, and Claire breathed it in. "If that's the Emperor, why can't I feel him?"

"It's a part of him. His breath. His spirit. His essence. Is your heart beating? Are your lungs filling with air? None of that would be without him. If you can feel life within you, you can feel him."

"What was the song they were singing?" Claire asked. "I know it was in the Startongue, but what were they saying?"

"It was a prayer."

"A prayer carried me like that? I thought it was some sort of spell."

"Prayers are a great deal more powerful than any spell or witchcraft. Especially in the Startongue," Caeli said.

"Can you teach it to me?"

"Sean can. The Emperor has chosen him to be his prophet. Sean will go to Tara and spread word of the Emperor, until you return from Drakaren. Then he will be your guide in the Faith."

"So, I won't learn anything more about the Emperor until this war is finished?" Claire asked.

"Ask Sean for the Gift. That will give you more than enough to ponder until you return," Caeli said.

"But Sean said the Gift came from the Emperor. Why would I ask Sean for it?"

"The Faith is a series of bridges between your world and the Emperor's. Sean is one of those bridges. The Emperor offers you the Gift, but Sean will be the one to carry it to you."

Claire was silent for a moment, staring down at Eris, which grew larger and larger as they descended. "You said until I return. Does that mean I will return? That I'll survive the war?"

"Astra told you about asking of the future. It will come in its own time, Claire. There are many possibilities. Only the Emperor knows which future will be written permanently into time. You surviving is one possible future. And if that comes to pass, then Sean will teach you."

"And if I never return from Drakaren?" Claire asked.

"Then you will have already received the Gift. And that will give you greater knowledge of him than any teaching." They descended back into the skies of Eris, passing through a cloud of golden sparks. As they flew lower, the sparks drifted down around them like golden snowflakes.

They landed atop the hill, where Astra, Kerry, and Sean were waiting. Golden sparks were floating into each of them. Caeli knelt, setting Claire down. Kerry shrank back from the star, but didn't cover her eyes this time.

"I'll bid you farewell, Claire," Caeli said.

"Will I see you again?"

"Of course. Just look to the sky."

"I meant here, in Eris," Claire said.

"Possibly. But I will watch over you from above. And I'll sing prayers for you. There will be nights when one star seems especially close, and you'll hear harpsong, and the Startongue. And you'll know I'm near."

"You would do that for me?" Claire asked.

Caeli nodded. "I'll watch over you like a mother."

Tears welled in Claire's eyes, and spilled out in hot traces down her cheeks. Caeli reached out and smoothed Claire's hair back. Then she leaned forward, and kissed Claire's forehead. Her touch had been cool before, but her kiss was as warm as sunshine on Claire's skin.

"When I leave, the veil will fall over you again, and you will lose sight of the sparks. But they will still be there. You'll see them again, for just a moment, when you receive the Gift. The shroud of this world obscures your eyes, Claire. But don't let it obscure the eyes of your heart. Always remember what you saw beyond the veil."

Caeli stood and spread her wings, her golden eyes flashing. Her wings snapped down, splitting the air like thunder, and she soared into the sky, trailing a streak of silver fire behind her.

CHAPTER 26

Claire

Claire blinked. The golden sparks were gone. In a heartbeat, they had vanished along with Caeli. Kerry came to her, tears streaking her face. She hugged Claire tightly. "I'm so sorry I didn't believe you."

"Has that changed?"

"After what I saw? Everything's changed. Astra and Sean told me about the Ancient. Did you see him?" Kerry asked.

"I saw the mountain that serves as his throne. I saw the crown of light surrounding him. And I even saw his spirit in this world," Claire said.

"Where?"

"All around us. He's hidden here, but Caeli told me that the Gift would let me see his spirit again."

"Sean told me about the Gift. He offered it to me when I decided to believe," Kerry said.

"Caeli talked of it. She never told me what it was, though."

"Come and see," Kerry said, pulling her over to Sean and Astra.

"Your Majesty," Sean said. "Welcome back."

"Did you know where Caeli was going to take me?"

He nodded.

"Why didn't you tell me?" Claire asked.

"You wouldn't have believed me."

"You're right. I wouldn't have. Has she ever brought you there?" Claire asked.

"No. I've seen it in a dream, though. And I see the Crystal Mountain whenever I receive the Gift," Sean said.

"Just what is this Gift?"

"It's him. It's his presence, in a way you can see and feel. It's the greatest bridge there is between this world and him," Sean said.

"A greater bridge than Caeli and Astra?"

"Much greater than us," Astra said.

"Then, please, give me the Gift," Claire said.

"And me," Kerry said.

"Guide me to the lake." Claire took his arm, and led him to the shore. "I'll need a shell," Sean said.

Claire found a large, scalloped shell, and gave it to him. He stooped, and dipped it in the lake. Then he lifted the shell toward the sky, and sang, *"Imploriuanus daenctae notas immacularum."*

A single ray of sunlight pierced the dark night sky, reaching down like a golden finger to touch the water in the shell. The water shimmered in the golden light for an instant, until the sunbeam vanished.

But the water still glowed. It was no longer golden, but shone a pure, brilliant white. Sean lowered the shell, the water rippling like white-hot molten glass. He took a sip from the shell. Then he held it out to her.

Claire took it, staring into the glowing whiteness of the transformed water. *Liquid light*, she thought, lifting the shell to her lips. A brilliant light flared across her vision, and warmth flooded through her. The light faded, and the mountain rose before her again—its heart of shimmering golden-orange encased in glittering crystal. A golden aurora crowned the mountain, and the soaring chorus of the singing stars echoed all around her. Their song lifted her again.

This time, Claire kept rising, straight into the glow at the summit. The golden light blocked out everything else, and grew larger and brighter as she rushed toward it. She entered the light, feeling it envelop her like a warm ocean.

The light's heat moved into her—not burning through her like the bloodberry wine had, but filling her like water fills a sponge. She closed her eyes, feeling tears etch down her cheeks before they vanished into the light. A voice echoed inside Claire— the same one that had spoken to her in the wind through the trees. "Peace," it whispered. When the voice spoke, a feeling of serenity blew through her like a summer wind.

Claire opened her eyes, and saw the trees and the lake. And she saw the golden sparks again. A stream of them flowed out of the shell she held, passing through her. A cloud of sparks danced and swirled around her and Sean. The sparks faded away after only a moment. But the feeling of their warmth lingered inside her.

Tears welled up in Claire's eyes as she passed the shell to Kerry. Kerry hesitated for an instant before lifting it to her lips.

She drank, and then gasped. A distant expression passed over her face. A moment later, she looked at Claire, blinking.

"Did you see it?" Claire asked.

Kerry nodded, tears running down her cheeks. She wiped them away, smiling. "It was everything I never let myself hope for."

Astra stepped toward them. "The hour is late," she said. "And you all have long journeys tomorrow. Rest now. I'll speak with you in the morning." Astra spread her wings, and soared up into the star-filled sky.

Claire and Kerry helped Sean down the hill, with Star following. They led him to his house, and then made their way to the camp on the seashore. Sloane stood watch next to the tents and slumbering dragons.

"Your Majesty," Sloane said, nodding to her. "I trust your vigil was peaceful?"

"You didn't see?" Claire asked.

"See what?"

"A star coming down to the hilltop," Kerry said. "You could hardly have missed that."

"I saw the three of you go up the hill. Several hours passed, and then I saw the three of you come down. I saw nothing in between," Sloane said.

Kerry stared at Sloane, her mouth open in surprise.

"Now you know how I felt," Claire said, laughing. "At least I'm not the only one seeing visions now."

"Visions, Your Majesty?" Sloane asked.

Claire shook her head. "It will keep until morning, Sloane. Perhaps you'll see a vision yourself then. Astra did say she'd be back."

Sloane frowned, a questioning look on her face. But she held her tongue.

Claire went to her tent, and wrapped herself in a bedroll. The warm feeling of peace still lapped inside her like a gentle tide, and she drifted off to sleep on it.

Claire woke to the smell of cooking fish. She stepped out from her tent. Mist drifted over the camp, rising thick from the sea. Sean knelt by a fire, turning pieces of fish on a stick. Star lay at Sean's feet. Sloane sat nearby, watching Sean cook. "We can make our own breakfasts, Sloane," Claire said.

Sloane shrugged. "I tried telling Sean that. He insisted on cooking."

"A good host provides for his guests. Sit and eat," Sean urged, holding out the stick. He had brought wooden plates, and they all took one and a piece of fish. They sat on logs the knights had arranged around the campfire.

As they finished their breakfast, more fog blew up on the warm wind. Sloane rose, and went to the sea to wash her plate. Claire had just swallowed her last bite when a plate clattered against a stone behind her. Claire turned just as a figure emerged from the cloud of fog on the shore.

Astra's pearl armor glistened in the sunlight filtering through the mist. Sloane jumped back, steel rasping against leather as she drew her sword. The other knights leapt to their feet, drawing their blades also.

"Put down your swords," Claire ordered. "She's a friend."

"Where did this friend of yours come from?" Sloane asked, eying Astra. "And why is she armed and armored?"

"For the same reason you are," Astra said. "I'm also a knight."

"I don't recognize your uniform," Sloane said. "You're not from any order I know."

Astra smiled. "My order isn't of this world." She stepped fully out of the fog, her wings emerging from the haze. The white light shining around her flared, glittering even more brightly.

Sloane gasped. "Are you one of the Fates?"

"No. Claire can tell you who I am. I'm here to speak with her and Sean."

"Put down your sword, Sloane," Claire said. "Let her pass."

Sloane sheathed her sword, and the other knights did the same. Astra walked over to Sean, who was sitting on a log by the fire. She reached down and helped him up.

"Astra," he said, smiling. "Have you come to send me off?

"I have. It's time for you to be on your way to Tara."

"Why should he go all the way there?" Claire asked. "Surely he can preach the Faith just as well in Port Laitha."

"Tara is the largest city in all Eris," Sean said. "There's nowhere else I can speak to so many people. And more than that,

Tara is the heart of the Syncrestry. Where better to bring the truth than to the very seat of the false gods?"

"I suppose you're right. I wish I could go with you, though. It's a long way to travel alone," Claire said.

"I won't be alone," Sean said, reaching down to scratch Star's ears. The dog wagged its tail at him. "And you have your own task. There are more allies to seek out than just Hynbarra and Kirosia. There are those within Drakaren itself who may join you against Minerva. Have you heard of the Merosians?"

"I know of a Lake Merosia in southern Drakaren. But I know nothing of Merosians. Are they a people who live by the lake?" Claire asked.

"They live by the lake. But they aren't people. Not human, at least. They're one of the First Races. Drakaren enslaved the Merosians decades ago, and they have no love for the Drakari," Sean said. "They may join you in this war. Go to Miral, their village, on the south shore of the lake. Meet with their ruler there, and see if you can persuade them to join you."

"You will find another ally in Drakaren as well," Astra said. "There is a castle called Darcann, on the Deral River. Minerva has turned it into a prison, and its dungeons are filled with those who have opposed her rule. There is a woman being held there named Brianna Graydare. She was the sister of King Valus, Minerva's late husband. Find her and free her. She's part of the Emperor's plan as well."

Astra reached out, clasping Claire's elbow. "The path ahead will not be easy. But it leads to the Crystal Mountain."

"Then it will be worth it," Claire said.

Astra took a step back, and unfurled her wings. "I will see you again, Claire." With a snap of her wings, she was gone, shooting up into the air.

"I'll have one of the knights fly you to Tara on a dragon," Claire told Sean. "Otherwise, it would take you weeks to get there by ship and foot."

"That's kind of you, Your Majesty."

"I think we're beyond titles, Sean. My friends call me Claire."

Sean smiled. "I'm honored to have you as a friend, Claire."

"I'm not sure how good of a friend I am. I'm sending you to Tara without a sword and without guards. The templers will hear of you soon enough, and the Faith will be heresy to them. I wouldn't put anything past Quaestor and the rest of the Syncrestry."

"Truth will be my sword. And the templers won't be able to stand against it. You'll be in much greater danger. Stealing into Merosia, and then into a Drakari prison…my prayers will go with you, Claire," Sean said.

A chilly wind blew in from the direction of Drakaren. The wind sent a stream of fog swirling and winding around her. The wind changed direction, blowing back to the east. It sent the fog swirling back toward Drakaren, tugging at Claire. *Like a snake's tongue pulling me into its jaws,* she thought, shivering.

CHAPTER 27

Minerva

Minerva's quick footsteps echoed through Darcann's dungeons. She turned the corner, her guards hurrying to keep up. At the end of the hall, two burly soldiers stood watch by a cell door. Minerva stopped beside it, glaring at the army sergeant who scurried along behind her guards. "Open it," she ordered.

The sergeant hastened to obey, pulling a ring of keys from his belt. He fumbled through them. "Hurry," Minerva said quietly.

"Yes, Majesty," he said, fear creasing his face. He sighed in relief as he found the right key and fit it into the lock. The key turned with a click, and he swung the heavy door open. Light from the hall lamps flooded into the cell. Jared scrabbled back from the door, shielding his eyes.

"Look at me," Minerva said. Jared lowered his hand from his face, squinting at her. "And what do you have to say for yourself this time?" she asked.

"Why was I thrown in here?" Jared demanded, his voice angry. "Sir Dral said he was bringing me to see you. But then he tossed me into this filthy cell."

Minerva turned to one of the guards at the door. "Hit him." The soldier grinned, and stepped into the cell.

"Minerva, what do you…" Jared began. The soldier's fist slammed into his stomach, and Jared doubled over.

"Again," Minerva ordered. "Harder. In the face."

The soldier grabbed Jared by the hair, yanking his head up, and punched him in the eye. Jared stumbled backward, cringing. Blood ran from his swelling eyelid.

"You destroy the eastern army, and all you can do is complain about your accommodations? Do you have any idea what you've done?" Minerva asked.

Jared winced, putting a hand to his face. "I took command after Dalrush's accident. I took advantage of an opportunity he was too cowardly to seize."

"Dalrush was an excellent general. He obviously saw a flaw in your plan. A flaw you were too arrogant to recognize. And look what happened. Now only the western army stands between the Keldari and Graydare. You've left our border defenseless."

"An archer failed to shoot down a pigeon. That was the only thing that went wrong with my plan. If that message hadn't flown, Dalrann would have been ours before Claire even knew we had crossed the border," Jared said.

"You shouldn't have made plans in the first place. I told you, you were to be Dalrush's assistant. Nothing more," Minerva said.

"Things changed after the General's accident."

"If it was an accident," Minerva said.

"Of course it was an accident. I doubt he meant to fall from the ramparts."

I know exactly what it was, Minerva thought, glaring at him. "No, I certainly don't believe he *meant* to."

Jared looked away. "I think I've been punished enough, Minerva. If you're finished making your point, I'd like to go put some salve on my eye. And bathe," Jared said, kicking at the filthy straw lining the floor.

Minerva looked at the guards. "Bind him."

"What is this?" Jared shouted as the soldiers grabbed him and tied his hands.

"I keep trying to teach you a lesson, Jared. It seems you require further instruction."

"What lesson?" he shouted, struggling.

"To stop being such an arrogant fool. To listen to me. I wish it didn't have to come to this." She gestured to the soldiers, and they hauled Jared to the door.

"Where are you taking me?" Jared yelled.

"To the courtyard. To be whipped," Minerva said.

"Whipped! I thought you loved me!"

"I forgave your failure at Connemara. But this is different. You defied me. I'm trying to teach you, Jared. But you insist on learning the hard way."

"No!" Jared wailed, as the guards dragged him out.

"Wait," Minerva ordered. "Bring him to the pit first."

Minerva followed them as they pulled Jared, kicking and crying, through the halls. Her disgust grew with every step.

Pathetic little maggot. If only I could have his head off, she thought. *But he may yet be useful.*

The guards reached a door set into a stone wall. They opened it, and forced Jared through. Minerva followed them into a cavern carved from the bedrock. They stood on a ledge overlooking the circular chamber. In the center of the grotto was a pit covered with iron bars. Cell doors lined the walls of the chamber.

The soldiers held Jared near the ledge. Below, more soldiers guarded the cells. "Bring him out," Minerva called. Soldiers entered a cell, and emerged dragging a slumped body between them. "Hold his head up," Minerva ordered.

The soldiers grasped the man under his shoulders, hoisting him up. His hands and feet were charred black, and speckled with raw, red patches of flesh. One of the soldiers grabbed his hair, yanking his head back.

"Roche," Jared gasped. "What have you done to him?"

"What the law mandates as punishment for treason. The traitor's hands and feet are burned. Not enough to kill them. But close. Infection sets in later, and that eventually finishes them off," Minerva said.

Jared shuddered. "Show him some mercy. Cut his throat and be done with it."

"I can't show him mercy. I have to do something that will stop any officer from even thinking of putting his own interests before Drakaren's."

"What are you going to do?" Jared asked, his voice quavering.

"Throw him in," Minerva ordered the soldiers below. One guard swung back the bars covering the pit. Roche screamed as the soldiers dragged him to the hole, and tossed him over the edge.

He tumbled down the rock wall, landing with a thud on the sandy floor of the pit. A chirping noise sounded from the shadows along the far wall. Roche wailed, using his elbows to try to drag himself away. A black shape emerged from the gloom. It was a giant beetle, as big as an alley cat. It scuttled toward Roche, its antennae waving. A second beetle appeared out of the shadows, following the first one. Another set of antennae appeared, and a third beetle scurried at him.

"Mercy, Majesty, mercy!" Roche screamed. His screams grew shriller as the insects drew near. He frantically waved his burned hands at them, but the beetles sidestepped his thrashing limbs. One jumped onto Roche's back and bit him. It hopped down, and the insects backed away, their bulging eyes fixed on Roche.

"What are they?" Jared asked, his voice laced with horror.

"Reaper beetles."

Roche's flailing slowed, and then he fell still. "One bite killed him?" Jared asked.

"No. Their venom only paralyzes. He's still alive. And awake. He'll be able to feel everything," Minerva said.

The beetles moved in, crawling over Roche's body. One beetle bent to nibble on his flesh. The others joined in gnawing at

Roche, and a cry of agony echoed up from the pit. Jared looked at her, terror flickering in his eyes.

"They'll only eat a little every day," she said, his fear filling her with cold satisfaction. She leaned closer to Jared. "I've heard of people surviving as long as a week. We'll see how many days Roche lasts."

Jared's lips twisted in disgust. "Monster," he whispered. Then he cringed, fear flooding his face.

"Do you think I enjoy this? I'd rather cut his throat. But an easy death wouldn't make a good example. Word of this death will spread across all Drakaren. The only thing that prevents betrayal is fear, Jared. Never forget that."

"Roche will serve as the example for this disaster. But you have to learn your lesson also. So you'll go out and take your whipping. Then you can come back to Graydare, and we'll talk about the future. We might still be useful to each other. If we survive the coming invasion, there may yet be a chance of you taking the throne someday," Minerva said.

Fear still marked Jared's face. But he nodded. The soldiers walked him to the door. "And Jared," Minerva called. He looked back at her. "If you ever defy me again, the beetles will be picking the flesh from *your* bones."

Claire

Kirosia stretched for leagues across the horizon, wreathed in spray from the waves crashing against its rocky shores. In the distance, the domed towers and rounded buildings of Kai Arann rose beside the city's harbor. The dragons turned, flying along the coast until they reached the city.

They landed in a square next to a tall, oval-shaped palace. The palace's curved walls were white limestone, glittering with flakes of mica. A silver dome crowned the building. As Claire and Kerry slid down from the saddle, a squad of Kirosian Marines gathered around the dragons.

The Marines wore peaked helmets with curved brims. Their armor was silver mail, worn over sea-green tunics. Each carried a short battleaxe slung over their back, and swords and hatchets sheathed on their belts. An officer emerged from the palace.

Claire removed her helmet, and straightened her crown. The officer bowed. "Your Majesty. You must be Queen Claire," he said.

"I am. I apologize for arriving unannounced, but I must speak with Queen Alexis."

"Of course. I'll take you to her." Claire and Kerry followed the officer through the palace gates and up a staircase. They came to a landing at the top of the stairs, where two Marines guarded a door.

"Please wait here, Your Majesty," the officer said. He knocked on the door, and entered, returning a moment later. "The Queen would be pleased to see you."

Claire went inside. Tall pillar candles bathed the room in pools of light. Alexis sat at a table, writing. The candlelight glittered off the crown of white gold atop her head. Alexis rose, her long brown hair swinging as she stood. She smiled warmly. "You've grown since I saw you last."

"I could say the same for you," Claire said, returning her smile. "I suppose that's to be expected after eight years. It's hard to believe it's really been that long since Father first brought me here."

Alexis' smile faded. "It grieved me to hear of your loss. King Colin was a great friend to Kirosia. And to my own father. I know how you must feel. People don't understand unless they've been through it themselves. Everyone just kept telling me that time heals all wounds."

"It dulls them. I don't know about healing."

"I think you're right. It's been a few years for me, and it certainly hasn't healed yet. I can't imagine having lost both parents at your age, Claire. At least I was older than you when my father died."

Claire felt her smile tighten, straining so much that the muscles in her cheeks hurt.

"I'm sorry," Alexis said, seeming to recognize her strained smile. "Let's talk of something else." She waved Claire to a couch. "I'm guessing your visit is more than just a social call?"

"Yes. You've heard of the attacks against Keldaren?"

Alexis nodded. "First Minerva attacks your palace, and then invades? She's after more than just a province this time."

"A great deal more. She helped my brother escape from the castle where he was imprisoned. And now Jared is trying to replace me on the throne."

"If they're in league together, and he became king…then Keldaren would no longer hold Minerva's armies in check," Alexis said.

Claire nodded. "And she would be free to threaten Hynbarra and Kirosia."

"But you mean to stop her. And you want our help."

"Minerva's armies are far larger than mine. Without Kirosian troops, we won't be able to defeat her," Claire said.

"An army of Marines will be at Tara within a fortnight. Kirosia will stand by its ally. And I'll stand by my friend."

"Thank you, Alexis. I can't tell you how much your friendship means to me. And to Keldaren."

"Can you stay the night? If there's a war coming, it will be some time before we'll have another excuse to hold a feast."

"I wish I could. But I have to get to Hynbarra and meet with Prince Hesperian," Claire said.

"You'll have a hard time convincing him to give you troops. As long as Minerva isn't marching her armies across his border, Hesperian won't see any reason to join a war against Drakaren," Alexis said.

"Then I'll have to make him see reason."

Alexis shook her head. "The only way he'll see reason is at sword point."

"If he doesn't listen, he might find himself on the wrong end of a sword someday soon. A Drakari sword," Claire said, standing. "Thank you again, Alexis. Come visit me in Tara when the war's over."

"I will. And whenever you're next in Kai Arann, that feast will be waiting," Alexis said as they hugged. "May the gods go with you."

"One does, Alexis. The only one. When we see each other again, I'll tell you about him."

"One god? That should be an interesting tale. Whatever god goes with you, I hope he brings you back safely."

"So do I," Claire said.

Claire rejoined Kerry on the landing, and the officer escorted them out to the square. They climbed aboard the dragons, and flew back over the ocean, heading for Hynbarra.

CHAPTER 28

Claire

Hours later, Hyperion appeared in the distance. The city was nestled deep in the rocky hills and mountains of Hynbarra's highlands. Breaus angled low over a mountain, and landed on the parade ground of a small fortress. As the other dragons touched down around them, soldiers came swarming out of the citadel.

The Hynbarrans wore armor of steel sunbursts linked by chain mail. The spikes crowning their helmets matched those atop the axe heads of the halberds they carried. Basket-hilted swords hung from their belts. The soldiers glowered at Claire, fingering the staffs of their halberds as she climbed down from the saddle.

"What's your business here, Keldari?" one of the Hynbarrans called out.

Claire removed her helmet. "I'm Claire, Queen of Keldaren. I want to see Prince Hesperian."

"And what makes you think the prince will want to see you?"

"I'm here to warn him of a grave danger to Hynbarra. I would think that might interest him," Claire said.

The soldier scowled. "Follow me to the palace." Claire beckoned to Kerry and Sloane. They followed him across the parade ground, and down a narrow, cobbled street. The city was noisy and crowded, with a bustling grittiness to it. Ox carts rattled across the cobblestones, and brawny Hynbarrans, all clad in simple roughspun, jostled through the streets.

After twisting through a maze of narrow lanes, and climbing the hills that seemed to sprout around every corner, they finally reached the palace. It stood alone on an island, surrounded by a pool of dark water. Its walls were polished black granite, sleek and stark against the afternoon sky. A dark blue flag flew over the castle. Hynbarra's blazon—a bronze torch flanked by two white mountains, rippled across the fluttering banner.

"Blackpool Palace," the soldier said. "The prince is holding court now." He nodded to the halberdiers guarding the drawbridge, and they walked across it into the palace. The soldier led them up a high flight of stairs to a set of tall doors, where two more halberdiers stood guard. "This one says she's Queen of Keldaren," the soldier told the guards. "Says she wants a word with the Prince."

"Wait here," one of the guards said. "I'll get the captain."

He and a captain emerged a few moments later. "The prince will see you," the captain said. They followed him into a high-ceilinged room filled with clusters of well-dressed noblemen. Beyond them, a middle-aged man sat on a silver throne. His long, blonde hair was tied back in a tail. His features were handsome, but there was a sharpness to them as well. A young man sat on a carved wooden chair next to him.

"Queen Claire, Sire," the captain announced.

"I'm Prince Hesperian. This is my son Ross, the Archduke of Hynbarra," Hesperian said, gesturing to the younger man.

Ross stood, smiling at her. He bowed. "Welcome to Hynbarra, Your Majesty," he said. He had thick, blonde hair like his father's, but shorter, and parted in the center. His brooding green eyes held Claire's. *Bewitching eyes*, she thought, staring into the emerald orbs. She looked away, feeling blood rush to her cheeks.

"What brings you to Hyperion?" the prince asked.

"I'm sure you know of the Drakari attacks against my kingdom," Claire said.

Hesperian nodded. "My generals keep me informed of such matters."

"Then the danger must be clear to you."

"What danger? I've heard you destroyed Minerva's army. She won't be trying to seize your territory again anytime soon," Hesperian said.

"She's tried to do a great deal more than that. She freed my brother from prison, and wants to put him on the throne in my place. Minerva also attacked my palace, and tried to kill me."

"What troubles you have in Keldaren nowadays, Your Majesty. An attack on the palace, siblings fighting over the throne...these are dangerous times. For you," Hesperian said.

"There's danger to you as well, Your Highness. If Minerva and Jared are in league together, and he becomes King of Keldaren, then nothing will stop Drakaren's armies from marching on the rest of Eris. If Minerva conquers Keldaren, Hynbarra will be next," Claire said.

"I hardly think Drakaren is interested in attacking us." Hesperian's smile was as haughty as his tone. *I should knock that smirk off his smug face,* Claire thought, fighting to keep her hand from curling into a fist.

"Your two countries have been squabbling over Dalrann Province for the past twenty years. I'm sure these attacks are just the latest chapter in that long story, and not the prelude to some Drakari conquest of all Eris," Hesperian said.

"And what of Minerva freeing my brother?"

Hesperian shrugged. "Perhaps Minerva thinks he'll give her Dalrann as payment for her help. There could be other explanations as well. I know there's a faction in Keldaren that objects to your rule. Perhaps they freed him, and made it look like the Drakari did. Either way, it's Keldaren's concern. Not anyone else's."

"Kirosia disagrees. They're sending Marines to help us remove Minerva from her throne. I came here to ask you to send troops as well."

"A wise ruler puts the good of his country above his friendships. Perhaps Alexis has forgotten that," Hesperian said.

"A wise ruler doesn't casually dismiss danger."

"True. But he doesn't chase phantom dangers. And he doesn't invade other countries on a whim. I can't give you any troops, Your Majesty. And I advise you to abandon this reckless plan altogether," Hesperian said.

"I'm sorry you feel I've wasted your time, Your Highness."

"It's quite all right." His smile appeared again. "You're still very young, after all. Once you have a few more years on the throne, you'll learn not to overreact like that."

Claire gritted her teeth. "We'll be on our way, then."

Hesperian looked surprised. "You must stay for the evening, at least. It would be discourteous of me not to extend hospitality to a queen."

"Thank you, Your Highness, but we really must be going."

Hesperian frowned. "And it would be discourteous of *you* to turn down my invitation. In fact, it would be insulting."

Claire smiled. "Why, Your Highness, don't overreact like that."

Hesperian leaned forward, anger darkening his face. "Claire," Ross said, walking over to her. "Please, stay. We can talk at dinner." He took her hand in his. "I'd like the chance to get to know you." He brought her hand to his lips, and kissed it.

"I suppose we could stay the night," Claire heard herself say. *No, there's no time for this*, she thought. *And I can't stand much more of Hesperian....* But then she looked into the deep green of Ross' eyes, and her hesitation melted away.

Dral

An oxcart rumbled through the streets of Hyperion. The cart was laden with large, covered baskets carrying vegetables for the palace kitchens. One basket, however, held more than vegetables. Dral stretched, trying to ease the pain screaming through his muscles.

The noise of the cart's wheels stopped, replaced by the sound of the driver unhitching the ox and leading it away. Dral waited until he was sure the driver was gone. Then he pulled out a knife and cut through the wicker side of the basket. He cautiously climbed out, hiding behind the cart. His muscles were on fire, and he stretched them carefully before he moved to look around. The cart was parked in its usual spot in the rear yard of the palace, near the kitchens.

Dral brushed a hand against his robe, feeling the metal tube still in place within a pocket. He reached into the basket, and pulled out a grappling hook and rope. Dral swung the rope, flinging the hook toward the palace roof. It caught, and he hauled himself up. He crept along, heading for the center tower.

Claire

Claire sat in one of the palace guest rooms, staring out the window. *Hesperian was no surprise at dinner*, she thought. *Predictably pompous. Ross, though…* a little thrill fluttered through her. *Witty. Clever. Definitely charming. And exciting. Even more exciting than Adrian.* She stared out at the stars, lost in thought.

After a while, she stretched, and stood. *Time for bed.* As she turned from the window, there was a flicker of movement below. She turned back. A dark-cloaked figure was crawling cautiously along the roof of the palace, heading toward the main tower. She leaned further back from the window. Her lamps were out, and the room was lit only by the moon and stars. *Little chance he'll see me*, she thought.

The figure crept to the base of the tower. *An assassin?* Claire wondered, her throat tightening. She reached for her sword and dagger, sliding them into place on her belt. The intruder reached a black-robed arm up, flinging a grappling hook toward a balcony. *Three floors down....the prince's apartments*, she realized. Claire raced off through the hallway and down the stairs.

She rounded the corner to the prince's chambers. The guards there turned toward her, bringing their halberds up. "Intruder!" Claire shouted. "An intruder in the prince's rooms!"

The soldiers looked at each other, then wheeled around. They jerked the doors open, Claire following behind them. They were in a parlor with doors on each wall. "Which one?" she yelled.

"There!" one soldier shouted, pointing. Claire threw the door open. Directly ahead of her, two windowed doors led out to the balcony. One stood ajar.

Hesperian was asleep in the bedroom. A black-robed Viper Knight crouched next to the bed, a metal tube in his hand. Something green emerged from the tube, slithering out onto the bedcovers.

The knight rose, the silver of his serpent helmet flashing in the moonlight. Keeping a tight hold on the tube in his right hand, he drew a slim, silver sword from his robes. But he drew the blade with his left hand, and that slowed him. *Just slow enough*, Claire thought, a plan bursting into her head.

She seized her dagger and flung it at the knight. His silver blade came up to intercept it. But not quickly enough. The dagger spun into his chest.

A strangled hiss sounded from the serpent-faced helm. Claire jerked her sword from its scabbard and charged. The knight slashed at her. She parried the blow and grabbed his wrist. Twisting his blade aside, she thrust her sword into the knight's throat. Claire looked into the eye slits of the serpent helmet as she twisted her blade. Anger and agony burned in the knight's eyes. Then they closed, his knees buckling.

Claire jerked her blade free. A halberd spike slammed into the knight's black robes. The second guard rushed to join the attack as well. Claire turned to the bed, where Hesperian was waking.

"Claire!" he shouted, blinking. "What's the meaning…" his voice trailed off, his eyes fixed on the bedcovers. A slender green shape rose up on his chest, a forked black tongue flicking from its mouth. Claire slashed out, and the snake's head flew off in a spray of blood. The green body twisted and writhed on the covers, and then fell still.

"What the nether is going on?" Hesperian screamed.

"Minerva just tried to have you killed. Come look," Claire said, pointing to the black-robed body.

Hesperian rose, and walked over to the corpse. "A Viper Knight, Sire," one of the guards said. "Drakaren's most elite warriors."

"I know what a Viper Knight is, fool," Hesperian snapped. "What is one doing in my apartments?"

"Delivering this," Claire said. She speared the snake's body with her sword, and held it up. "See the black swirls on the skin? This looks like a Blackwatch Adder. Very poisonous. And very rare. They're found only on Blackwatch Mountain in Keldaren."

"And why would Minerva want to poison me?" Hesperian asked.

"Isn't it obvious? You'd be found dead, next to a snake from Keldaren. If you had allied with us, the suspicions raised by this would break the alliance. And if you had refused to help us, it would look as if a Keldari had killed you for refusing. Either way, it would turn Keldaren and Hynbarra against each other," Claire said.

"And guarantee that Hynbarra doesn't interfere with Minerva's plans."

"Exactly," Claire said. "Now do you see a deeper plot here?"

"I do. I believe I will join your war against Drakaren after all. I'll send an army to Tara right away," Hesperian said.

There was a clatter of steel at the door, and a squad of Hynbarran soldiers rushed inside, halberds at the ready. Kerry and Ross followed them.

"What happened here?" Ross asked.

"A Viper Knight," Kerry said, staring at the black-clad corpse. "Are you all right, Claire?"

"I'm fine," Claire said. "He came for the prince."

"I've changed my mind," Hesperian told Ross. "I'm sending troops to help Keldaren fight Minerva."

"Then send me as well," Ross said. He turned to Claire. "I won't let you stand alone against Drakaren. I'll lead the Hynbarran army myself." He looked into her eyes, flashing his perfect white smile.

CHAPTER 29

Claire

The next morning, Claire and Kerry met Sloane at the parade ground, where the dragons had spent the night. "Back to Tara, Your Majesty?" Sloane asked.

"Not yet. Have you ever heard of the Merosians?"

Sloane nodded. "One of the First Races. I've passed over their domain on scouting flights."

"Good. You can lead us there. I want to meet with their leader, and ask them to fight Minerva alongside us," Claire said.

"Are you sure that's wise?" Sloane asked. "We know so little about them. No one from Keldaren had any contact with them even before the Drakari invaded their lands. There's no way of telling where their loyalties lie."

"I've heard the Drakari keep them enslaved. That should tell us something of their loyalties," Claire said.

"They keep them captive, to be sure. The Merosian Domain is surrounded by Drakari guard towers. But that doesn't mean there aren't some Merosians loyal to Drakaren," Sloane said.

"That's a risk we'll have to take," Claire said. "We need all the allies we can get."

"The towers are a problem, though," Sloane pointed out. "If we fly into Merosia, the Drakari will see us."

"What if we go at night?"

Sloane thought for a moment. "On a cloudy night, it might work. The watchtowers are only stationed along the borders of the Merosian Domain. But there is a Drakari fortress near Miral, the Merosian village. If we stay up high until we're right above Miral, we might be able to avoid being seen. We can only take one dragon, though. Any more, and we'd surely be spotted."

"We'll take Breaus, and leave the other knights and dragons in Keldaren just before we cross the border," Claire said. "Kerry, I'm afraid I'll have to leave you with them. I need Sloane to show me the way to Miral."

"Sean did tell you to seek out the Merosians. But going so deep into Drakaren without guards is a bad idea. A *very* bad idea," Kerry said.

"I'm a Dragon Knight. I go where duty takes me. No matter the danger. Besides, not even a hundred guards could protect me if we were discovered there."

"I suppose you're right about that," Kerry said.

Hoof beats came from behind them, and Claire turned. Hesperian and Ross rode up to the fort, along with an escort of Hynbarran soldiers.

"We came to bid you farewell," Hesperian called out to her.

"I'm honored, Your Highness," Claire said. "But you needn't have ridden all the way here just to see me off."

"I owe you my life. Seeing you off was the least I could do. And my son wished to speak to you."

Ross slid down from his horse, and walked over to Claire. "I was hoping to travel with you to Tara. Father is sending

General Ecca to march our army to Keldaren, and if I fly with you, I can meet our troops in Tara when they arrive. That way, we'll have some time together before we go off to war. To discuss battle strategies…and other things," he said with a smile.

The morning light seemed to highlight him, making his hair shine like a field of golden wheat, and his eyes sparkle like jades. Claire opened her mouth to say yes.

"I'm sorry," Kerry said, "but there's no room on the dragons, Your Highness."

"I see. Well, I'll see you when I reach Tara, then?" he asked.

Claire smiled. "I'm looking forward to it."

He smiled back. "As am I," he said, mounting his horse.

"Good luck, Your Majesty," Hesperian said. He spurred his horse, and rode away. Ross rode after him, turning back to wave before he disappeared around the corner.

Claire turned on Kerry. "Why were you so rude to Ross?"

"I'm sorry, Claire. I know it wasn't my place. There's something about him I don't trust. I can't put my finger on it, but there's something…wrong about him. My instincts told me to keep him from coming with us. And in the Crown Guard, you learn to trust your instincts."

"He seems trustworthy enough to me, Kerry. And he's the son of an important ally. Next time, be more diplomatic." They climbed up onto the dragons, and were soon flying off to the west.

It was dusk by the time they reached Keldaren's western border. They landed by a stand of trees, and Kerry dismounted to help the knights set up camp. Sloane swung up into the saddle behind Claire, and then they were airborne again, crossing over into Drakaren.

A cloudless night had fallen by the time Lake Merosia appeared on the horizon. They flew high above the lake, until Sloane pointed out Miral along its shore. Claire nudged Breaus, gesturing to the village. He nodded, and dove toward it. Claire's stomach leapt into her throat. Just before they hit the ground, Breaus pulled up, spreading his wings to catch the air. He landed hard just outside the village, his body shaking with the impact as they touched down.

Claire and Sloane climbed off him, and Claire removed her helmet. A faint scent of fish hung in the air. The lanes between the mud huts were dark, but a distant light glimmered in one of the alleys, and Claire dropped her hand to her sword. Two figures came hurrying around the corner. One held a lantern. Both carried harpoons. The first raised the lantern, and his face came into view.

By the nether, Claire thought, recoiling. The creature's skin was a shiny lime-green, with a fin-like crest atop his hairless head. His lips were thick, and his eyes bulged in their sockets. Webbed fingers held the lantern and harpoon. The other creature looked much the same, except that his skin was a darker shade of green. Both Merosians wore simple brown tunics that left their legs and feet bare. The fish smell was even stronger now.

"You don't look like Drakari," one of the Merosians said, in a low, gurgling voice.

"We aren't. I'm Queen Claire of Keldaren. I came to speak with your leader."

The Merosians looked at each other. "Send them away," the second one said. "If the Drakari find out they've been here…"

The first Merosian looked at Claire again. "No. We have to bring them to the Archon. He will decide what to do with them. Follow me," he said, motioning with his harpoon. Claire gestured for Breaus to wait. They turned, and followed the Merosian through the narrow lanes between the thatched-roof huts. Two more Merosians stood watch by the lakeshore, harpoons in hand.

"I see you station sentries," Claire said. "Are they watching for the Drakari?"

The Merosian shook his head. "Quellcrabs come ashore sometimes at night, looking for food."

"You post guards against a crab?" Sloane asked.

"A Quellcrab is as big as a horse," the Merosian said. "We lose several guards each year to them."

They turned a corner, and came to the center of the village. A large, round building rose in the middle of a grassy square. Like the huts, it was built of mud and sticks, but on a much larger scale. "This is the Merhall," the first Merosian said. "The residence of our Archon, and the seat of our assembly. The Drakari Viceroy leaves us with some trappings of independence."

A pair of Merosians stood watch at the door. They shrank back at the sight of Claire and Sloane. "It's all right," the

Merosian with the lantern said. "They're Keldari. They want to speak to the Archon."

"He's with his son," one of the guards said. "Wait here." He went inside, and returned a few moments later, gesturing for them to follow.

Inside, they passed through a large hall, and into a sitting room. A thin Merosian sat in a chair next to a brazier, his long legs crossed in front of him. His skin was baggy and faded, and his shoulders were stooped with age. His tunic was crimson, instead of the drab brown the other Merosians wore. A slender crown of polished red coral rested atop his head.

A younger Merosian sat nearby, staring at them with narrowed eyes. "Archon," the guard said, "the visitors from Keldaren."

"I am Jeral," the old Merosian said. "Archon of the Merosians. Who are you?"

"I'm Claire, Queen of Keldaren. This is Dame Sloane."

"What are you doing here?" the younger Merosian growled. "We'll all suffer if the Drakari learn we've spoken with you."

"This is my son, Panga. Who will hold his peace from now on," Jeral said, giving him a sharp look. "But the question is fair. Why have you come here?"

"We're here to ask for your help in fighting the Drakari."

"Our help. Do you know what we are here? Slaves. The Drakari hold us prisoner in our own lands. They force us to fish for them in peacetime, and to fight for them when they go to war.

The Drakari have utterly conquered us. We're in no position to help you fight them," Jeral said.

"I know the cost of war can be terrible. Especially when you've already lost so much. But we're fighting to remove Minerva from her throne, and after she's gone, I promise you Merosia will be free again. Isn't your freedom worth the price?" Claire asked.

"The price?" Jeral's laugh was grim. "You don't understand the price. You haven't had the education we have in the cost of defying the Drakari. When King Azeras came to conquer us, we fought a long and bloody battle against him on the land. A war he won. We retreated into the lake, and we were safe there for a few weeks. We thought they couldn't reach us underwater."

"You lived underwater?" Claire asked.

Jeral nodded. "We can breathe water just as well as air. We thought all we had to do was wait them out. We were wrong. They poisoned the lake. You have to understand, that lake is our life. We hunt the fish, and eels, the crabs and the sharks. We even farm the seaweed. When the Drakari dumped their poison into the water, everything began to die. When even our people started getting sick, we surrendered. From that day since, we've been slaves."

"It took a decade for the lake to recover from the poison. Most of those years, we starved. But even after we had enough food again, we were still hungry for freedom. So we rose up against the Drakari. Several times, in fact. All of our rebellions failed. And many Merosians died afterwards," Jeral said.

"The Drakari executed the rebels?" Sloane asked.

"At first they killed rebels. But that only increased the uprisings. The Drakari realized they were creating martyrs. So they stopped executing rebels. And they started executing our children instead."

Claire gasped. "Your children?"

"Every time a Merosian rebels against the Drakari, they behead some of our children. They torture the rebel first, and then force them to watch the beheading," Jeral said.

"That's hideous," Claire said, nausea curdling in her stomach.

"Hideous, but brilliant," Panga said. "They choose the children at random, by drawing lots. No parent ever knows if their child will be chosen. So this turns all parents against any acts of rebellion. Most parents inform on rebels, rather than face the possibility of their child being killed. It turns us against each other. And it's almost totally effective at keeping us under control."

"Once you see a child murdered for something you've done, you lose all stomach for rebellion," Jeral said, bitterness sharp in his voice. "Fifteen years ago, I tried to slip across the border and meet with an ally to plan an uprising against the Drakari. But they caught me. Thankfully, the Drakari thought I was just trying to escape, and never realized what I really intended."

Jeral sighed. "But they still whipped me half to death. Then they made me watch as they killed five children. I still see those five little heads falling. I never *stop* seeing them. That's the price of defying the Drakari, Queen Claire. Five little heads."

"I'm sorry," Claire said. "I had no idea."

"I'm sure you didn't," Panga said. "Why would any outlander know anything about our suffering? And why would any outlander care? Now, it's time for you to be gone before the Drakari discover you."

"I haven't refused them yet, Panga," Jeral said quietly.

"If the Drakari ever find out we even talked about a rebellion, they'll kill five hundred children. Not five. Five hundred," Panga said.

"Only if we fail. A country the size of Keldaren offering to help us…that changes things."

"They aren't offering us help! They want us to fight for them. They're no different than the Drakari," Panga snarled.

"We're asking you to fight alongside us, not for us," Claire said. "And whether you help us or not, I will make sure Merosia is set free after Minerva is defeated. But the Drakari greatly outnumber us. Your help might make the difference in defeating them."

A guard burst into the room. "Archon, Ineris is coming!"

Panga cursed. "He must know they're here!"

"I don't know what else would bring him out at night. How much time do we have?" Jeral asked the guard.

"The watchers said he just left the fortress. It's a half-hour ride."

"We have to hide them," Jeral said.

"Who's Ineris?" Claire demanded.

"The Drakari viceroy," Jeral said. "Even if they saw you arriving, it will go worse for us if they find you here. If you're hidden, we can claim to have never seen you. But where to put you?"

"The roof," Sloane suggested. "We can hide under the thatching."

"But what about Breaus?" Claire asked.

Jeral looked confused. "Who is Breaus?"

"The dragon that brought us here," Claire told him. "He's waiting on the outskirts of the village."

Panga slammed a hand against the arm of his chair. "We'll never be able to hide a dragon! Our children's blood will be on your hands, outlander!"

"Be quiet, Panga," Jeral said. "The lake. Have your dragon hide there. There are reefs a short distance from shore. He can submerge himself there, and keep his head above water so it looks like part of the reef."

Claire rushed out, and sent Breaus hurrying into the lake. One of the Merosians fetched a ladder, and Claire and Sloane climbed up to the roof of the Merhall. They covered themselves with piles of straw, leaving small gaps to see through.

Panga helped Jeral outside as five horsemen rode up to the village. Four of them wore gray uniforms. The last rider was clothed in silk, and had the black, gold-trimmed cape of a Drakari noble draped across his shoulders. A contingent of Berserkers marched behind the horses.

The riders entered the plaza, and reined in their horses at the Merhall. The nobleman leaned down from his saddle. "Jeral," he said, a sneer echoing in his voice.

"Lord Ineris," Jeral said, bowing stiffly.

"I've just received a pigeon from Graydare. Queen Minerva has ordered me to summon the Merosians to do their duty for Drakaren. You will have all your men assembled here by sunset tomorrow, ready to march to Graydare."

"As my lord commands."

"I'll return tomorrow. I trust I needn't explain the consequences if you aren't ready to march." Ineris turned his horse, and the Drakari riders followed him out of the village. The Berserkers marched after them, their wary eyes watching the Merosians as they went.

After the Drakari were out of sight, one Merosian brought the ladder, while another went to fetch Breaus. Claire and Sloane climbed down, and joined Jeral and Panga.

"So, they're sending us to Drakaren," Jeral said. "To defend Graydare from you, I would assume?"

"Yes. I'm sure they expect our invasion," Claire said.

"Well, you have your answer, then. We can't help you. We must fight you instead. I'm afraid that when we next meet, it will be in battle. They'll send us ahead to soften up your lines for their troops."

"They use you as skirmishers, then?" Claire asked.

"Yes. To bear the brunt of the initial clash. Once we wear down the enemy, the Drakari soldiers charge, and the battle is truly joined."

"Then you can help us after all. When you charge, stop short before you meet our steel. I'll have my troops break ranks, and you can step between our lines to join us."

"Then the Drakari will kill *all* our children. The women too. And burn Miral. Our entire people will be destroyed," Panga said.

"Only if Minerva wins. With your help, we can defeat her. Your men are going to war no matter what, Jeral. And some will die. Wouldn't you rather they fall fighting for their freedom, instead of fighting for the people who keep you enslaved?" Claire asked.

"I would," Jeral said. "But do you understand what you're asking me to risk?"

"Yes. Do you understand what you'd be risking it for?"

"Father, I can't believe you're even listening to her!" Panga growled. "Think of my children. Your grandchildren. Is this outlander queen worth risking their lives for?"

"No. But freedom might be." Jeral turned back to Claire. "I will consider what you've said, Queen Claire. I'll consider it carefully. And I'll make my decision by the time we meet you on the battlefield."

"How will we know whether you'll be friend or foe?" Sloane asked.

"We'll have to arrange some sort of signal."

"Will you be leading the Merosian troops?" Claire asked.

"Ineris will keep me with him behind the lines. If we turn against the Drakari, I'll be the first to die. But I won't die quickly," Jeral said, grimacing.

That stopped Claire short. "Jeral, I'm sorry...I didn't realize..."

He shook his head. "What happens to me isn't important. What happens to Merosia is."

Breaus came up from the lake, dripping and glowering. Claire went to him, and scratched his scales to calm him. She took her helmet from its fastening on the saddle. Reaching inside it, she pulled out the black cloth that padded the helmet. She wrung the lake water from the cloth, and handed it to Jeral. "If you decide to join us, have one of your warriors in the front lines tie this to his harpoon. If we see the cloth, we'll know to let you pass between our ranks. If we don't see it...we'll know we have to fight you."

Jeral took the cloth. "I can't guarantee you anything."

"I know."

"I can tell you one thing. We aren't the only people enslaved by the Drakari. The Graithans would be happy to join you in fighting Minerva."

"I've never heard of them," Claire said.

"They're humans, like you. They dwell in the great desert to the south. They lived in seclusion there until the Drakari learned of the Graithans' gold."

"Their gold?"

"Their capital, Garat, lies between three mountains. One of those mountains holds the richest gold mines in all Eris. Ever since the Drakari conquered the Graithans, they've used them as slaves to mine the gold."

"And do the Drakari use the Graithans as soldiers?" Claire asked.

Jeral shook his head. "They trust the Graithans even less than they trust us. They wouldn't let a Graithan anywhere near a weapon."

"Why?"

"The Graithans were never truly defeated. When Garat fell, their Emir escaped, along with many of their warriors. They've been living in hiding ever since, waging a rebellion against the Drakari."

"How is it the Drakari haven't destroyed them yet?" Sloane asked.

"The Graithans know the desert. The Drakari never could adapt to it like they have. The Drakari hide behind the walls of Garat. When they dare to venture out, the Graithan rebels appear out of nowhere to attack them, and then vanish back into the sands. They also attack the mines, steal gold, and free slaves. The Graithan rebels call themselves Raiders. And they live up to their name."

"How do you know of this rebellion of theirs?" Claire asked.

"Fifteen years ago, Faran, the Graithan Emir, had a letter smuggled to me. He proposed that our peoples join forces to fight

Drakaren. I was trying to leave Merosia to meet with him when I was captured. That was when the Drakari…punished me."

Jeral squatted down, drawing a crude map in the dirt. "Fly southwest, until you come to a single mountain beside an oasis. That is Mount Ziggurat. I was supposed to meet Faran there. That's all I can tell you, I'm afraid. After the Drakari caught me, I never tried to leave Merosia again. And Faran never tried to contact me after that. I've heard the Raiders are still fighting the Drakari. Other than that, I know nothing more about them."

"Thank you, Jeral. Your people will be free. I promise you that," Claire said.

"But only if we help you."

"No. They'll be free at the end of this war, whether you help us or not. But when you reach Graydare, you'll have to choose what your people fight for—for freedom, or for Minerva." Claire turned, and swung up into the saddle. Sloane followed her, and then Breaus' wings pulled them up into the air.

Dawn was breaking when they crossed back into Keldaren. Breaus landed at the knights' camp, and Sloane and Claire slid down from the saddle. "You should have told him we would only free the Merosians if they help us," Sloane said.

"I believe he'll make the right decision. He seems like an honorable man. And he wants freedom for his people."

"You heard what he said. If they join us, Jeral will die. The Merosians have been beaten down by decades of slavery.

They won't risk defying their masters. Worse, they might fly that cloth, and then still attack us when our troops step aside to let them join our ranks," Sloane said.

"Why would they do that?" Claire asked.

"If they take us by surprise, they'll lose fewer men. They would kill many of our troops, and that would win them favor with the Drakari."

"I can't believe slaves would be that loyal," Claire said.

"A beaten dog will still come running when its master calls. These Merosians are beaten dogs, Your Majesty. You can see it in their eyes. Threats are the only thing that will move them."

"We're not the Drakari. The Merosians have been threatened enough. And gaining them as an ally would be worth the risk. We'll have to trust that they make the right choice," Claire said.

"As you wish. I suggest we get a few hours of sleep before we leave for the desert."

Hours later, they were in the air again, crossing over the flashing expanse of the Silver Sea. Eventually, a khaki-colored haze came into view on the horizon. As they flew closer, the haze turned into a vast stretch of sand. They crossed over the shore, and the warm, sea-scented breeze died away. The formation of dragons flew into a cloud of hot, dry air hanging like a shroud over the blowing sands.

The air burns like the netherworld, Claire thought, as Breaus' wings churned steadily through the parched sky. A craggy peak eventually appeared on the horizon. Next to the mountain, a blue pool shimmered like a gemstone amidst a green swath of palm trees.

Claire gestured to Breaus, and he descended toward the oasis. As they flew lower, the waves of heat intensified. Breaus landed gingerly near the edge of the palm trees, the other dragons following him down. Claire slid down from the saddle, the sand's heat baking up through the soles of her boots.

The other knights dismounted also, and they all went over to the pool. The ground next to the water was cooler, at least, than the sands surrounding the oasis. "There's no sign of any people," Claire said.

"We should search the mountain for these Raiders," Kerry suggested. "If they are here, they're likely hidden."

"Jeral was supposed to meet them years ago. They may have moved on since," Sloane pointed out.

"We'll spread out and search around the mountain. Go in groups of two," Claire ordered the knights. The knights all paired off and started out. Kerry and Claire set off together around the mountain.

The swirling sands and scorching wind of the open desert enveloped them as soon as they left the shelter of the palm trees. The sand burned at their boots as they walked. Only a few minutes had passed before dragon roars sounded from the oasis.

CHAPTER 30

Claire

Claire and Kerry drew their swords and raced back. The dragons had formed a snarling circle, surrounding a group of white tigers along the shore of the pool. The huge tigers stood their ground—their lips curled back to show their teeth, their eyes wild and angry. The tigers were as tall as a horse, and a rider sat astride each one.

The riders wore white robes, with headscarves twisted over their faces, leaving only their eyes visible. Scabbards hung from their cloth belts. Each rider pointed a curved scimitar at the Keldari.

"They appeared out of nowhere!" Breaus growled.

"They're dripping wet," Kerry said. "There's only one place they could have come from."

Claire stepped forward, her sword at the ready. "Who are you? What do you want?"

The lead tiger growled at her. "First tell me who you are. And why you're trespassing here," its rider demanded.

"I'm Claire, Queen of Keldaren. I'm looking for Faran, the Graithan Emir."

The rider sheathed his scimitar and dismounted, walking toward Claire. "Faran is no longer with us. I'm Emir now." The rider pulled the scarf aside, revealing his face.

Her face, Claire realized. *A woman.* Her jet-black hair was pulled back under the headscarf, and her eyes were the same shade of light brown as her skin.

"My name is Azaira. Faran was my father. I've led our people since he died in battle. What business did you have with him?"

"The Merosian Archon told me your people are fighting the Drakari. I'm gathering allies for an invasion of Drakaren. I came to ask for your help," Claire said.

"Our help? Where were you when the Drakari invaded Graitha? Where have you been for the decades my people have been enslaved? We never had any help from Keldaren when we needed it."

"We never even knew your people existed until Jeral told me about you. You're already fighting the Drakari. Join us. Together, we can defeat them. After we depose Minerva, I promise that your people will be free again," Claire said.

"No one wants to see Minerva gone more than I do. But we won't leave our homeland until it's free. A war will take months, if not longer. With the Raiders gone, the Drakari would have free run of the Graithan Desert. Our raids are all that keep the Drakari trapped behind Garat's walls. I'm sorry. We can't leave to help you."

Claire thought for a moment. "The Drakari are only in Garat? They have no other fortresses in your lands?"

"No. They hold only our capital," Azaira said.

"What if we were to help you take Garat back from them? Would you join us then?"

Azaira frowned. "I'm sure your fighters are skilled. But I see only nine of you. The garrison in Garat is small enough, to be sure. In fact, my Raiders outnumber the Drakari soldiers there. But the city walls are stone, and built high. We have no siege engines or rams to bring them down, and nowhere near enough fighters to breach the gates. Nine Keldari knights won't make much of a difference, I'm afraid."

"But if you got inside the city…could you take it then?"

"Yes. But I told you, there's no way through the walls," Azaira said.

"Not through them. Over them. We have dragons."

"And you could open the gates for us from within. A bold plan. But there are enough Drakari in Garat to keep you from reaching the gates. As soon as the sentries saw your dragons landing, they would sound the alarm, and the entire garrison would turn out."

"The dragons would never touch down," Claire said. "They'll fly us high over the city at night. We'll use sky sails to land within the walls."

"Sky sails?"

"Sails sewn out of steelsilk that a Dragon Knight wears tied to their back," Claire explained. "The knight jumps from their dragon in mid-air, releases the sail, and it catches the air like a wing. The knight floats down to the ground on the sail. They're dyed black, so they're next to invisible at night," Claire said.

Azaira looked thoughtful. "It might work. Let's go in and discuss it."

"In? In where?"

"The mountain, of course. It's been our home since my grandfather fled Garat."

"We couldn't find an entrance," Claire said.

"I wouldn't think so," Azaira said, smiling. "The Drakari have searched this mountain many times, and they've never found it." She went to her tiger, and swung up onto its back. "Follow us. Don't forget to hold your breath."

Azaira nudged the tiger, and it turned toward the pool. Its paws splashed into the water. Then it dove, disappearing into the blue depths. The other Graithans and their tigers followed.

"What should we do?" Kerry asked.

"Follow them." Claire swung up into the saddle atop Breaus' back. Kerry and the knights mounted up as well, and Breaus walked to the edge of the pool. He growled deep in his throat as the water welled up around his feet.

"Go on," Claire said. "But pull up if it gets too deep," she added quietly. Breaus plunged in. Cool wetness swallowed her boots, and then rose to her chest. She took a deep breath as the water came rushing over her, covering her head.

The walls of the pool were rough rock. There was an overhang on one wall, shielding a tunnel from view. Breaus swam for what seemed an eternity, pulling hard through the water with his wings. He swam into the tunnel, and when a glimmer of light appeared above them, he streaked upward.

They shot to the surface. Claire and Breaus both gasped air back into their lungs. They were floating in a river that flowed through an underground tunnel. Lamps hanging from the ceiling cast a flickering light down over them. The Graithans and their tigers waited on a rocky ledge beside the river. Behind them, a huge passage gaped in the wall of the tunnel.

Breaus swam to the ledge, and clambered up onto it, as the other dragons surfaced behind him. "You could have warned us how far a swim that was," Claire told Azaira, who stood next to her tiger, wringing the water from her hair.

"That's what makes this such an excellent hiding place. We train ourselves to swim long distances underwater. Anyone other than a Raider would have a hard time reaching these caverns."

"And how do you teach a tiger to swim?" Claire asked.

Azaira laughed. "It's more like they teach us. These are Sea Tigers, from the southern coast. There's no game big enough to sustain them in this desert, so they hunt fish instead. They start swimming when they're a few weeks old. Come," she said, gesturing for them to follow.

They walked through the opening in the wall, into a huge chamber. "Your dragons can rest here," Azaira said. "I'll have food brought for them."

"Get some rest," Claire told Breaus. "I'll be back soon." They went into the next chamber, where the tigers ambled off into lairs carved into the rock.

The air was blessedly cool in the tunnels, but was still as arid as the desert winds outside. "Don't worry about your clothes and armor. They'll dry quickly enough," Azaira said, leading them deeper into the mountain. They came to a room furnished with a long, low table, with pillows set on the ground beside it. Hanging oil lamps lit the room.

"Please," Azaira said, gesturing for them to sit. Claire found a place on one of the pillows, as servants appeared with trays of honey-soaked pastries. Azaira spoke to one of the servants, who went out. He returned with a rolled-up tapestry, and spread it on the table.

"This is a map of Garat. It's one of the few things my grandfather was able to take with him when he fled the Drakari invasion." Azaira pointed to the image of a large building. "This is the Emir's palace. It's the tallest building in Garat, and it has a large, flat roof. We know from our spies in the city that the palace's lower floors are guarded, but the roof isn't."

"A good place to land," Claire observed.

"Exactly. And the city's north gate is nearby. But most importantly, Xithrac, the Drakari viceroy, is there. If he escapes, he could rally the garrison. But if we capture him, the battle will be over quickly."

Claire nodded. "And where will he be in the palace?"

"The Emir's apartments are on the north side of the top floor. That's where you'll find him."

"Good. We'll attack tonight."

"We'll ride out and wait by the mountains," Azaira said. "Wave a torch when the gate is open."

"Kerry, you've never trained with a sky sail. I'll have you ride with Azaira," Claire told her. "We should all get some sleep. We have a long night ahead of us."

A thick sea of clouds hid the moon and stars. Claire turned in the saddle to look back at the outlines of the dragons following them. Breaus rumbled when three mountains appeared on the horizon. Claire reached behind her, checking the bundled silk tied tightly to her back. They flew between the mountains, and Garat appeared below.

Breaus turned to circle over the city. Claire swallowed. *We weren't nearly this high on the training jump*, she thought. Then she smiled. *The ground's no softer from a thousand feet than it is from three times higher.* She pulled her feet out from the saddle's stirrups, and tugged the release rope. The sky sail caught the air, unfurling with a snap. The canopy yanked back the steelsilk cords sewn to her vest, and jerked Claire from the saddle.

She freed the control ropes from their ties, and pulled to the left, curving the sky sail toward the northern walls of Garat. The dark outlines of more sails bloomed above her. The wind blew fiercely, and Claire concentrated on steering toward the palace below.

The roof came rushing up at her, and she bent her knees, bracing for the impact. She landed with a jolt, and undid the fastenings of the vest she wore over her armor. The other knights landed around her and freed themselves from their sails. Claire loosed a coil of rope and a hook from her belt, and went to the edge of the roof.

Sloane and the other knights followed her as she set the hook and wrapped the rope around herself. Claire tightened the rope, and rappelled down the wall. She stopped on a ledge beside a set of tall windows. Claire drew her dagger, and wedged it between a window and the frame. She gently pushed, until the latch broke with a soft snap. She opened the window and slipped into an ornate bedchamber.

A fire burned on the hearth, casting a flickering light over the room. A huge canopy bed stood against the far wall, its gilded pillars glistening in the firelight. The other knights slipped into the room behind her as Claire drew her sword and crept to the bed. Sloane came up next to her, reaching out to pull back the bedcovers.

A heavy, broad-shouldered man lay asleep in the bed, his arms wrapped around a pillow. Claire brushed his cheek with the tip of her sword. The man shifted, mumbling in his sleep. His eyes stayed shut. Claire laid the sword point against the man's cheek, and pressed. A single drop of blood reddened her steel. The man gasped, and his eyes flew open.

"Lord Xithrac," Claire said.

"Who are you? What do you want?" Xithrac muttered, his voice thick with sleep.

"I'm the Queen of Keldaren. And I want you to get up. The Graithan Emir would like a few words with you."

Xithrac's eyes moved from Claire to Sloane, and then to the other Dragon Knights.

"Get up. Now," Sloane said, gesturing with her sword.

"Of course," he said, stretching his arms under the pillow. "Just let me shake the sleep from my head first."

"Enough stalling," Claire said. "Move."

He moved. Xithrac jerked a fist out from under the pillow, steel flashing in his grip.

CHAPTER 31

Claire

Claire swung instinctively, the tip of her sword stabbing into Xithrac's arm. Sloane was faster. Her blade smashed through his throat, pinning Xithrac to the bed. Xithrac gave a gurgling cry as a flood of red spread across the linen sheets. The knife dropped from his hand, clattering to the floor.

Claire pulled her sword free. "Let's go." They went back to the window, and grasped the ropes, rappelling to the ground. The other knights took cover behind a corner of the palace, while Claire leaned out to look at the gate. A squad of Drakari soldiers was gathered around a fire next to the guardhouse. Three of them were talking, while the other two snored in their bedrolls.

Claire ducked back behind the wall, and gestured to the knights. Rows of mesquite and chaparral were planted between the palace and the city walls, forming a desert garden. Claire started crawling behind the bushes toward the gate. Sloane and the other knights followed. When they drew close to the Drakari, Claire slipped her dagger from its sheath. She rose, and burst silently out from the brush.

There were quiet footfalls behind her as the knights followed her charge. Claire grabbed the nearest Drakari. She clamped a hand over his mouth, sinking her dagger into his throat.

Claire glanced into his eyes. They were glazed with shock and fear.

Her stomach churned. It was one thing to fight blade to blade with an enemy, but sneaking up on one like this, and holding him down as he died…that felt more like murder than war. *It is war, though*, she reminded herself. Claire held his gaze until his eyes went blank, and he slumped over in her arms.

Claire lowered the soldier's body to the ground. The knights had finished off the remaining Drakari, and she gestured for them to open the gate. Then she lit the end of a stick in the fire. She carried the torch to the gate, and waved it back and forth. A cloud rose up behind a mountain to the north. The cloud drew closer, carrying with it the sound of hundreds of paws thumping against the sand. Bursts of flame erupted high above Garat as the dragons answered her signal. Dark wings soared down toward the city, flames streaking along behind them.

Dawn revealed the red stains on the sand in Garat's streets. Drakari survivors sat huddled behind the bars of the former slave barracks, while freed Graithans filled the city with the sounds of shouting and laughter. Many gathered in the square in front of the Emir's palace, hugging and cheering the white-robed Raiders.

Claire stood with Azaira on the portico of the palace, watching the celebration. "It's been many decades since Garat heard laughter. I can never thank you enough for my people's freedom," Azaira said.

"Your help against Minerva is all the thanks I need," Claire said.

"You'll have it. We'll make sure the Drakari can never enslave anyone again."

A roar went up from the crowd. Graithans pointed to the roof of the palace, cheering wildly. Claire and Azaira went down the steps, and turned to see two Raiders hauling the Drakari flag down from the roof. In its place, the Raiders raised a white pennant bearing the image of a golden fox. The Graithans in the square erupted in applause.

"Our flag," Azaira explained.

"Why the gold fox?" Claire asked.

"My people left Edera as yours did, fleeing the Nazra invasion. They came ashore in the south of Graitha. It was a land like their old home in Edera, so they abandoned their ships and journeyed through the desert, in search of an oasis where they could build a city."

"But after several days of traveling, a sandstorm hit them. When the storm cleared, they were lost in the desert. My ancestor, who was named Graitha, went out searching for water, and saw a sand fox. Seeing a sand fox is a rare event. Their fur blends in with the sand, and makes them almost invisible in the desert. The only reason he saw this fox was the streaks of gold in its fur," Azaira said.

"Gold?"

Azaira nodded. "He followed the fox, hoping it would lead him to water. And it did. The fox had a den in the caverns beneath

Mount Arel, where the gold mines are now. It had picked up gold dust in its fur from the caverns. The fox led him here, to the site where Garat stands today. Graitha found a spring here, and led my people to it. The people made Graitha our first Emir, and named the nation after him."

"Your people were lucky there was a spring here," Claire said.

"It's not really a spring. Just a place where the Deral River surfaces."

"The Deral? The Deral River is Drakaren. It flows north from Lake Merosia. This can't be the Deral," Claire said.

"That's just the north branch of the river. This is the South Deral. It flows down from Lake Merosia through underground caverns. Then it turns, and runs to meet the north branch at Toldan. It's the same river you swam through to get into Mount Ziggurat."

"And it flows all the way to Toldan?" Claire asked.

Azaira nodded. "There's a Drakari castle on the outskirts of Toldan. The river emerges from a cave in the hill the castle is built on. It actually flows right through the castle's lower levels before it reaches the cave. That's how the Drakari managed to keep Garat supplied with food, since we raid all the convoys that try to cross the desert. Our spies tell us the Drakari sent supplies on the river from Toldan by raft."

"If the river flows north, how did they send rafts south to Garat?"

"There are paths carved into the side of the river caverns. Donkeys walk the paths, pulling the rafts upstream. Then they load the rafts with gold to ship back downstream," Azaira said.

"If this river connects to the oasis at Mount Ziggurat, why couldn't your Raiders just float down it into Garat?"

"The caverns carrying that portion of the river are too shallow, and the water fills them completely. The caverns between Garat and Toldan have higher ceilings, with plenty of room for a raft."

"The castle that it flows through—would that be Darcann?" Claire asked.

"I believe that is what the Drakari call it. Why?"

"We're headed there next. Minerva is holding someone prisoner there. Someone we need to free. Can we get there by raft?"

"We took the city before the garrison had a chance to send any pigeons, so the Drakari won't know Garat has been liberated. They certainly won't be expecting Keldari and Graithans to come down the river. Yes. We can get you there," Azaira said.

Brianna

Brianna Graydare sat on the floor of her cell, staring at the dim light seeping underneath the door. Footsteps and the clank of armor echoed through the hall. Brianna shuddered. *They're coming for someone.* It was a daily occurrence in the cell blocks.

The lucky ones were taken off to be executed. The unlucky ones were brought to the torture chambers, and then returned to the longer, slower torture of existence in the cells.

The footsteps stopped outside her door. *Oh gods, no,* Brianna thought. The stripes on her back had just barely healed from Minerva's last visit to Darcann. "Open it," a muffled voice came from outside. A woman's voice. *She's back.* Terror seemed to squeeze the air from Brianna's lungs.

A key clattered in the lock, and the door swung open. Torches blazed in the hallway, and Brianna raised a hand to her eyes. An armored figure stepped into the cell. Brianna squinted into the dazzling light of the torches. *That's not Drakari armor.*

"What is this?" Brianna demanded.

The warrior stepped forward, reaching up to remove his helmet.

Her helmet, Brianna realized, as an auburn braid came into view. Green eyes stared out at her from the woman's freckled face. A slim circlet of gold rested atop her head.

"Freedom," the stranger said.

CHAPTER 32

Claire

The cloud of smoke hung low over Tara. Row after row of army tents crowded the fields outside the city walls. The smoke from their campfires rose, mingling in the air to form a black veil shrouding the city. The dragons entered the cloud, smoke roiling and churning under their wings.

They passed over Tara, and Breaus landed in the outer courtyard of Connemara Palace. Shanra, carrying Sloane and Brianna, landed next to him, while the other dragons flew on.

"I'll fly back with them to Mount Draconis," Breaus rumbled, nodding at the other dragons.

"Must you?" Claire asked.

"There are younger dragons there, just joining the order, who weren't at the Spearcrags. They haven't been blooded in battle yet, and we'll be at war in a matter of weeks. I have to make sure they're ready."

"Does no one train the new dragons?"

"Of course. But I test them," Breaus said.

"Like you and Sloane tested me. I never thanked you for that, Breaus."

"We were hard on you."

"That's what I'm thankful for. You made sure I was ready," Claire said.

Breaus leaned down to touch noses with her, his scales hot and smooth against her skin. "It was an honor to train you. And it will be an honor to carry you to victory when I return." He lifted his wings, and leapt into the sky, sending a flurry of air gusting down around her. Shanra followed him up.

"I have some things to attend to, Brianna," Claire said. "But after that, we'll talk more."

"As you wish, Your Majesty," Brianna said.

"Escort the princess to a guest room, Sloane," Claire told her. Sloane nodded, and led Brianna off.

A Crown Guard met them at the palace stairs.

"Is all well, Eloc?" Kerry asked.

"Yes, my lady. The palace and the Regent are secure. Your Majesty," he said, bowing to Claire. "It's good to see you back in Tara."

"Thank you, Legate. How is my cousin?"

"Princess Elsie has adjusted to being Regent, Your Majesty. But I think she'll be quite relieved to see you back in Tara."

"I can't stay long, I'm afraid. I'll be leaving for Drakaren now that the legions are here. Have the Hynbarrans and Kirosians arrived?"

"Yes, Your Majesty. Their generals presented themselves to the Regent a few days ago."

"Summon them at once," Claire ordered.

Eloc nodded, and hurried off.

Claire and Kerry found Elsie in the throne room. "Claire!" Elsie exclaimed. She leapt up from the throne and hugged her.

"How are you holding up, Els?"

"Well enough. I've been looking forward to giving this back to you, though," Elsie said, tapping the signet ring on her finger. "But not just yet, I suppose."

"You can step down when I return from Graydare. But it seems you have things well in hand."

"Well, there was a bit of a crisis the other day. Involving Sean."

"What happened? Is he all right?" Claire asked.

"He is now. When I met him, though, he was in the city stockade. The constables arrested him for inciting a riot."

"A riot? Sean?"

"He's been preaching in the marketplace every day since he arrived here. It seems there's some opposition to his teachings," Elsie said.

"Is he still in the stockade?"

"No. Sir Flynn was the knight who brought Sean to Tara. It seems Sean converted Flynn on the journey. He came to me, and told me Sean had been arrested. He told me Sean was your friend, and asked if there was anything I could do to help. So I went and spoke to the constables. They looked into it further, and found that all of the supposed rioters were actually templers, masquerading as normal citizens," Elsie said.

"They *staged* a riot?"

Elsie nodded. "When the constables learned the truth, they arrested the templers, and released Sean." She raised an eyebrow. "But not before he had converted most of the prisoners in the stockade."

"And what about you? Did he convert you as well?"

"No. One conversation didn't convince me to give up the gods I've known since I was a child. He didn't even try to convince me to convert, though. He only wanted me to question things. To seek the truth."

"A true religion can withstand questioning. Unlike a false one," Claire said.

Elsie raised an eyebrow. "Sir Flynn told me Sean has also converted you."

"Sean was very convincing. But he didn't convert me. What I saw did."

"And what was that?"

Claire smiled, and began telling her.

Brianna

"Is the room to your liking, Your Highness?" Sloane asked.

"Yes, thank you. It seems strange to be asked that. Almost as strange as having a door without bars."

"Well, you're no prisoner here."

"What will your queen do with me?" Brianna asked.

"You'll be free to return to Drakaren, if you like."

"Will there be a Drakaren left to return to?"

"Of course," Sloane said. "Why wouldn't there be?"

"Claire doesn't plan on annexing our country? Or burning our cities?"

"No. She has no interest in conquest. Or in punishing your people. She only wants Minerva gone, and a treaty to settle our borders."

"Then yes, I would like to go back," Brianna said.

"I assume you'll want to wait until the war is over, and Minerva is removed from the throne?"

Brianna shuddered, her stomach tightening at the sound of Minerva's name. "I'd rather not set foot in Drakaren again until she's gone. Five years in her dungeons was more than enough."

"Only five years? Minerva's been on the throne for ten. I would have thought she'd rid herself of you right away. You are the rightful heir, aren't you?" Sloane asked.

"Yes. When my brother died, by our laws, the throne should have passed to me. But I didn't believe Valus died of a fever, as Minerva claimed. And I knew Viper Knights would be coming for me as soon as Valus breathed his last. So I fled Graydare, and for five years I managed to stay beyond Minerva's reach."

"The Dragon Order made inquiries after you disappeared. But our informants couldn't find any trace of you. We assumed Minerva had you killed," Sloane said.

"Braydon DeSora, the Duke of Aedan, sheltered me in his castle. We had met years ago, and we kept in touch by letter.

Sometimes I visited him at Aedan Island." Brianna felt the blush flare on her cheeks. "He proposed to me once. But I knew Valus had other plans for who I'd marry. So we kept our affections a secret."

Brianna shook her head. "It was far too convenient for Minerva that Valus fell ill just before the peace talks began. I knew once he was gone, I'd be next. So when it was clear he wouldn't survive, I disguised myself as a courier, and left for Aedan."

"The Dragon Order always thought it suspicious that Valus died just before he was supposed to meet with King Colin," Sloane said.

"There was no suspicion in Graydare. No one would ever say it aloud, but everyone knew Minerva murdered my brother. She always told him that there would only be peace with Keldaren once we had conquered it. Valus wanted a real peace, though. He wanted a treaty, and an end to the border wars between our countries."

"Those wars only started when Lord Inverin Graydare turned traitor, and marched off into the Western Wildlands with his band of rebels," Sloane said, raising an eyebrow.

"My ancestor was no traitor," Brianna snapped. "He was a reformer. And when Keldaren rejected his reforms, he left to carve a new nation out of the wilderness. You call his followers rebels. In Drakaren, we call them heroes. And he was *King* Inverin. He renounced his lordship when he renounced Keldaren."

Sloane smiled. "You see, Your Highness? Two hundred years of hostility is hard to overcome."

"I suppose it is. You were trying to provoke me, though."

"I was trying to test you. To see if you really want peace between our countries."

"I do want peace. No matter what our differences are. And so did my brother. He was going to renounce Drakaren's claim to Dalrann Province. And he wanted to arrange my betrothal to Prince Jared to seal a peace treaty between our nations."

"Five years in the dungeons must have been terrible. But I think marrying Jared might have been worse," Sloane said.

"From what Claire's told me, that may be true." Brianna shook her head. "But if Jared is in league with Minerva, then he's found his match in her. She's the most ruthless person I've ever met."

"How did she manage to capture you?"

"I hid in Braydon's castle, in old apartments that had been sealed off decades ago. There were only two servants who knew I was there, who brought me food and whatever else I needed. We thought we could trust them, but one of them must have betrayed me in the end. Braydon's brother Thorne found out where I was, and told Minerva."

"And now Lord Thorne is Duke of Aedan," Sloane said.

Brianna nodded. "The title went to Thorne after that. Along with all the lands and the family fortune." She blinked back tears. "They made me watch Braydon die," she said, feeling the quaver in her voice. "They brought us both to Graydare from the island. They put me in a cell with a barred door, and chained him up outside. They burned him, and I had to watch him suffer for days until he finally died. Then they took me to Darcann." She wiped her eyes, her stomach crawling at the memory.

"Why did Minerva keep you alive?" Sloane asked gently.

"She wanted me to recognize her as the rightful queen. She told me that if I publicly supported her claim to the throne, she would release me, and let me go live in exile."

"But you didn't."

"I knew that even if I did acknowledge her as queen, she wouldn't have let me live long."

"And after five years, she was still trying to break you?" Sloane asked.

"She always kept trying. She would have me whipped from time to time. But no worse than that, thankfully. She could hardly have me proclaim her queen looking like I had been tortured."

Sloane stood. "Well, you're beyond her reach now. I'll leave you be, Your Highness. Feel free to explore the palace, if you like." Sloane went to the door.

"I hope Claire realizes who she's dealing with," Brianna said. "Minerva is relentless."

Sloane smiled. "So is Claire."

CHAPTER 33

Claire

Ross was the first to arrive. "Claire!" he called, striding into the throne room. He walked boldly up to the dais, and took her hand in his. Armor clinked on her right as Kerry moved toward him. Claire gave a quick shake of her head. Kerry returned to her position beside the throne, her mouth set into a tight line. Ross kissed Claire's hand, his emerald eyes gazing up into hers.

She smiled as he released her hand. "Archduke Ross. I'm glad you arrived safely."

He smiled back, stepping down to stand before the dais. "I wouldn't have let anything stand in the way of seeing you again," he said. Claire felt the blood rush to her cheeks.

The doors opened, and Adrian walked in with the Hynbarran and Kirosian Generals. Adrian bowed. "Welcome home, Your Majesty." His smile was as bright and warm as the Silver Sea.

"Adrian. It's good to see you again." Claire couldn't keep a tremor of excitement from her voice.

Ross' eyes narrowed. "Claire," he said, stepping in front of Adrian, "allow me to introduce General Ecca, commander of the Hynbarran Army. For this war, though, my father has given me the command. General Ecca is here as my adviser."

Unease churned in Claire's stomach. "You've had experience, then, commanding armies?" she asked.

Ross smiled. "I'm a quick learner. And General Ecca will help me."

"Be that as it may, we need one overall commander for this invasion. And that will be General Dalraiden. Did you send the scouts to Graydare?" Claire asked Adrian, ignoring Ross' frown.

"I did, Your Majesty. It seems that Drakaren's western army is larger than we thought. Apparently Minerva has recently added several regiments to it. Even with our allies, I'm not sure we have enough soldiers to defeat them," Adrian said.

"Drakari soldiers are nothing more than raw conscripts. Whether they outnumber us or not, we can outfight them," Ross scoffed.

"Your Highness, this is their western army. They defend Graydare. They're picked from the best soldiers in Drakaren. They're the equal of any Keldari soldier," Adrian said.

"I don't know about your troops, General, but my Halberdiers are more than a match for these Drakari rabble."

Adrian raised an eyebrow. "Your Highness, the scouts' report makes the threat they pose quite clear. Perhaps you'd care to read it."

"What's clear is that you don't have the stomach to win this war," Ross said. "Claire, give me command of all three armies. *I'm* not afraid to lead our troops to victory."

He's just like his father. The realization turned Claire cold. "Thank you for your offer, Archduke. But I have faith in General Dalraiden."

Ross' face fell. "As you wish, Your Majesty." He glared at Adrian, his jaw set tightly.

The Kirosian General stepped forward. "Your Majesty," he said, bowing. "I bring you greetings from Queen Alexis. I am General Maran, commander of the Kirosian Marines."

"Welcome, General," Claire said. "We're grateful for your assistance. We'll need the help of all our allies to win this war." She told them about the Graithans and the Merosians.

"Let's hope the Merosians do join us," Adrian said.

"Either way, we have to stop Minerva. Defeat isn't an option, Generals. Draw up your battle plans for General Dalraiden's approval. We march for Drakaren in two days," Claire said.

Brianna

Brianna walked along an upper balcony, staring at the frescoes and statues lining the palace halls. *Proterian Palace can't hold a candle to this place*, she thought, remembering the dim, stark corridors of the palace in Graydare. *If I ever get home, I'll have to make a few changes.*

A group of people walked into the great hall below her. Most of them were in uniform, although one wore the clothing of a nobleman. As they headed toward the doors of the palace, the nobleman stopped. "Dalraiden," he said, grasping the arm of a Keldari General, "I'd like a word."

Brianna shrank back, peering between the railings to watch the two men below. When the others had left, the nobleman leaned toward the General. "What are you playing at, Dalraiden?"

The General pulled his arm free. "I don't know what you mean, Archduke."

"Address me as 'Your Highness,' peasant."

"I'm no peasant, *Your Highness*," the General growled.

"Peasant, commoner, it's all the same. And you know exactly what I mean. I saw the way you looked at the queen," the Archduke said.

"Just how was I looking at her?"

"As if you had feelings for her. It's absurd."

The General stiffened. "Is it so absurd?"

"Of course it is. She's royalty. You're a low-born soldier who's managed to worm his way up the ranks. How could she ever have any interest in someone like you? Stay away from her, Dalraiden. You'll only embarrass the Queen, and yourself."

"I'm Commandant of the Keldari Army. And the Queen's friend. Who are you to tell me to stay away from her?"

"I'm royalty. I have a duty to protect the Queen's honor. I'll tell you again—stay away from her. Otherwise, honor will demand that we duel."

"I'd gladly cross swords with you. But Claire can make her own decisions about who she spends time with. You may have royal blood, Your Highness, but you have the manners of a tavern lout. I see you for what you really are. And Claire will, too." The General stormed out through the palace doors.

The Archduke turned and disappeared back into the depths of the palace. *Like a snake slithering back to its hole*, Brianna thought.

Claire

Claire and Kerry passed through the city gates, riding across Tara's cobblestone streets, with a squad of Crown Guards following them. Making their way to the marketplace, they found Sean standing atop a merchant's table, preaching to the crowd gathered around him. Star lay curled at his feet.

They dismounted, leaving their horses with a guard. Claire stood at the edge of the market, watching. There was eagerness on the faces in the crowd as they listened to Sean. Eagerness…and something else. *Hunger*, she realized. *They're starving for the truth.*

Sean finished speaking, and the people swarmed around him, bombarding him with questions. A man helped Sean step down from the table, and Star followed him. The man looked at Claire, and said something to Sean. Sean nodded, and excused himself from the crowd. The man led Sean over to her.

Claire grasped his hands and squeezed them. "Sean. It's so good to see you again." Star barked up at her, wagging his tail.

Sean smiled. "This is Liam," he said, gesturing to the man beside him. "He's been guiding me. Star doesn't quite know what to make of the city yet. It's a blessing to have you safely back, Claire. Did you make the alliances?"

"Yes. But I see you've won over more people than I did. A great deal more."

Sean's smile widened. "It's amazing, isn't it? People flock here every day. So many are joining the Faith."

"Your preaching is quite persuasive," Claire said.

"My preaching has very little to do with it." Sean drew a crystal flask from his robe. A brilliant whiteness rippled inside it.

"The Gift," Claire said, her pulse quickening.

"This is what draws them. Him. I brought a single flask from the island, and I've given a drink from it to everyone who joins the Faith. It's never gone dry."

"A sign from the Emperor?" Claire asked.

Sean nodded, and held the flask out to her.

Claire took it. The crystal was cool in her hands, but the liquid within glowed as if it were white-hot. She put the flask to her lips, and drank. The light and warmth enveloped her again. This time, though, there was also a smooth, sweet taste, like honey on her tongue. Claire closed her eyes, feeling currents of warmth moving through her, lifting her up to the crystal mountain.

She bathed in the light at the mountain's summit, letting it soak into her. When the light faded, the feeling of peace lingered. Claire opened her eyes, and handed the flask to Kerry. Even after

Kerry drank, the flask was still full. Kerry returned the flask to Sean.

"You've been through a great deal since we last saw each other," Sean said.

Claire nodded. "And won another battle."

"The next one will be harder, though. Much harder."

"Adrian told me the Drakari army is larger than we thought. But how did you know that?" Claire asked.

"I had a dream."

"And in this dream, did you see victory or defeat for us?"

"Both," Sean said.

"What does that mean?"

"I'm not sure. It was a confusing dream. But have faith, Claire. The Ancient will help you."

Liam leaned closer to Sean. "He's back."

"They are persistent, aren't they?"

"Who?" Claire asked.

"The templers. They've been following Sean around the city. That one's been watching him for the past three days." Liam pointed to a man in the crowd. He wore a gray cloak wrapped tightly around him, the hood pulled up. A bit of bronze-colored cloth showed beneath the edge of his sleeve.

A templer's robe, Claire realized. "Come with me. We'll put a stop to this." They followed her as she moved through the crowd. The templer saw her coming and turned, pushing people aside as he hastened away. Claire ran after him, catching him by the hood. Kerry grabbed one of his arms, pinned it behind his back, and spun him around.

Claire stared into the defiant face of a young man. "What's your business here, templer?"

"Listening to the preaching, Your Majesty."

"Listening…and reporting back on it, perhaps?"

"This man has the gift of a silver tongue. We templers preach as well. We could all learn from his style of preaching."

"You expect me to believe that? That you're here only to improve your sermons?" Claire asked.

A deep voice rang out from behind her. "Ethra is here on my orders."

Claire turned. Quaestor stood there, resplendent in his golden robe and headcloth. His diamond and ruby-encrusted sashes glittered in the sunlight. Two templers stood beside him.

"And what did you order him to do, Grandmaster?" Claire asked, gesturing for Kerry to release the templer.

"To keep an eye on a dangerous man."

"How can you call Sean dangerous?"

"He's preaching blasphemy, and leading people away from the gods and the Syncrestry."

"Perhaps the Syncrestry is the real danger," Claire said.

Quaestor's mouth twitched. "He's converted you, hasn't he?"

"Yes. I've joined the Faith."

Quaestor stared at her. Then he smiled. "Perhaps, Your Majesty, a new god *has* revealed himself to you and Sean. There's room in the Syncrestry for all gods. Our next convocation is this coming year. I promise that I'll personally champion this new god of yours for recognition by the Syncrestry. I believe I can guarantee you a successful vote."

"So, you would recognize him as one god among many?" Sean asked.

"Of course. But with the amount of followers you've been attracting, he would soon be one of the most popular gods in the Syncrestry," Quaestor said.

"But he isn't one god among many. He's the only one. Your Syncrestry is a collection of lies and false gods. The Emperor has no place in it," Claire said.

Quaestor's face darkened. "Be careful, Your Majesty. The gods curse heretics. And unless you renounce this blasphemy, they will curse you."

"It's truth. Not blasphemy," Claire said.

"Then you leave me no choice. Claire Erinn, the gods curse you as a heretic," Quaestor intoned, his voice booming across the marketplace. "I disavow you from the Divine Syncrestry. Unless you repent and rejoin the Syncrestry, the gods will take a terrible vengeance on you, and you will die in the upcoming battle. When this prophecy is fulfilled, all the people will see that your god is a false one!"

"And what if this prophecy of yours doesn't come true?" Claire asked.

"The prophecy of real gods can't fail to come true. When it does, the people will know that the gods I serve are the true rulers of the world."

"And if it doesn't come to pass, the people will know that you and your gods are frauds," Claire said. "Once we've defeated the Drakari, I intend to build a temple to the Emperor. I'll build it taller than the Holy Hill, so it overshadows your temple. Just as the Faith will overshadow your false religion."

Quaestor shuddered. "I see that this hermit has poisoned your mind with his heresy. Come, we're done here," he told the templers. Ethra and the other templers followed as Quaestor stormed off.

"Hopefully he won't give you any more trouble. If he does, let Elsie know, and she'll assign you some guards," Claire told Sean.

"That won't be necessary. I have no fear of Quaestor. I'm protected by a power far greater than him. Besides, I'll be gone from Tara soon enough, and beyond his reach," Sean said.

"Gone? Where are you going?" Claire asked.

"With you, of course. To Drakaren."

"No. Sean, we're going to war. It's much too dangerous."

"I know the danger. But I also know I have to go with you. I have…suspicions of what's happening in Drakaren. I need to see for myself that those suspicions are wrong."

"And just what do you suspect?" Claire asked.

"That something else is behind Minerva's aggression. Something more than just politics and grasping for power."

"What?"

"Something deeper. Darker." Sean shook his head. "It's probably nothing. I won't worry you with my farfetched fears. When do we leave for Graydare?"

"The day after tomorrow."

"I'll meet you at the palace that morning," Sean said.

"Where are you staying?"

"An inn on the Dock Road."

"That's not a good part of the city," Claire said.

"No, it's not. But the room was the right price."

"Well, that's settled easily enough," Claire said. "You can stay at the palace. That inn must be crawling with thieves and cutthroats."

Sean smiled. "It is. It's full of lost souls. And they all need to hear of the Ancient. I go where I'm needed, Claire. And I'm needed there more than at the palace."

"If you say so," Claire said. "Then I'll see you on the march to Drakaren." Sean smiled and nodded. He and Liam waded back through the crowd to the table. Liam helped Sean up, and he began preaching again. As she rode off, Claire glanced back at Sean. People crowded around him, their hungry faces turned upward, like plants to the sun.

CHAPTER 34

Jared

Jared rode along the hills, following Minerva and General Vanar along the lines of trenches. Guard towers crowded the ridges, standing sentinel over the Graydare Valley below.

"The trenches are dug and the stakes are set," Vanar said. "We've held these hills before, Majesty. If we held them against the Ravek two hundred years ago, we can certainly hold them against the Keldari now."

"Your confidence is admirable, General. But it isn't just the Keldari. It seems the entire world is marching against Graydare," Minerva said.

"My army will hold, Majesty. And the southern army is here also."

"But not the Garat regiment," Minerva said.

"No. There's still no word from Lord Xithrac."

"There can only be one reason for that. If we win this battle, I'll personally hunt down every last Raider. And then I'll add another tower to these hills. A tower of Graithan bones." Minerva looked over the ridges. "Your preparations are sound, General. I'm giving you command of our defense. Keep them away from my city."

Vanar bowed his head. "Yes, Majesty."

Jared shivered when Minerva turned in her saddle to face him. "And what about you, Jared? Any military wisdom you'd like to share? Any advice for the general?" One of the guards escorting them smirked, and Vanar chuckled.

Jared shook his head.

"Good. You're finally learning," she said.

She doesn't love me, he realized, a sick feeling burning through his stomach. *And maybe she never did.* He looked into her eyes. There was only contempt blazing in their depths.

"Yes," he said. "I am."

Claire

Claire gazed out at the hills shielding the Graydare Valley. "Two weeks to march what we could have flown in a day," she told Sloane and Kerry.

"Flying does have a way of spoiling you," Sloane said. "But when an army marches, its queen should march along with it."

"The knights are all here?"

Sloane nodded. "Breaus arrived today with the new knights and dragons. Even the Prefect is here."

"And the Graithans?" Claire asked.

Kerry shook her head.

"I thought I could trust Azaira. It seems I was wrong."

"Perhaps. The Graithans might still come," Sloane said.

"When? We attack in the morning," Claire said.

"We could certainly use their help," Kerry said quietly.

Claire nodded, staring across the plains between their camp and the hills. Towers bristled like spears atop the ridges—dark islands in a blazing sea of Drakari campfires. "No wonder we didn't meet any resistance on the march."

"It looks like they've pulled all of their troops back here," Kerry said.

"There are too many, aren't there?" Claire asked, her heart sinking.

"They outnumber us. Almost two to one, from the look of it," Sloane said. "But we have dragons."

"I hope that's enough." Claire turned away from the hills. "Let's find Adrian. I want to go over his battle plan again." They walked toward the headquarters tent.

"Claire," a voice called. She turned to see Ross walking up. "I was wondering if I could have a word with you. In private."

"Of course. I'll see you tomorrow," she told Kerry and Sloane.

Kerry frowned. "Your Majesty, we're only a league from the enemy lines. I can't leave you unguarded."

"I suppose you're right. We'll go to my tent. That's certainly well-guarded enough," Claire said.

Kerry nodded, but her frown remained. She escorted them to the tent, where Crown Guards opened the flaps for them. "Get some rest, Kerry," Claire said. "You'll need it for the battle."

"I'll see you in the morning, Claire," Kerry said, her narrowed eyes lingering on Ross. She turned and left.

Ross followed Claire into the tent. "I've known a few bodyguards before, but never one that suspicious," he said.

"She takes her duties very seriously. And after all that's happened, she has good reason to be wary."

He smiled. "But not of me, I hope. I wanted to explain why I questioned your choice of General Dalraiden back in Tara. I was just trying to look out for you."

"Thank you for your concern, Ross. But I can look out for myself."

"I know. But I can't help feeling protective of you." He stepped closer.

Her muscles tensed. "Why?"

"Because of how I feel about you." He leaned in, his lips aimed at hers.

Claire's skin crawled, and she took a step back. "Don't."

"It's all right," he said, gripping her arms and leaning in again.

"No!" Claire wrenched an arm free and punched him.

Ross reeled back, a spurt of crimson flowing from his nose. "You hit me!" he screamed.

"Get out! Before I hit you again," Claire shouted.

Guards burst into the tent, their swords drawn. "Your Majesty?" one of them asked, his sword pointed at Ross.

Claire took a deep breath. "Archduke Ross was just leaving. Escort him out," she ordered.

"You'll pay for this, wench," Ross growled. He turned and stormed out.

Brianna

Brianna sat outside her tent, watching the officers come and go from the headquarters pavilion.

"Ecca!" Brianna jumped at the roar. The Hynbarran Archduke came storming through the lanes between the tents. "Ecca!" he shouted, blood trickling from his nose.

The Hynbarran general emerged from the pavilion, his hand on his sword. "Your Highness? What's wrong?"

"Gather the troops. We're leaving."

"Right now? What about the war?" Ecca asked.

"This is Claire's war. Let her fight it."

"That isn't what your father decided."

"Things have changed."

"What's changed, Your Highness?" Ecca stared at Ross. "She rejected you, didn't she? That's what this is about."

"The alliance is over, Ecca. That's all you need to know."

"That's a decision only the prince can make, Your Highness. And you're not the prince."

"No. Not yet. But I am commander of this army. And I say we're leaving. Have the men pack up the camp."

Brianna's heart quickened. *Claire's army is too small as it is,* she thought. *Without the Hynbarrans, we won't have a chance.*

"No," Ecca said.

"What did you say?" Ross snarled.

"I said no. If this is how you command the army, I'll have no part of it. I resign my commission. I'll offer my sword to Queen Claire. She's fighting for all of us. I won't abandon her," Ecca said.

"Fine. Stay here. Stay here and be damned. The rest of us will be on our way back to Hyperion."

"If you leave, you're the one who'll be damning yourself, Highness. Damned as a coward. As a deserter."

"Better damned than dead. Which is what you'll be after tomorrow." Ross spat, and stomped off.

I have to warn Claire. Brianna rose, and hurried off toward the queen's tent.

Minerva

"A dark dawn. That must be a good omen," Minerva said.

Anastasia was staring out between the tower's battlements, toward the armies massed across the plain. "That isn't," she said, pointing.

"We outnumber them."

"They have dragons. And you know what happened the last time dragons met a Drakari army," Anastasia said.

"We have rocs this time. Their dragons will be too busy fighting for the sky to help in the fight on the ground."

Anastasia turned. "I can ensure our victory. But only if you let me make the sacrifice. Then I'll have enough power to kill them all."

Minerva suppressed the shiver rippling through her. "No. We've discussed this already. It's going too far."

"What's the life of one man compared to victory?"

"Losing one soldier is nothing. But if I lose one soldier that way, I'll lose them all. Can't you see that?"

Anastasia shook her head. "No. You'd become more powerful than ever. Your troops wouldn't abandon you. They would respect and fear you even more."

"It would show us for what we are. They would never follow me if they knew."

"And what are we?" Anastasia asked, her voice harsh. "Witches? Demon-worshippers?"

"They'd call us that, and worse. You know that," Minerva shot back. *And they'd be right*, she thought.

"You lack faith. Don't be afraid to embrace Zahara. Follow him fully, and he'll make you more powerful than you could ever dream," Anastasia said.

"I lack faith in my soldiers, not in him. They wouldn't understand. Not now, anyway. When we've won this war, then I can reveal my beliefs. Gradually. So the people have time to accept the new religion. And then, we'll be able to eliminate any who oppose it. We'll make the sacrifice then. Not now."

Anastasia stared at her. Minerva's heart ached at the disappointment on her sister's face. "Trust me," Minerva said.

"This time, you should trust me. Without the blood, my power is limited."

"You can still kill them, though?" Minerva asked.

"Many of them. But not all."

"Then our army will have to do the rest. Along with your knights."

"I did as you told me, and divided the knights up. Some will fly with the rocs. Some will stay and guard the city," Anastasia said.

"And the ships?"

Anastasia frowned. "I sent some knights to the harbor. Along with a large contingent of Berserkers. Too large, Minerva. Those troops could help defend Graydare."

"They'll defend you. You're more important than the city."

"What do you mean? I'll be on the front lines, not at the harbor. I'm a Viper Knight. I don't need protection."

"You're not just a knight," Minerva said. "You're my sister. My heir. I won't risk your life in this war. You'll do what you can today, with what power you have. After that, you'll board one of those ships. And sail away."

"Sail where?"

"Somewhere safe. Far from Graydare."

"You're asking me to abandon you. You're the only family I have left."

"I'm also your queen. I'm *ordering* you to leave. And to live. To save our family."

"I thought you said we'd win this battle?" Anastasia asked.

"I believe we will. But if we do lose, I won't lose you too. You'll summon his help if we need it. But after that, you'll take ship. You can return after we've won."

"No. I won't leave you," Anastasia said.

"Then you're defying your queen's orders. I'll have you arrested for treason, and put aboard a prison ship. One that will sail far from Drakaren's shores."

Anastasia blinked, wiping her eyes. "Why are you doing this? Let me stay and fight for my family."

A flood of tears strained against the dam of Minerva's heart. She held them back, willing her eyes to stay dry. "If Graydare falls, you'll be all that's left of our family. I have to protect you. I won't lose you. I won't."

"But if I leave, I'll lose you," Anastasia said, her lip trembling.

The dam broke, and hot tears spilled into Minerva's eyes. She held her arms out, and Anastasia came to her, hugging her tightly. "Pray to Zahara that we win," Minerva said. "Perhaps your prayers will move him to help us."

"It takes more than prayer to move him. It takes blood," Anastasia said.

Minerva let go of her, giving her a kiss on the forehead. "This field will become a lake of blood today. Enough blood to quench even the thirst of the Crimson God."

CHAPTER 35

Claire

Clouds filled the dawn sky—hanging like dark harbingers over the empty plain. *Not empty for long, though*, Claire thought, walking into the headquarters pavilion. Adrian was there with Ecca and Maran, looking over a map.

"Are you ready, General?"

Adrian straightened. "Your Majesty, we've adjusted our plans to make up for the loss of the Hynbarrans. We're as ready as we can be."

"Still no sign of the Graithans?" Claire asked.

"I'm afraid not."

She nodded. "Very well. I'd like a moment with General Dalraiden, if you wouldn't mind, Generals." Maran nodded, and left.

"I'm afraid I'm not a General anymore, Your Majesty," Ecca said.

"I'm giving you a battlefield commission in our army," Claire said. "Adrian will still be in command, of course, but you'll be a General again, if you're willing to join us."

Ecca bowed. "I'd be honored." He saluted and left.

"Can we win?" Claire asked Adrian.

"It will be difficult without the Hynbarrans. But the dragons tip the balance in our favor."

"If you were Minerva, would you send your army into the field against dragons?"

"No," Adrian said. "I'd keep them in Graydare, under cover. Especially after what happened at the Spearcrags."

"So why is the Drakari army camped on the hills, instead of hiding in the city?" Claire asked.

"You think she has some way to deal with the dragons?"

"Minerva is no fool. She wouldn't send her troops out against us otherwise," Claire said.

"Should we call off the attack?"

"No. They would just charge down on us as we retreated. But be wary. Minerva is cunning. I'm sure she has some surprise in store for us."

"I will, Claire. But I have a surprise of my own for her."

Two hours later, Claire stood with Adrian, Kerry, and Brianna atop the small hill where the headquarters pavilion had been set up. A squad of Crown Guards stood watch around the tent. The Keldari and Kirosian troops spread out across the plain below them. In the distance, Drakari soldiers darkened the hills, teeming in their trenches like a horde of gray locusts.

Watch over us, and bring us victory, Claire prayed silently. "Signal the advance," she ordered. Adrian gestured to an officer, who waved a signal flag.

The sounds of trumpets rose up from the ranks, and the soldiers started marching. As the allied troops drew closer, white-clad figures emerged on the hills, clambering out of the Drakari trenches.

Claire raised her spyglass. They were Merosians, wearing some sort of white quilted vests. "What are they wearing?" Claire asked Brianna. "Some kind of uniform?"

Brianna raised her own spyglass. "It's armor. They sew cotton vests and soak them in saltwater. The cotton dries stiff, and strong. It's much lighter than metal, but it can stop sword slashes and arrows."

"Ingenious," Claire said.

"They're beginning their attack," Kerry called. The Merosians formed into battle lines, and started marching down the hills.

Adrian stepped closer. "One of them is flying the cloth." He lowered his voice. "Dame Sloane spoke to me about the Merosians, Claire. She's still worried they might betray us. What orders should I give?"

Claire searched with her spyglass, and found the black cloth fluttering from a Merosian harpoon. "We'll take the chance. Order the men to break ranks for them."

Adrian nodded, and shouted to the signal officer. The officer waved a flag, and the trumpets blared out the order. The Merosians were halfway down the hills now, and they broke into a run, their harpoons lowered.

The allied troops hesitated to move aside, remaining in place in their ranks. "Sound the order again," she said, trying to control the tremor in her voice.

"Are you sure?" Adrian asked quietly.

No, she thought. "Yes," she said. "Do it."

Adrian nodded, and the trumpets blared once more. This time, the allied ranks split, as each soldier stepped aside, opening a gap in the lines, and lowering their spear tips to the ground. The Merosians kept thundering down the hills toward them. *Let me be right*, she prayed silently. She stared through the spyglass, watching her troops stir nervously as the Merosians bore down on them.

The Merosians were only a few hundred feet from the Keldari lines when one of them blew a seashell trumpet. As one, they swung their harpoons up into the air, and came to a halt. They greeted the Keldari and Kirosian soldiers as they blended into the gaps in the allied ranks. "I suppose they had to make it look good for the Drakari, but they held that charge too long for my liking," Adrian said.

"Far too long," Claire said. "Let's hope they charge as fiercely against the enemy lines."

The Keldari trumpets blew again, and the allies resumed their march. When they reached the base of the hills, Drakari arrows and spears began raining down from the ridges. The troops raised their shields and pressed on. Soldiers fell, but the advance continued. Halfway up the hills, the allies started jogging. As they neared the crest, they broke into a run.

The soldiers leapt over the sharpened spikes guarding the trenches, and crashed down like a wave of steel onto the Drakari lines. Clashing metal and the sound of screams floated back across the field to Claire. She paced restlessly.

"Calm yourself," Kerry said. "You'll be out there soon enough."

"I should be fighting alongside them, not sitting back here watching them die."

"Have patience, Your Majesty," Adrian urged. "If we don't hold to the plan, we'll lose this battle. And then those men will have died for nothing."

Claire's entire body burned with the urge to join the fight. The minutes passed as if they were hours. Finally, Adrian gestured to the signal officer. The flag waved again, and the trumpets blew a retreat. The allies pulled back, half of them fighting to cover the retreat while the other half withdrew.

The Drakari roar of triumph echoed across the plain. Enemy soldiers streamed out from their trenches and towers, rushing down like a gray tide after the retreating allies.

Yes, Claire thought, watching the Drakari pour out from their defenses. Adrian shouted an order, and the signal officer waved his flag frantically. In the camp behind them, a trumpet blared a charge. Cavalry horses exploded out from the tents where they had been hidden. The cavalry thundered out of the camp, curving around to encircle the charging Drakari.

As the horses came around behind the enemy, the retreating allies stopped. The cavalry troopers lowered their lances and smashed into the Drakari, while the allied soldiers turned and charged the gray-clad ranks.

"Like a hammer and anvil," Claire said, smiling.

"She'll send the Berserkers next," Adrian warned.

Claire lifted her spyglass. Figures appeared on the ridge—figures clad in black and silver steel, wearing silver skull-faced helmets. The Berserkers charged down toward the cavalry. "Sound the horn," she ordered.

One of the officers unslung a metal horn from its strap on his shoulder. He took a deep breath, and gave it a mighty blast. A deep growl like a dragon roar echoed from the horn. A real dragon's roar answered from the forest beyond the camp.

A flight of thirty dragons rose from the woods. They soared overhead and swooped at the Berserkers, flooding fire down on them. One dragon hung back, flying to the headquarters pavilion. Breaus landed, and Claire and Kerry ran to him. They leapt into the saddle, while four Crown Guards climbed onto his feet, clinging to his legs. Breaus took off, heading for the front lines. The other dragons landed ahead of them, letting their knights off into the battle.

Breaus touched down at the edge of the fighting. They slid out of the saddle, and he swiveled his head down. "Come back in one piece," he growled.

Claire touched his nose. "You too." Then, with a flurry of wings, he was off. She drew her twin lance, while Kerry and two of the Crown Guards drew their swords. The other guards drew their bows, stringing arrows. They all followed Claire as she ran toward the fight.

Claire's blood pulsed hot within her. *The dragon blood awakening,* she thought. She leapt into the battle, her twinlance whirling. Claire caught glimpses through the fray of other Dragon Knights fighting nearby. Mostly, though, she saw only the swarms of Berserkers ahead of her.

Her steel wailed as the blades whipped through the air, cutting down enemies. Dragons shot overhead as Claire fought, their claws and fire carving gashes through the enemy ranks. Claire found herself next to another Dragon Knight, facing down a group of Berserkers.

They charged the Ravek warriors, their lances at the ready. Suddenly, a young woman appeared, striding toward Claire. Her white hair floated behind her, and her tattered black cloak flapped wildly in the wind. Claire skidded to a halt. *Death.*

Death smiled triumphantly as she advanced. Her black wings spread, curving around toward Claire. Death stretched out a hand, her fingers extended like talons toward Claire's throat. An icy wind gusted against Claire's neck, and she jerked her head back. The pale hand closed, grasping only air. Death vanished into a cloud of mist, an angry cry echoing after her.

There was a rush of air next to Claire's head, and a black blur sped past, right where her neck had just been. It arced in front of her, sticking itself into the ground. *An arrow,* she realized. She spun around. One of the Crown Guards was stringing another arrow onto his bow. He aimed, letting the arrow fly. She ducked, and it clanged harmlessly off her helmet, the metal ringing with the impact.

She charged. *I'll kill the traitor.* As the guard reached for another arrow, a second Crown Guard charged at him, stabbing him from behind. The archer dropped his bow, twisting to face his attacker. The second guard hit him with a shield, knocking him down. The guard ran the traitor through again, pinning him to the ground with a sword.

A group of five Dragon Knights, fighting as a team, emerged from the chaos of the battle. Claire signaled, and they ran to her. She pointed to the other knight fighting the Berserkers. "Help him," she ordered. "And keep the rest of the Drakari back while we deal with this traitor." The knights charged into the fight.

Claire ran to the second guard, who lifted her helmet. It was Kerry.

"Are you all right?" Kerry asked.

"I'm fine. Who is this turncloak?"

Kerry reached down and ripped the helmet off the fallen guard.

Claire gasped. "Ethra!"

"You again," Kerry snarled. "Why are you trying to kill the queen, templer?"

Ethra moaned, looking at the blade buried in his stomach. "Quaestor sent me."

"So his prophecy would be fulfilled," Claire said. Rage coursed like molten steel through her veins. "He'll pay for this."

"So will I," Ethra gasped. "I'm sorry, Your Majesty. I was wrong to follow Quaestor. And to help defend his lies."

"Then you know they are lies?" Claire asked.

"Yes. I believed in the gods when I first joined the Syncrestry. Most templers do believe. Only the high templers, and the ones assigned to the Great Temple, know the truth about the gods. It was only when I came to the Great Temple that I learned that all I knew of the gods was a lie."

"Why didn't you leave?" Claire asked.

"The Order rewards those who cooperate. Richly rewards them. And they punish those who don't. There's a small order of assassins that hunt down and kill any templer who reveals our secrets, or who tries to leave the Syncrestry after learning the truth." Ethra winced, putting a hand to his wound. "They're called the Blood Brethren. I was to become one of them. Killing you was my final test."

"You failed," Kerry spat.

"I'm glad I did." Ethra coughed, gasping in pain. "Listening to Sean preach...it gave me doubts. And now I see how wrong I was." His voice weakened. "Tell me...is this god of yours real?"

Claire nodded. "He's the only real god."

"Then, please...have pity...on me...Your Majesty," Ethra said, his breath coming in gasps. She leaned in to hear over the noise of battle. "Speak to him...for me. Tell him...I'm sorry. Tell him..." His breath gave out, and his head slumped back. His eyes shone with fear for a heartbeat, and then went dull.

"I'll tell him," Claire said softly.

"He tried to kill you, and you're still going to pray for him?" Kerry asked.

Claire nodded. "If I believe in a merciful god, I should be merciful as well." She was whispering a prayer for Ethra when dragon roars erupted from the sky above her. Claire looked up. Dark wings were rising from Graydare, headed their way. *Rocs.*

The huge ravens attacked the dragons, drawing them away from the fighting on the ground. Talons slashed, and columns of fire scorched out as the sky became a second battlefield.

CHAPTER 36

Minerva

Minerva turned as Vanar climbed the last stairs to the tower roof. "Why did you wait so long to send the rocs?" she asked quietly.

Vanar paled. "They were guarding the city, Majesty. I waited until I was sure they were needed before I sent them to the front."

"And while you were waiting, those dragons killed thousands of our troops."

Vanar grew even paler. "Forgive me, Majesty. You told me the city's safety was the first priority. I did leave a second contingent of rocs and Viper Knights to protect Graydare when I sent the others to fight the dragons."

"If that army gets past the hills, Viper Knights won't be enough to save Graydare. You should have sent them sooner, General. Now it's too late." *I should be furious*, Minerva thought, wondering at the bleak calm she felt. *No. Calm's the wrong word. Resignation.*

"We can still win, Majesty." Vanar's face was a bloodless white, and his hands trembled. "Give me a chance to redeem myself."

"We have one more gambit left. If it works, it will be the perfect opportunity for a counterattack. I want you to go and personally lead the charge."

Vanar swallowed. "Personally?"

"Yes. I can't think of anything that would rally our troops more than to see their commander charging ahead of them into battle. Come back victorious, General, and all will be forgiven."

"And if we're defeated?" Vanar asked.

"Then if I were you, I would make sure you fall in battle. Because if you come back defeated, I'll burn you alive," Minerva said, her mouth filling with the iron taste of fury.

A hint of gray colored Vanar's face. "Then I'll be sure to bring you victory, Majesty," he said. He bowed, and walked stiffly away down the stairs.

"I'm surprised you didn't kill him," Anastasia said.

"I did kill him. I put him at the front. At least this way he might take an enemy or two with him." Minerva looked out at the battlefield below. "Time for you to kill a few enemies yourself."

"Let me make the sacrifice," Anastasia said. "We can use him," she whispered, nodding toward Jared, who stood on the other side of the tower. "Let him bring us victory for once. Let me destroy them all."

The pleading in Anastasia's eyes almost moved her to say yes. Almost. "I can't. There's no way to keep it quiet. Once news spread, the people would call me a savage, and a heathen. And they would rise up against me. What good would it do to win the battle but lose my kingdom?"

Anastasia looked crestfallen. "You'd lose nothing. And gain everything. Especially faith."

Minerva forced a smile, trying to ignore the hurt of Anastasia's disappointment. *How many times must I suffer that look?* she wondered. "I have faith in *you*. I have faith you'll save Drakaren. Prove me right."

"I'll do what I can." Anastasia snapped her fingers at a Viper Knight. He walked over to them, holding out a long bundle wrapped in black cloth. Anastasia opened the cloth, pulling out a twisted, knobby staff carved from the mud-black wood of a gnarltree. A ruby in the head of the staff glowed with a dim red light.

Anastasia turned the staff sideways, holding it above her head. "ENCORDAT DIVANI MORAS," she roared, her words seeming to shake the very air around them. Red smoke poured from the ruby. The smoke tumbled to the ground, and ran along it like a river, racing down the hills, running between the Drakari soldiers.

When it reached the Keldari ranks, the smoke split, the river turning into streams of red mist. Soldiers on both sides of the battle shrank away from the mist, and the fighting ground to a halt as the fingers of red smoke wound through the Keldari lines. The mist sank into the ground, disappearing like water into a sponge.

Anastasia slammed the base of the staff against the roof. "TREMERUS!" she shouted. The shaking was barely noticeable at first. But it grew until Minerva felt it even from atop the tower. The ground that had absorbed the fog was quivering and buckling.

The enemy soldiers ran, as the battlefield turned into a stormy ocean of earth beneath their feet. The ground broke, and yawning chasms opened to swallow up the retreating soldiers.

Yes. Yes, Minerva thought, feeling a smile spread across her face. She glanced over her shoulder at Jared. His look of horror was almost as satisfying as the dying screams floating faintly through the air. "I knew you'd save us," she told Anastasia as the chasms rumbled closed, slamming shut over the soldiers they had engulfed.

Anastasia touched the head of her staff. The red light in the ruby was so dim that its faint glow was barely visible. "I only killed half of them, from the looks of it. And now my power is spent. I can't do any more."

"Half of them is more than enough. The army can handle the rest. Thank you. Now it's time for you to go," Minerva said. "Let me finish wiping out what's left of them. When you get back, we'll drink a toast over their bodies."

"If you say so, sister," Anastasia said, doubt hanging in her voice. "Zahara be with you."

"He's already given us what we needed to win. The rest is up to me." She hugged Anastasia tightly, and then let her go with a kiss on the top of her head. "I'll see you soon."

"I hope so," Anastasia said, with a sad smile. "I feel an ill omen in the ether."

"Now whose faith is lacking? Zahara wouldn't have brought us this far to let us fail now. Don't worry. Soon we'll be toasting our victory," Minerva said.

Minerva turned back to the battlefield, watching as the last traces of the fissures in the ground disappeared. She willed herself not to turn around until Anastasia's footsteps on the stairs had faded. *I can't let her see me cry*, she thought, swiping at her eyes. *Even a novice like me can feel the disturbance in the ether. A dark omen, indeed. All the more reason for her to be far from here.* Below, Anastasia and another Viper Knight mounted their horses, and rode off toward Graydare. *Toward the docks. And safety.*

"Signal the troops," Minerva ordered one of the officers atop the tower. "Prepare to charge."

Claire

The river of red smoke reached the allied lines. *Witchcraft.* The realization sent a chill through Claire. *We have to pull back.* She signaled the officers to retreat. Then the tremors started. The ground turned into a bucking, roiling nightmare beneath her feet. Fissures opened in the ground behind her. Claire and Kerry both turned and ran.

A shadow fell over her. *A roc*, she thought, bringing her twinlance up. A flash of green shot overhead, and a dragon roar split the air. "Breaus!" Claire yelled. Breaus turned and snapped his wings out, catching the air. He dropped, slamming down onto the shaking ground.

"Get on!" he roared. Claire grabbed a stirrup and hauled herself into the saddle. Reaching back, she helped Kerry up. A fissure raced toward them, and Breaus leapt into the air ahead of it. "Go to the headquarters tent!" Claire shouted at him.

The tent was far enough back to escape the tremors. Soldiers fled from the chasms splitting the ground, streaming back in retreat. Breaus landed next to the hill as the earthquake subsided, and the fissures began to seal. As soon as Claire and Kerry slid down, Breaus leapt into the air, soaring back toward the rocs. They ran to the tent. Officers swarmed around it, barking orders. Claire made her way to Adrian.

He stood at the edge of the hill, staring out through a spyglass. He turned to Claire, looking grim. "They've destroyed at least half our forces."

"There's no way we can win now, is there?" Claire asked.

"Win? We'll be lucky to make it off the field without losing what troops we have left. Look," he said, pointing to the base of the hills. The Drakari were gathered there, re-forming their battle lines. "They're getting ready to charge."

"Where is the Emperor?" Kerry asked. "Why doesn't he help us?"

"I don't know. I've been praying," Claire said. "Maybe he's not listening anymore."

"He is," a voice said from behind her.

"Sean! What are you doing this close to the front?"

"When Liam saw the smoke, I knew we had to ride up. It's as I feared. Minerva has joined Zahara."

"Zahara?" Claire asked.

"An enemy of The Emperor. He once was a star, like Caeli. Now he wields the dark powers, and claims to be a god himself. He has a cult of followers who practice his breed of sorcery. It would seem Minerva has joined it."

"What should we do, Sean?" Claire asked quietly. "We can't fight sorcery."

"The Emperor can. When Liam told me about the smoke, I prayed. And I heard an answer. Stand your ground, Claire. The Emperor will stand with you."

Claire bit her lip, indecision stabbing through her like a knife.

"Have faith," Sean urged.

She took a deep breath. "Adrian, signal the troops. Tell them to re-form the battle lines."

Adrian stepped closer. "Claire, we need to retreat while we still can," he said, his voice quiet, but firm. "Standing our ground is suicide."

"No. It's faith. Send the signal," she ordered.

Adrian hesitated for a heartbeat. Then he nodded. "As you command." He gestured to the signal officer.

"Now will he come to help us?" Claire asked Sean.

"They will," Sean said.

"Who?" Claire asked.

"Them," Liam said, pointing.

Claire turned to look. A line of white tigers, each bearing a white-robed Raider on its back, rode up toward them from the woods beyond the camp. *There must be at least two hundred,*

Claire thought. Then the halberds appeared behind the tigers. Line after line of halberds, bobbing up and down in time with the marching of the Hynbarrans carrying them.

CHAPTER 37

Claire

"You knew?" Claire asked.

Sean nodded. "He showed me."

"You could have told me."

Sean smiled. "And deny you the chance to have your faith rewarded?"

The Graithans rode up to the pavilion. The lead rider pulled the scarf from her face, and slid down from her tiger.

"Azaira. You were supposed to be here days ago," Claire said.

"We marched through Amira on our way up into Drakaren. We found that the Stenari had left a contingent behind to defend their capital. It took us several days to fight our way through the city," Azaira said.

"Well, you've come just in time," Claire said. "Ride to the front, and wait for the signal." Azaira nodded, and climbed onto her tiger. She waved her arm, and the other Graithans followed her to the field.

The Hynbarrans came next, led by a group of mounted officers. Ross rode at the front. He reined in his horse beside the hill, and stepped down from the saddle.

"And what brings you back?" Claire asked. There was a hard, icy feeling in her chest—as if the sight of him had frozen something deep within her.

Ross hung his head, and knelt down in front of his entire army. "I came back to beg your forgiveness, Your Majesty. And to offer our swords to you, if you'll have them."

Humility? Regret? Can this really be Ross? "Forgiveness for what, exactly?" Claire asked.

"For the way I behaved toward you. For deserting my allies right before the battle. For my arrogance." Ross looked at her, a pained expression on his face. Then he hung his head again.

"That's a great deal to forgive," Claire said. "What prompted this change of heart?"

"I was leading the army home when she appeared to me. And showed me how wrong I was," Ross said.

"She? Who is she?"

"Her," Ross said, pointing behind Claire.

Claire turned, her movement stirring the white fog drifting at her feet. *Fog?* The flash of pearl armor confirmed her suspicion. "Astra."

Astra smiled from beneath her winged helmet. "The Emperor heard you, Claire. And he answered. He's giving you a second chance to win this battle. Give Ross another chance, too. He's part of the Emperor's answer."

"How?"

"He has a role to play in this battle. His heart's changed, Claire. Give him the chance to prove it."

Claire looked at Ross. "Then I forgive you."

He rose. "Thank you, Your Majesty."

Claire turned to Astra. "Will you stay for the battle?"

Astra smiled. "Who do you think revealed Death to you? I've been here the whole time. Whether you see me or not, I'll always be watching over you." Astra shimmered—dissolving into a plume of mist, and rising to vanish into the sky.

"I thought the Drakari were the ones using sorcery," Adrian said, his face pale.

"It's a long story, Adrian. But it's far from sorcery. For now, though, we have a battle to win," Claire said.

"As you say, Your Majesty," Adrian answered, tearing his eyes from the spot where Astra had disappeared. He turned to Ross. "Lead your soldiers to the front. The Graithans will charge first. We'll be right behind them."

"We?" Claire asked.

"I'll lead our remaining soldiers in the final charge, Your Majesty," Adrian said.

"You're the Commandant. Your place is here, at the headquarters."

"Half our troops are dead, and the rest are terrified. They won't charge the hills after that smoke came down from them. But they will follow their commander if he charges. So I'll lead them. And we'll finish this."

Claire looked at him, his words sending a fiery shiver through her. "I chose you for courage, General. I see I chose well.

Ride out, and bring us the victory. I have one last order for you, though."

"Yes, Your Majesty?"

Claire leaned in toward him. "Be careful," she said softly. "Don't let me lose you." She took his hand in hers, and squeezed it.

Color crept into Adrian's cheeks, but this time, he didn't look away. His smile glowed like sunlight. "As you command, Claire."

She released his hand, and Adrian walked to his horse. He swung up into the saddle, and then turned back to look at her as he rode off.

"We do still have a battle to win," Kerry murmured next to her.

Now it was Claire's turn to blush. "Yes, we do. Find us some horses."

Kerry sent an officer to bring horses for them and the remaining Crown Guards. As they mounted up, the Graithans began their charge. The foot soldiers followed them, churning up a cloud of dust over the trampled battlefield.

Claire rode through the cloud, with Kerry and the guards behind her. The battle ahead was hidden by dust, but the screech of steel and screams of the wounded were easy enough to follow. Claire drew her sword as the sounds of battle grew closer. She emerged from the cloud, charging into the enemy lines.

She killed the first Drakari from the saddle, leaning over to catch his throat with her blade. She jumped down from her horse, cutting out a hole in their ranks with her sword. Kerry and the guards followed her into the fray. Claire slammed her sword back into its sheath and drew her twin lance, carving a bloody trail through the Drakari.

The minutes seemed to stretch into hours. Slash after slash, and enemy after enemy all whirled around her in the melee, until everything else faded away, and only the fighting remained. By the time the sound of the horns woke her from the trance of combat, it felt as if she had been fighting forever.

Claire looked around. Drakari horns were sounding the retreat, and their lines were melting away as the gray-clad soldiers fled for the hills. "They're running!" Kerry called to her. Keldari and Kirosian officers held the allied troops in their lines, waiting for orders.

But on the far side of the field, a dozen Raiders broke away from the Graithan ranks, spurring their tigers forward. Claire trained her spyglass on them. The Graithans charged after the Drakari, catching them near the crest of a hill. Within a stone's throw of a guard tower.

"Pull back, you fools," Claire muttered, watching the Graithans attack. A moment later, figures clad in black and silver armor came boiling out of the tower. The tigers and their riders fought fiercely, but soon, all twelve of the tigers were dead, and the Raiders fled down the hill, the Berserkers close behind them.

A single rider galloped up from the Keldari lines toward the Raiders, and Claire turned her spyglass toward him. "Adrian," she gasped. "What in the nether is he *doing*? "Is he trying to kill himself?" she shouted to Kerry, hearing the panic lacing her voice.

"One of those Raiders is Azaira," Kerry said, peering through her own spyglass.

"Even she's not worth his life. Get the horses," Claire ordered. "We have to go help him."

"The horses are gone, Claire. They've probably run all the way back to the camp by now."

Claire peered through the spyglass as Adrian reached the Berserkers, his sword flashing out in the sunlight. He killed one, and was about to down another when a warhammer blow knocked him from his horse. Three Ravek warriors surrounded him. Adrian dragged himself to his feet, holding his blade up to ward them off.

"Look," Kerry shouted.

Claire dragged her eyes away from him. Another rider charged toward the Berserkers. Claire brought the spyglass around. *Ross.* She watched his horse thunder closer. A Berserker turned and raised his warhammer.

A heartbeat before the horse reached the Berserker, Ross jumped from the saddle. He smashed into the Ravek, stabbing his blade into the warrior's throat. Ross leapt up and spun around. Two more Berserkers swung at him. He caught the first warhammer on his sword. But not the second.

The axe blade sliced into his arm, leaving a bloody ruin in its wake. Ross' sword fell from his hand. Another blow cut into his stomach, dropping him to his knees. A Ravek towered over him, raising his warhammer. *No,* Claire thought, a sick, sinking feeling gripping her. The Berserker smashed the warhammer down.

Claire turned away, a lump hardening in her throat. *He sacrificed himself. For Adrian. Or maybe it was for me.* She swallowed, and turned the spyglass back to Adrian. A group of Berserkers clustered near him, gesturing at the rank insignia on his collar. One gave an order, and they rushed at him.

Adrian's sword caught one Berserker in the throat. He drew it back to strike again—but a Berserker blade smashed into his hip. Adrian stabbed out wildly as he fell, burying his blade in the Ravek's leg. The other Berserkers swarmed in, beating and kicking him.

Tears streamed down Claire's face as she watched the Berserkers haul Adrian toward the tower. He was still fighting as they disappeared inside it. "No!" Claire screamed. She sank to her knees, burying her face in her hands.

CHAPTER 38

Claire

"Get up, Claire." Kerry shook her. "Get up! You can't help him from down there."

Claire stood. "We have to save him, Kerry. They must realize he's a General. They'll torture him for information."

"Or worse," Kerry said. A cloud of dust came rolling toward them from the front of the allied lines. The cloud slowed, clearing to reveal a group of white tigers, each carrying a Raider. One tiger also carried a second rider.

"Sean! What are you doing? You'll get yourself killed out here!" Claire exclaimed.

"Helping you," Sean said.

"You knew this would happen?"

"I knew you would need my help. And that you'd need the Raiders."

"You can't come with us, Sean. We're going into battle. You might be killed."

"I know. But I also know I have to go with you."

"I suppose the Emperor told you that?" Claire asked.

Sean nodded.

"Then I won't try to stop you. But you'll take guards along," she said, gesturing to the two remaining Crown Guards. They all mounted the tigers, seating themselves behind the

Graithans. "Head for the citadel," Claire told the Raider ahead of her. "And pick up your Emir on the way." They raced to the base of the hills, where they met the Raiders straggling back from the citadel.

Azaira led the limping survivors. She had lost her headscarf, and her dark hair whipped in the wind. A bloody slash was carved across her cheek, and anger burned in her eyes.

"What in the nether were you doing?" Claire demanded.

Azaira looked away. "I thought the rest of the troops were behind us. I wanted to press the charge and destroy them when we had the chance."

"Our soldiers wait for orders before charging. They don't let their bloodlust send them racing off into a trap!"

"If the Drakari had enslaved your people for two generations, you might have a bit of bloodlust yourself," Azaira shot back.

"I wouldn't throw my men's lives away like that. Or my allies' lives," Claire snapped.

The fire in Azaira's eyes dimmed. "I'm sorry about that," she said. "I can't tell you how sorry I am. Your Generals died bravely."

"One died bravely. We're going to save the other one," Claire said.

"We are?"

"You wanted Drakari blood?" Claire asked. "Come with us, and you can drown your sword in it."

Azaira nodded. She climbed onto a tiger, and they continued toward the citadel. As the tigers drew closer, arrows flashed out at them from the roof. They sped up, darting from side to side. Tigers and riders alike fell under the storm of arrows.

They reached the citadel, hugging the wall as they slid down from the tigers. Arrows rained down a few feet away, the overhanging wall shielding them from the archers. A heavy wooden door was set into the stone wall. Kerry felt the thickness of the beams, running her hands along the iron strips holding the door together. "We'll need a battering ram to bring this down."

"There's no time," Claire said. She drew her sword, flashing a signal toward the swirling cloud of rocs and dragons above. *I hope he's watching*, she thought, signaling again.

He was. A dragon peeled away from the fight, descending toward them. Breaus soared over the citadel, shooting a burst of fire at the archers on the roof. He made another pass, and then landed heavily next to the citadel. "Take out the door!" Claire shouted.

Breaus spit a ball of fire. It erupted against the wall, leaving a smoking wreck where the door had been. "Stay close," Claire told him. "We'll need you after we're done here."

Breaus nodded, and snapped his wings down, pulling himself back up into the air. Claire drew her sword, and kicked the scorched wood of the door. It crumbled beneath her boot. Claire and Kerry led the way into the citadel, with Azaira close behind.

The first two Berserkers were waiting around the corner. Claire killed one, and then ran the other through as he fought Kerry and Azaira. Kerry slashed the Berserker's throat as he fell, finishing him off. "There's probably more waiting around every corner."

"I know. We don't have time to fight floor by floor," Claire said. "Who knows what they're doing to Adrian."

"These hallways are wider than I thought they'd be," Azaira remarked.

"What of it?" Claire asked.

"They're wide enough for a tiger," Azaira said.

"You're right. Call them in," Claire ordered.

Azaira whistled, and the tigers stalked inside, crowding into the corridor. Azaira snarled to them, gesturing down the hallway. The tigers bared their teeth, and bounded off.

Claire called the rest of the riders in. "Stay here with Sean," she ordered the guards. "Kerry and Azaira, you and the Raiders come with me."

They passed through the hallways, stepping over broken and bleeding Ravek bodies. They came to a tall flight of stairs. Dead Berserkers and soldiers lay scattered at the base of the steps. A tiger lay among them. His blood-stained sides heaved as he struggled to breathe.

Azaira sheathed her sword. She knelt next to the tiger, talking softly to him, and smoothing his fur. She held her other hand out to Claire.

Claire's eyes grew wet. *I'm glad I don't have to do it*, she thought, handing Azaira her dagger. Azaira showed the knife to the tiger, still stroking his head and gently talking to him. Light gleamed silver along the blade, reflecting in the tiger's blue irises. The tiger licked Azaira's hand, and closed his eyes.

Claire turned away, squeezing her own eyes shut, a tear trickling down her cheek. Azaira's hand touched her shoulder, and Claire turned. Azaira wiped the dagger on her sleeve, and handed it back to Claire.

Claire looked into Azaira's eyes. The reflection of the blade glistened in the tears there, and for an instant, her eyes looked as blue as the tiger's. "I know now," Claire blurted out.

"Know what?" Azaira asked, wiping her eyes.

"How sorry you are."

Azaira's voice was soft, and sad. "I've known Zeran ever since he was a cub. He's carried me into battle many times. And now my foolishness has cost me him. I don't think you do know how sorry I am, Claire."

"Azaira, I..."

Azaira shook her head. "It's my own fault. We've both lost enough today. Let's go find your General. Before we lose anything more."

They made their way up the stairs, and through another hallway littered with bodies. Two more tigers lay dead amongst them. Another flight of stairs brought them to the top floor of the citadel. The remaining tigers waited in the corridor there, beside a narrow door.

"We're on our own from here," Azaira said. "They won't fit through that."

"No, I suppose they won't." Claire ran her hand over the heavy beams of the door. It wasn't nearly as thick as the one below. But it was thick enough. *It'll take hours for us to break this down*, she thought. "But can they open it?"

Azaira looked at the door. "I think so." She purred at the tigers, scratching one's head. She slapped her hand against the door and growled to them. "Stand back," Azaira warned. They went to the far end of the hall. The first tiger took a few steps back, and then raced down the corridor. It leapt up onto its rear legs, crashing its front paws against the door. Wood splintered beneath its weight. It stood aside, and a second tiger came crashing against the door. Then a third. The fourth tiger sent the door flying off its hinges.

Claire rushed into a large room, with Kerry and Azaira right behind her. Three Berserkers faced them. Their warhammers were slung on their belts, and swords filled their fists. A Drakari officer stood behind the Berserkers. Adrian slumped in a chair next to him. Adrian's face was covered in bruises, and blood trickled from a dozen wounds all over his body. A noose was cinched tight around his neck. The rope was slung over a beam in the ceiling, and the officer gripped the loose end. "Kill them!" the officer roared.

The Berserkers charged, their steel slicing through the air. Claire traded blows with one Ravek, until she managed to slip her blade under his. She finished him with a quick stab to the throat, and turned to face the others. Azaira and Kerry fought one Berserker, while the other cut his way through the Raiders.

Claire ran to help Kerry. The third Berserker killed the last of the Raiders, and turned toward her. Claire caught his blade with hers. Their steel screeched as they dueled.

"Kill them! Kill them!" the officer shrieked. He pulled on the rope, hauling Adrian up out of the chair. Claire's eyes darted to Adrian. His body twisted in the air; he clawed at his throat, choking and gasping.

In the corner of Claire's eye, a steel-encased fist appeared, flying at her face. Time slowed to a crawl as the armored fist grew closer. Her eyes flicked to the Berserker's sword, locked with her blade. Only one of his hands held the sword hilt. *Scite*, she thought, just as his fist hammered into her face.

The room spun as she fell and slammed into the floor. Claire caught her breath and rolled on her side, jerking her dagger from its sheath. She buried the dagger in the Ravek's thigh. He howled, purple blood spurting from his leg. Claire stabbed her sword into the Berserker's stomach, just below his chestplate. She twisted the blade, cutting off his cries of agony.

Pain pounded in Claire's face. She jerked her sword free from the falling body, and looked at Adrian. His face was a horrible shade of blue, and his hands flailed weakly at the rope. Claire spun at the scream from behind her.

The last Berserker jerked his sword free of Azaira's leg, the steel dripping with blood. Azaira crumpled, clutching her maimed leg. Kerry was on the floor behind the Berserker, crawling toward her fallen sword. The Berserker turned, swinging his blade up as he advanced on Kerry. Claire charged. *I won't make it in time,* she realized.

Azaira lifted herself up on one elbow. Her scimitar flashed out, slicing through the back of the Berserker's knee. The Ravek dropped with a roar. He fell onto his good knee, and pivoted, swinging at Azaira. She weakly parried his blows.

The Berserker spotted Claire coming, and swung at her. Claire caught his blade on her steel, twisting it downward and out from his grasp. He drew his warhammer.

Claire jerked her blade up, stabbing it into the eye socket of his helmet. The Ravek convulsed, the warhammer slipping from his hand. Claire pulled her sword free and leapt over the falling Berserker.

The officer dropped the rope, letting Adrian fall. He fumbled at the hilt of his sword, but Claire ran him through before his blade cleared the scabbard. He wailed, and crumpled to the floor.

Leaving her sword buried in the officer, Claire knelt by Adrian's side. His face was as gray as a Ravek's skin, and his chest barely rose with each sporadic breath. Panic boiled through Claire. She touched his neck, feeling the veins. His pulse was weak beneath her fingers.

Claire shook him. "Adrian!" she shouted. She shook him again, harder. "*Adrian!*" she screamed.

Kerry knelt next to her, and bent to listen to his chest. "His heart is too slow, Claire. He won't make it."

"No," Claire whispered, pulling Adrian up and wrapping her arms around him.   "No."   Tears flowed from her eyes.

CHAPTER 39

Claire

Kerry put an arm around her. "I didn't know he meant so much to you," she said softly.

"I didn't either," Claire sobbed. "Until now."

There was a sound behind them. Kerry grabbed her sword, jumping to her feet. Claire glanced over her shoulder. Sean stood there with the two Crown Guards. "What are you doing up here?" Claire asked.

"I had a feeling I should come," Sean said. "I felt a call."

"I felt a call also," a voice spoke from behind Claire.

Azaira gasped, pointing a trembling finger at Adrian. Claire turned. Death knelt on the other side of his body, her dark wings spread out to encircle him. The black fire of her gaze burned into Claire's eyes.

Kerry pointed her sword at Death. "And what is she? Another valkyrie?"

"No. Put your sword away, Kerry. Steel is no use against Death," Claire said. Kerry's face went white.

"What call?" Claire asked Death.

"A summons. From his spirit."

"No," Claire said, tears spilling down her cheeks. "Please."

Death's voice was gentle, almost kind. "Look at his suffering, Claire. It's a mercy for me to take him. Sometimes I'm a hunter. But sometimes I'm a blessing."

"It's not his time," Sean said.

"Then why does his spirit still call to me?" Death asked, touching her fingers to Adrian's forehead.

"Because The Emperor hasn't called him back yet. Bring me to him," Sean told the guards. They led him over, staring with wide eyes at Death. They helped Sean kneel down next to Claire, careful to stay as far from Death as possible.

"Can you save him?" Claire asked.

"No. But The Emperor can." Sean pulled the crystal flask from his robe and laid it on Adrian's chest. The liquid inside cast a pure, white glow over Adrian's gray face. Sean started singing a prayer in the Startongue. His voice rose, then fell, like waves rolling against the shore. He sang the final verse, and fell silent, his voice echoing faintly off the chamber's stone walls.

Adrian's chest shuddered, and then fell, his breath leaving him. Death looked at Adrian, and then at Claire. There was no triumph on Death's face. No gloating. Just something that looked almost like sympathy.

"Have faith," Sean told Claire.

"It's time," Death said. She leaned down, her lips brushing Adrian's, as if she were giving him a kiss. Suddenly, Death's head jerked back. A glowing strand of light stretched from the flask to Death's pale lips, hanging in the air like a frozen bolt of lightning.

The flask glowed brighter, illuminating the entire room. Luminous tendrils stretched out from it, winding themselves around Adrian's body, enveloping him in a cloud of light. The strand of light pushed Death's head away as the flask flared into an almost unbearable brightness. Then the light dissolved into a shower of white sparks.

Adrian opened his eyes…and breathed. Color flooded back into his skin. Blood still seeped from his wounds, but he was alive. He moved, and groaned in pain. "Just lie still," Claire told him, joy flooding through her. "Save your strength." Adrian closed his eyes. A moment later, he was asleep. But his chest still rose and fell, his breathing deep and steady.

Death's wings rustled, folding behind her back. "You were right, prophet," she told Sean. "It's not his time." She reached out and touched Claire's face.

The fingers were frigid against Claire's skin, but she forced herself not to pull back. Claire held Death's gaze, staring into the dark currents churning in her eyes. "But today may yet be your time," Death said. "Today, I am *everywhere*."

"Now you sound like yourself again. Like a hunter," Claire said.

Death withdrew her hand. "I told you. I can be a hunter, or a blessing. Sometimes both. But to me, you'll always be prey. Prey I've learned to respect. But prey nonetheless."

"And why are you so eager to hunt me?" Claire demanded, a shiver rippling through her.

"You're marked."

"Aren't all people marked for death?" Claire asked.

"Yes. But you are marked for greatness. And those with that mark call to me all the more strongly. People like you burn brightly, and die young. And make tantalizing trophies."

"I'm no one's trophy," Claire said.

"Someday, you'll feel my kiss. Then you will be my trophy. And until you are, I'll always be nearby. The mark calls to you also, Claire. Like a moth to a lantern. It draws you close to the flame. One day, it will lure you too close. And on that day, I'll be there to claim you." Death smiled. "It may yet be today. Minerva awaits you in Graydare. Wherever she is, I'm always nearby."

Death stood. "Minerva will be waiting at Proterian Palace. And so will I." She dissolved into a cloud of gray mist. The cloud rushed at Claire, passing through her. Claire gasped. It was like being stabbed by a thousand icicles. Then the mist vanished, dissipating into the air. Claire took a deep breath. The pain was gone, but the chill remained.

Kerry stared at her. "First Valkyries, and now Death," Kerry muttered. "What next?"

"Minerva. That's what next," Claire said. She reached out and touched Adrian's cheek. "But we can't just leave him here."

"I'll stay with him," Sean said. "Leave one of the guards here, and have the other take a tiger to bring help."

"A tiger won't let just anyone ride him," Azaira said, struggling to sit up. "Not without a Raider riding along. I'll go with you."

"Can you ride?" Claire asked, looking at the bloody gash in Azaira's leg.

"I think so. Bind the wound, and I can make it. Besides, I'd rather risk the journey than stay here and wait for that demon to come back," Azaira said with a shudder, looking at the spot where Death had vanished.

Kerry bandaged Azaira's leg, and one of the guards helped her limp downstairs to the tigers. "Take care of him, Sean," Claire said, pausing at the stairs.

"I will. Be careful, Claire. I'll be praying for you," Sean said.

"I'll need it."

Claire and Kerry helped Azaira out of the citadel, and onto a tiger. "I'll send a surgeon back for Adrian," Azaira promised. As Azaira and the guard rode off, Claire looked into the sky. Two dragons circled overhead. She gave a roar, and Breaus answered.

Breaus and Shanra landed next to them, and Sloane slid down. "We've finished off the last of the rocs. We lost several dragons, but the skies are ours again," Sloane said.

"And what of their army?" Claire asked.

"Broken. The survivors are fleeing into the city. Some of them may try to fight us through the streets. If they do stand and fight, it will take our armies days to reach the palace, Claire. And I saw ships in the harbor. If we wait for the army, Minerva will slip through our grasp," Sloane said.

"I don't think Minerva is going anywhere. She'll make her stand at the palace. But you're right. We don't have time to wait for the army to fight through the city. If we kill Minerva, they might not have to," Claire said.

"Cut off the head of the snake, and the body will die," Sloane said. "Their army will probably surrender once Minerva is dead. But the Viper Knights and Berserkers never will."

"That will still save many lives. The fewer enemies our troops have to face, the better. Gather as many dragons as you can," Claire ordered. "We're going after Minerva."

"I'm coming with you," Kerry said.

"Of course." They climbed onto Breaus' saddle. Breaus leapt into the air, and they circled while Sloane and Shanra flew off to gather more dragons.

They were twenty dragons strong when they set off for Graydare, soaring over the hills and into the valley. Soon, the gray, gloomy city sprawled out before them. Breaus growled low in his throat. "What is it?" Claire shouted.

"Trouble," he rumbled, nodding toward a gray castle. Dark, winged shapes rose from the castle's roof. *More rocs*, she thought, a heavy stone of dread forming in her stomach.

The rocs formed a dark cloud, heading toward them. As they drew closer, the dark-robed figures they carried came into view. Claire turned to Kerry. "Viper Knights!" she shouted.

The huge ravens closed in on them. One roc headed straight for Breaus, slamming into him like a tidal wave. Breaus snapped at the bird's head. The roc screamed, digging its talons into him.

The roc's rider stood in his saddle, and jumped. The Viper Knight landed on Breaus' back, near the base of his tail. The knight half-crawled, half-walked toward them, struggling to keep his balance as Breaus rocked and pitched, battling the roc. Behind her, Kerry rose from the saddle, drawing her sword and screaming a challenge. The knight drew his own sword as Kerry charged.

The knight caught her blade with his, and kicked her in the knee. Kerry stumbled. The knight forced her sword back, and smashed his fist into her face. Losing her balance, Kerry tumbled over Breaus' side.

"KERRY!" Claire screamed. A horrible, gutted feeling tore through her as she watched Kerry fall. A screech rent the air. Claire turned. Shanra's jaws snapped around the neck of the roc she was fighting. Shanra gave her head a shake, releasing the roc's body. As the raven fell, the dragon dove after it, her wings pulling hard through the air.

There was a hiss behind her. Claire spun, drawing her sword. A flash of silver flew toward her. Claire jerked her gauntlet up just in time to deflect the helmet away from her head. She yanked her blade from its scabbard, her eyes snapping to the Viper Knight. He moved toward her, his long hair streaming in the wind.

"Captain Varin?" Claire gasped.

"*Sir* Varin, usurper," he spat. "Knight of the Viper Order. Servant of the true king. And executioner of the false queen." Varin advanced, his sword raised. He swung, and she parried his blow. Claire slashed at him. He caught her blade with his, the impact rattling her arm. They fought back and forth, lurching and jolting along with Breaus as he and the roc clashed.

Breaus pitched forward just as Varin lunged at her. Varin lost his footing, and slid along Breaus' body. He managed to grab the dragon's tail, clinging to it as Breaus jerked and rolled in the air. Claire crawled along Breaus' back, holding on to the ridges running along his spine. Reaching the base of his tail, Claire stood, raising her sword.

The roc kicked Breaus in the head. Stunned, the dragon pitched downward. Claire lost her balance and fell, just as Varin fell also. Clinging to her sword, Claire managed to grab the horn of the saddle as she fell past it. Varin slammed into one of Breaus' feet. He wrapped his arms around it, clinging to the dragon. Breaus righted himself, flying back at the roc.

Varin hung from Breaus' foot, far from the reach of Claire's sword. An idea flashed into her head. She crawled to the side of the saddle, and gripped its leather strap. Claire slid down the strap, jerking to a stop when her hand hit the metal buckle against Breaus' belly. Varin clung to Breaus' foot, within reach of her blade.

Claire thrust her sword into Varin's shoulder. He gave a cry of pain, and his sword slipped from his grasp. His arm dropped, hanging limp at his side. Varin wrapped his other arm tightly around Breaus' leg, and used his feet to propel himself up at her. He bared his teeth in a snarl, his face a mask of hatred. Claire kicked, her boot smashing into his head. He kept climbing. Claire

kicked him again, feeling his nose crunch beneath her heel. Varin
lost his grip and fell, screaming in rage.

CHAPTER 40

Claire

Sheathing her sword, Claire hauled herself back up to the saddle. Breaus kicked the roc, slashing its stomach with his claws. He whipped his tail into the raven's neck. Bones snapped, and the bird plummeted to the ground.

Breaus leveled out, and turned his head back to her. "All right?" he bellowed.

"I'm fine," she said.

"Kerry?" he asked. Claire shook her head.

I'm sorry," he rumbled. Claire nodded, tears rushing to her eyes. *Later. Deal with it later*, she thought. *Or you'll never be able to finish this*. She shook her head, forcing her feelings down deep inside her. Shanra flew up alongside them. *At least Sloane is safe*, she thought, looking over at the dragon. Then she stood straight up in the saddle.

Kerry was sitting behind Sloane. "Breaus!" she screamed. "It's Kerry! Shanra has her!"

"I wondered why she was diving after a dead roc. She must have gone down to catch Kerry. No wonder she was flying so hard," he said.

Claire waved to Kerry, her eyes swimming with tears. Kerry gave her a quick wave back, and then resumed her death grip on the saddle.

"The other rocs are gone," Breaus said. "The way is clear."

"Take us to the palace," she ordered. Breaus landed on the roof of the sprawling castle. Claire slid down, counting the other dragons as they landed. *Fifteen left.*

Claire ran over to Shanra. As soon as Kerry's boots hit the roof, Claire hugged her tight. "I thought I'd lost you," Claire said, holding back a sob.

"You almost did. If it weren't for Sloane and her dragon…" Kerry's voice trailed off.

"You're alive, and that's all that matters. We have a battle to win. Focus on that," Claire said.

Kerry nodded. "I'll take a horse back to Tara after the battle is over, though. I'm not flying anywhere again. At least not for a long time."

Claire smiled. "I don't blame you."

Sloane shouted from the other side of the roof, waving them over. She pointed out a door set into a tower. "Locked. Of course."

"We have a key." Claire gestured to Breaus. He walked over, his steps shaking the roof. Lifting his foot, he smashed it through the door. The knights drew their swords and started down the stairs into the palace.

Breaus lowered his head to her, and Claire stroked his nose. "I'll see you soon," she said.

"I'll wait for you above."

Claire shook her head. "Don't wait for me. Take the other dragons to the edge of the city. Our troops will be there soon. Help them fight through whatever defenses the Drakari have left."

His eyes darkened, a frown etching across his mouth. But he nodded. "As you say. I'll see you after..." his voice trailed off.

There was a tremor, almost hidden beneath the stone and thunder of Breaus' growl. *But I can hear it*, she thought. She stared into the golden fire of his eyes. "Don't worry, Breaus. I'll be fine."

"It's just another test, Claire. Just another wolfworm to kill. You did it once. And you can do it again."

"I know." But Death's face flashed in her mind, and her words echoed in Claire's head—*Minerva will be waiting at the palace. And so will I.*

"I'll use my fire," she promised Breaus, giving him a kiss on the cheek. "Our soldiers are coming. Go light their way."

Breaus took a step back, and leapt into the sky, his wings sending air gusting down around her. He bellowed to the other dragons, and they followed him up. Claire paused at the top of the stairs. Breaus turned his head toward her, and she roared up at him. He answered, the other dragons joining in. Claire turned and descended the steps, their roars echoing after her.

She emerged into a long, dusty corridor, filled with faded paintings and worn tapestries. The knights spread out along the hall, their swords drawn. Claire took the lead. "Where are the guards?" she asked.

"Waiting for us, most likely," Kerry said. "Protecting the only thing that really matters in this palace—Minerva." They turned a corner, and came out onto a balcony.

A grand staircase stretched out below them, descending into a great hall. The hall was filled with palace guards. Their weapons glittered in the sunlight streaming through the windows. A squad of Berserkers guarded a tall wooden door at the far end of the hall. A door with the outline of a crown carved into it.

The Drakari bellowed at the sight of them. They began beating their swords against their shields, marching toward the staircase.

"Look," Sloane said quietly, pointing to the huge windows lining the hall. Outside, swarms of Drakari soldiers were converging on the palace. "Survivors from the battle?"

Claire nodded. "There must be a hundred of them."

"At least. All flocking here to defend their queen."

"After we've killed the guards here, send the rest of the knights down to the lower levels to hold off those soldiers," Claire ordered. "You and Kerry come with me after Minerva." Sloane nodded.

Claire sheathed her sword, and drew her twinlance. She went to the head of the stairs, turning to look back at the knights behind her. Claire lifted her lance. "For Keldaren!" she shouted.

"Keldaren!" they roared. She turned, and led the charge down the staircase. Guard after guard fell beneath her swirling blades. She and the other knights fought through the hall, Kerry never straying far from her side. Finally, they reached the Berserkers.

Claire charged at one, feinting high, then slashing his arm when he moved to block her. She stabbed him in the stomach, and twisted the lance, sending him crumpling to the ground. She kicked the next Berserker in the face. As he stumbled backward, she slipped her blade behind the greave protecting his leg. Claire cut into him, hitting an artery. He fell in a spray of purple blood.

Around Claire, knights clashed with the other Berserkers. One more Ravek warrior stood between her and the door. He raised his warhammer, baring his needle-point teeth. His empty white eyes glistened behind his skull-faced helmet.

"Die," he snarled, swinging at her. Claire ducked under the warhammer. He kicked her, and she lost her balance, crashing to the ground. Her armor rang with the impact, and her lance fell from her hand. The Berserker stood above her, hoisting the warhammer high over his head. Claire flailed out with her hand, and felt the knurled steel of the lance shaft. She grabbed it, stabbing the blade into the Ravek's armpit. He gasped as she twisted it inside him.

Claire jerked the lance free, scrambling to her feet. The Berserker sank to his knees, his white eyes wide in shock. She kicked him onto his back and slashed his throat. Claire stepped over the spreading pool of purple blood, and tried the handle of the door. *Locked.*

"Your Majesty!" Sloane called. "The Drakari have reached the gates!"

Claire turned to the knights. "Go and hold them in the lower levels. This castle must have at least a dozen stairwells. Find a narrow one, and you can kill them all as they try to fight their way up."

"We'll hold them, Your Majesty," a knight promised. All the knights except Sloane followed him out of the hall.

Claire, Kerry, and Sloane were left standing alone before the door. It was tall and heavy, fashioned from dark ebony. The polished wood reflected the light of the oil lamps hanging on the wall beside it.

"We need a dragon to break this door down," Kerry said.

"We don't have a dragon. But we do have fire," Claire said, grabbing one of the lamps. She poured the oil over the door, and stepped back, hurling the lamp at it. The glass shattered, and the wick set the oil alight. The flames spread, burning through the door until only a few smoldering pieces still clung to the stone frame.

Claire held her twinlance at the ready, leading the way up the stone steps beyond the door. They ascended into a throne room. Rows of braziers cast flickering shadows between the statues lining the chamber. A narrow strip of black carpet ran down the middle of the room, leading to a dais against the far wall. An ebony throne, carved into the shape of a raven, stood atop it.

A woman sat on the throne. A spiked crown of bronze rested atop her blond curls. She wore a black dress, and a sheathed sword on her belt. "Minerva," Claire said.

"You must be Claire," Minerva said, tapping her fingers on the hilt of her sword. "The girl who just won't die." Two Viper Knights stood guard behind the throne, and two Berserkers waited at the foot of the dais. Jared stood between them, his sword drawn.

"It's over," Claire said. "Surrender. No one else needs to die today."

Minerva smiled. "One more person needs to die, Claire. You."

CHAPTER 41

Claire

The Berserkers growled, and started toward Claire, raising their warhammers. "Stop," Minerva called. "Jared will do it."

Jared turned to look at Minerva. "You wanted revenge," Minerva said. "Take it."

Jared turned back to Claire, and raised his sword.

My brother, Claire thought. *I have to kill my own brother.* She spun her twinlance around, pointing it at him as he advanced. "Don't make me do this, Jared."

The sword trembled a little in his grasp. He clasped the hilt of the blade with both hands, holding it steady. Claire looked into his eyes. Hesitation flickered in his gaze. *He doesn't want this,* she realized.

"Save him," a voice whispered. It was a man's voice, deep and soft. A voice she knew from the island, and from the wind in the trees.

I can't.

"You must," the voice whispered.

How? she thought. But the voice was silent. Kerry moved between her and Jared, her sword raised. "No," Claire said, pulling Kerry back. "Don't interfere. You, too," she told Sloane. "Both of you stay back. Whatever happens, don't intervene."

"Claire, you can't expect me to just..." Kerry began.

"*Don't interfere*," Claire said, cutting her off. "No matter what. That's an order. Understand?"

Kerry stared at her. Her eyes were filled with confusion, and worry. "No," she said. "I don't understand. But I'll stay back."

Claire turned to Jared. "Don't do this. This isn't who you are."

"This is exactly who I am," he said, starting toward her.

"It's not the brother I remember. You were distant. You were even cold sometimes. But you were never evil, Jared. Remember the time we were wading in the lake?"

Jared stopped advancing, and his sword lowered a little. "You went in too deep. You didn't know how to swim yet."

"I started going under," Claire said. "And then you came and pulled me out. You saved me." She lowered her lance. "Now you're in too deep. It's my turn to save you."

"I don't need to be saved."

"We all need saving, Jared."

"There's no saving me from what I've done. From what I've become," he said quietly, sadness falling like twilight over his face.

There it is, she thought. The same look she had seen so many times when they were children. Suddenly, all she could see was the scared, lost-looking boy she had grown up with. Jared's lip trembled, his sword wavering.

"There's always a way back," Claire said. "You always have a choice. Choose to change. Put down the sword, and let me help you."

"Put down the sword, and she'll kill you," Minerva said. "Do you really think she's just going to forgive you for everything you've done?"

I can forgive him, Claire realized. *I really can.* "I do forgive you," she said, looking at Jared.

"Have faith." The words were Sean's, but the voice that whispered them to her was the Emperor's. Claire laid her twinlance on the floor.

Behind her, Sloane gasped, while Kerry muttered a quiet curse. Jared looked at the lance, and then at her, confusion written across his face.

"Kill the fool, Jared. Kill her and erase your failures. Kill her and take back what's yours. Kill her *now*," Minerva ordered.

Jared tightened his grip on the sword, his eyes hardening. "Pick up your weapon."

Claire shook her head. "No."

"Then I'll kill you where you stand."

"You have a choice, Jared. Remember that. There's always a way back," Claire said.

Fear and anger flashed across Jared's face. He came at her again, his sword raised. Kerry moved forward. "Stay where you are," Claire said, gesturing her back.

Jared advanced, lifting his blade above his head. Claire closed her eyes. *Faith is trust*, she thought. She felt a gust of air against her neck. A heartbeat passed—then another, and there was still no sting of steel against her skin.

Claire opened her eyes. Jared stood in front of her, his sword hovering inches from her neck. The blade shook in his hands. Jared's eyes glistened, and he bit his lip, a trickle of blood running down from it. His eyes met hers. "I can't," he said. "I can't do it." He threw down his sword.

Tears swam in her eyes, and a tremor of relief rippled through her. *Thank you*, Claire prayed silently. She held out her arms to him. From the corner of her eye, she saw Minerva's arm snapping down. There was a silver sparkle in the air, and then a look of shock on Jared's face. He reached behind him, and pulled his hand back, staring at the blood on his fingers.

Jared stumbled a few steps, and collapsed into Claire's arms. The thin handle of a throwing knife protruded from his back, the steel shining brightly against the dark stain spreading across his tunic.

Jared coughed. A tear rolled down his cheek. "Sorry," he gasped, his eyes catching hers. "I'm sorry, Claire."

"I forgive you," she said, touching his cheek.

"Why?" He coughed again, blood flecking his lips.

"Because you're my brother. Because I love you."

He smiled. *The first smile I've seen from him in years*, she realized, a lump forming in her throat. Jared coughed again, his body shuddering. A thin stream of red trickled from his mouth. "Thank you," he whispered. His eyes closed, and his head slumped against her shoulder.

Tears coursed down Claire's face. She gently laid Jared down on his side. His hair fell down over his eyes, and she brushed it back.

"How touching," Minerva said. "I wouldn't have thought you'd shed any tears for him."

"You'll pay for this, Minerva."

"You should be thanking me. He and I planned your father's death together. Just as we planned to poison you. He attacked your palace and invaded your country. The blood of thousands of Keldari soldiers is on his hands. Your father is dead because of him. *You* would be dead because of him, had the poison worked." Minerva shook her head. "Yet you weep over his body."

"He changed. He was sorry, in the end. And he was my brother. I suppose you don't have anyone you love. Anyone that you'd care enough about to cry over if they died. I wouldn't expect you to understand. You're just a cold, heartless monster."

Minerva sighed. "I wish I really was the monster you think I am. It would be so much easier. I don't need your understanding, Claire. I just need you out of my way."

"Then you have a problem," Claire said, picking up her twinlance. "I'm not going anywhere."

"We'll see. Kill them," Minerva ordered, gesturing to her guards.

The Berserkers started forward, hoisting their warhammers. Even for Ravek, these two were giants, standing at least eight feet tall. The Viper Knights followed, drawing silver swords from their robes. A Berserker and one of the knights came at her, while the others headed for Kerry and Sloane.

The Berserker charged, swinging his warhammer. Claire ducked under the blow. She kicked him, and he stumbled. Claire swung her lance around and parried an attack from the knight. She thrust the lance out, aiming for his head. He ducked and slashed at her knee, but Claire deflected his blade. She whipped her lance up, grasping it with both hands. Claire smashed the center of the shaft into the knight's helmet, knocking him onto his back.

The Berserker roared behind her, swinging his warhammer. Claire dropped to her knees, the warhammer passing above her helmet. Her steel greaves clanged as her shins hit the floor. She spun on her knees to face the Berserker. She slashed at him, her lance blade carving a purple trail across his gray cheek. He swung the warhammer up, then down at her head.

Claire caught the warhammer with the shaft of her lance. A clang rang out as the lance split in two beneath the hammer head. The Berserker pulled his weapon back for another blow. Claire dove between his legs, drawing her dagger. She leapt to her feet behind him and buried the dagger in his neck. The Berserker slumped to his knees. Claire freed her blade, and he toppled over, a purple pool spreading beneath him.

Claire sheathed the dagger and drew her sword. The knight stepped over the Ravek's body, heading for her. His sword flashed out and she parried it. They fought, her ears ringing with the smash of steel. *This one's strong*, she thought. *Not fast for a*

Viper Knight. But strong. Every blow against her blade sent waves of pain rippling through her wrists.

Claire's arms grew heavy, her muscles burning. The knight pushed her back, driving her toward the wall. Across the room, Kerry killed the Berserker she was fighting. She rushed to help Claire.

The knight shot a glance at Kerry as he slashed at Claire's head. Claire moved to block him. He shot out a steel-gauntleted fist, striking just below her chest plate. The blow was like a kick from a horse. She doubled over. The knight brought the hilt of his sword crashing down on the back of her helmet. Claire fell flat on her stomach, her sword flying from her grasp.

Kerry stabbed at the knight. He darted aside, slashing her thigh. Kerry clutched her leg, and the knight's blade darted past hers, tearing into her shoulder. She screamed in pain, dropping her sword.

The knight kicked Kerry's leg, driving her to her knees. He aimed his blade at her face, and pulled his arm back. *He's going to kill her*, Claire thought. Alarm shot through her, slicing through the dizziness and pain clouding her head. Claire tore off her helmet and hurled it at the knight.

The helmet hit his arm just as he swung. The blade jolted, missing Kerry's head by inches. The knight kicked Kerry in the chest, knocking her onto her back. He turned, and advanced on Claire.

Claire staggered up onto her hands and knees, crawling toward her sword. The knight stomped his foot down onto her back, slamming her flat to the ground. "Stay still," he hissed. "Or it may take more than one blow." He raised his blade, lining it up with her neck. Claire's gaze fell on half of her shattered twinlance.

She darted her hand out, her fingers closing around the knurled metal. She thrust the lance under the knight's helmet. The blade shot up through his chin, filling his mouth with steel.

Blood spurted from the silver fangs of his helmet. The knight's eyes widened, and he gave a muffled cry of pain. Claire shoved the lance deeper. The knight's arms and legs convulsed. His sword fell to the floor, and his body followed it down.

Claire sat up, her head ringing. On the other side of the room, Sloane was battling the remaining Viper Knight. Claire found her sword, and went to Kerry. "How bad?"

"I'll live," Kerry gasped. "But I won't be much help."

"Don't worry," Claire told her. "Sloane and I can handle Minerva."

"Can you?" Minerva asked. She stood, removing her crown. She set it down on the throne, and drew her sword. It was black steel, with ripples forged into the blade.

"The Black Blade of Drakaren," Minerva said, walking down the steps of the dais. "Forged for King Inverin, and carried by every Drakari ruler since. No one bearing this sword has ever been defeated."

Claire turned toward her. "Then you'll be the first." She charged, swinging at Minerva. Minerva leapt into the air, somersaulting above Claire and landing behind her. Claire barely had time to block the black steel flashing at her.

Minerva shoved Claire's blade with hers, pushing her back. "I trained as a Viper Knight. I'm as good with a sword as you," Minerva growled.

The steel flashed toward her, and Claire jerked her head back, feeling the puff of air across her neck, the sword slicing bare inches from her skin. *As good?* Claire thought, the acrid taste of fear filling her mouth. *She might be better.* A cry of pain came from behind her. Claire looked just as the Viper Knight stabbed Sloane's thigh. Sloane's sword whipped around, slashing through the knight's throat. As the knight dropped, Sloane fell too, his sword buried deep in her leg.

Claire ripped her attention away from Sloane, her eyes searching for Minerva's sword. The black steel stabbed at her, light rippling along the wavy blade. Claire brought her sword up. *Too late*, she thought, bracing herself. Her blade caught Minerva's sword, deflecting it. But as the sword shot by her, pain ripped across her left arm. Her arm dropped, blood running from the gash Minerva had carved into her.

Minerva jerked her sword back, slashing at her again. Claire parried the blade, her left arm hanging uselessly at her side. Minerva attacked furiously, pushing her across the room. Her blows pinned Claire up against the back of the throne. Claire jumped, flipping backward in the air, and landed atop the throne.

She rained blows down on Minerva. The throne rocked unsteadily beneath her, and Claire shifted her weight, tipping it over. Minerva jumped clear just before the throne crashed down onto the floor. Claire leapt after her. Her sword sliced into

Minerva, cutting deep into her side. Blood spread in a dark circle over Minerva's dress.

Minerva smashed her blade into Claire's, pushing her back across the room. As she forced Claire past a table, Minerva grabbed a glass pitcher from it. She locked her blade with Claire's, and swung the pitcher.

It smashed into the side of Claire's head, bursting into shards. Pieces of glass fell in a glittering cloud around her, while others bit deep into her skin. Claire fell, pain shrieking through her head. Through a dull haze, she saw Minerva turn and run to an alcove at the back of the throne room. Minerva opened a door, and disappeared up a flight of stairs.

CHAPTER 42

Claire

Claire groaned, her head swimming, and pain stabbing through her skull. She raised herself to all fours, her stomach heaving. Claire pulled herself to her feet, and reached up to touch her head. Her hair was slick with blood. She stumbled over to Sloane, who lay on her side, clutching her thigh. A silver sword hilt, shaped like a snake's body, protruded from her leg. The blade was buried deep in her skin, surrounded by a pool of blood.

"Sloane," Claire gasped.

"It looks worse than it is," Sloane said, with a grim smile.

"It looks bad enough."

Sloane shook her head. "I'll survive."

"Let's get you over to Kerry." Claire helped Sloane up onto her good leg, supporting her as they made their way over to where Kerry lay. She helped Sloane sit down. "Hang on, Kerry," Claire said. "I'll go for help when I get back."

Kerry grabbed her arm. "When you get back? You aren't going after her. Not alone."

"I have to. She might escape, or try to work some other sorcery against our troops. Someone has to go finish her off. And you two aren't in any shape to help me."

"Wait for our soldiers to get here," Kerry urged. "Or at least wait for the other knights to come back from the lower levels."

Claire shook her head. "That could take hours. I'm going after Minerva now."

Kerry released her arm. "Be careful," she said quietly.

"I will."

"At least let me bandage your arm, Your Majesty," Sloane said. She tore a strip of cloth from her uniform, and wrapped it tightly around Claire's wound. "Watch yourself up there."

Claire nodded. "I'll be back." She went to the stairs, and climbed the twisting stone steps, her sword at the ready. Finally, she reached a door. She cautiously pushed it open, and found herself on the roof of the castle's tallest tower.

Minerva stood on the far side, staring out from between the battlements. Her sword hung sheathed at her side. The only dragons in sight were far away, flying near the edge of the city. They were all alone atop the tower.

"Jump," Claire said. "Save me the trouble of killing you."

Minerva turned. "I thought about it," she said, a sad smile on her face. "But that would be too easy. I have to at least try to win." Her side glistened in the fading sunlight, dripping with blood.

"I thought you'd be eager to kill me," Claire said.

"Why? Graydare is about to fall. No matter what happens, my rule is coming to an end. What reason would there be to kill you? Besides revenge."

"And that isn't enough of a reason to kill me?" Claire asked.

"It is. But not enough to make me eager to do it." Minerva shook her head. "You have no idea how tired I am."

"You have no idea how little I care."

"You should. After ten years on the throne, you'll feel this way too. You don't know how much it takes out of you," Minerva said.

"I'm sure all your plotting and killing was exhausting. Drakaren wasn't enough for you, was it? You had to have more. And now you've lost everything," Claire said.

"It was the only way to keep what I had. The world is a ruthless place. There's always someone trying to take what you have. You're a warrior, Claire. You arm yourself, and you wear armor. But you don't realize that power is a weapon, and that territory can be armor."

Minerva shook her head. "I needed a sharper weapon. And more armor. I did what I had to do to survive. And unless you learn to do the same, you won't be Queen of Keldaren for long."

"I could never be as ruthless as you," Claire said.

"Claire," Minerva sighed. "You sound like a child. I did what had to be done."

"You murdered people. You started a war that killed thousands. And that's all you have to say for yourself. That you did what had to be done."

"That's all I need to say. I'm not a sheep like you. Someone tells you what's right and what's wrong, and you trot right along after them," Minerva said. "Don't you see? There is no right or wrong. There's only what works, and what doesn't."

"And what about the price of what works for you? What about the cost to everyone else?" Claire asked.

Minerva glared at her. "Don't talk to me about the price. Don't talk to me about the *cost*. You were born in a palace. I was born in a gutter. What do you know about the cost of anything? Did you have to steal food to survive? Did you grow up watching your mother sell herself to keep a roof over your head? I was ten years old when my mother died. I took her place. I did what had to be done to keep my sister fed. When you've done that, then you'll know something about paying a price."

"But you wouldn't know anything about that, would you? You were born a princess. You had everything handed to you. I had to fight, and scheme, and *work* for everything I have. And look how far I came," Minerva said, gesturing to Graydare. "From a peasant in a hovel to a queen in a palace."

"You took the wrong path to get there. And now you've lost it all."

"It was the only path I could take. The only way out of the gutter. I made a gamble. My luck held for a while. Now it's run out." Minerva winced, her hand going to her wounded side.

"Then give up," Claire said. "Put down your sword and surrender. Then I won't have to kill you."

Minerva raised an eyebrow. "You wanted me dead when you came up here. I thought you wanted revenge for Jared."

"Revenge isn't enough of a reason to kill. Not for me. And I don't want revenge any more. I see you for what you truly are now. And I pity you."

Minerva's mouth tightened into a thin, hard line. "Keep your pity."

"Feeling sorry for you won't stop me from killing you." Claire raised her sword. "Yield, and live."

"I'll never surrender. Better to die standing than live kneeling." Minerva drew her sword, the fading sunlight shimmering off the wavy blade.

"That depends on what you're kneeling to," Claire said.

"I never kneel. Not to anyone or anything," Minerva said.

"We all kneel to what we worship."

"I worship nothing. I keep no gods. There are powers in this world, to be sure. But none worthy of being called a god. Not the myths of the Syncrestry. And not the demon my sister worships."

"Power is your god. You order your whole life around it," Claire said.

Minerva shook her head. "You don't understand. If you weren't highborn, you might. If you had known poverty, and hunger, you would understand. Power isn't a god. It's safety. If you have enough power, no one can take things from you. No one can force you back into a brothel, or turn your sister back into a beggar. No one can cast you low enough to spit on you again."

"And what safety did it give you in the end? You still lost everything."

"That proves the point. I didn't have *enough* power. Take care you don't make the same mistake, Claire. Otherwise you'll find yourself all alone someday, watching the sun set on your kingdom, and staring at the point of an enemy sword." Minerva raised her blade. "Enough talking. It's time we finish this." She charged.

Their blades rang as they clashed. Minerva fought with a growing fury, forcing Claire back across the roof of the tower. Toward the edge. *I have to stop her*, Claire thought, glancing back at the battlements. *Quickly*.

She feinted, exaggerating her swing as she slashed at Minerva's head. Minerva ducked underneath the blade. Claire let her momentum carry her. As she passed Minerva, Claire smashed an elbow into her wound.

Minerva screamed, and slammed her sword hilt into Claire's face. Claire's blade dropped from her hand as she fell. Pain beat through her head, and blackness lapped over her vision.

Get up! Claire screamed at herself. She forced herself to crawl over to her sword. She grasped it, and stood. Minerva dragged herself to the edge of the tower, leaving a trail of blood behind her. She held on to the battlements, hauling herself to her feet.

Claire rubbed her throbbing head. *Press the attack*, she told herself. She shook her head to clear it, and charged.

Minerva parried her blade, and knocked her down with a blow that left a dent in her chestplate. Claire scrabbled back across the roof. But Minerva didn't pursue her. She leaned heavily against the battlements, her dress soaked with blood.

Claire stood, raising her sword. Minerva straightened herself, moving into a combat stance. A grim defiance burned in her eyes.

Claire charged, and Minerva moved to block her. At the last second, Claire dropped to her knees. She skidded across the stone roof on the greaves covering her shins. Black steel flashed down toward her. Claire slid underneath it and punched her sword up between Minerva's ribs.

Minerva screamed. She dropped her sword, the Black Blade falling off the tower. Claire jerked her sword free, and Minerva crumpled. She slid backwards, over the edge, clawing for a handhold.

Claire peered over the tower. Minerva hung a few feet below her, clinging to a groove in the wall. *Let her die*, Claire thought. *She'd do the same to you.*

Claire sighed. *That wouldn't make it right.* She laid down her sword, and unbuckled her belt. Leaning over the edge of the tower, she braced her feet against the battlements. She stretched the belt down to Minerva. "Grab it! I'll pull you up!"

Minerva stared at her. Grim resolve still burned in her eyes. "No."

"Are you mad? I'm trying to save you!"

"And why would you save me?" Minerva asked.

"So you can stand trial. So all of Eris can see justice done to you."

"Justice." Minerva said the word as if she were spitting. "You mean an execution."

"No. I mean a lifetime in prison. A lifetime to live with what you've done. A lifetime to learn right from wrong."

Minerva shook her head. "Claire," she sighed. "You sound like a child." Then she let go. Minerva fell, her dress whipping around her in the wind. She crashed to the ground, and the dress fell around her in a dark puddle, covering her body like a burial shroud. Only the distant speck of her golden hair showed against the black. Then a stream of red appeared, flowing out from beneath her body.

CHAPTER 43

Claire

Claire turned away. She buckled the belt around her waist, and slid her sword into its scabbard. The clatter of armor and the tramp of feet echoed from the streets below. *More Drakari soldiers*, she thought, tensing. They turned the corner, marching toward the palace. Claire sighed in relief. The soldiers wore black and crimson. *Our troops are finally here.*

She made her way to the stairs, and descended back to the throne room. The last of the Dragon Knights were coming up the stairs from the lower levels. "The Drakari?" Claire asked.

"Dead, Your Majesty. The palace is ours," a knight said.

Sloane sat in a chair, her injured leg swathed in blood-soaked bandages. Two knights held Kerry up while another bound the wound on her shoulder. "Are you all right, Claire?" Kerry asked. "What happened up there?"

"Minerva's dead," Claire told her. "That's what happened." She turned to the spot where Jared had fallen. The floor was empty. "Who moved him? What happened to his body?"

"No one moved him," Sloane said. "I only realized he was missing after you left."

"Then who took his body?" Claire asked.

"There was no body to take," Sloane said.

"What do you mean, there was no body? I was holding him when he died."

"Did he? Go look," Sloane said. Claire walked over. There was a small puddle of blood where Jared had fallen. But there were also bloody streaks leading away from it, toward a tapestry hanging on the wall. Claire went over, and moved the tapestry aside. She felt along the wall behind it. One of the stones felt different than the others, and she pushed it. There was a click, and a section of the wall swung open, revealing a dark stairway.

"Dame Sloane sent me down when we found the passageway, Your Majesty," one of the knights said. "It leads to the palace stables. All the horses were in their stalls. Except for one."

Claire looked at Kerry. "Jared is *alive*?"

"It looks that way," Kerry said, wincing as the knight finished wrapping her shoulder. "He must have dragged himself away during the fighting."

"Why? Why would he do that? I could have helped him, Kerry."

"You did help him. Maybe you helped him enough. Maybe he couldn't stay and face you after what he's done." Kerry shook her head. "Jared always was a strange one. Who can say why he left?"

Claire turned to one of the knights. "Form a search party to go look for my brother," she ordered.

"Yes, Your Majesty." He hesitated. "With the state of the city, though..."

"I know. But try."

He nodded. "We'll do our best."

"Before you go, summon dragons to carry us back to the camp. We could all use a surgeon, I think," Claire said, wincing as she tried to move her left arm. She eased herself down, sitting next to Sloane and Kerry. "And have guards stationed here. I want this room sealed until I return."

The next day, Claire stepped past the guards into the Drakari throne room. Her bandaged arm hung in a sling around her neck. Liam led Sean in behind her, followed by a pair of Crown Guards. "And you have no idea where this sister that she mentioned is?" Sean asked.

"No. But I can tell you she's not in the throne room. Why did you want to come here?" Claire asked.

"She may have left certain...materials behind. Implements of her sorcery. Things that must be destroyed, lest they fall into the hands of other Zaharim," Sean said.

"Zaharim?"

"The followers of Zahara," Sean explained.

"Why look here?"

"This is a seat of power. Worldly power enhances the black arts. She would have worked her sorcery here, or nearby," Sean said.

"There was power here once. But not today. Now there's just this." Claire walked over to the dais, where the throne lay on its back. "A fallen throne for a fallen queen." She looked closer at it. "Move that over," she ordered the guards. They dragged the throne aside.

"What is it?" Sean asked.

"There's an opening beneath the throne," Claire told him, staring down into a hole that gaped like an open mouth in the dais. Stone steps spiraled tightly down into the darkness below. "A hole with stairs leading down it."

"Then we've found her lair," Sean said. "We'll have to go down."

Claire led the way. The guards followed close behind her, while Liam helped Sean down the stairs. A pale, sickly green light glimmered in the blackness below, growing brighter as they descended. Finally, they reached the bottom of the shaft. Claire stepped through a doorway cut into the stone wall.

She entered a large chamber filled with the eerie green light. A glass orb stood on a pedestal in the center of the room. The orb was filled with a pulsing, glowing green liquid. It cast rippling waves of light across the ceiling, like sunlight off the surface of a wind-swept lake.

No sunlight ever looked so foul, though, she thought. The putrid green light sent a wave of nausea through her. Torches lined the chamber walls, and when she walked further in, they all lit at once, burning with greasy yellow flames. Claire froze. "There's sorcery at work here, Sean."

"I can feel it. Be eyes for me, Claire. Tell me what you see."

She described the room to him. "There'll be more," Sean said. "Keep looking."

A small table stood further back, and Claire walked toward it. There was something in the air, something that seemed to push back at her as she moved through the room. *Like walking through cobwebs*, she thought, shuddering.

"There's a small table, made of stone," she told Sean. "A black cloth is hanging from the ceiling above it, like a flag. The cloth has a sword embroidered on it, with a flame curled around the blade. There's also a plain black cloth covering something on the table."

"See what it is."

She pulled the cloth away. "There's a book underneath it. It's very thick, bound in black leather, with a large clasp holding it shut. It has the same image on it as the flag…a sword and flame."

Claire reached for the book, touching the rough, thick leather. It was warm beneath her fingers. *Warm. How can that be?* Her hand moved to the clasp. The book seemed to almost pull at her, to draw her hand closer.

Claire unlatched the clasp, and opened it. The book trembled under her fingertips, growing even warmer, almost hot to the touch. She looked at the first page. The writing was strange— flowing, whirled symbols, inscribed in red ink. The letters ran up and down the page, instead of from side to side, and were linked together by curved lines weaving in and out of the script. "I can't read what it says," she told Sean. "I've never seen writing like this before…it looks almost like music, not words."

"It's the Startongue. It would be written in that."

"Then you know what this is?" Claire asked.

Sean nodded. "It's the Book of the Blade. The Zaharim scriptures. It tells the story of Zahara, and his war against The Emperor. It also contains the incantations the Zaharim use in working their sorcery."

Claire looked at the words again. Stared at them. The red ink shimmered, seeming to turn liquid before her eyes, and dripped like blood down the page. Claire shivered, slamming the book shut. "Why would it be written in the Startongue?"

"Zahara *is* a star. At least, he was once. He's become something else now. The Startongue...there's great power in it, Claire. Power in the words, but also power in the language itself. It's a distant echo of the Paean. And it carries some of its power."

"The Paean? What's that?" Claire asked.

"It's a story. A poem. A language." Sean rubbed his forehead. "How to explain it? You and I have imaginations, Claire. And so does The Emperor. Eris and the other worlds were all born in his mind. He told the story of what he imagined, and as soon as he spoke the words, his creations came into being. The stars were his first creation. They listened as his words gave birth to everything else, and they learned the Startongue by listening to him. They named his language, and the story he told on that first day, the Paean."

"Then the Startongue is the same as this Paean?"

Sean shook his head. "No. The Startongue is only a dim echo. Only The Emperor knows the Paean. Only he can wield its power. Even humans can eventually learn the Startongue. But no one can learn the Paean."

"The Startongue carries an echo of the Paean's power. Only an echo. But an echo is powerful enough. The ground swallowing up our troops yesterday...that was the power of the Startongue," Sean said.

"The same Startongue I heard being sung at the crystal mountain? It caused all that death?" Claire asked.

Sean nodded. "It can be used as a prayer. Or as a curse. The Startongue is the power behind the Zaharim's sorcery. Like most things, it can be perverted...twisted, to be used for evil."

"If just one of these Zaharim can destroy a whole army, how are we supposed to defeat them?"

"Only a few have the skill to do something like that. It takes a great deal of study and practice to become a mage—one of the Zaharim sorcerers. But even mages have their limitations. They must perform sacrifices to grow more powerful," Sean said.

"Sacrifices? You mean animals?"

"No. Not animals," Sean said.

Claire's blood went cold in her veins. *Savages.* "How do you know so much about the Zaharim?" she asked. "That didn't all come from dreams and visions, did it?"

"Astra and Caeli have told me a great deal. Sometimes too much. Especially when it comes to the Zaharim," Sean said.

There was something red on the far wall of the chamber. Claire walked over, leaning in to look closer in the torchlight.

"There's writing on the wall also," she told Sean. "It looks like the Startongue. It's hard to see, though. The paint is chipped."

One of the guards came over, staring at the wall. He drew his dagger, and rubbed the point against the writing. He looked at the blade. "This isn't paint, Your Majesty. Neither is that," he said, pointing to a dried stain of red on the floor behind the table.

The gorge rose in Claire's throat. "Let's leave, Sean. I need to see some sunlight."

"Yes, we've been here long enough. But first, you must destroy what we've found. Burn the book," he said.

Claire looked at it. *So many secrets inside*, she thought. *So many mysteries. Maybe even…answers.* There was a tingling in her fingers. Her hand moved toward the book, touching its cover. She felt the heat on her skin, and her fingers moved to the latch. Then her eyes went to the floor, and the red stain there.

She jerked her hand back, and threw the cloth over the book. Claire pulled the flag down, laying it atop the table. She strode to the wall, and snatched a torch from its holder. Dropping the torch onto the table, she watched the flames flare.

An oily smoke rose as the book burned. A wail rose also, growing louder and louder, until it became a piercing scream. *Even the book is possessed*, Claire thought, shuddering. The flames consumed the book, and the scream stopped as the pages fell into ashes.

"Now the orb," Sean said.

She picked it up, the green liquid sloshing inside the glass sphere. "What is this?"

"The Zaharim use the orbs to communicate with each other. And with Zahara himself. They're the Zaharim's link to his world. And his link to ours."

Claire lifted the orb above her head, and threw it to the ground. The glass smashed, the green liquid spreading over the floor. A thick smell of decay filled the room. The liquid hissed and bubbled in a frothing puddle, eating away at the stones until it dropped through the floor.

They all hurried to the stairs, fleeing the putrid stench. "I want this chamber filled with rubble and sealed off," Claire ordered the guards. "That vile pit must never be opened again."

The next day, Claire waited with Brianna, Azaira, and Panga on the steps of Proterian Palace. Azaira sat next to Claire, her injured leg propped up in front of her. A line of Crown Guards stood between them and the crowd of Drakari gathered in the square below.

Claire went over to Panga. "I'm sorry about your father."

"He was a brave man. I once thought him a fool for taking the risk he did. But he was braver than me."

"You were courageous enough to fight with us against the Drakari. And now you have a chance to be brave enough to honor your father's sacrifice, and to lead the Merosians like he did," Claire said.

"We don't inherit titles amongst my people. Our assembly will choose the new Archon."

"But you would be eligible?" Claire asked.

"Any adult Merosian is eligible, if they tell the council they wish to be considered."

"Then tell them," Claire urged. "Tell them you want to follow in your father's footsteps."

He looked at her, blinking his bulging eyes. "Perhaps I will," he said. "Perhaps I will."

Claire walked over to Brianna. "Has there been any sign of them?" Brianna asked.

Claire shook her head. "We sent knights to search their villages. But there's no trace of either the Stenari or the Ravek. They're all gone. Even the females and the young. We'll find them though. We won't stop looking until we do."

Brianna looked into the sky, squinting as she checked the sun. "It's time," she said. Claire stepped forward.

"People of Drakaren!" Claire called. "The Hynbarran and Kirosian armies are already marching east. In six months, all Keldari soldiers will follow them. Until then, Keldari troops will remain here, to keep the peace, and to train a new army to defend Drakaren. But in six months, all Keldari will be gone."

"We didn't come to conquer Drakaren," she continued. "We came to free you from the reign of a tyrant. Minerva is dead. But she was never the rightful queen. By Drakari law, when King Valus died, the throne passed to his sister. Minerva stole the throne. But today, Princess Brianna is here to claim it."

Brianna stepped forward, carrying the Drakari crown. "By our law and tradition, this is mine to take," she said, holding up the crown. "But I think we've had enough of rulers who take. I won't take this crown. I will only accept it if you give it to me. If you choose me as your queen, then I'll lead our nation. If you don't, then I'll put the crown aside, and the people can choose another to rule."

A stunned silence filled the square, the crowd standing as still as a windless lake. Then the first ripple started. "Long live the queen!" a voice shouted. "Queen Brianna! Brianna the queen!" Other voices joined in, until the roar was as loud as waves crashing against the seashore.

Brianna raised her hands for silence. "Then I accept," she said.

"Crown her!" someone shouted.

Brianna looked out at the crowd. "The people chose me as queen. It seems fitting that one of the people should crown me."

A young girl stepped forward. "May I, Your Majesty?"

Brianna smiled. "I'd be honored," she said. Brianna walked down the steps to the square. She handed the crown to the girl, and knelt down in front of her. Claire watched the girl gently lower the crown into place, its polished bronze shining against Brianna's black hair.

Brianna gave the girl a hug, and then rose. When the cheering died down, she climbed the steps, rejoining Claire. "The Keldari will leave soon," she told the people. "But they could just as easily have chosen to stay. To conquer us. To force Drakaren back within their borders, as it once was long ago. But they've chosen to act with honor. To help us rebuild, and then to leave us in peace. In freedom. Our nations have been enemies for a long time. But now, they've proven themselves to be friends. So, I've decided to make a peace treaty between us and the Keldari."

Brianna turned to Claire, and they embraced. Brianna signaled to a servant, who brought them two glasses of wine. Brianna held up her glass. "To peace," she said.

"To peace. And freedom," Claire said, holding up her own glass. Cheers erupted from the square as they drank.

When the noise died down, Brianna turned back to the people. "The Keldari are giving us our freedom back. We have to follow their example. From this day forward, Graitha and Merosia are sovereign, independent nations again. I renounce all Drakari claims to their territories." She turned toward Azaira and Panga. "And I apologize to their leaders for the occupations they endured for so long. We were wrong to take your freedom away. Today, we offer it back to you. Along with our friendship, if you'll have it."

"The Graithans would welcome friendship with Drakaren," Azaira said. "A friendship of equals."

Panga said nothing. He merely nodded to Brianna. Most of the Drakari in the square were silent as well. But some muttered angrily, glaring darkly at their new queen.

Brianna turned back to the crowd. "We've ruled Merosia and Graitha for many decades, and conquering them has made Drakaren wealthy. But look at the price we've paid for that wealth. We had to maintain an enormous army—an army supported by massive conscriptions of our young men. And every year, soldiers died fighting to keep our hold over the conquered territories."

"But worst of all, it turned us into a nation that steals from others. That's what led us into this war—trying to take more of what wasn't ours. We need to change what we've become. We're going to do that by freeing the Graithans and Merosians. I know this won't be popular. But it will be right," Brianna said.

There was silence for a moment. And then, a single person in the crowd began to clap. Another started clapping, and then another. Soon, the entire square echoed with applause.

CHAPTER 44

Claire

A week later, Claire and Elsie stood outside of Adrian's room at Connemara Palace. "Are you sure you don't want this back, Els?" Claire jested, touching the signet ring on her finger.

Elsie smiled. "I wore that long enough. It's back where it belongs now."

Claire grinned. "Oh, I don't know. You did such a good job as Regent that I might consider making the position permanent."

"That sounds like an excellent opportunity," Elsie said. "For someone else. I've had more than enough of governing."

"I hope Isabelle doesn't feel the same way."

"I would, if I had just been elected to a five-year term as Chancellor." Elsie shuddered. "More like a five-year prison sentence. I don't know how you talked her into it, Claire. I can't think of anything worse than that."

"There's a great deal worse that can happen in this world, Els. A great deal," Claire said, looking at Adrian. All the humor was gone from her voice.

"The surgeons say he'll recover, Claire. It's just a matter of time."

"Kerry and Sloane are both much further along than he is. I heard Sloane may even be walking by next week."

"Adrian was almost beaten to death. They weren't. It's a miracle he even survived. Be patient, Claire. Damien examined him. He's certain Adrian will wake up soon."

"But the surgeons aren't sure he'll ever walk again. Or that being strangled didn't cause him any permanent damage," Claire said.

Elsie sighed. "No. Damien wasn't as sure about that. But wait and see what happens. Aren't you supposed to be the one with faith?"

"You're right. I am. But having faith doesn't mean you don't worry." Claire smiled. "It just means you don't panic." She looked at Elsie. "And what of your faith? We haven't talked about that since I returned."

Elsie sighed again. "Well, I certainly don't believe in the Syncrestry any more. No one does now. The news of the templer trying to kill you changed that." Elsie shook her head. "I would have liked to get my hands on Quaestor, Claire. He should have spent the rest of his life in prison."

"It would have been good to see him face justice," Claire said.

"I sent the constables as soon as I got your message. But he must have had an informant within the army...someone he sent along to keep an eye on his assassin. He knew what had happened before we did. The surgeons said he had been dead for hours by the time the constables found him. And the other templers had plenty of warning as well. They had all fled by the time the constables reached the Holy Hill," Elsie said.

"I'm sure they wanted to be gone long before the mobs arrived," Claire said.

"It's a good thing they were. Otherwise, more templers would have hung that day. And not by their own hand, like Quaestor."

"So, if you don't believe in the Syncrestry any more, what do you believe in?" Claire asked.

"I'm not sure. But I *am* sure I'm not ready to be converted."

"I understand." Claire smiled. "Let me know when you are."

Elsie laughed. "I will. If Sean doesn't get to me first. That reminds me; he sent a message for you. He wanted you to meet him at the Holy Hill today."

Claire nodded. "I'll go this afternoon. I still have to see General Ecca off this morning. He's bringing Ross' body back to Hyperion."

"It was good of you to have the palace gravesmen preserve him."

"It was the least I could do. Ross chose to change. He found his courage, and he found a way back. He died a hero. He deserves a hero's memorial," Claire said.

Elsie looked through the open door. Claire followed her gaze to the bed where Adrian slept. "And Adrian?"

"What about him?" Claire asked, feeling her cheeks flush.

"What does he deserve?"

Me, Claire thought. *He deserves me.* "His queen's thanks," she said. She went in and sat next to the bed. She pulled her chair closer, watching the rise and fall of his chest as he breathed.

An hour had passed before she noticed the angle of the sun through the window. *Time to meet Ecca,* she realized. She stood, and reached out to touch Adrian's face. Then she leaned over, and kissed him.

That afternoon, Claire rode with a squad of Crown Guards to the Holy Hill. Workers swarmed around it, digging a set of foundations on either side of the hill. Claire climbed the broad marble steps. At the top of the steps, the temple's bronze doors stood open, and she and the guards went in.

Inside, the sun streamed through the skylight, glistening off the polished marble floor. The silver wall dividing the temple in two was gone, leaving the interior open. The pulpit was gone as well. The chairs had been replaced by long rows of wooden benches.

At the far end of the temple, a large stone platform was set against the wall, with steps leading up it. A marble table stood at the center of the platform. Candles burned atop the table, and between them stood the crystal flask. The liquid light glowed a brilliant white—outshining the candles; and brighter even than the sunbeams pouring through the skylight.

The first few benches were filled with people. Some sat with their heads bowed. Some sat staring at the flask. They all recited a prayer in the Startongue. A prayer Sean was leading. Claire slipped into an empty bench behind them, and waited.

When the prayer was finished, Claire stood and walked up to him. He raised his head at the sound of her footsteps. "Sean," she said.

A smile broke across his face. "Claire. It's good to hear your voice again." Liam rose from the bench, and helped Sean to his feet. "Keep practicing the words," Sean told the others. "You're doing well."

He and Liam walked with Claire to the doors of the temple. "Your followers?" Claire asked.

Sean shook his head. "*His* followers. I'm only a guide. A guide to him."

"You're teaching them the Startongue?"

"A few prayers in it. Did you see the foundations being built outside?" Sean asked.

"Yes. I was wondering about those."

"We're building two monasteries. One for an order of monks, and one for nuns. These are the first of them. After the templers were exposed as frauds, the Faith has grown even more quickly. Too quickly for me to handle alone. But there are many interested in joining our orders. Soon, we'll be able to build monasteries beyond Tara, and carry the Faith to all of Eris," Sean said.

"I see you've converted the temple into a shrine to the Emperor," Claire said.

"The templers abandoned this place. An actual mob showed up looking for them, Claire. It's a good thing the templers left, or there would have been blood spilled. After they found the templers gone, the mob destroyed the statues of the gods, and knocked down the wall that protected the sanctum. They destroyed all the trappings of the false gods, leaving this building empty. One of our converts petitioned the Chancellor to let us use it, and this land. And the Chancellor granted it to us."

"You don't have a problem with using a temple that was built to honor false gods?" Claire asked.

"No. I'm told it's a beautiful building. We can put it to use honoring the true god. We can take a monument to lies, and convert it into a temple of truth. The Emperor takes fallen people and redeems them. If he can do that with people, why not with a building?"

"I suppose you're right," Claire said. "I realized the other day that I never thanked you for leading me to faith, Sean."

"Don't thank me now," he said, with a smile. "You aren't there yet. All I did was get you started."

"What do you mean?"

"Faith isn't a destination. It's a journey. A life-long one. You only reach the end of the journey at…well, at the end of life. And it's a difficult trek. Some journeys are easy. When you get aboard a ship, you simply ride it until you reach your destination. Faith is different. You have to walk the whole path. Sometimes you run. But mostly you walk. And a great deal of the journey is uphill."

"Everything's been uphill for me lately," Claire said. "I had hoped most of that was over."

"You've been through much since your father died," Sean said, reaching out to find her arm. He put his hand on her shoulder. "You suffered a great deal. But you learned, and you grew. Suffering is the path to wisdom. It's the only way you really learn things in this life. True wisdom is nothing more than pain, distilled by experience. I'm afraid your journey to wisdom is far from over. It's only just beginning."

"The Emperor gave me a vision, Claire. A vision of Keldaren in the near future. I saw our country burning. I saw oceans of spears and swords flooding across Keldaren, carried by invading armies. Steel and Fire. That's what the future holds for us. The future you'll face as queen. The Emperor will stand with you. But can you walk that path, knowing what awaits you?"

Claire turned, looking back toward the glowing flask. "I took the crown, and I swore the oath. I am Queen of Keldaren. Through war and peace. Through steel and fire."

Anastasia

Anastasia finished her prayers and leaned over to kiss the orb. She covered it and the Book with the cloth. The prayer flag hung on the cave wall behind the orb. She gazed at the fiery blade emblazoned on the flag. *A reminder of the Crimson God's power*, she thought. *Of how he turned defeat into a glorious victory.*

She touched the Book. Even through the cloth, she felt its warmth. Its power. *Thanks be to Zahara that I had another orb and Book to bring with me. All would truly be lost without them.*

Anastasia sensed the Viper Knight approaching. She turned. "You asked me to tell you when it was dawn, Majesty," the knight said, bowing, and holding out her staff.

Anastasia took the staff. The familiar feel of the gnarled wood was comforting in her grasp. "Very well. You're dismissed." The knight inclined his head, but didn't leave. "Was there something else?" she asked.

"Might I ask a question, Majesty?"

Anastasia nodded.

"Forgive me, but we're all wondering what we're doing here."

"All of you?"

"Not the Ravek and Stenari, of course. They would never ask such questions. But the knights...we're trained in espionage. We're supposed to ask questions. To seek answers. And we're asking why you've brought us here."

"A fair question. My sister was a great woman. A great queen. But she did have a flaw. She claimed to follow the Crimson God. But I don't know if she ever really worshipped him. Perhaps she just coveted his power. I know one thing for sure— she was never close enough to him. Never devoted enough to him. I won't make the same mistake," Anastasia said.

She touched the ruby atop her staff, watching the dim light flicker inside it. "I brought us to Askilaira because the caverns

here are a perfect place to take shelter while we rebuild our forces.
We could hide an entire army in these caves."

Anastasia looked at him. "But there is another reason.
This place is sacred to Zahara. These caverns are where the scrolls
of the Book were found. We'll stay here while I pray and study
the Book. While I grow in faith, and power. When I'm strong
enough again, I'll lead our forces out from this valley to re-take
Graydare. And then we'll march on Tara."

The knight bowed. "We will follow you to Tara, Majesty.
And to victory."

Victory, and vengeance, she thought. *A vengeance that will
teach the entire world the power of the Crimson God.* She gazed
into the ruby, staring at the vision flickering in its red depths. A
vision of crimson flames burning across a curved blade. The fire
rose, spreading to engulf all of Eris.

Acknowledgements

First, thank you to Mary South for all of her help in editing this book, and for her invaluable feedback and suggestions. Thanks to Scott South and Mike South for their suggestions as well. Thank you to all of those on absolutewrite.com who helped me edit and hone the beginning of this book. Thank you to Rebecca Weaver and Maja Nesic, the artists I worked with, for their excellent artwork!

And, last but certainly not least, thank you very much to my readers. I really appreciate you taking the time to read my book. I hope you enjoyed it. I would welcome any feedback (positive or negative) you might have. You can share any feedback, comments, or questions with me on my Facebook page for this series:

 www.facebook.com/queenofsteelandfireseries

CPSIA information can be obtained
at www.ICGtesting.com
Printed in the USA
LVHW081757091019
633690LV00011B/709/P

9 781500 973735